# The Ghost Writer

# The Ghost Writer

## A Novel

# Brian Warner

ISBN-13: 979-8-9920059-6-7

The Ghost Writer

Book Cover by Brian Warner

Illustrations by Brian Warner, Seth Warner

1st edition 2024

Jupiter &
Phoebus
Publishing
House

# CONTENTS

For Angie, Seth, and Josh
My Family and Ka-Tet

"The information was false."
"No. The information a book provides is an objective given. It may be presented by a malevolent author who wishes to mislead, but it is never false. It is the reader who makes a false reading."
Corso seemed to be thinking carefully. He shifted to face the garden in darkness. "Then there must be another author," he said quietly.

**THE CLUB DUMAS** - Arturo Perez-Reverte

# Tommy Comes A Knockin'

Novel By MARTIN KNIGHT

Jupiter &
Phoebus
Publishing
House

# PROLOGUE
## Tommy Comes A Knockin'

*October 31, 1987*

"Jesus wept, Tom, sober up!"

He slapped himself across the face, which did little to change his inebriated state. Taking his hand off the wheel almost caused the car to veer off the snow-covered road. The heater on the rust bucket '72 Oldsmobile Cutlass could barely hold back the frost creeping down the windshield. At least the cold helped keep him awake, but he also switched on the radio.

*...on track to be the worst blizzard we've seen in a hundred years. Expect snowfall between twelve to eighteen inches in most parts of the listening area, with some receiving over two feet. If you can stay off the roads for your safety...*

"Thanks, asshole," Thomas grunted as he mashed the station buttons until he found Johnny Cash on and turned it up. "Of all fucking nights."

The blizzard had rolled in while he was at the VFW Halloween party getting shitfaced. He had heard the weather report while driving to Iowa City from Old Ahnen. He wasn't about to turn around since he'd already spent an hour putting on his clown makeup. His efforts were rewarded as he had harassed the barmaids all night as part of his act and won the costume contest to boot.

Tom glanced at the trophy in the seat beside him, a gold cup glued to a cheap wood stand with a red helium-filled balloon tied to one handle. It was a stupid thing to be proud of, but it would be going on the mantle next to the bowling league championship trophy the Ahnen Volunteer Fire Department had claimed three years ago.

His attention was distracted by the shiny bauble long enough that the car drifted over again. "OH FUCK!" Tom's heart leaped into his throat as he cranked the steering wheel to the left, then back the other way as the Cutlass fish-tailed about. He was breathing so hard it fogged up the windshield, and he had to wipe it off with his sleeve.

If he put his car into the ditch in this weather, he would be stuck until the snowplows came through tomorrow. It wouldn't be the first time he spent the night drunk in his car, but he didn't have a death wish. The snow was coming down so thick that the windshield looked like a TV screen filled with static. He doubted anyone else would be stupid enough to be out on a night like this.

The wind died down as he approached the first bend in the road, and his headlights reflected off a pair of eyes in the field ahead. At first, he thought it was a deer, but it seemed to be standing on its hind legs. Tom slowed down to a crawl as he turned and tried to get a better look at it without crashing.

"Is that a fucking bear?" The snow picked up again and obscured the field from his view. Whatever he had seen had run off, or maybe it had never been there.

He slowed down as he came to the next turn and headed northward again. A blur of movement out of the corner of his eye made him risk looking over at the field. His eyes widened as he saw an enormous creature moving so fast it was pulling ahead of his car. The front tires hit a slick patch, and he nearly lost control. His knuckles were turning white from gripping the steering wheel so tight. When he glanced out the window, the animal was gone. (*It had to be a bear. Are there bears in Iowa?* he wondered. *Or maybe a moose, they can run fast.*)

Tom was starting to freak out that he was seeing things. He pushed down on the accelerator as far as he dared. He was a grown-ass man, but he was scared by shadows in the dark. Even if it was Halloween with a full moon, that was no reason to believe that the stories he'd heard were real.

He only had a moment to react as a giant beast emerged from the snow-filled ditch up ahead and launched its body at his car. Tom's reflexes were slowed down by too much alcohol, and all he managed to do was throw his hands up to cover his face as the windshield shattered. The Cutlass spun out before it hit the ditch. Tom slammed his face against the steering wheel, and the pain caused him to vomit all over himself before he passed out.

When he came to, dazed and now with a pounding headache, the spider-webbed windshield was covered with a thin layer of snow. He recoiled at the smell of sour beer and bile coating his legs. The haziness lifted enough for him to remember what had caused the crash. Tom jabbed at the seatbelt lock to get it to release. He grabbed the trophy, which was still buckled into the passenger seat, as it was the only weapon he had at hand. His vision was blurred from the pain as he searched for any sign of the thing that had attacked his car.

Tom couldn't think straight (*he would have one hell of a hangover tomorrow*), but he knew he was a sitting duck in the car if that creature was still alive. It took him a couple of tries to shove open the door far enough to squeeze out. His costume caught on the door handle as he climbed through, sending him tumbling face-first into the snow. Cold, angry, and with an even greater pounding in his head, Tom scrambled out of the ditch and back onto the road. He had somehow held onto the trophy and raised it above his head, ready to strike. The blowing snow made it hard to see further than the other side of the road, but nothing was moving within the confines of the wintry veil.

Tom's fingers were going numb as he struggled to unlock the trunk. He popped it open and dug through the contents until he found the first-aid kit. The best he could scrounge up to stop the bleeding from his crushed nose were a couple of cotton balls. He gingerly packed them inside his nostrils, and it sent lightning bolts of pain coursing through his skull.

"Fuck, that hurts!"

The cold air carried the sound of tree branches rustling behind him over the howling of the wind. Tom froze and cursed himself for letting his guard down. He was suddenly aware of how full his bladder felt. His eyes landed on the fireman's axe he kept in the trunk for emergencies, and he snatched up its wood handle. Tom scrambled back up to the road, whirled around with the red-painted steel blade ready to strike, and his feet went flying out from under him on the slick ground.

The snow cushioned his fall, but fresh pain shot up his broken nose. Tom groaned as he rolled onto his shoulder, the elbow of his right arm smarting from having hyperextended. Footsteps crunched in the snow, and he tilted his head back even as his hand groped around for the axe.

A pair of slender bare feet stood on top of the snow. Tom's eyes traveled up the connected legs until they disappeared beneath the hem of a long green cloak. The shadow of a deep hood concealed the woman's face. The wind ruffled the cloak, and he was shocked to get a glimpse of her naked body. Even with the bitter cold, he could feel himself growing hard. His headache faded, and a pleasant sensation of warmth spread throughout his body.

She bent down in front of him so that he could see her face. His hand closed around the axe's handle, but he had forgotten why he wanted it as he fell into her mesmerizing green eyes.

*I have a job for you, Thomas Hickman.* He could hear her voice even though she didn't move her lips. *Will you help me?*

"Yes, my Queen," he heard himself saying, "anything for you."

Tom wanted nothing more than to please this woman. Spotting the half-buried trophy in the snow, he picked it up and offered it to her. He listened raptly as she spoke. When she was done, a whirl of snow enveloped her, and she vanished into thin air. Tom got to his feet, then trudged up the road into the thick of the blizzard, carrying his trophy and dragging the axe behind him. He headed towards a streetlight at the top of the hill where the woman had said there was somebody he needed to save.

Catherine Schreiber sat in her recliner watching television, a quilt draped across her legs, as she sipped a cup of tea. She was usually fast asleep at this hour, but the snowstorm was causing her arthritis to act up. Weather like this brought back memories of her husband's death three years ago. She pushed the thought out of her mind and took another drink. Cathy grimaced and spat the tea back into the cup as it had already turned cold.

The wind started blowing harder, cutting out the television signal and filling the screen with snow. Cathy set the teacup down and lifted off the blanket, her knees popping as she stood up. She hobbled over to the TV set and rotated the channel dial around. After pounding her fist on top of the wood frame, she smacked the power button in frustration.

It wasn't the first time the antenna on top of the house had broken in a storm, but without Elias to climb up and fix it, she would have to call in a repair service from Iowa City. There were so many things she had to learn how to do for herself now that he was gone, but nothing could fix the emptiness his death had left in her heart.

The loneliness almost made her cry, and she struggled to hold it back. Cathy went over to the window, pulled back the curtain, and glared at the raging snowstorm that had robbed her of a cozy evening in front of the television. "At least it waited until Carson was over," she sighed. "Can this night get any worse?"

Since she wasn't likely to get any sleep, she decided to do some writing for her book. She freshened up her tea and slowly climbed the stairs. Her office had a view of Bailey

Grove to the north, but she had placed her desk underneath the window facing the open fields to the west. It provided a tranquil, less distracting scene that was especially lovely at sunset. There wasn't much to see tonight as the blizzard nearly choked off all light from the streetlamp at the end of her driveway.

She set her teacup down on the desk and picked up the last page she had been working on from the drawer underneath the Underwood manual typewriter. The machine was over forty years old, but electric typewriters were too complicated. God help her if she ever had to use a computer. Cathy had seen several professors switching to those garish contraptions that used a screen instead of paper. She couldn't trust such an invention, no matter what promises of convenience were used to lure people into staring at its sickly green text for hours. She suspected that sitting in front of a computer too long would cause blindness, cancer, or probably both.

Cathy looked over at the framed wedding photograph hanging on the wall. She hadn't noticed how few nice pictures there were of her and Elias together until after he died. He had gone out after receiving a late-night phone call even though it was snowing. That wasn't unusual since he was a volunteer firefighter, but she had heard him yelling into the phone before he left. His pickup truck had skidded off the road and crashed into a tree, bursting into flames. Catherine never found out who had called him, but it hadn't been the fire department. She also couldn't remember if they had said goodbye to each other.

She had met Elias shortly after what was left of her family had immigrated from Germany to the United States following World War II. Elias had grown up in the Ahnen Villages, a cluster of six small farming towns founded by a close-knit religious group. Most of the families who populated the community had descended from a group of Germans who left Europe to escape persecution, eventually settling in what would become eastern Iowa to establish a communal farming society that was wholly self-sufficient. Although the townsfolk relied more on tourism dollars these days, many still adhered to the old ways and made their living off the land.

Before retiring, she had been a professor and head of the German department at the University of Iowa. She had authored three books during her career and contributed to several more, but her current project differed from anything else she had written. It began as a history of the Ahnen Villages, something she had wanted to do since moving to the area. That changed when Elias confided to her a secret while he was drunk one night. Cathy had brushed it off as another of his wild stories that he rolled out when he had a few too many beers. After his death, she found some books in the university's library that seemed to confirm what he told her that night was not made up. Or at least not entirely.

Cathy switched on the desk lamp, plopped down into the wooden swivel chair, and rolled a blank sheet of paper into the typewriter. She was reading through the notes she kept in a leather-bound journal when she looked out the window. The blizzard had let up some, and she could see a person standing under the streetlamp.

"What idiot would be out in this?" Cathy got to her feet, slipped the journal into the pocket of her robe, and pulled back one of the curtains to take a better look. It was too difficult to make out the stranger's face from this distance. He stood there for a while, seemingly impervious to the snow and the cold. Cathy worried he might be lost or hurt, but something about him made her nervous.

The man started walking towards her house, so she headed downstairs as fast as her swollen knees would allow. She tightened the sash on her robe and peered through the front door window. The stranger was still twenty feet from the porch, far enough that she felt safe unlocking the door. Cathy opened it just enough to stick her head through.

"Hello, who's there?" The man stopped at the bottom of her porch. He wore a white with red polka-dots clown costume while holding a trophy with a partially deflated balloon attached. In his other hand, though, was the handle of a large axe. "If this is a Halloween prank, you had better leave before I call the sheriff."

"I need...need to...help," the man said in a strange, monotone voice. "Have job...job...to do. Need to...need...to help."

Cathy thought she caught a whiff of alcohol when he spoke, and she could see dried vomit staining the lower half of his costume. Even though his speech was slurred, she thought his voice sounded familiar.

"Thomas Hickman, is that you?" she asked, but he didn't respond. Tom and her husband had volunteered at the fire department. "Have you been drinking tonight, Tom? Did you have a car accident?"

"Need...help," he muttered as his eyes remained unfocused. She suspected from the blood around his nose that he had been driving drunk and crashed, but his behavior disturbed her. "Have to...rescue..."

"Come sit down on the porch. I'll see if I can get someone out here with the weather and all," Cathy said. Again, he gave no indication that he heard her. She thought about telling him to come in out of the cold, but the axe he was holding frightened her. She stepped back inside and closed the door. After a moment's hesitation, she decided to lock the deadbolt. Cathy glanced out the window, then went to the kitchen to use the telephone.

Looking up at the farmhouse, Tom could see the flames growing stronger as the smoke poured out from under the rafters. His head was throbbing, but he had a job to do. He wondered why no fire trucks had arrived yet. Maybe he should wait for them, but he could hear somebody calling for help inside the home. He had an axe with him, so it was up to him to break down the front door and brave the flames. *You've got a job to do*, a voice urged him on. *You need to help her.* He climbed up the wooden steps, raised the axe, and swung it at the door.

Catherine picked up the receiver from the phone mounted on the kitchen wall and rotated the dial around from the number nine, followed by two rotations from the number one. It was only the second time she had ever dialed the emergency number, the other being when her husband hadn't come home the night he died. The line didn't ring on the other end, so she tapped the switch on top several times. She listened for a dial tone, but there was only silence. Cathy screamed when a heavy thud rattled the front door and dropped the receiver.

The tip of an axe blade was sticking through a crack in the door. It pulled out, and the door shook again as another blow widened the hole. The next hit shattered the window, sending a shower of glass flying across the entryway. Cathy knew the door wouldn't hold much longer, so she hurried to the back door and unlocked it. While she didn't have a coat on, she wasn't about to stay here with a psychotic clown. The next thud brought the sound of splintering wood, and she threw open the door.

From out in the dark, glowing amber eyes stared up at her. A hulking shadow crept towards her on four legs across the backyard. The creature issued a low, chilling growl from its throat and she slammed the door shut before it could leap at her. Cathy twisted the lock and grabbed a butcher knife from the wooden block on the counter. There was no escape from the house, so her only way out was to fight. The front door was still closed, but the hole had widened to the size of a dinner plate. Cathy saw the clown's face peer through the jagged opening, and a white-gloved hand reached inside to feel around for the lock.

Although her knees were in agony, she hurried to the basement door tucked away in the kitchen. Cathy locked the door behind her, not that it would slow down a maniac with an axe for long. There was another set of stairs in the cellar which led outside, but that would do her little good. She would freeze to death in this storm if that thing lurking in the darkness didn't hunt her down first. Butcher knife in hand, she would have to take her chances with the threat that was at least human.

Thomas could feel the heat from the fire raging upstairs as he unlocked the front door and stepped inside. He recognized the house from the street since it belonged to his friend Elias Schreiber. Tom had been first on the scene the night Elias died, but there had been nothing he could do to save him. His truck was wrapped around a thick oak tree, and the engine had caught fire. Tom had arrived in his own car and had no way to extinguish the flames. It wouldn't have mattered, as Elias was already dead. His friend's head had been nearly decapitated in the accident even though the truck's cab had sustained little damage. Tom had watched helplessly as the truck was engulfed.

He wasn't about to let Elias's widow die on his watch, not without doing everything he could to rescue her. A wall of flames blocked the stairway, but the ground floor was clear. He checked the bedroom, the dining room, and the kitchen but didn't find her. The back door was locked, so she couldn't have left that way, which meant she had to be trapped upstairs in the inferno. He turned back towards the hallway but spotted a light coming from underneath a door in the corner.

Tom tested the handle before turning it to ensure there wasn't a fire on the other side. A light bulb was on at the top of the stairs, and he figured Cathy must have taken shelter down below. He was walking down the steps when a sharp pain flared up in his left ankle and sent him tumbling down to the cement floor. Howling in agony, Tom saw that the back of his leg was bleeding where his Achilles tendon had been sliced open. Cathy came out from behind the stairs, wielding a large knife dripping with blood. She started climbing the steps, and he reached out to stop her from returning to the burning house.

He caught her foot with his hand, making her stumble as a book went flying out of her robe pocket.

She kicked his hand away and scrambled up to the kitchen, apparently oblivious to the waves of black smoke roiling across the ceiling. Tom thought she must be confused by his costume and didn't understand he was there to rescue her. He grabbed the axe and used it to get to his feet, then hobbled up the stairs after her.

"Cathy!" he hollered. "I'm coming for you, Cathy!"

His left leg was useless, dragging behind him as he limped along on his makeshift crutch. A door slammed somewhere in the house as he neared the top of the steps. The back door was still locked, so he went to the hallway. It was getting harder to see through the thick smoke. He noticed the bedroom door was closed when he was sure he had left it open after clearing the room. Tom shuffled up the hallway and tried the handle to find it locked. He braced his shoulder against the wall to stand on his good leg and swing the axe without falling over. It still took a couple of blows to open the door.

The bedroom was dark, but cold air hit his face as soon as he limped in. There was another door to his left that led to an attached bathroom. A window above the claw-foot tub stood open to the night. It looked wide enough for Cathy to squeeze through if she were desperate to escape. He also saw that her robe had been dropped on the floor by the tub. Tom picked it up, wondering why she would discard it unless she couldn't fit through wearing it. He was about to climb into the tub to look outside when he heard the door close behind him.

Cathy charged him from her hiding spot in the small bathroom closet. The butcher knife sank all the way to the handle in his stomach and made him swing out with the axe in reaction. The flat of the blade struck Cathy's shoulder, knocking her backward where she hit her head on the sink. She crumbled to the floor and remained motionless, a streak of blood dripping from the porcelain fixture.

Tom wanted to help her, but his bowels were a pit of molten lava. He dropped the axe as he stumbled out of the bathroom, leaving a bloody handprint on the door as he steadied himself. Tom careened down the hallway towards the front door. Blood was already turning the lower half of his costume bright red. He slumped down on the porch steps as his legs lost all feeling. His body felt cold, and his eyes grew too heavy to hold open. Before he passed out, he thought he saw a hulking shape with glowing eyes approach the house.

Cathy woke up with a splitting headache and found blood when she touched her hair. Her vision was also blurry because her glasses were missing. She tried to pull herself up using the edge of the sink only to become lightheaded, forcing her to lie back down. The dizziness started to pass, but the sound of footsteps from the bedroom stopped her heart. Cathy feared it was Tom returning to finish her off. The man who stepped into the doorway was taller and completely naked. Despite the darkness and her poor eyesight, she thought he looked like her late husband.

"Elias, is that you?"

The man reached down and picked up something off the floor. Cathy's hand found her glasses and she put them back on. Although he bore a strong resemblance to Elias, it wasn't him.

"I know you," she said, "you're one of Elias's friends. You're...you're one of them, aren't you? Just like Elias."

"He couldn't keep his mouth shut," the man said, "and I wish you would have left it alone."

"You don't have to do this," she pleaded. "I won't tell anyone."

"I'm afraid I don't have a choice."

"No, please don't!" Her words were cut off as the axe split her head open.

Deputy Edgar Blackburn squeezed the steering wheel of his Ford Bronco cruiser tighter as the tires swerved on the slick road. The snowplows wouldn't be through here until morning, so he was at the mercy of the elements and his truck's four-wheel drive to make it out to the crash site. A caller had reported a car wreck about half a mile from Bailey Grove. Why any idiot would be driving at night in a blizzard was beyond his comprehension, but he imagined alcohol was involved.

He hoped that he would find a passed-out drunk behind the wheel, not an injured or dead drunk lying in the ditch. Otherwise, he would be stuck out in this storm while he waited for the ambulance to arrive. The Bronco's headlights reflected off something metallic up ahead. Edgar slowed down as he approached the wrecked car.

"Son of a bitch, this isn't going to be good," he grumbled. He zipped up his coat, pulled on his gloves, turned on the cruiser's flashing lights, and stepped out into the bitter cold. Edgar removed the flashlight from his belt and pointed it at the car as he approached.

When the beam shone upon the vehicle, the first thing that struck him as odd was that the trunk had popped up. He sank almost to his knees in the snow as he climbed into the ditch to reach the open driver's door. There was nobody inside, and he recoiled at the smell of puke. A quick check of the back seat verified that the car was vacant, so he crawled in and retrieved the registration from the glove box.

The vehicle belonged to Thomas Hickman, whom Edgar recognized as the chief of the Ahnen Volunteer Fire Department. Searching around, he found footprints leading away from the accident scene and going up the road. He returned to his truck and drove slowly with his window open, his flashlight trained on the trail in the snow. The tracks led into the driveway of a farmhouse, and he pulled in until he was off the street.

A man in a clown costume was sitting on the front porch, leaning against the railing on the steps. That wasn't unusual given that it was Halloween night, but to be passed out in a snowstorm suggested that he had found the missing driver of the wrecked car. Edgar approached the porch and trained his flashlight on the drunk clown. A bloody axe was cradled in his lap. He unholstered his .38 revolver, and as he got a few steps closer, he spotted a knife sticking out of the man's gut.

"You on the porch, let me see your hands," he called out. "Hey, can you hear me?"

The clown stirred and looked up with bloodshot eyes. "Wha...huh?"

"Chief Hickman, is that you?" Deputy Blackburn asked. "Were you driving the car in the ditch, Tom?"

"I...I was...trying to...trying to help," Tom replied in a slurred voice.

"Tom, what happened? Were you injured in the accident? I'm going to call an ambulance for you, but I need you to set aside your weapon. Is there anybody else in the house?"

The fire chief looked down at his lap and seemed surprised he was holding the axe. He let it slide off his legs and drop into the snow at the bottom of the steps.

"I think I did a bad thing." Tom reached up and took hold of the wood handle sticking out of his stomach. He yanked the butcher knife out with a grunt, unleashing a torrent of blood that poured down the stairs. Before Edgar could reach him, Tom had fallen over. He knelt beside him and checked his neck for a pulse, but the man was already dead. The front door of the house had been battered open, and there was a trail of blood leading inside from the porch.

With his revolver and flashlight in hand, Edgar entered the farmhouse and followed the blood splatter down the hallway and into a bedroom. His hands were sweating as he pushed in the bathroom door and discovered another body lying on the floor. This one belonged to an older woman, he guessed the homeowner, and there was no need to check her for vital signs. Brain matter was visible from the large gash in her head, most likely made by the clown's axe. Edgar barely made it outside before his stomach let loose and he vomited into a snow-covered bush in the yard.

Stumbling back to his truck as he wiped his mouth off, he climbed into the cab and keyed the radio under the dashboard. "Dispatch, this is Unit 19, I'm at, um...1408 Motte's Ferry Road. I've got, ah, multiple fatalities. I need an ambulance and backup here and see if you can get a snowplow out to clear the goddamn road. Copy, Dispatch?"

"Copy, Unit 19, sit tight."

Deputy Blackburn knew he should go back inside and check for more victims, but he wasn't about to set foot in there until backup arrived. He had been with the department less than a year and seen a couple of dead bodies while working traffic accidents, but this was his first murder scene. His father was the sheriff of nearby Linn County, and he would have been furious if he knew his son had thrown up while on the job.

Edgar was wondering if he had made a mistake following in his father's (*and grandfather's and great-grandfather's*) footsteps, when he felt like he was being watched. His eyes went to the rearview mirror, which reflected a hooded person standing behind his truck. Edgar stepped out with his gun drawn, but there was only snow and darkness surrounding him.

That same night, in a cheap apartment near the campus of the University of Iowa, an English professor named Martin Knight awoke from a troubled, alcohol-induced stupor. He searched around blindly until he found his glasses on the nightstand. Someone moaned behind him, and he looked over his shoulder to see the naked back of a woman lying in his bed.

Martin remembered talking with a beautiful, raven-haired graduate student at his faculty Halloween party that evening. The same woman now appeared to be sleeping beside him without any clothes. He also had nothing on except for a pair of white cotton briefs, which had a couple of holes in them, but he was sure they had still engaged in sexual relations. The details of how he had managed that impressive feat were murky, but the nightmare he had woken up from was fresh in his mind.

As quietly as he could to avoid disturbing her, Martin slid open the nightstand drawer and removed the leather-bound notebook he always kept with him. He dug around in the drawer until he found a pen, which he used to jot down what he could recall about the lucid dream.

Scary clown with red balloon
Psycho with axe breaking door
Werewolf and witch?

He closed the notebook, returned it to the drawer, took off his glasses, and then nestled back into bed beside the nude sleeping beauty. Martin hoped that he could remember her name when he woke up in the morning. It was too bad he hadn't thought to scribble that down in his notebook.

# PART I:

# HOMECOMING

# A Colorado Kid Comes To Iowa

Novel By **MARTIN KNIGHT**

Jupiter &
Phoebus
Publishing
House

# CHAPTER 1
## A Colorado Kid Comes To Iowa

*June 9, 2019*

The single-aisle regional jet touched down with a jarring bump at the Cedar Rapids Regional Airport. The pilot braked hard enough that John Sterling had to brace his hand against the seat ahead. He hated flying and was grateful there was no turbulence on this flight. The plane was packed, and it took fifteen minutes to debark since he was near the back. At least he only had a carry-on bag, so he didn't have to wait for his luggage to be unloaded.

His interview at the University of Iowa was in an hour, and he still needed to get his rental car. Iowa City was a good half-hour drive away on top of that. John texted his wife, Karina, to let her know he had arrived safely as he hurried through the terminal. He had flown out of Denver International this morning, and any of its terminals were larger than this entire airport.

There wasn't a long line when he reached the car rental counter, but the clerk behind the desk seemed in no hurry to process anyone. It was another ten minutes before he was heading out to the parking lot, and he was so annoyed he forgot the parking spot number where his car was located. John walked down the aisle, pressing the unlock button on the key fob until he spotted lights flashing on a bright red convertible.

When he got to the vehicle, he held down the trunk-open button on the remote to be sure he had the right car. The lid popped open, but he pulled out his rental agreement to double-check that there wasn't a mistake. Sure enough, the form showed he was paying the fee for a compact car but had been provided with a brand-new Chevy Camaro.

"Oh, fuck yeah," he said, then winced when a woman walking by glared at him. John tossed his bag in the trunk, started the engine, and put the top down. He pulled out onto Interstate 380 heading southbound, and before he knew it, the speedometer showed he was going 95 miles per hour.

"Whoa, slow down there, girl." It was like the damn car had a mind of its own, and he was grinning like a teenager on his first joyride. Jack eased his foot off the gas and breathed a sigh of relief there wasn't a cop around running radar. It would be just his luck to get a speeding ticket on his way to a job interview.

While he grew up in Colorado, this trip was a homecoming since he'd earned his Bachelor of Arts degree in English and Creative Writing from Iowa. He had just completed his doctorate in English Literature from the University of Colorado at Boulder (*he still wasn't used to having the title of Dr. Sterling*). Now, he hoped to land a position as an assistant professor at his first alma mater. Boulder was where his children were born, and John loved the view of the mountains. However, his wife wanted to be closer to her parents, who lived in the Ahnen Villages.

He was nervous about his chances of landing this job, given that his only recently published work was a short story in a literary magazine. He had also written a novel inspired by the pulp horror stories of his favorite author, Martin Knight, but after collecting a stack of rejections, he had given up on it. He had almost thrown it away, but Kari had convinced him to keep working on it. He had eventually found a small publisher that had offered five thousand dollars for it, which had helped pay for his doctorate. The book had yet to make back the advance, and his subsequent attempts to produce a more literary novel had resulted in writer's block.

John pulled into the parking lot next to the English-Philosophy Building with ten minutes to spare. He put the top back up and did his best to brush his thinning, wind-blown hair back into place (*driving a convertible to an interview may not have been the best idea*) before getting out of the car. John pulled on his suit jacket and did a final check of his hair in the side-view mirror. He thought he remembered the way to the department head's office, but he got turned around and had to ask for directions. He finally found his way to her office and checked in with her assistant, a preppy young man dressed in a black polo with a yellow Tigerhawk emblem and khaki pants. Dr. Kellie Wilkens stood up to shake his hand when he was shown into her office.

"Good morning, Dr. Sterling. Please have a seat," she said. "I hope your flight went smoothly?"

"Yes, it did. Thank you, Dr. Wilkens," he replied. "I appreciate the opportunity to join the English department. It's a pleasure to be back on campus."

"I'm glad to hear that. You did your undergrad work here if I remember correctly?" Kellie asked. "I found your thesis on the evolution of female protagonists in literature quite intriguing. Congratulations on your doctorate from the University of Colorado Boulder. I hear they have nearly as good of a program as we do."

"They're comparable, but Iowa gave me a solid educational foundation."

"That's a good political answer," she replied. "I imagine that the campus there has us beat hands down in terms of scenery. What made you want to come back to Iowa?"

"Well, besides being the best college for writing programs, my wife's family lives in the Ahnen Villages," he said. "We want to be closer to them, and the schools in this area have excellent resources for special needs children. Our ten-year-old son, Patrick, is on the autism spectrum."

"I have a nephew with Asperger's. It's always good to have family around to help," Kellie nodded. "We always like it when alumni return here to teach. Your published work is a bit light, but I'm impressed by your doctoral work. I must tell you that we've already met with several other well-qualified candidates. I decided to interview you because a friend helping me with the applicant selection put forward your name after reading your work. I can't say who that is, but that endorsement carries much weight."

"Thank you," Jack replied, unsure of what to say. "And I guess thank you to your friend also." He cringed at his awkward response, and Kellie smiled politely before checking the time on her watch.

"The other members of the Selection Committee should be gathered in the conference room by now," she said. "Let's head down the hall and find out, I don't want to keep them waiting too long on a Friday afternoon. I hope you don't feel like I'm putting you in front of the firing squad, but I like to ensure that candidates are a good fit with the rest of the staff."

"Not at all. It will be nice to meet the other professors," he answered, hoping he didn't sound too nervous.

The two-hour interview left him mentally exhausted. His necktie was cutting off circulation to his brain, so he yanked it off as he climbed into the Camaro, took out his phone, and dialed his wife.

"Hi babe, I'm done with the interview. How are you doing?"

"Just fantastic, Patrick's been playing *The Wonder Pets* all day," she replied. "If I hear that theme song one more time, I'll lose my mind. When will you know if you got the job?"

"I don't know for sure," he answered. "Dr. Wilkens told me that they would be deciding soon. I know how much you want this to happen, but it sounds like they have a lot of people who applied for this opening. I might not have enough experience to qualify."

"Yeah, you're right, I shouldn't get my hopes up," she sighed dramatically. "I don't know how many times I've had to correct you on the use of *there, they're,* and *their*. I'm just a simple elementary school teacher, not a learned word doctor like you." This was a running joke between them, and the teasing had become even more brutal since receiving his doctorate.

"You're hilarious, Kari," he groaned, "you missed your true calling as a stand-up comedian or a high school guidance counselor. I'm going to check into my room, get out of this monkey suit, and maybe take a nap before getting some food. There's a steakhouse near my hotel, I think I'll order a ribeye tonight."

"For someone technically unemployed, you sure eat like you're living high on the hog. I hate to spoil your evening's dinner plans, but I've got you set up to meet with a realtor in an hour to look at rental properties around town. You can stop at my parents' house afterward for dinner tonight. It would be rude to be so close and not drop in to see them."

Jack had to force himself not to let out a groan. He had been looking forward to a nice dinner and then touring the campus, but now he would have to spend the afternoon driving all over the city and his evening listening to his in-laws talk about the weather, crop prices, and the local gossip.

"Yes, dear, send me the contact number for the realtor," he sighed.

"I already texted you and emailed all the listings I've been looking at online," she replied. "I'm hoping to find something that would also be close to my parents so they could help watch the kids, but we need to make sure we're in a school district that has a good special needs program. I haven't seen much in our price range, so make sure she doesn't show you anything outside our budget. I know you talked about buying a house, but I don't see how that's feasible."

"Okay, babe, I'll go check them out and send you photos," he said. "Did you get the picture of the rental car I sent you?"

"Yes, I did, Dr. Sterling and you better not get any bright ideas driving around in that with all those college girls there."

"Don't worry; school is out for the summer, and why would I need to go looking for a younger model when I have a perfectly good MILF waiting for me back home."

"I told you not to call me that, but that is a good answer. Please don't argue politics with my father, no matter what he says about You-Know-Who. I really hope this job works out, Jack, I want to get back to Iowa."

"Yeah, me too. This could be a new beginning for us," he replied. "Who knows, maybe we'll wake up tomorrow, and it will be like all the bad shit from the last ten years never happened."

There was a heavy pause on the other end of the line. "I know neither of us was ready for parenthood, especially not with all of Patrick's issues, but I wouldn't wish our lives to be any different. Say hello to my parents for me and be on your best behavior."

Jack hung up and texted the realtor to confirm he would arrive at her office in an hour. On the way to his hotel, he grabbed a cheeseburger at the nearest drive thru. After changing into jeans and a T-shirt, he scarfed down his greasy lunch as he sat on the bed watching a baseball game. Jack allowed himself a quick ten-minute nap before he zipped across town to the realtor's office.

While the interview had gone well, he didn't think there was any chance he would get the job. He needed to at least go through the motions to keep his wife happy. It wasn't like he hated the thought of moving back to Iowa. Jack had enjoyed his college days here before Kari got pregnant, forcing him to put his academic career on hold for five years.

In fact, he wasn't exactly thrilled about being an English professor, but it paid a lot better than being a grad student and having to work odd jobs to make ends meet. Before unexpectedly becoming a father, he dreamed of living abroad and becoming a writer like Ernest Hemingway. Having spent the better part of a decade changing diapers and raising kids, he was resigned to trading in Paris for the land of endless cornfields if it meant keeping his marriage alive. Jack wondered how he would ever come up with something to write about if he did end up in Iowa.

The realtor was a tall, thin, middle-aged woman wearing an expensive-looking pantsuit. It was already mid-afternoon, but she drove him around town to view a dozen apartment buildings. He tended to get carsick when he wasn't driving, another reason why he hated airplane travel. By the time they returned to the office, he felt queasy from sitting in the passenger seat for so long.

Jack stopped at the hotel to freshen up before getting back in the car. His head was pounding, and he wanted to get some rest before flying out tomorrow morning, but he had promised his wife that he would visit her parents. The drive would take him almost half an hour. Maybe he would feel hungry when he got out there, especially if Margrit, his mother-in-law, had baked her rhubarb coffee cake.

He took the Interstate out of the city, grinning like a fool as he opened up the throaty V8 and zipped past the lumbering semi-trucks. Despite his headache, he had put the top back down. Jack was going so fast that he almost drove past the turn-off for Bailey Grove. Luckily, nobody was behind him as he hit the brakes and whipped onto the exit ramp. The fresh air and thrill of driving such a magnificent automobile had reinvigorated him as he reached the Ulmer's farm.

His stomach started growling when Margrit set a plate before him piled high with homemade fried chicken, mashed potatoes with gravy, corn on the cob, and cottage cheese with chives. By the time he pushed away from the table, too full to take another bite, he had already stayed later than he had intended. She insisted on making coffee and getting out the rhubarb cake for dessert, and Jack found a few more inches of space in his stomach.

It was getting dark outside as he said his goodbyes to his wife's parents, gladly accepting a generous piece of cake for breakfast. Heading back towards the Interstate, he passed through Bailey Grove again. Jack noted what a quaint little town it was, tucked away in a valley surrounded by tree-covered hills. Coming over the top of a hill south of town, he had to slam on the brakes to avoid hitting a large deer carcass lying in the middle of the road.

"Jesus wept," he said, his heart beating wildly. He wasn't an outdoorsman by any stretch of the imagination, but he could tell from the antlers that it was a sizable buck. Jack had to drive onto the shoulder to get around it, the rear passenger wheel spinning in the gravel as it slipped off the road. He thought about leaving it there, but the next car that came through might be unable to stop in time. Jack pulled into a driveway up the road and parked with the hazard lights flashing.

He took out his phone to call the police to come get the dead animal off the road. Jack dialed 911, but his phone beeped three times before displaying **No Service** on the screen. He stepped out of the car and tried the call again without any luck.

"Goddamn backwater Iowa. Not even decent cell service out here. What else can go wrong today?" He leaned against the car, wondering if he should try dragging the deer off the road, only to have the Camaro sputter and die.

Jack turned off the ignition and tried restarting the engine, but the starter only gave a dry clicking noise. He leaned forward and rested his forehead on the steering wheel.

"You've got to be kidding me," he muttered as he exited the car and slammed the door shut. "Whoever lives here better have a working fucking phone."

The car's headlights pointed up at a quaint, two-story farmhouse. A streetlight to the right of the driveway had a sign nailed to the wooden pole with ***FOR SALE BY OWNER*** printed on it. The sodium lamp at the top of the pole was flickering in its death throes. Jack walked around the car to get a better look at the sign. He was taking down the phone number when the Camaro's headlamps turned off, leaving him only the streetlight to see by.

He stood there debating whether to continue to the house or walk back to town. Jack shook his head, ashamed that he was acting like a kid afraid of the dark, and marched towards the farmhouse. He switched on the flashlight feature of his cell phone and used the narrow beam of light to pick his way across the rutted driveway, careful not to trip over the deep runnels cut throughout the gravel by rainwater.

His last hopes of being able to call for help faded as his repeated knocking on the front door drew no response. The house appeared to have been sitting empty for some time, but it wasn't in a state of neglect. He thought about checking it out in the morning before his flight.

Jack decided to walk down the hill to the convenience store he passed on the south side of Bailey Grove. Hopefully it had a working phone, or maybe he could get a signal and call a tow truck. He reached the spot where the massive roadkill had been, but the light from his phone showed only a few streaks of blood leading off into the far ditch. It was possible that the animal had only been knocked unconscious after being struck by a passing car, woke up, and stumbled away. Then again, something big enough to drag off a couple hundred-pound buck might also be lurking nearby.

He hadn't heard of bears roaming around the middle of Iowa before, but he wasn't about to find out if one had wandered down from Wisconsin or Minnesota. Jack ran back to the safety of the Camaro, breathing a sigh of relief as he locked the doors. He tried the key in the ignition again, and the engine roared to life.

The tires spun in the loose gravel as he backed out of the driveway. If a car came over the hill, he would be roadkill, but he didn't care as he tore off with a squeal of rubber. Jack didn't slow down until he turned onto the Interstate and was heading back toward the city. He glanced at his reflection in the rearview mirror and gave a nervous laugh.

*June 10, 2019*

With his flight scheduled to depart at 10 o'clock, Jack debated whether there was time to revisit the farmhouse for sale that morning. Shortly after waking up, he received an alert that his flight was delayed until 2 that afternoon. Jack contacted the realtor, Pam, to tell her about the property and see if she could arrange a tour with the homeowner.

While he and Kari had gotten pre-approved for a mortgage, the home prices in Iowa City were way beyond their means. A fixer-upper out in the country might be something they could swing. Pam called him back about ten minutes later to say that she had received the code for the key locker on the front porch and would meet him there to let him in. He had driven away from the farmhouse the night before like his ass was on fire, but he risked heading back on his own so he could get a look at it before the realtor arrived.

The two-story home, painted off-white with hunter green trim, was even more quaint in the daylight. It was landscaped with some lilac bushes and shrubs that heightened the austere aesthetic of the house. Jack knew once his wife got a good look at the place, she would fall in love with it.

He doubted they could afford it, but he wanted to see if it was within the realm of possibilities. Jack was trying to peek in through the windows when Pam's pearl-white Cadillac Escalade pulled into the driveway and parked behind his car. He stepped off the porch to greet the realtor as she exited the gaudy SUV.

"Good morning, Pam. Thank you for coming out here," he said as he shook her hand. "I found this place when I was coming back from my in-laws. If its out of our price range, I apologize in advance for dragging you out here."

"It's really no problem. This property is something of a curiosity in the local real estate market," Pam replied. "As far as I know, it's been sitting empty for the past thirty-five years and never been put up for sale. One of the oldest law firms in Iowa City holds the title, and several of my colleagues have inquired about it with them. They were told it wasn't for sale, but somebody has been paying to maintain it."

"That does sound odd. I wonder why they suddenly decided to sell it now?" Jack asked. "The outside looks to be in pretty good shape. It could use a fresh coat of paint, but those look like new shingles on the roof. I bet the inside is probably trashed. I wouldn't be shocked if an isolated house like this hasn't been used as a meth lab."

"I spoke to the head of the law firm this morning, and he assured me that nobody except for the property management company they hired has set foot in there and that all the utilities and appliances are in working order. Why don't we go in and look around for ourselves?"

"Yeah, good idea," he nodded. "Why would a law firm have the deed to an old farm-house? And why wouldn't they have sold it off long ago instead of paying to keep it up?"

"I don't know, but I've heard some rumors..." Pam seemed about to say something more, but she stopped herself. "I mean, it's just small-town gossip. I'm sure that every-thing about this place is fine. Nothing I found in the records raised any red flags."

He was about to press her further about these rumors, but she climbed the porch steps and opened the lock box by the door. The interior was even more immaculate than the outside, yet it had a dusty, stale smell that told him it had been closed up for a long time. "This is in much better shape than I was expecting."

"Yes, indeed. I hope you won't mind if I take some pictures of the house while we look around," she said. "Don't take offense, but if you pass on it, I won't have much trouble finding another buyer."

He chuckled but also felt anxious about making such an important decision without his wife seeing the house. That thought inspired him to pull out his phone and photo-graph the rooms as he went through them.

Jack toured the first floor, which included a living room, kitchen, master bedroom with a small ensuite bath, and a laundry room. Upstairs were two bedrooms and a bathroom, which would be perfect for the kids, but no room he could use as an office. He opened the curtains in one of the bedroom windows when his phone started ringing. Jack saw the number had an Iowa area code, and his heart raced as he pressed the button to answer the call.

"Hello, this is John Sterling."

"Good morning, it's Professor Wilkens. Did I catch you at a bad time?"

"Not at all. I was just doing some house hunting before I flew back home," he replied.

"That's not a bad idea, actually, since I'm calling to offer you a position on our staff," Kellie said. "Congratulations, and welcome to the department."

"Thank you, that is excellent news," he answered. "My wife will be thrilled to hear that, and I'm very excited about this fantastic opportunity as well."

They discussed the particulars of the offer for a few minutes before Jack hung up the phone and headed back downstairs. "I was worried you got lost up there," Pam said as she typed on her phone.

"Sorry about that. I had to take a phone call. I think I'd like to put an offer down on the house," he grinned. "I accepted a position at the University, so maybe it's my lucky day. Let's see if we can work out a deal for this place."

"That's great news, and congratulations on getting the job," she replied. "I was told that if you wanted to make an offer, you should send a text to this number."

Pam showed him her phone screen with a ten-digit number displayed on it.

"I'll be the first to admit that I don't know a thing about real estate deals, but is this how these sorts of things are normally conducted?" Jack asked. "I mean, without ever meeting the seller?"

The realtor shrugged her shoulders. "Maybe in the big cities, but usually not around here. These are the instructions the lawyer gave me." Jack nodded as he copied the number into his phone. He typed out a brief message and almost immediately received a reply to his text.

> Hello my name is Jack Sterling

> I'm interested in buying the house at 1408 Mottes Ferry Road

> What's your offer?

Jack was caught off guard and stared at the screen. "I guess I might as well put all my cards on the table," he said as he punched in the total amount the bank had approved him for a loan, which felt too low for what the house had to be worth.

He showed Pam the figure, and a brief grimace crossed her face before she smoothed it over. "Well, here goes nothing." There was about a minute delay before the seller responded, but it felt like forever to him.

> Offer accepted

> Paperwork sent to your realtor

"Holy crap, I think I just bought a house," Jack whistled as he showed Pam his phone's screen. "Oh man, I better call my wife. She's going to be pissed I didn't talk it over with her."

"I'm sure she will be delighted with the deal you made," Pam said. "This will be a great home to raise a family in."

# The Long Drive

Novel By **MARTIN KNIGHT**

Jupiter & Phoebus Publishing House

# CHAPTER 2
## The Long Drive

*June 30, 2019*

J ack remembered a joke one of his college professors from Iowa had told on the first day of class. *An Iowa farmer goes to his doctor after not feeling well and learns that he has terminal cancer. The doctor recommends that he move to Nebraska, and the farmer asks him if that will help him live longer. The doctor replies, 'No, but it will definitely feel like it.'* He had laughed with the rest of the class but didn't appreciate how true it was until he drove across the state with two kids in tow. Yesterday, they had gone from Boulder, Colorado, to Grand Island, Nebraska, in eight hours, and it had certainly felt like the longest day of his life. Not that Iowa would be all that more exciting, but at least there were the occasional signs of civilization.

Since this was their fourth trip back to Iowa after the kids had been born, Jack thought they were prepared, and like each time before, he was sadly mistaken. They had stocked Patrick with a case of his favorite DVDs and installed a headrest-mounted player so he could change them out by himself. Instead, he wanted to repeatedly watch videos he had recorded on his electronic tablet from streaming YouTube on the TV. All these videos were of cartoon shows being interrupted by tornado warning alerts interspersed with tests of tornado sirens being conducted. For reasons known only to Patrick, these homemade movies were downright hysterical and provided hours of entertainment. By the time they hit the Nebraska border, Jack hoped a tornado would swoop down and carry him off to a nice quiet wheatfield in the middle of Kansas.

Their eight-year-old daughter, Jennifer, had her own video player and was watching movies until her headphones died. After that, she began complaining about her brother's videos, prompting Patrick to turn up the volume on his tablet. The argument escalated until Jack was forced to stop at Walmart to buy her a new pair. Both kids were bouncing off the walls from being cooped up when they reached the hotel, but thankfully Kari had booked a place with an indoor swimming pool.

The second day of the trip had started out better. The kids were worn out from playing in the pool all evening, and they were watching movies with headphones on. The plan was to drive the four hours to Des Moines for lunch, and then they would only have a couple of hours left until they reached Bailey Grove. A little over two hours into the drive, Patrick began repeatedly talking about "Stop at Big Smiley Face" and "Lunch at eleven."

"No, buddy, we're not stopping for lunch until noon," Jack said.

"Lunch at smiley face!" his son yelled. "McDonald's at eleven."

"Jack, if he wants to eat lunch early, what's the problem?" Kari asked.

"The problem is we're out in the middle of Bumfuck, Iowa."

"Watch your language, Jack."

"They've got their headphones on," he replied. "Look, I'll stop if I see someplace along here, otherwise we keep-"

"There it is! There's Big Smiley Face!" Patrick called out excitedly as he pointed towards the windshield. On the horizon was a bright yellow water tower with two black dots and a black curved line painted to resemble a smiling face.

"Holy crap, we stopped there for gas two years ago," Jack said. "How the hell did he remember that thing?"

"Because he remembers everything, so knock off the cussing," she answered. "If I have to say it again, you won't be a happy camper later."

Jack was about to argue with her, but the possibility of sex after two long days on the road and the three longer days of packing before that shut him up. The road sign listing restaurants located at the Adair turnoff showed that Patrick was also right about there being a McDonald's. He got off at the exit and drove the short way into town. The familiar golden arches elicited excited arm flapping from his son as they pulled into the parking lot.

Patrick would tolerate eating food from only a handful of restaurants, most of which served breakfast all day. Otherwise, if they went out to eat, they had to pack a thermos full of Spaghetti-Os or Kraft Mac'n Cheese for him if there was nothing on the menu he liked. Patrick was a picky eater because he had sensory processing disorder, so most foods tended to make him gag or throw up. The smell of certain foods could also make him ill, so they had to be careful about where they ate even when they packed food for him.

"I don't want to go to McDonald's," his daughter whined.

"I know, Jenny, but your brother wants to eat here," Kari answered. "How about you get a Happy Meal with a toy? If you're not hungry, I packed plenty of snacks. We're going to a nice restaurant tonight with grandma and grandpa. I promise you'll like it."

Jack found a parking spot as close to the entrance as he could, and his son had already unbuckled his seatbelt before he shut off the engine.

"Patrick, wait for daddy," Kari said as Jack hopped out of the driver's seat.

"I'll take the kids and find a booth if you could get me a Big Mac meal," he told his wife. "Are you going to eat anything, babe?"

"No, I've got some peanut butter crackers and Twizzlers in the van," she replied. Kari often got car sick on long trips and usually ate only enough to keep from getting dizzy. "Jenny can stay with me and help carry the drinks."

Jack held his son's hand as he led him into the restaurant and steered him towards the seating area. Patrick slipped free and made a beeline for the counter, cutting in front of an elderly couple trying to order breakfast despite it being lunchtime.

"Say hi to the kitchen," his son announced as he brought up the camera on his tablet and started recording the workers preparing the food.

"Excuse me, young man, but we were in line here first," the gray-haired woman told Patrick sternly, but his son didn't acknowledge that she had spoken to him.

"Sorry about that," Jack said as he slipped around them to reach the counter. "He likes to see all the activity happening in the kitchen." His explanation didn't appease the elderly couple's annoyance as they both scowled as he pulled Patrick away.

His wife was also glaring at him for not keeping Patrick under control, and he gave her a shrug of the shoulders as they walked past. The booth in the back he'd hoped to snag had been taken, so he had to settle for a four-person table in the center of the dining room. The restaurant was quite busy and judging by the number of elderly patrons milling about drinking coffee and chatting, Jack guessed it was a hangout for retired folks who gathered here to socialize. To make matters worse, the pair from up at the counter sat at a table beside them.

"Patrick, look what I have," Kari said as she brought the tray full of food. "Yummy pancakes, and they're all mine!"

"Mine!" Patrick laughed at their usual game during mealtimes. Kari sat down across from him, opened the lid of the pancakes, and smelled them in an exaggerated display of delight. Patrick hummed and shook his hands in anticipation.

"Mmmmm, I think I'm going to eat up all these pancakes," she teased as she peeled back the cover on the syrup container.

"Mine! Patrick's pancakes!" he exclaimed as he jumped up and knocked over his chair. Jack righted the chair while Kari sat him down and started cutting up his meal. The entire restaurant was looking in their direction. The worst was the old couple at the adjacent table, blatantly staring at them. Normally he would have ignored them, but he stared back until they turned their attention to their breakfast. Jack had to hurriedly eat his sandwich while his son was scarfing down his plate of hotcakes.

"Slow down, Patrick, you don't want to get a belly ache," his wife said. "We need to use the bathroom after we finish eating, and then we'll get back in the van."

"Uh-uh, No Van, No Bathroom!" Patrick shouted with a mouth full of food. "SWIM-MING POOL!"

"Patrick, please be quiet," Jack told him. "We need to use our inside voice in here. We went to the swimming pool last night, but we'll be sleeping in our new home tonight. Now doesn't that sound exciting?"

"NO HOME! HOTEL! POOL!"

"Calm down, let's go over our schedule," Kari said. "First lunch, then bathroom, back in van, drive to new home, and then see grandma and grandpa. Can we do that?"

Patrick was silent for a few seconds as he thought it over. "Yes," he finally said. "Lunch is check, next is bathroom."

"That's good, Patrick. Follow daddy and wash your hands when you're done." Jack had to leave the last few bites of his burger as he helped Patrick stand up without knocking over his chair this time. They were walking past the rude old couple when the woman's phone on the edge of the table rang, and Patrick picked it up. He held it next to his ear to listen to the musical ringtone.

"Hey, that's my wife's phone!" the man snapped. "Give that back."

"Patrick, we don't touch other people's things," Jack scolded him as he grabbed the phone from his son and handed it to the man. "I'm very sorry about that. He has autism and likes to-"

"I don't care what he has. You need to teach him to keep his hands to himself."

Jack felt anger bringing a nasty retort to his mouth but forced it back down. If he shouted at the old codger, it could send Patrick into a full-blown meltdown, and he didn't want to cause a bigger scene. His wife's head whipped around at the commotion. Jack knew that even if he held his tongue, she would go full mamma bear on the man, so he needed to defuse the situation quickly.

"Yes, thank you for that," he said curtly, ushering his son to the restroom. He got Patrick back to the van without any further incidents. Jack put a new disc into the DVD player for him and sat down in the driver's seat to close his eyes for a bit. Kari was buckling Jenny into her car seat when he overheard his daughter asking her a question.

"Mommy, what is a retard?"

"Where did you hear that word?"

"That mean old man called Patrick it." Jack didn't remember the man saying that, but it could have been after they were in the bathroom.

The look in his wife's eyes was one of murderous rage, and Jack worried she would storm back into the restaurant. Her nostrils were flaring in anger, and he knew if she confronted them, it would end up on the evening news. Or even worse, YouTube. That was the last thing they needed, to be some kind of viral freak show.

"Honey, calm down, it's not worth it," he pleaded. "Let's just get the hell out of here." Kari was still seething, but she saw that Jenny was on the verge of tears.

"It's a very bad name, sweetheart, so don't ever repeat that, okay?" Jenny nodded, and Kari kissed her forehead before shutting the sliding door. As he backed out of the parking spot, he noticed his wife looking at the old couple still eating their meal.

"Choke on it," Kari muttered under her breath. Jack shifted into gear and sped off toward the Interstate.

Grant shook his head as he watched the van drive off through the restaurant windows. He was a retired middle school art teacher, and if there was one thing he couldn't stand anymore, it was loud, annoying children, especially while he and his wife, Nan, were enjoying their breakfast. It also annoyed him that McDonald's stopped serving breakfast at ten-thirty, but the manager here knew better than to piss off her clientele and would extend it until eleven.

"I tell you, parents these days just don't know how to teach their brats to behave in public," he grumbled to his wife. Grant took a bite of his sausage biscuit right as the top palate of his dentures came loose, causing him to swallow the chunk of food without chewing it. The thick biscuit formed a plug in his windpipe and cut off all air to his lungs.

His hands clutched at his throat while his mouth opened and closed soundlessly, but it took a few seconds before his wife noticed he was unable to breathe.

"Grant? Grant, what's wrong? Oh god, somebody help, he's choking!" Nan called out.

His lungs were burning as one of the restaurant workers rushed over, wrapped his arms around Grant's stomach, and began administering the Heimlich maneuver.

"Please don't die on me, Grant!" With the third compression, the morsel flew from his mouth and smacked his wife squarely in the eye. He sucked in a deep breath before coughing and sputtering. Nan wiped her face off and began crying as she came around the table and hugged him.

*June 30, 2019*

Jack turned into the farmhouse's driveway shortly after two o'clock and pulled up beside the Cadillac Escalade parked on the grass. Pam was standing in the shade of the porch, talking on her cell phone as they piled out of their minivan and stretched from the long trip. Patrick ran up the front steps and peered inside the house through the windows, his arms flapping wildly in excitement. Kari hurried to move him out of the realtor's way until she finished her phone call.

"Sorry about that, I've got three open houses going on today, so I'm having to coordinate with my staff," she said. She held out her hand to Kari. "Hello, I'm Pam. It's a pleasure to meet you. I must say that your husband is a brave man to buy a house without having his wife see it first. I think you'll agree he made a good purchase."

"Yes, well, I hope he made the right choice for his sake," Kari replied, giving Jack a sideways look. Pam fished around in her purse before pulling out a set of keys.

"Here you go. Have a look around and see for yourself."

Kari took the keys from her, unlocked the front door, and then hesitated.

"You know, this house looks so familiar," she said to Pam. "Out of curiosity, do you know who lived here before?"

"I'm afraid not. The law firm only said it was an investment property," the realtor replied. "I had my assistant check for any existing records on the property, but she could only find that it was part of a working farm until 1985. The home inspector I hired to look it over said it was in excellent condition even though nobody's been living here in a while, so I think you got a fantastic deal on the place."

"See, I know what I'm doing," Jack said. "I'm sure you probably remember seeing this place when you lived here."

"Did your husband tell you about the great view of Bailey Grove?" Pam asked. "I'll admit, the interior does look a bit dated. I'm sure with some minor renovations, you'll feel right at home." Kari opened the front door, and Patrick took off running.

"It looks like somebody is excited about the new house," his wife said. Jack chased after their son while Pam took her around the ground floor before heading upstairs.

"I want the bedroom on the left," Jenny called out.

"Sure thing, sweetheart," Kari replied. He corralled Patrick and herded him up the steps.

"This one will be your bedroom, Patrick," his wife said. "Look, you can see the town from up here."

"What do you think about the house, babe?" Jack asked her.

"It needs a good deal of work, but it's not bad. That doesn't mean you're off the hook."

"I'll take that as a win," he replied with a grin.

"If you don't need anything else from me, I'll get out of your hair so you can settle in," Pam said. "Enjoy your new home, and welcome to Iowa."

Jack unloaded their luggage from the minivan. They had packed only enough things to get by for the few days before the moving truck arrived with the rest of their belongings. Somehow, they had managed to fit air mattresses, sleeping bags, towels, clothes, and toiletries into the rear of the van, along with all the food for Patrick. Jack was drenched in sweat when he finished carrying everything in and dropped the last two bags on the floor with a thud.

"Careful, the floors are scuffed up enough already," Kari scolded him. "It's about time you got all that in. I've been keeping Patrick from trying to flush the toilet for the last ten minutes. I hope this dump doesn't have a septic tank that overflows easily. You need to go to the hardware store tomorrow morning and get locking doorknobs for both bathrooms. I don't know how I'm going to watch him across two different floors. Does this hellhole also have a basement for him to get into?"

"Whoa, I thought you said you liked the house?"

"I said it wasn't bad, and I was also saying that in front of the real estate agent," she replied. "This wallpaper is disgusting and will be a nightmare to remove. Maybe once you get all that stripped off, I can look around without my eyes hurting. The first thing that needs to happen is for you to Patrick-proof everything before I can even relax. I'm also worried about living near Bailey Grove. How many times have I told you that the people in this town can be snobbish."

"I get that, babe, but you said you wanted to be closer to your parents. The mortgage is the same as renting something in Iowa City would cost. Give it a year, and if you don't like living here after that, I promise we'll sell it and find something else."

"Like we could find another sucker to buy it." Kari sniffed. "Okay, fine, I'll give it a year. You're right, it will be nice to have a real house instead of another apartment. Why don't you make yourself useful and put my suitcase in the bedroom? We're meeting my parents for dinner at the Yoke and Plow. Do you think you can watch the kids while I grab a quick shower?"

"Sure thing, babe. Let me know if you need your back scrubbed while you're in there." Jack reached around and grabbed her rear end, and Kari responded by kneeing him in the groin. "Ooof, that's some kind of gratitude I get around here."

"Then keep your hands to yourself," she said as he pretended to double over in pain. "Suck it up, buttercup. I'm shocked you chose this house since there's no place for an office. I thought you'd want someplace to do your writing?"

"I know, but I guess I'll have to make do."

Since he learned to read a clock, Patrick insisted on eating dinner at 5:00 pm sharp. Jack's brain and stomach were still on Mountain time, so he wasn't hungry. It didn't matter as Patrick went by what the clock on his tablet showed. Karina had anticipated this and arranged to meet her parents at the *Yoke and Plow* restaurant at quarter to five. Jenny complained that she was too tired to go out, and his wife promised her that she could have cereal when they got home if she didn't want to eat. Jack didn't have that same luxury, but he knew once the aroma of authentic German cooking filled his nose, that wouldn't be a problem.

When they arrived, the parking lot behind the rustic wood and brick building was only half full. Hopefully, that meant the place wouldn't be packed yet. Jack didn't feel like having an audience while they ate after what happened at lunch. Both kids were cranky after two days of driving. A single-cab Ford F150 pickup rumbled into the lot, parked beside them, and Kari's parents got out.

"Hi, mom. It's so good to see you again," Kari said as she embraced her.

"Yes, it's been too long," her mom replied. Even at her age, Margrit had a striking beauty that she seemed to be trying to hide by putting her blond hair up in a tight bun and only wearing minimal makeup. Her black, wire-framed glasses also made her look more severe, and she seemed to have a permanent scowl on her face like a librarian daring anyone to make a noise. Jack knew she was a kind, caring woman underneath the cold exterior, as evident by the warm hug she gave her grandchildren.

The tall, stocky man who followed behind her had a perpetual jolly personality in stark contrast to his wife. He had a graying beard, and his weathered, lined face was quick to light up with a smile. The quintessential Iowa farmer, Albert was wearing a flannel long-sleeved shirt and denim overalls despite the heat, but he had traded his work boots for black cowboy boots to go out for dinner.

"There's my girl," Albert said. "I'm so happy to see you, and your little munchkins are growing like weeds."

"Hi, daddy, how are you?" She grinned as she hugged him and planted a kiss on his cheek. "I can't believe it's been almost two years since we've seen you guys."

"Hi grandma, look I lost a tooth last week!" Jenny said as she opened her mouth wide and pointed at the gap in her front teeth. "I got five dollars from the tooth fairy. Daddy said I should save it for college, but I want to buy a coloring book with it."

"Well, your father has been in college longer than you've been alive," Margrit commented, "so he probably knows what he's talking about."

"Patrick, can you say hi to your grandma and grandpa?" Kari prompted their son, but he didn't acknowledge her question and continued playing with his tablet.

"I see the boy is still not speaking much," Margrit noted.

"Mom, he can understand what you're saying even if he doesn't answer," Kari bristled. If she was offended by the rebuff, Margrit didn't show it. Instead, she bent down to be at eye level with him and got his attention.

"Hello, Patrick. Can you say hi to me?"

To Jack's surprise, his son briefly made eye contact with her as he said, "Hi to me." Margrit smiled and gave him a peck on the cheek, which he wiped off with his hand. Patrick did this whenever somebody kissed him, but she didn't appear to mind.

Albert hugged Jenny and lifted her off the ground as she laughed. He put her down and held his hand out to Patrick with the palm facing up. His son reached out and touched his grandfather's hand with his fingertips. His father-in-law had taught Patrick how to do a high-five this way the last time they had come to visit. Jack and Kari exchanged a quick look of disbelief at their son's display of social interaction.

The interior of the Yoke and Plow was made to look like a Bavarian cottage high up in the Alps. To create a cozy atmosphere, the large dining area was sectioned off by walls into smaller rooms decorated with flowered wallpaper and paintings of mountainous landscapes. Karina asked the hostess to seat them out of the way if possible, and the young woman in a white and blue dress escorted them to a big round table in the back corner of the room. Their waitress, a smiling, plump woman with the bosoms to properly fill out the traditional German outfit that the servers were required to wear, soon appeared at their table.

"Guten Tag, wilkommen zurück im Joch und Pflug," she recited a practiced phrase that was clearly intended to amuse the tourists. "My name is Helena. I'll be your waitress today. Can I take your drink order?"

Albert answered her back in fluent German. "Wir werden vier pints ihres dunkelsten deutschen Bieres, zwei gläser milch für die kinder und einen blick auf diese milchkrüge in deiner bluse." Jack had no idea what his father-in-law had said, but neither did the waitress by the deer-in-headlights look on her face. Albert chuckled until he was silenced by an icy glare from his wife.

"Ignore my husband. He is a babbling fool who should never be allowed off the farm," Margrit said. "Please bring us four dark German beers and two glasses of milk." The waitress nodded as she jotted down the order on her pad.

"You are a dirty old coot," Jack heard his mother-in-law hiss at Albert, which made him wonder even more what he had said to the waitress.

"Bah, can't a man have a bit of fun?" he replied, earning him another withering look from Margrit.

"Actually, make two of those beers iced tea with no lemon," Kari called to the waitress as she started to walk away. "It's been a long day. I don't think a beer would be a good idea right now."

"I don't know, hon, I think a beer sounds pretty..." he stopped when he saw his wife raise her eyebrow. "I mean, iced tea sounds fine. I'll take lemon with mine, though." The waitress nodded and hurried back to the kitchen.

While Margrit was busy asking Jenny what she thought of the new house, Kari leaned over and whispered, "I thought we agreed you weren't going to drink anymore." Jack started to argue with her but then decided it would be best to avoid this topic.

He had not been a heavy drinker when he was an undergrad, apart from getting hammered at a couple of parties. As the pressure started mounting from the rigors of his academic studies, on top of having to raise two kids, he found himself turning more often to alcohol to take the edge off. He hadn't realized it had become an addiction until it was almost too late.

Jack came home drunk one night to find that Patrick had flushed several pages of a dissertation he was working on down the toilet, clogging it up. He had woken his son up, yelling at him until his wife slapped him across the face. Jack had passed out on the couch in the living room while Kari dealt with Patrick's resulting meltdown, which lasted well into the early morning hours. She hadn't spoken to him for three days when she issued him an ultimatum. Either get his drinking under control or else move out and agree to a divorce.

"How do you like your new home?" Albert asked. "We will have to come and see it once you are ready for guests."

"It's going to take some remodeling," Kari replied. "Do you happen to know who used to live there?"

"No, I can't say we do," Margrit replied. Jack thought a bit too quickly. "I think that house has been empty for quite a while. I don't remember who might have owned it last."

"I feel like I know that house for some reason, but I can't think of how." Kari shook her head. "It's driving me nuts."

The waitress soon returned with their meal. Dinner was served family style, with a heaping plate of both smoked ham slices and fried chicken set in the center for everyone to share, surrounded by side dishes of steamed corn, coleslaw, cottage cheese with chives, pickled beets, and sauerkraut.

Patrick and Jenny turned their noses up at most of the food, but they did eat some ham, corn, and cottage cheese. Jack loaded up two plates worth of food and had probably put on ten pounds when he threw in the towel. The only thing that would've improved his dining experience was a pint of dark German beer, but it wasn't worth bringing his wife's wrath down upon him.

"I shouldn't have to eat for a week after that," he said, patting his stomach.

"That's good because we could be eating frozen meals until the moving company arrives with our things," Kari replied. "That reminds me, we need to stop at a grocery store on the way home. I need to get something to make the kids for breakfast."

"The children need to have good home-cooked meals," Margrit said. "Why don't you come to our house for dinners until you have your kitchen in order."

"Mom, we can't impose on you like that."

"Nonsense, we would enjoy having the company. Isn't that right, Albert?"

Her husband set down his empty beer glass and let out a loud belch. "Yes, you are always welcome."

Margrit rolled her eyes at him. "Besides, I'm greedy and want to see my grandchildren. There are also several projects around the house that your father has been too lazy to take care of, so I intend to put your husband to work. He could use the exercise if he keeps eating like that."

Jack felt his face turn red, but he let out a belch, and the table broke out in laughter. "I'll be happy to help with whatever you need after I make the house safe for Patrick. Or I guess I should say safe *from* Patrick."

"We had better get going," Kari said. "The kids could use baths, and we still need groceries. Thank you so much for dinner. It feels good to be back home."

The kids were nodding off when he pulled into the driveway, and they had to be carried inside. However, when Kari announced it was bath time, they found the energy to take off running. Jack chased them down, threw them in the tub, slapped pajamas on them, and tucked them in bed.

Jack's clothes were soaked, so he headed downstairs to change. The door to the bedroom was closed, and he gave it a quick rap with his knuckle. There was no answer, and he had the inexplicable urge to break it down. He gave another knock before he turned the knob and peeked inside. The room was dark, but in the light from the hall, he spotted his wife's discarded clothes on the floor beside the inflated air mattress.

He slipped inside and turned the lock behind him. Kari wasn't in bed, but the sound of running water came from the bathroom. This door was slightly ajar, so he eased it open the rest of the way. The only light in the bathroom came from a single candle sitting on the windowsill above the clawfoot tub. The curtain covered most of the tub, but his wife must have heard him come in. She sat up and pulled back the curtain, her breasts peeking above the water. The candlelight bathed her in a warm, luminous glow that gave her pale skin an ethereal appearance.

"Did somebody invite you in here?"

He started to answer with a juvenile quip, but she silenced him with a finger raised to her lips. To his surprise and pleasure, she stood up to reveal her naked, dripping-wet body and motioned for him to come closer. Jack walked over to the tub, scooped her up in his arms, and lifted her out.

"What do you think you're doing?"

"I'm going to make love to my sexy, slippery wife in our new home," he said as he carried her over to the bed. "Oh crap, this won't work, we're going to get the sheets all wet."

"Don't worry, I packed an extra set. I figured you wouldn't wait until our furniture arrived before you pestered me for sex." He laid her down and started stripping off his clothes. "This is crazy. We haven't done it on a mattress on the floor since college."

"I only graduated from college a month ago," he grinned. "At least we don't have to worry about roommates interrupting us like in the old days."

"That depends on whether you wake up the kids."

*July 1, 2019*

Patrick woke up with a buzzing sound in his ears. He was fast asleep one second and the next wide awake, but that usually happened at 5:30 every morning. His dad called him the human alarm clock, which confused him because he didn't make a ringing sound when he awoke. It was still dark in the house, and when he turned on the tablet lying next to his bed, it showed the time to be 2:27. He had trouble falling asleep last night, not only because he was in a strange bed, but also from the house being so quiet that he could hear everything. He finally drifted off after his parents had finished wrestling in their bedroom. His sister had woken up crying an hour later, and his mother had sung to her until she fell asleep again.

He watched YouTube videos on his tablet when he couldn't sleep, but they didn't have any Internet. Before they moved, his dad gave him an old stereo with headphones and a collection of Christmas music CDs to help him fall asleep. Patrick liked Christmas music because it made him feel calm and happy. He also liked messing around with the radio tuner on the stereo because it was fun to turn the knob back and forth fast to go through all the stations. The noise the radio made between stations—his dad called it static—sounded like the buzzing that had woken him up.

Patrick could also feel a vibration through the floor that grew stronger and faded away like somebody was using a vacuum cleaner nearby. He loved to watch video reviews of vacuum cleaners that people posted online. This sound, however, set his nerves on edge and made his stomach muscles clench tight like he was trying to throw up. He slipped out of bed, tip-toed to his bedroom door, and pressed his ear against it.

No sound came from the hallway, but he could feel the strange vibration through the door. He put his hand on the doorknob and jerked it back in pain. The metal was so cold it burned his palm, leaving it throbbing. Patrick grabbed his blanket and used it to turn the knob. He stuck his head into the hallway but didn't see anything. The buzzing in his head intensified as he stepped out of his room. He crept towards the stairwell when a woman's voice whispered behind him.

*Patrick*

Whipping around, he thought someone was standing in front of the window in his room. Patrick felt scared until he saw it was only the shadow of a passing cloud. He noticed a faint green glow on the floor outside his bedroom door. The hallway felt colder here, and the buzzing seemed louder. The light formed the outline of a rectangle on the ground, and it was coming from around the opening of a small door in the ceiling. A white rope hung down from a metal loop on the door, but it was too high up for him to reach.

"Patrick, is that you?" his mother called in a hushed voice as she came up the stairs. "What are you doing up? Is something wrong?"

He looked up, but the light from the ceiling had gone away, and the buzzing in his head had stopped. Kari knelt and took hold of his shoulders, looking directly into his eyes.

"Did you have a bad dream? Your skin feels cold. I hope you're not getting sick." She placed the back of her hand against his forehead. "You don't seem to be running a fever. Let's put you back in bed, and I'll get you a drink of water."

Patrick wanted to tell her about the light but couldn't make his mouth form the words. His mother tucked him in underneath his blanket, gave him a drink of water, kissed him on the forehead, and he was soon fast asleep.

# A Draft with no Wind, Lock with no Keyhole

Novel By MARTIN KNIGHT

Jupiter & Phoebus Publishing House

# Chapter 3
## A Draft with no Wind, a Lock with no Keyhole

*July 1, 2019*

Jack woke to blaring sunlight shining in through the curtainless window. That was unusual since Patrick was up at 5:30 every morning like clockwork. His back was stiff from sleeping on the air mattress. He was vaguely aware of running water when a scream came from the bathroom. Jack jumped out of bed, but a charley horse shot through his hamstring. He flopped back down on the mattress, writhing in agony as he tried to get his leg to straighten out. Karina stormed out of the bathroom, dripping wet and naked except for a bath towel. He thought about pulling the blanket over his head as she glared at him, but the view was too good to miss.

"Jack, there's no fucking HOT WATER!" she snapped. "This house you bought is a piece of shit. I swear to god, if the water heater is broken, I'm getting a hotel room until it's fixed. Get your ass out of bed and go check on it."

"Alright, calm down, I'm not even awake yet-"

"Then go jump in the shower, that should wake you up pretty damn quick."

"Okay, I get that, but why are you hating on the house? I thought you were okay with it?"

"What I would have liked was to have a say in the decision, and now I'm standing here cold and naked in a house that's older than dirt. All I want is to take a hot shower!"

"Mommy, I can see your butt," Jenny giggled, peeking around the bedroom door. Jack couldn't help but let out a snort. Kari's towel had fallen open in the back as she chastised him, and she snatched it closed while giving him the look of death. "I'm hungry. Can I have some breakfast?"

"Wait at the kitchen table, and daddy will be right there," his wife said as she shut the door. "As for you, go make your kids some food. And then find out what's wrong with the water heater." She stomped off back to the bathroom.

"What about all these puddles you left on the floor?" Jack called after her. "What should I use to clean these up with?" His wife opened the door and threw the wet towel she had been wearing at him, giving him a glimpse of her bare chest before slamming it shut again. "Thanks, babe. Nice rack!"

Both kids were sitting at the folding table his in-laws had loaned them. Jenny played with her dolls while Patrick drew on his sketch pad. Jack switched on the coffee maker they had brought before getting two cereal boxes down from the otherwise empty cupboard.

"Okay, guys, do you want Magic Charms or Sugar Flakes?"

"I want Magic Charms," Jenny replied.

"Pancakes," Patrick said.

"We don't have any pancakes, buddy," he sighed. "Can you have Sugar Flakes this morning?"

"No, try again," he answered without looking up from his drawing. "Pancakes."

"Don't be difficult, Patrick. How about some Magic Charms?"

"NO CHARMS, PANCAKES!" Jenny jumped from her brother's outburst and fell backward in her folding chair, hitting the floor with a thud. Jack ran over and scooped her up as she started crying.

"Damnit, Patrick, you can't yell like that. You scared your sister."

"What's going on? Who's shouting?" Kari poked her head out of the bedroom with a towel wrapped around her hair.

"It's nothing, babe. I've got everything under control. Patrick got upset because he didn't want cereal for breakfast, and he startled Jenny."

"Pancakes!"

"So, make him some pancakes. We bought frozen ones at the grocery store. That's why we packed the microwave in the van. Plug it in on the counter, get one of the paper plates from the cupboard, and cook two pancakes for one minute. Do you think you can handle that?"

"Sorry, I didn't know we had all that," Jack fumed. "I know how to heat up pancakes."

"I guess that's why you're the big, smart professor," she replied. "Can I finish getting ready with no hot water in the world's smallest bathroom now?"

"Yes, dear," he said. "What would I do without you?"

"Watch it, Sterling," she snapped at him. "When you're done with that, you need to find out if we need to call a plumber. Tuesday's a holiday, so they'll get booked up quickly."

Jack fixed breakfast, dressed, and went to find the water heater. He soon discovered that he had no idea where it was located. His search of the house finally turned up a locked door tucked away in the kitchen, but the house key wouldn't work. Kari found him trying to pick the lock with a couple of paper clips in a futile attempt to open it.

"What are you doing? I thought you were going to look at the water heater?"

"I am, but first I have to get into the basement."

"Don't you have the key for that?"

"No, I'll have to call the realtor," he replied. "The home inspector must have gotten down there somehow."

"Hold on. I think there's another entrance on the side of the house," Kari said as she looked out the bay window. "Yeah, there it is. Go see if you can get that open."

Jack went outside to the wooden bulkhead doors covering the exterior cellar entrance. He gave the padlock securing them a tug, and the hasp latch it was attached to wiggled. Jack yanked hard on it several times until the screws holding it to the wood pulled free. Just another thing he'd have to fix, but at least he now had access to the basement.

The bulkhead doors lifted with a grating creak of rusted hinges. Underneath was a set of cement steps leading down to another door. Jack didn't have a flashlight, so he hoped there would be a working light when he got below. This door was unlocked and opened onto a large, cinderblock-walled room. He felt along the inside wall until he found an old-fashioned toggle switch and pushed in the top button.

A naked bulb in the center of the room hummed to life, putting out only a faint glow until the filament had time to warm up. The walls were lined with rows of sturdy, hand-made wooden shelves that he guessed had been used for storing canned fruits and vegetables. In one corner was an antique washing machine, the manual kind with an enameled metal wash basin and a set of wooden rollers to wring out the wet laundry. There was also a red metal toolbox with a few spots of rust, which contained a mixture of worn but usable hand tools.

Jack crossed the room to the wooden staircase on the other side, which he assumed led to the kitchen. Beside the stairs was the water heater, which appeared to be from this century at least. A piece of paper was taped to the tank with something written in red marker. He pulled it off and stepped back into the light to read it.

*IF NO HOT WATER*
*CHECK PILOT LIGHT*
*— THE CARETAKER*

"The caretaker, huh?" Jack said. "I guess that's my job now."

Whoever had left the note had also provided him with a box of long stick matches atop the water heater to reignite the pilot light. Sure enough, no blue flame burned inside the compartment at the bottom of the tank. Jack took a match, struck the sulfur head across the sandpaper on the side of the box, and it flared to life. A draft of frigid air wrapped itself around his arm and blew out the fire. Jack shuddered as a chill ran up his back, but he didn't see where it could have come from. He slid open the box to get out another match, but it was upside-down. All the matches spilled onto the floor and scattered everywhere.

Feeling like an idiot, Jack knelt to pick them up. He worked his way over to the space underneath the staircase. It was too dark to see the floor, so he had to grope about blindly. His hand recoiled when it touched something soft. Jack lit another match and saw that it was a dust-covered book.

He picked it up and scooted back into the light to get a better look at it. The small book had a brown leather cover that showed some patches of discoloration from water stains. He wiped it off and opened it to find pages full of tight, cursive handwriting in faded black ink written in a language he didn't know. Jack flipped back to the front cover and saw that the owner had thankfully put her name on the inside.

*Prof. Catherine Schreiber*

That was the most information he could decipher from the book and only served to make it more of a mystery. It certainly didn't look like something he would expect to find abandoned in the basement of an old farmhouse. The woman was likely a professor at the University of Iowa, so perhaps she had been the house's former owner. He figured it would be easy to look her up and see if she was still alive. He tucked the book under his arm, struck another match, and lit the pilot light.

Jack climbed the stairs leading to the kitchen and spotted a key hanging on a hook by the door. Kari was still in the bathroom, blow-drying her hair, and she jumped when he spoke.

"I found the key to that door inside the basement. I had to break the lock off the outside doors to get in, but you'll never guess what else I found-"

"I don't give a crap if you discovered gold in the basement. Did you fix the damn water heater, or do we need to call a plumber?"

"Yeah, the pilot light just went out, so I took care of it. I won't know if it's working until the water in the tank heats up, but it should be good now."

"For your sake, you had better hope so," Kari replied. "The air mattress might be uncomfortable, but it will seem like heaven compared to sleeping outside on the porch."

"Okay, I'll schedule a plumber to come over and cancel if it's fixed. I'm considering using the basement for my office. It's dingy but should be fine once I clean it up. It already has shelves on the walls that I can use for my books."

"There's a lot of other things around the house that need to be taken care of before you start decorating your man cave. Patrick said he heard bees in his room, and he was standing underneath the door to the attic in the middle of the night."

"Bees in the attic? What am I supposed to do about that?"

"I don't know, Jack. Buy some goddamn bug spray when you're at the store," she sighed. "If it's bad, then call a pest control company. Do I have to tell you everything? Why don't you take your son with you? He loves going to the hardware store."

Jack slipped the leather notebook into his suitcase before heading upstairs. Patrick was sitting on the floor of his bedroom, a cartoon playing on his tablet while he worked on a drawing. He never got tired of seeing his son sketching away on his pad. Patrick had been doing it since he was old enough to walk. They discovered his artistic abilities when he got ahold of a marker and covered his bedroom walls with pictures of animals. Patrick had started to show real talent with his artwork lately, and he could spend hours on his drawings. During those periods, Jack thought he almost seemed neurotypical. It also reminded him of how special Patrick was and that he wouldn't change a thing about him.

"Hey buddy, you want to take a ride to the store?" Jack asked. He waited for his son to respond, but he continued drawing. "Patrick, did you hear me? Do you want to go to the hardware store with daddy?" He leaned down to see what his son was working on, but he flipped the cover closed.

"Go to store."

"Yeah, come on, let's go to the store. You need to listen to me when I say it's time to go, understand?"

Jack decided to take Ahnen Trek over to Coralville because it was a shorter trip, but he had to drive right at the speed limit because a white SUV with a police light bar followed behind him almost the entire way. He pulled into the parking lot of the home improvement store and picked a spot with few other cars nearby. Kari was quite protective of her minivan, and he would be up shit creek if he got a scratch on it. His vehicle, an old Toyota Camry, was being delivered by the movers. It was a piece of junk, but he would be glad when he was driving it instead.

He only needed a handful of items, but they had to go up and down each aisle so Patrick could take photos with his tablet of the EXIT signs hanging from the ceiling or mounted above doorways. Jack picked up a flashlight, two cans of wasp spray, a padlock, and two locking knobs for the bathroom doors. He was comparing the gate latches to replace the broken one on the cellar doors and noticed Patrick was no longer with the shopping cart.

A wave of panic swelled up in his chest as he spun around and saw no sign of his son. He ran towards the main aisle and scanned the crowd of people for him. Jack didn't see him anywhere, so he raced back to the checkouts and the front doors. Patrick wasn't there, so he hurried past each aisle until he reached the last row without finding him. The urge to sprint through the store shouting his son's name at the top of his lungs was overwhelming. Jack knew he needed to keep a cool head and think what to do. He was about to have one of the cashiers call the manager when he saw Patrick walking with a stranger towards the registers.

The man had to be at least six-foot-four, muscular but rail thin, and probably in his fifties with a tanned, weathered face that made him look older. He wore dark blue jeans, a chambray shirt, and cowboy boots. Jack thought he wouldn't have looked out of place on the back of a horse herding cattle. What kept him from calling the man out for trying to kidnap his son was the pistol holstered on his hip. The old cowboy approached a cashier and started talking to her as Jack rushed up.

"Patrick, you can't disappear on me like that," he said. Jack knelt beside his son and hugged him. "Please don't do that again. You scared the hell out of me."

"I came across this little guy wandering around alone. Couldn't get a word out of him, so I brought him up front," the cowboy said. Jack noticed the man had three faded white scars down his left cheek. "I assume he's your son?"

"Yes, sorry, I'm Jack Sterling, and this is Patrick. I turned my back on him for a second, and he wandered off. He has autism, so he has trouble talking to strangers. Thank you for finding him."

"It's a good thing I came across him," the man said as he shook Jack's hand. "The name's Edgar Blackburn. I'm a detective for the Johnson County Sheriff's Department. Make sure you keep a close eye on him. You never know what can happen, even in a small town."

Jack returned to the aisle where he had left their shopping cart. A large box containing an outdoor spotlight with a built-in motion detector had made its way into the basket. Patrick must have grabbed it while he was looking for him.

"Let's put that back, and daddy will get you-"

"No! Patrick's light!"

He didn't want to cause a scene and draw the detective's attention again, so he gave in and bought the light. As they crossed the parking lot, a white SUV with Johnson County Sheriff's Department markings drove by. Jack couldn't be sure it was the same one that had followed them here, but Detective Blackburn was behind the wheel.

By the time they returned home, Karina had lunch prepared for them. She helped Patrick wash his hands while Jack scooped up a plate of macaroni and corn with a hot dog for his son, careful to keep the three foods from touching each other. She and Jenny had already eaten, but Kari sat down at the table beside Patrick in case he needed help. Jack got his plate ready and joined them.

"How did your shopping trip go?" she asked.

"It was fine," he lied. "Patrick did great."

"What's with the giant outdoor floodlight? Are you trying to guide passing airplanes in for a landing on our front lawn?"

"Oh, I thought installing it over the porch would be useful. There's only the streetlamp to see by at night, and you wouldn't want somebody to trip on the steps if they're coming home late."

"Uh huh, I think Patrick conned you into buying it," Kari said. "It's not a bad idea. I forgot how few lights there are in the country. It freaks me out how quiet it is, too. You'd think it wouldn't bother me since I grew up on a farm, but you get used to all the noise after living in a city."

"Yeah, this is probably going to take some getting used to," he agreed. "You have to admit it's nice and peaceful, though."

"I know I was harsh to you this morning. This last week has been stressful, and I was angry that you made a big decision without me," she said. "It's not that I hate the house or would rather be living in an apartment. There's something about this place that bothers me."

"What do you mean by that?" he prodded. "You've been acting odd since we got here. What's going on?"

"I don't know, I can't put my finger on it. This sounds ridiculous, but I thought somebody was lurking outside the door when I was getting ready in the bathroom this morning. Nobody was there, but I felt so scared it almost made me cry."

"Mommy sad?" Patrick asked. He didn't like it when she or Jenny cried and would get upset if he saw either of them doing so.

"Mommy's fine, Patrick," she replied, giving him a big smile. "See, mommy was only talking, okay?" He looked at her for another few seconds before resuming eating. Jack gave his wife an apologetic shrug.

"Is it because you're upset about the condition of the house?" he asked in a more hushed tone. "I know it needs some work, but I think it will be great once we get it fixed up."

"No, it's not that, although it does need a good deal of renovations." She stopped and shook her head. "I don't know what's wrong with me, forget I said anything. I guess this move has been a lot to deal with and I'm overly emotional."

"I'm very sorry, babe. I wouldn't have bought the house if I knew it would upset you this much. Let me get this place in decent shape, and then we can put it back on the market. We'll get an apartment in the city until we find another place we can afford. It would be a better commute for me anyway."

"Don't be silly. The kids would be heartbroken. I'll feel better once the rest of our things arrive." She leaned over and gave him a quick kiss on the cheek. "You're a good husband, Jack—when you're not being annoying."

"Does that mean I might get lucky again tonight?" he whispered.

"As I said, when you're not being annoying."

After he cleared the table off from lunch, Jack hoped to sneak in some writing. He powered up his laptop, opened the file browser, navigated to the directory where he kept his collection of various projects, and stared at them in dismay. Between a half dozen short stories, two novels, and a clunky attempt at a screenplay, he had spent the last five years banging his head against a brick wall with nothing to show for it but a thinning head of hair. What he needed was a fresh start.

Jack brought up the word processor, opened a new file, and then typed **Chapter One** at the top of the page. He sat there for a couple of minutes with his fingers hovering over the keyboard, staring at the dreaded blank page spanning down into the void of electronic emptiness, and finally sat back in his chair. He had been trying to write what he thought he was supposed to write. Or rather, what his college professors had taught him he was supposed to write, but that hadn't inspired any passion in his writing. The only time he had felt excited about a story he wrote was the Martin Knight-inspired pulp novel he had churned out. He loved writing horror stories, but his fellow intellectuals looked down upon that type of genre.

Martin's novels were interconnected by shared characters and settings from story to story, forming an overarching world that his fans had dubbed *The Knightmare Verse*. If there were one question Jack could have asked the man, it would have been how he kept coming up with all those story ideas. Martin had published at an almost supernatural rate, but he had never achieved more than a cult following in his readership. It was like he had made a deal with the devil or had access to a magic box that could spit out a new story every time you opened it. Martin had retired and became a recluse three years ago when a car accident killed his wife and left him crippled. Jack wished he had been a student at Iowa while Mr. Knight was still teaching there.

"Doesn't look like you're getting much writing done," Kari said, carrying a handful of laundry.

"I was just taking a quick break," he replied. "You know, collecting my thoughts."

"Um hmm, why don't you take a break from your break and go check out the attic or fix the lock that you broke outside? A little manual labor will help stir the creative juices."

Jack groaned but headed down to the basement to get the toolbox. He hauled it upstairs and carried it around to the bulkhead doors. He pulled out a hammer and screwdriver, removed the old hardware, and then fastened the new latch below where the previous one had been mounted. With the padlock attached, he gave the handles a couple of good tugs to be sure it held. Jack brushed his jeans off and looked around for something else to fix, but he would have to tackle the next chore on Kari's list instead.

He left the heavy chest by the door to the basement, then armed himself with a can of bug spray and a flashlight before heading upstairs. Patrick was lying on the air mattress in his room and playing with his tablet, so Jack shut his door. He spotted the pull rope hanging down from the folding attic ladder and grabbed it. The hinges groaned as he yanked down with all his strength. It seemed like the spring arms were too rusted to move, and then the entire thing popped loose and almost unfolded on his head. Jack swore under his breath as he extended it the rest of the way.

He clicked on the flashlight and pointed it at the opening, listening for any buzzing sound before he climbed up. The attic turned out to be more than bare rafters and insulation. It had been finished off with a floor and walls to form an L-shaped storage area. A small window at the far end provided a thin shaft of sunlight. A light socket with a string to switch it on was mounted near the opening. He tugged at the cord, but the bulb had burned out.

Jack inched along the length of the storage area, bug spray at the ready as he searched for any sign of a nest. He only came across an old steamer trunk near the window. He cautiously pulled it away from the wall to check behind it. Jack bent down to lift the lid, but it was locked. He didn't see an opening to insert a key, so he pushed it back into place. He made a second pass of the attic, but his inspection found no sign of an infestation.

Satisfied that he didn't have a bug problem to deal with, he returned to the trunk. Jack tried to pick it up, but it was too heavy. He dragged it closer to the ladder but unless he dropped it through the opening there was no way he could carry it down. There was enough light coming up from the hallway that he could get a better look at the lock. It consisted of a clasp made of brass with a raised, circular dial embossed to look like a snake eating its tail. He knew there was a word for such a thing, *oingo boingo*, or something like that (*or was that the name of an 80's band?*). There were symbols etched into the snake's body, which made Jack wonder if it was a combination lock. He tried turning the snake, but it didn't budge.

"Jack, are you up here?" Kari asked as she poked her head up through the attic opening. "Are there any bees? Did you get stung?"

"No, there aren't any bees or wasps or anything. Not that I could find," he answered. "Looks like somebody left this trunk behind, but I can't get the damn thing open."

"Great, more junk I don't care about. Go lock that poison up in the basement and take that nasty, rusted toolbox you left sitting in my kitchen with you as well."

"Yes, ma'am."

*July 2, 2019*

Patrick's eyes snapped open to the buzzing in his ears again. When he turned on the electronic tablet beside his bed, it showed 2:27, the same time it had happened the previous night. He switched on the tablet's built-in flashlight, the beam blinding him as it lit up the room. Once the spots cleared from his eyes, he rolled out of bed and stood up. He knew several floorboards in his room creaked, and he had already memorized their location to avoid stepping on them. Patrick picked up his drawing pad and crept to the bedroom door, opening it slowly so the hinges wouldn't squeak.

The buzzing noise was much stronger tonight. The ladder to the attic was down, and a faint green glow was coming from the opening. The hallway was also freezing, and he shivered as he stepped out. Patrick stood at the bottom of the ladder and pointed his tablet up. He did not want to climb up there, but he couldn't resist the pull of the buzzing. Holding the tablet and drawing pad with his right hand, he grabbed onto the ladder with his left. The green glow was coming from a large trunk near the top of the ladder.

Patrick knelt beside the trunk and flipped open his drawing pad to the page he had been working on this morning. He wasn't sure why he had continually drawn the same three symbols for hours; it had been like someone else was controlling his hand. There were times when he became deeply involved in doing an activity, such as when he lined up his Hot Wheels cars bumper-to-bumper all around his bedroom so that they were very close but did not touch. He would go so far into his mind that he seemed to step outside his body.

The light from his tablet illuminated a metal snake forming a circle on the trunk, just as he had drawn in his pad. Along the snake were marks that looked like letters. He loved to watch videos on his tablet of children's songs in different languages. These reminded him of the songs in Japanese, with the letters that looked like little pictures.

He pressed down on the snake's head, which made a clicking noise and allowed him to rotate it. Patrick located the first of the symbols he had drawn and turned the snake until it was at the top. He spun it in the other direction to the second symbol and back around to the third. There was another clicking sound, this one louder, and the clasp on the trunk popped open.

The light on his tablet turned off, leaving him in the dark except for the moonlight from the window. Patrick shivered as the air grew colder and something moved further in the attic. When he looked up, a woman in a bathrobe was standing in front of the window. The side of her head looked like it was covered in black paint, and he could see through her body. Her lips didn't move when she spoke to him.

*Hello, Patrick*

# Desirable Wares

Novel By **MARTIN KNIGHT**

Jupiter &
Phoebus
Publishing
House

# CHAPTER 4

## Desirable Wares

*July 2, 2019*

K ari stood on the front porch, holding a paper cup of coffee, watching the line of daybreak crawl towards her across the cornfield to the west. Surprisingly, both kids were sleeping in, and Jack was also snoring away (*not surprisingly*). It wasn't often that she got to watch the sunrise in peace, so she drank it in along with her morning coffee.

She had enjoyed her life in Colorado, raising her children amid the gorgeous scenery with the bustle of a busy city surrounding them. There was something to be said, though, about the tranquility of the farmlands where she grew up. Kari hated the small-town snobbishness when she lived here and wanted nothing more than to escape it. Maybe things were different now, but she doubted people like that truly changed. At least not for the better.

The smell of coffee must have stirred her husband from his thunderous slumber. He shuffled onto the porch wearing only boxers and a short-sleeved shirt, nursing a cup of the steaming black liquid. "Mmmmm, that's the good stuff," he said as he slurped loudly. "Are the kids still in bed? I don't remember the last time Patrick slept past six o'clock. Why are you up so early?"

"I guess I'm just used to being up at the crack of dawn," she replied. "Since I was awake, I figured I might as well enjoy a quiet breakfast for a change."

"Oh, sorry if I interrupted," Jack said. "I'll leave you alone."

"No, you're fine. It's nice to spend time alone with you before the chaos begins."

"Yeah, I think I'll grab a shower before the kids get up." He took another gulp of coffee and turned to leave, but she stopped him by putting a hand on his forearm.

"Did I pressure you into taking this job and moving us here?" she asked. "Should we have looked at other universities? I'm worried it was a mistake to come here because of my family."

Jack put his arm around her and pulled her closer. "Honey, I wouldn't have come here if I didn't want to. I don't know that I'm all that crazy about being so close to my in-laws, but that's a burden I'll have to bear with stoic silence." She slapped his butt, and he grinned at her. "Careful, you don't want to make me accidentally spill hot coffee down your shirt."

"Do that, and you'll be sleeping on the couch for the next month," she replied. "Once our couch arrives, anyway."

"Can I ask why you're having second thoughts? I thought you wanted to move back here. Are you really that upset about the house?"

"It's not my dream house by any stretch of the imagination, but it's better than an apartment," she replied. "I think I'm having a hard time because I want my kids to feel like they belong here, which will be hard enough for Patrick with all his issues. You don't know what it's like to grow up in a small town. School can be hell if you don't fit in."

"I'm sure that won't happen, but if it does, we'll deal with it. Why don't we take the kids into town for lunch? I'm sure once we settle in and make some friends, you'll start feeling like this is really our home." Jack gave her a kiss and went back inside.

"I hope you're right," she muttered into her coffee.

They loaded the kids into the van shortly before eleven and drove into Bailey Grove. Motte's Ferry Road took them to the town square, a tree-covered park with a wooden gazebo in the center and a small playground with swings and a slide. The square was lined with picturesque brick-fronted buildings, most dating back to the early part of the previous century. The downtown area had seen a revitalization since she lived here. Half of the buildings had been vacant back then, and now only a single storefront was empty.

"Oh, hey, there's a Mexican restaurant," Jack said, pointing to a building on the square's east side. "Do you think the kids would eat there?"

"I guess we can try," Kari replied. "It doesn't look open yet. Why don't you take Patrick over to the playground while Jenny and I do some window shopping?"

Several cars were in front of the Catholic church on the north side, but the rest of the square and the park were deserted. Kari was happy to see that because she didn't have to worry about other kids or parents staring at Patrick while he played. She wasn't ashamed of how her son acted when he was excited, but she knew it looked odd to people who hadn't been around someone with autism. He tended to flap his arms and hum loudly, and Kari made it a point to glare at anyone who was openly staring at him when he did so. She couldn't help getting her back up if she thought anyone was judging her child, which was probably why Jack handled him most of the time.

Patrick caught sight of the swing set and jumped out of his seat as soon as the van stopped. Kari waited on the sidewalk with Jenny until Jack had gotten him safely across the street to the playground. She held her daughter's hand as they strolled along the sidewalk, stopping in front of a clothing boutique with an unusual name painted across its display window.

# DESIRABLE WARES

"I like that shirt, mommy," Jenny said, pointing to a pink, short-sleeved shirt. "Can we go inside?"

"It's Sunday, honey, they're probably closed." The sign on the front door showed the store was open for business, and two women were standing at the sales counter folding clothes. "Okay, let's go in. Just remember, we're only looking, not buying."

"Welcome to Desirable Wares," one of the salesclerks called out, "we'll be right with you."

Kari soon found several nice tops that she liked, and despite what she had told Jenny, she was considering buying one for the holiday. She couldn't afford to get clothes for herself on Jack's graduate student salary. While they would still be living on a tight budget, his new paycheck would be a considerable step up. Although the price tags on the shirts weren't cheap, Kari thought she could indulge in just one. She was trying to narrow her selection when she overheard the two ladies talking.

"Did you see that new store coming in next door?" asked the tall, blonde-haired woman with her back to Kari.

"Yeah, I noticed the sign hanging up this morning," the other clerk replied. She was shorter and curvier with dark brown hair. "It's strange, I haven't seen anybody going in or out of there, but everything looks like it's already set up."

"Yeah, I didn't see anyone either. Maybe the movers came in overnight. I think it's going to be a used bookstore." There was something familiar about the blonde woman's voice, but Kari couldn't see her face.

"I need to go check on our customers. Would you mind unpacking the boxes that got delivered yesterday?" the dark-haired woman asked, then approached Kari. The blonde-haired clerk disappeared into the back room before she could get a good look at her. "Good morning, I'm Rose. Is there anything I can help you with?"

"I was looking for a new shirt for the Fourth," Kari said, holding up two shirts. "They're both pretty, I can't decide between them."

"I think the one with the flowers would look good on you, and I have a lovely skirt over here that would complement it beautifully." Kari was not typically one for wearing skirts, but when the saleswoman paired one with the flowered shirt, she found it hard to say no.

"Mommy, can I get this?" Jenny asked, carrying a stuffed toy cat. "He's so cute. Can I buy him with my allowance?"

"Jenny, that costs nine dollars, and you only have five," Kari replied. "Besides, your brother will be jealous if you get something."

"Please, mommy, I won't tell him, I promise," she begged. "I'll do extra chores if you let me get it. Please, please, please?"

"Alright, I'll give you ten dollars, but that means no allowance for next week. And you have to help me with the dishes every night this week, deal?" Kari held out her hand and took the toy. "You know, you're supposed to be saving up to buy your dad a birthday present at the end of the month."

"I can get him something with any money I have left."

"Um, that will be a whole dollar. I don't think you can buy him anything with that." She paid for the stuffed cat, her outfit, and the pink shirt Jenny wanted. Jack would have a stroke when she told him how much money she had spent, but he'd forget about it once he saw her in the skirt.

"I'm impressed by your selection of clothes," Kari told the saleswoman. "I wish this store would have been around when I was in high school."

"Oh, did you attend school here?" the clerk asked. "I only moved here recently, but you look about the same age as Susan." The blonde-haired clerk came out of the storeroom carrying a large box that obscured her face. "Susie, dear, do you know...I'm sorry, I didn't ask your name."

The woman set the box on the counter, and Kari felt her stomach tighten into a knot. Susan Salisbury had been the most popular girl in town when she was in high school, and she had treated her like she was nothing but a poor farm girl. She was about the last person Kari had expected to see still living in Bailey Grove, especially working in a clothing store since her family had been quite well off.

"Kari Ulmer, is that you?" Susan asked as she came over to hug her, which was not the reaction she had expected. "Oh my god, I haven't seen you in forever. Wow, you haven't aged a day since high school. Are you here visiting your parents?"

"Actually, we just moved back to Iowa two days ago."

"You're kidding, that's great. I'm so happy you're living here again."

"Thank you. It's been quite a hectic week. We bought a house south of town, and the movers haven't arrived yet," she explained. "This is my daughter Jenny."

"Very nice to meet you, Jenny. My name is Susan. I went to school with your mother." Jenny suddenly turned bashful and ducked behind her, but Susan didn't seem offended. "She's adorable, and she has your eyes. When you get settled in, we should meet for lunch and catch up."

"Yeah, that sounds great," she said with a forced smile. "It's nice to see you again, Susan."

Kari returned to the van and put the bag with her new clothes into the back. She made Jenny put her toy cat in the bag as well. She could hear Patrick laughing from the playground. He was having a blast as Jack pushed him on the swing. Kari closed the van's tailgate and turned to cross the street, but her daughter was no longer with her. Jenny was standing in front of the recently vacant store at the end of the block. A wooden signboard hung down from the awning with a carving of a black bird as the apostrophe in the store's name.

# THE RAVEN'S PERCH

Kari locked the van and rushed over to her daughter. "Jenny don't wander away like that. You scared me."

"Look, mommy!" she said. "I found a present for daddy's birthday."

Jenny pointed at the building's display window. Kari had to tilt her head to see underneath the sign announcing **OPEN SOON** hanging on the inside of the glass. What had her daughter excited was a black manual typewriter sitting between two stacks of leather-bound books.

Kari pressed her face against the window to get a better look at the machine. A handwritten price tag hanging from a red string showed it cost $175. She cupped her hands around her eyes to block out the light, and she could see several shelves of books, antiques, and other knickknacks inside the darkened store.

"I'm sorry, honey, that costs way too..." She was interrupted by the sound of a metal bell tinkling as her daughter turned the knob on the unlocked front door.

"Hello?" Jenny called out as she entered the store. "Are you open?"

Kari tried to pull her daughter back outside before anyone noticed, but she heard a door open from somewhere within the shop. The overhead lights turned on, and then a tall, lanky older man leaning on a cane emerged from behind a bookcase. He was distinguished-looking with slicked-back white hair, a neatly trimmed beard, and piercing blue eyes. To Kari's chagrin, Jenny was not deterred by the scowl on the shopkeeper's face.

"May I help you?" he asked.

"Can we buy the old computer in the window for my daddy's birthday?"

"I assume you saw the sign on the door saying that the store was opening soon?" he snapped in a thick British accent. Kari started to apologize, but he held up a hand to silence her. He turned and addressed Jenny directly. "I must have left the door unlocked, but it is not polite to trespass. Even if this is a place of business. Since it is a birthday present, and you are my first customer, I would be happy to sell it to you. That is a typewriter, though, young lady. Do you still wish to purchase it?"

"Yes, my daddy is a writer," Jenny replied. "He's going to teach other people how to write."

"You don't say. My late wife was a poet. Her favorite writer was Edgar Allan Poe. Have you heard of him?" Jenny shook her head. "His most famous poem was about a bird called a raven that torments a poor fellow deep in mourning for his dead wife, Lenore. I find Mr. Poe a bit morbid, but my wife dreamed of opening a bookstore in his honor."

"My husband is a fan of horror stories, but I prefer Jane Austen myself," Kari said. "I'm sorry about your wife and for intruding on you."

"It's quite alright, my name is Thynne. Ryland Thynne, at your service," he announced with a bow. "I lost my own dear Lenore three years ago. She was from this area and always spoke so highly of it. I decided to move here and open this store in her memory."

"Why do you sound funny when you talk?" her daughter blurted out.

"I have an accent because I am from England," Ryland chuckled at her question. "Now then, I don't mean to be rude, but I'm rather busy. So, would you like to make a purchase?"

"The typewriter is very nice, but I'm afraid-" Kari started to say.

Ryland again held up his hand to stop her from talking. "No offense, ma'am, but I have only agreed to enter into an exchange of goods with this young lady. What is your offer for the typewriter displayed in the window?"

Jenny cocked her head at him like she was trying to figure out what he was asking. Kari was about to put a stop to the whole thing when her daughter reached into her pocket. "I have a dollar." She held out the bill the store clerk had given her as change.

"Then a dollar it shall be." He reached down and took the money from her. "Since this is the first dollar my store has made, I will have to frame it and hang it on the wall."

"I don't mean to sound ungrateful, Mr. Thynne, but we can't possibly accept it at that price."

"Nonsense, that was my wife's typewriter, and I am more than happy to see it go to somebody who will appreciate it."

"Are you sure you want to sell something like that?" Kari asked. "I would hate for you to regret giving up an item with sentimental value."

"It's really nothing to worry about. I have plenty of other mementos," he said with a sad smile, then regained his composure. "I'm afraid I didn't ask your names. It's not good salesmanship for me not to know who my first customers were."

"I'm Kari Sterling, and this is my daughter Jenny." Mr. Thynne shook both of their hands. "We're sorry for barging into your store like that. My daughter can be impatient sometimes."

"I am not," Jenny huffed. "I don't even know what that means."

"There's no need for any apology. I had hoped to have the store open for business before the holiday, but I'm having trouble hiring enough staff."

"Oh, that's too bad. I hope you don't miss out on too many sales because of it."

"It is a minor inconvenience, nothing that won't sort itself out in the long run, but enough about my troubles. Now, let's get your purchase boxed up so you can get on your way."

Ryland went into the back room to fetch a cardboard box for the typewriter. "I hope this is not too heavy for you to carry. Your husband, has he published anything I might have read?"

"Probably not. He's been struggling to find his voice."

"This machine may not seem like much, but I can promise that if he lets it do its job, it will open the door to all kinds of new worlds." He handed her the box, and Kari grunted as she took its full weight. Ryland showed them to the door and held it open as they left. "Thank you for your patronage. I look forward to seeing you again soon."

Kari stood on the sidewalk outside the store, staring at the box. Her daughter tugged on her sleeve and pointed towards the park. "Can I go play on the swings?"

"Sure, be careful crossing the street. Look both ways first."

She placed the box in the back of the van and joined her family at the playground. Jack raised his eyebrow as she approached him. "Are you going to tell me what's in the box, or is it a surprise?"

"It's a surprise, daddy!" Jenny scolded him. "No peeking."

"You heard your daughter, best keep your nose out of where it doesn't belong."

"Okay, I'll behave myself," he laughed. "What kind of store is that? It doesn't look like it's open yet."

"It's not, but that didn't stop your daughter," Kari said. "I think it's some kind of bookstore, and the owner is short on help."

"Oh yeah, are you thinking of going back to work? I thought you wanted to take some time off. Wouldn't you rather find a teaching job?"

"I was only thinking about it. I might return to teaching, but it would also be nice to try something different."

"Yeah, that's cool. I'll support whatever you want to do."

"The restaurant should be opening soon. Why don't I drive the van over and get us a table?"

"Okay, I'll bring the kids when Patrick's done swinging," Jack said as he rubbed his shoulder between pushes. "Or my arm falls off."

Kari got in the van, backed out of the parking spot, and then drove past The Raven's Perch. She looked at the shop while going by, and something caught her eye. Stopping at the intersection, she glanced back at the store.

The window reflected the park now, but Kari thought she had seen a building engulfed in flames in the glass. She could have sworn it was the local high school, but that was impossible since it was several streets over. Perhaps the sun had hit it at a weird angle. Kari wondered why her mind would have imagined such a disturbing vision.

⊗

*July 3, 2019*

The moving truck pulled into the driveway without warning and blared its horn. Jack had to rush out and move the van so the truck could pull up to the front porch. The moving crew consisted of an overweight truck driver, who immediately got on his wife's bad side by dropping a nuclear bomb in the upstairs bathroom, and two young college boys who did all the actual work. The driver spent the rest of the day sitting on the front porch, checking off the inventory on a clipboard as the two other men brought everything inside.

"I'm taking Jenny to the grocery store," Kari said, glaring at the driver out of the corner of her eye. "Can you open some windows while we're gone? I hope a frozen pizza is good for tonight."

"Yeah, that works," Jack replied. "I imagine we'll be busy unpacking."

The sun was beating down on the movers, but they seemed unfazed by the heat as they worked. Jack felt exhausted just watching them hustle back and forth, hauling heavy furniture and boxes inside before heading back for the next load. The truck driver was sweating profusely despite being in the shade, and Jack worried he might collapse from heatstroke.

One of the first things that came in was the living room couch, and Patrick promptly staked claim to it as he watched the procession of their belongings going by. The furniture from their two-bedroom apartment back in Colorado barely took up half the house, so it took the movers only a couple of hours to unload everything. Jack brought another armful of water bottles to the porch for them as one of the college guys carried a box full of books down the loading ramp.

"Where do you want this?" the mover asked.

"Um, I think it will have to go into the attic for now. Come on, I'll show you." Jack set the water bottles down and led him to the second floor, then pulled down the folding ladder from the ceiling. The guy lifted the heavy box up the ladder with one hand and set it beside the steamer trunk. The box bumped up against the trunk, and the clasp popped open. After the mover returned down the ladder, Jack knelt beside the trunk and lifted the lid just enough to peek inside.

He was worried it might be the source of the buzzing Patrick heard, but the only thing that came out was a whiff of musty air. The light from the small window was bright enough to show him that it contained stacks of textbooks. He was slightly disappointed in the contents, especially since such a clever lock had guarded it. While he hadn't expected it to contain a horde of gold doubloons and jewels, keeping old books under lock and key still seemed odd. Jack was also curious how the lock had suddenly sprung open since it hadn't budged the day before.

The books looked to be in good condition. Jack picked up the top one and read the title on its spine: *Ahnen Villages: A Photographic History*. He opened the cover and saw a faded ink stamp on the title page.

## UNIVERSITY OF IOWA LIBRARY

Whoever had checked out the book probably owed a crap ton of money in overdue fees. The books were about German history and literature, but one near the bottom was surprising. *Occult Secrets of the Third Reich* was the title above a black-and-white photograph showing a parade of goose-stepping Nazi soldiers carrying swastika flags through a throng of cheering citizens. That one also belonged to the library. The same person had checked out all these books based on the last ID number written on the borrower cards.

Jack set the Nazi book back in the trunk and spotted a small metal cube tucked into the corner. The cube was rather heavy for its size, and it felt cold as he picked it up. Hieroglyphic-like patterns were etched across the shiny black surface. He examined it closer in the light and could see seams along the surface as though it were meant to be moved or rotated in some manner. Jack tried to figure out a way to manipulate it, but nothing he did worked. He traced his finger along the outer edge and felt a stinging pain.

"Fuck!" he snarled as he dropped the cube back into the trunk. Blood welled up on the tip of his finger. While it looked no worse than a paper cut, it seemed to be deep from how profusely it was bleeding. Jack climbed back down the ladder and folded it back up using only his left arm.

"Hurt?" Patrick asked from behind him. His son pointed at the blood trickling down his hand. "Daddy hurt?"

"Daddy's okay. I just cut my finger like an idiot." He went into the bathroom to run water over his hand, trying to ignore the lingering foul odor as he wrapped a towel around his finger.

Patrick poked his head into the bathroom. "Daddy cut?"

"Daddy will be fine, Patrick. There's nothing to worry about. Why don't we go see if mommy has any bandages?" Kari was in the kitchen unpacking a box full of dishes.

"Cut hand," his son announced as they walked in. "Daddy cut hand."

"Thanks for tattling on me, buddy."

"Oh lord, what did you do to yourself now?" Kari asked. "Please tell me that Patrick isn't hurt."

"No, he's fine. I just sliced open my finger," he grunted as she removed the towel. "See, it's only a little cut."

Blood quickly sprang up along the wound, and Kari shook her head. "I can't leave you alone for five minutes. What did you cut yourself on?"

"Thanks for caring. Remember that old trunk in the attic I told you about? I opened it, and it was full of books. I also found this strange black cube, which must have had a sharp edge."

"Will you stop messing with every piece of junk you find around this house?" she replied. "There's a first aid kit out in the van. Do you think you can get it?"

"Yeah, yeah, I can take care of myself."

"I wouldn't go that far. You're not getting out of unpacking, Jack, no matter how much of a hot mess you are."

# Fireworks Starter

Novel By **MARTIN KNIGHT**

Jupiter &
Phoebus
Publishing
House

# CHAPTER 5
## Fireworks Starter

*July 4, 2019*

Karina couldn't remember the last time she had been in Iowa during the Fourth of July. There was going to be a parade around the town square in Bailey Grove this morning, and then they would head out to her parent's house for lunch. She knew the kids would love seeing all the floats, and the parade always started with a line of fire trucks, police cars, and ambulances. She hoped that the sound of the sirens and people yelling wouldn't overwhelm Patrick. Kari made a note to bring headphones for him in case he got aggravated.

Planning for such contingencies had become second nature whenever they took Patrick somewhere new. There was a feeling of walking on eggshells during such an outing until they knew how he would take to it. Ever since Patrick had been diagnosed on the autism spectrum, Kari had lived in a constant state of worry. It wasn't simply about keeping him from getting hurt or wandering off. They also had to stick to his rigid schedule and ward off any detrimental situations that could upset him.

She had this dreadful sense of uncertainty about what his life would be like when he grew into adulthood or, god forbid, both she and Jack were to die. She knew that day would eventually come, or they would both be too old to care for him anymore. At least Jenny would be there to look out for her brother when it did. It was a heavy burden to put on her daughter's shoulders. She held out hope that her son could live on his own someday. There was nothing more frightening than leaving your child to an unknown fate with nobody to protect them.

From early on, she had suspected something wasn't right with Patrick's development. He had been slow to sit up, barely attempted speech other than the occasional babbling, and was very slow to begin walking. Jack was dismissive of her concerns, assuring her

Patrick would catch up. She thought his attitude was more about not wanting to be distracted from his writing.

He had been upset when she went ahead and had Patrick tested, mainly because it cost two thousand dollars for the diagnosis. Her husband struggled to accept the reality of what the doctor explained they could expect as their son got older. It was shortly after that when Jack started drinking.

Kari hadn't said anything about it right away because she knew he was trying to cope with having his world turned upside-down. After the incident when he had lost his temper with Patrick, she had laid down the law, and he had made a complete turnaround. He became supportive of her efforts to get their son the therapy he needed or as much as they could afford to provide him with. Jack had even devised a plan to hire on as the summer caretaker of a ski lodge in the Rocky Mountains to make extra money while he worked on his writing. Kari hadn't been keen on spending three months isolated from civilization. She had told him she would only do it if her mother could come along, which had put an end to it.

At nine o'clock, they piled into the minivan and drove into town, then spent ten minutes looking for a parking spot before finding one three blocks west of the square. Kari was not thrilled about walking that far, especially if Patrick went into full meltdown mode and had to be carried back to the van. Jack had to keep a firm grip on his arm to prevent him from running ahead, which wasn't easy since he also had two camping chairs tucked under his other arm.

The sidewalks around the square were already crowded, and the park was filling up with people sitting on chairs and blankets in the grass. Patrick was fidgeting, and Jenny complained that her legs were tired as she and Jack looked for an open spot. She was about to suggest they try the other side when someone called her name.

"Kari! Hey Kari, over here," a woman's voice rose above the noise. She looked over at the park and spotted Susan waving at them. They crossed the road, which was already closed to traffic, while Susan made room for them. Jack set up the chairs and the blanket for Patrick and Jenny to sit on.

"Hi Susan, thank you so much," Kari said. "I didn't know the parade would be this busy. This is my husband, Jack."

"Nice to meet you. I went to high school with Kari."

"Are you here with someone?" Kari asked, spotting the empty chair beside her. "Did you and Tony end up together?"

"Um, yeah, we did, but we're not together anymore. That's my wife, Rose, over at the swings with our daughter, Sara. She was Tony's parting gift before he left me for a stripper."

"I'm so sorry. I shouldn't have mentioned him."

"You're fine. He was a jerk, and I wasted too many years on him," Susan replied. "If it weren't for Tony, I wouldn't have Sara. I should have introduced you to Rose at our store yesterday, but we don't usually discuss our relationship at work. Small town and all, you know?"

"I'm so happy for the both of you. How long have you been married?"

"We're coming up on our second anniversary. It was right before we opened the store. Being away from Bailey Grove for a while made me realize how stuck up I was in high school. I owe you an apology for how I treated you back then, especially going along with that prank Tony tried to pull on you at the homecoming dance."

"What are you talking about? What prank?"

Susan bit her lip and hesitated for a moment. "I imagine it must have come as a surprise when you were elected homecoming queen. That's because Tony had me rig the vote so the two of you won."

"You never told me you were the homecoming queen," Jack said.

"Why don't you go take the kids to the playground before the parade starts," Kari replied.

"Swing! Daddy, swing!" Patrick exclaimed, and Jack gave her a look as he got up from his chair. He trudged away with both kids dragging him by the arms.

"Yeah, I was shocked at the time. Was that supposed to be the prank?"

"No, that was only the first part of it. Tony was mad at you because you told the science teacher that he didn't help with the group project about oil spills. He ended up getting detention, so he couldn't play football. They lost that game and didn't go to State. His friends were going to dump a bucket of oil and a bag of feathers on you during the coronation."

"Are you kidding me? Why didn't they do it then?"

"Because I found out what Tony was planning, and I told him I'd break up with him if he did," Susan answered. "That was also the first time he threatened to hit me."

"Oh god, I didn't know he was like that."

"I didn't either until then. I wish I had left him before he went from threatening to hit me to doing it. I don't know why I'm telling you all this."

"I'm glad you got away from him. Aren't you scared he'll return and take Sara from you?"

"Hopefully that's not something I have to worry about. He's spending the next twenty-five years in jail for manslaughter and selling meth. Knowing his temper, I doubt he'll get off for good behavior. Unless he tunnels his way out, Sara will graduate college before he sets foot outside of prison."

The wail of multiple sirens announced the start of the parade. Several emergency vehicles drove slowly up Mottes Ferry Road from the south. Jack and Rose returned to their seats with the kids, and she wasn't surprised that Jenny and Sara had already become fast friends.

"Mommy, I can't find Mr. Whiskers," Jenny said. "I must have dropped him!"

Before Kari could stop her, Jenny ran into the road where the parade was coming up. Jack took off after her and snatched her up. "Whoa there, kiddo, let's not give your parents a heart attack today," he said, setting her back on the blanket.

"You have to save Mister Whiskers, daddy! Please!"

"Daddy will get your cat for you, but you can't run out into the road like that," Kari scolded her.

Jack jogged back towards the corner where they had crossed and picked up the stuffed kitten in the middle of the road. He hurried out of the way as the lead police car held up the parade for him and handed Mister Whiskers back to Jenny. "Here, no worse for wear," he said. "I guess toy cats must have nine lives as well."

All three kids were jumping up and down in excitement as the emergency vehicles turned left and crossed in front of their viewing spot. When somebody from the floats threw out candy, she sent Jack to scoop it up so they wouldn't go near the street. Patrick settled down once the emergency vehicles went past, but he became excited again as a line of antique tractors rumbled past after the floats, followed by a group of riders on horseback. Kari kept a close eye on him in case he got up from his seat.

The end of the parade was marked by a wooden box bed wagon pulled by a team of six Clydesdale horses, with Santa Claus and a group of children riding in the back. Patrick laughed hysterically when one of the horses took an enormous dump in the street. The smell made Kari gag and reminded her why she hated growing up on a farm.

"Okay, guys, time to get going," Jack said.

"More parade! Patrick want more parade!"

"Do you want to watch the horses as they leave?" Kari asked him, then turned to Jack. "I'll take him, we'll meet you back at the corner there."

She and Patrick cut across the square to catch the parade as it headed back around. Once the Santa Claus wagon passed by, they were swept up in the throng of people heading back to their cars. She guided her son through the crowd, keeping a firm grip on his wrist. Jack and Jenny were waiting for them in front of The Raven's Perch, which had a new sign on the door.

### HELP WANTED
### PART-TIME SALESCLERK

The cookout wouldn't start until noon, but Kari wanted to be there early to help her mother prepare the food. She also wanted to let Patrick settle down for a while before everyone else arrived. He was already overstimulated from the parade, and she worried that too much excitement could set him off like a firecracker.

With it being a holiday, the shops and restaurants of Old Ahnen were swamped with tourists ambling back and forth across the street. Once outside town, the pedestrians were replaced by RVs and pickup trucks pulling boat trailers heading to the nearby lake. Jack turned west at the lake, and they passed a large factory that looked out of place alongside the tranquil village of quaint houses and stores. Even though it was a holiday, several vehicles occupied the sprawling parking lot.

"Good lord, that place never seems to close down," Kari said. "I don't understand why Kurt would want to work there."

"Yeah, it gives me the creeps every time we pass by. Seems like an odd place to put a pharmaceutical factory," Jack mused. "Kind of like if there was a nuclear power plant next to Disneyland."

"Please don't say anything about it at my parent's house. You know how upset they get when anyone mentions MasterPharm. I think Kurt took the job just to irritate them."

"Of course I won't," he replied. "You know, the only thing that sticks out more than the factory is that mansion up on the hill. I would love to see the inside of that place." He pointed at the enormous house on a tree-covered hill behind the factory. The thick foliage hid most of the house from sight, but it would have a commanding view of the town and the river valley.

"I think it belonged to the man who built the factory, but he passed away long ago. I don't know who owns it now, and I doubt it's open to tours."

Margrit and Albert Ulmer had bought a farm three miles west of Old Ahnen forty years ago. They had sold most of the farmland when her father retired, but the homestead had changed little in all those years. Her mother raised chickens for eggs and meat, and the birds roamed freely around the yard during the day. Kari wondered if her son would remember the chickens from their last visit two years ago. As soon as they entered the driveway, he started singing Old MacDonald and flapping his arms.

"Here chickens! Here chickens!" Patrick called as he got out of the van. He ran after the birds, and they scattered before him. "WITH A CLUCK CLUCK HERE!" The chickens fled towards their coup as he chased them about the yard.

"Jack, go get your son!" she said, and he jumped out of the van. Kari knew it would be a long day of watching him, and they'd both be exhausted when they got home. "Jenny, can you help carry in the tableware?"

Kari opened the trunk and handed her daughter a bag of paper plates, plastic utensils, cups, and napkins. She picked up the container of potato salad and shut the liftgate. Margrit stepped out the back door, wiping her hands on a flour sack towel. "I told you not to bring anything. I've got plenty of food for everyone. What's all this? I have real plates and glasses. We don't need to waste all that stuff."

"I know, mother, but I don't want you spending all afternoon washing dishes," Kari replied. "You've got your grandchildren here. You should be enjoying time with them instead." Margrit shook her head but didn't argue with her any further.

The back door opened onto a small landing with an old steel refrigerator to the left, a set of stairs that went down to the cellar, and to the right were a couple of steps that led up to the kitchen. The house was already hot and stuffy from the oven, but the smell of fresh bread, strudel, and cookies was intoxicating. It was also noisy since her parents had never installed air conditioning and instead relied upon box fans and open windows for circulation during the summer months. That could be a problem with Patrick since he liked to stick his fingers in the fans, so she would have to keep him away from the windows.

"What time do you think the rest of the family will arrive?" Kari asked.

"Knowing your brother, they'll get here right after everything is set up."

"It'll be good to see Kurt again. It's not like he ever bothers to call or email. If Jessica weren't on Facebook, I wouldn't know anything happening with his family." She and Jenny sat down at the kitchen table where Margrit had a pitcher of fresh lemonade and glasses waiting for them.

"You know what your brother is like: mistrustful of technology and not exactly the social type. Once they get a few beers in, he and your father will probably start arguing politics or whether the Hawkeyes need a new coach. Did I tell you that Kurt recently got promoted to head of security at the factory?"

"No, I don't think so. Jessica hasn't posted anything about it either," she replied. "I'll be sure to congratulate him on it. That must be a lot of responsibility."

"Just don't mention it around your father," Margrit said. "You know how worked up he gets about that place."

"I'm glad that Kurt is doing better. He seemed to be in a bad place after returning from Iraq. I can't imagine the kinds of horrors that he saw over there."

Margrit sighed as she pulled a hot tray of apple strudels from the oven. "I worry his problems readjusting were because he enjoyed what he was doing over there too much. I wish he never would have enlisted, but it is what it is."

Kari wanted to ask her mother what she meant by that, but Jack came in carrying a crying Patrick in his arms. "It's okay, buddy. You're fine. Let's go see mommy."

Her son's knees and forearms were scratched up and covered with grass stains. Margrit turned on the faucet as Kari knelt and took Patrick in her arms to comfort him. "Oh no, my poor angel, are you all right? Jack, what happened? Weren't you watching him?"

"He was chasing after the chickens and tripped. I was behind him but couldn't grab him in time." Kari frowned at him as she took the wet dishcloth from her mom and gently dabbed at the wounds. Patrick seemed more annoyed than hurt about his game being interrupted.

"Hey, I know what will make you feel better," she said, kissing his scraped elbow. "Do you remember the chicken dance I taught you? I bet grandma will dance with us if we teach her. Should we show her how it goes?"

"Ugh ungh, No Dance!"

"I want to do the chicken dance, mommy," Jenny piped up as she got out of her chair. "Come on, grandma, do what I do! Nah-na-na-na-na-na-nah Nah-na-na-na-na-na-nah Nah-na-na-na-nah-nah Nah Cluck Cluck Cluck Cluck!"

Kari took out her phone and found an online video that played the music for the song. Patrick buried his head against her shoulder and refused to look up as his sister sang and danced. He soon began to open and close his fingers during the clucking part as though they were beaks. When Margrit joined in and mirrored Jenny's movements, he clapped and laughed along with them.

"Do you feel better now?" she asked him when the video finally ended after the third round, much to the relief of an exhausted Margrit. Patrick nodded, and she kissed him on the forehead. "Let's get you a snack. Would you like to sit at the table and draw a picture for grandma?"

"Yes," he said, allowing himself to be led to the table. "Patrick draw."

"Okay, daddy will get your drawing kit from the van."

"Yep, I'm on it," Jack replied.

"I want a snack, too, mommy," Jenny said. "And some more lemonade, please."

She put some freshly baked strudels on a plate and stuck them in the freezer for a minute. Jack returned with a paper pad and colored pencils as she served the dessert. Patrick shoveled a strudel into his mouth before going to work on his art project.

"Albert has the Cubs game on in the living room if you want to watch it with him," Margrit told Jack as she sat beside Patrick. "There's cold beer in the other fridge. I hope you like Busch."

"Sounds good," he said and headed toward the back door, but Kari stopped him by clearing her throat. "Actually, I think I'll just stick with the lemonade." He took one of the plastic cups and filled it with lemonade from the pitcher on the table. "Mmmm, yep, that hits the spot."

After he left the kitchen, Margrit looked at her curiously. "Did I say something wrong?"

"No, mom, it's okay. I told him he needed to cut out drinking as he was gaining weight. You know how sensitive men can be about their waistlines." Kari forced herself to smile as she chopped the vegetables. Jack would get one hell of an earful later for embarrassing her in front of her mother. She wasn't responsible for reminding him what would happen if he fell off the wagon.

"Someone is coming," Patrick announced. A few moments later, she heard the low rumble of an engine in the driveway. Kari peeked out the window and saw a four-door red and black pickup truck pull in and park beside her minivan.

"That would be your brother, earlier than I expected. Good, he can help Albert with the grill. The man almost burned off what little hair he had left last year."

"Wow, that's quite a fancy truck. How can he afford that?" Kari asked.

"I guess they pay pretty well at MasterPharm," Margrit answered. "I hope he's smart enough to put some of that into a retirement account."

The back door swung open, and her brother walked in wearing blue jeans, a sleeveless Harley Davidson T-shirt, cowboy boots, and a distinct red-and-white baseball cap she wanted to knock off his head. He grabbed a can of beer from the refrigerator before entering the kitchen.

When she had seen him two years ago, he had been skinny and pale. It had seemed like he was wasting away even though he ate ravenously at every meal. Kurt could still use some sunlight, but he had returned to the peak physical condition he had been in before leaving for boot camp. His eyes had not lost the wariness to them he had picked up on active duty, like those of a hungry predator, and he scanned the room quickly before he came over and hugged Margrit.

"Hi, mom. Hey, sis."

"Hi Kurt, it's good to see you again," Kari greeted him. "Kids, can you say hello to your uncle?"

"Hi, Uncle Kurt!" Jenny said.

"Hey, pipsqueak," he replied and ruffled her hair.

"Can you say hi, Patrick?" she asked her son.

"Hi, Patrick," he answered without looking up from his sketch pad. Kurt snorted before chugging down his beer.

"Where's Jessica and the kids?" Kari asked. "I thought they would be coming with you."

"They're on the way over. I drove down to the Missouri border this morning. They sell fireworks half-off on the Fourth. Do you know those pussies in Des Moines won't even let honest, hard-working folks celebrate their national holiday with so much as a goddamn bottle rocket? Stinks of fucking communism if you ask me, but the man in the White House is going to do something about all that. Trust me on that."

"Kurt Edwyn Ulmer, watch your language," Margrit spat. "And that's enough talk of politics. I don't want to hear any of that today."

"So, how have you been?" Kari changed the subject. "I don't remember the last time we spoke. Mom said you got a new job?"

"Yeah, just got promoted last month, been working a lot of hours," he said. "You guys bought the old Schreiber place, huh?"

Kari thought she saw her mom turn and shoot him a look as she rinsed off the dishes. "What was that?"

Kurt took another swig of his beer instead of answering her. "Do your kids like fireworks? I've got some sparklers and Black Cats. Those are safe enough for kids unless they do something stupid."

"I'll have to talk to Jack about it."

"Oh yeah, I forgot you were one of those-"

"Kurt, go start up the grill before your father tries to set himself on fire again," Margrit cut him off. "The bags of charcoal are in the shed next to the house."

"I know where they are," her brother replied as he drained the rest of his beer, snatched one of the strudels from the hot pan on top of the oven, and then grabbed another beer from the fridge. He shoved the screen door open and let it slam shut behind him.

"Don't pay him any mind. He came out of the military with a bunch of foolish ideas in his head," her mother said.

"It seems like half the country has those same foolish ideas these days."

Kari heard another vehicle arrive and looked out the window to see a minivan parked on the other side of the truck. Kurt's wife, Jessica, got out of the driver's seat and was followed by her teenage son, Stefan, and her twin eight-year-old girls, Brandy and Mandy. Her sister-in-law was a short woman with wide hips and a large chest, which she suspected was why her brother had started dating her. The two of them couldn't have been any further apart personality-wise, with Jessica being perpetually cheerful and overly chatty and her brother...not.

"Oh my god, Kari, it's so good to see you again!" her sister-in-law beamed as she came into the house. "I'm sorry if we're a bit late. I had to get everyone ready by myself. The girls were so excited to come over that they were awake at five this morning."

"I know how that goes. Jenny, do you remember your cousins?"

"Hi," she said, looking nervous.

"Come outside and play with us, Jenny," the twins said in unison.

"Can I take Mr. Whiskers out there?" her daughter asked.

"All right, but don't lose him again." Jenny nodded in agreement.

"Stefan, why don't you take Patrick out and show him your new drone," Jessica suggested. "I bet he would like that."

"I don't know if that's a good idea," Kari replied. "Patrick just hurt himself chasing after the chickens earlier."

"Stefan will keep a close eye on him, don't worry."

"Do you want to go outside, Patrick?" she asked. Surprisingly, her son put down his pencil and followed Stefan out the back door.

"I can't tell you how happy I was when Kurt said you guys were moving back to Iowa," Jessica said. "It will be so nice having you this close. We'll be able to grab lunch and go shopping together. Kurt only takes me out to eat without the kids on my birthday and our anniversary, and it's either to a steakhouse or Red Lobster. He doesn't like any place that's too fancy, and he can't eat anything too spicy. I'm dying to try that new Mexican restaurant in Bailey Grove. Do you like Mexican food?"

"Yes, of course, we went there this weekend," she replied. "We don't go out to eat all that often. Jack and I haven't been out alone since before the kids were born. It was too hard to find a babysitter in Colorado who I could trust to handle Patrick's issues."

"We're family, so you can trust us. You'll have to let us watch the kids so you two can go on a date night. Isn't Jack's birthday coming up soon?"

"Yeah, at the end of the month."

"Why don't you plan something and take him out to celebrate? The kids can come to our house and have a sleepover."

"Oh, um, it might be too soon to do that. I don't know if Patrick can handle spending the night in someone else's house yet."

"Bring your kids over on a weekend before then so he gets used to it. The girls are already bugging me about inviting Jenny to spend the night. Stefan is a few years older than your son but loves playing video games. I'm sure he would be happy to show Patrick. I think the two of them will get along great. Not to be rude, but you'll have to cut the apron strings sooner or later."

"Okay, let me talk it over with Jack," she answered, trying not to let Jessica get under her skin. "He doesn't like to make a big deal about his birthday."

"Kurt's the same way, a big ol' party pooper. I tried to throw a birthday party for him when he first got back from Afghanistan, and he turned around and walked out. He didn't come home until the next day and never apologized for being rude. Albert's the only adult in this family who still enjoys his birthday. He says every year above ground is another year he doesn't have to settle his tab with the devil yet! Goodness gravy, he is such a hoot, you know what I mean."

"Jessica, would you mind taking the hamburger patties and bratwurst out to Kurt?" Margrit asked. "Remind him not to undercook the meat this time. Not all of us like our burgers rare."

"Of course, mom," she said. Jessica opened the fridge, took out the large platter of raw meat, and carried it out through the back door.

"Honestly, that woman can wear me out some days," Margrit sighed.

Jack wandered into the kitchen. "Hey, what time is lunch going to be ready?" he asked, and she and Margrit turned to stare at him. "I'm just, ah, asking for Albert, he's getting hungry."

"Lunch will be ready when you and Kurt are done grilling it," Kari said. "Take the buns and tableware out with you." His shoulders sagged as he grabbed the stack of paper plates and the package of hamburger buns from the counter and shuffled outside.

"That's the best thing about the Fourth of July, the men folk having to do all the cooking for a change," Margrit chuckled.

"Yes, it's a shame it only happens once a year," Kari agreed. "I better go check on the kids. Do you want me to carry anything out?"

"Sure, if you don't mind, there are two Tupperware bowls in the new fridge," her mom replied. "Grab some serving spoons from the drawer by the sink."

"When did you guys buy this one?" she asked. "I don't remember you telling me about it."

"Kurt bought it for us when the freezer on the old one died. Your father refused to throw it away since the refrigerator part still works, which is why it's now filled with beer."

"That sounds like something dad would do."

Kari took the bowls out of the fridge and headed to the lawn on the east side of the house. She set the bowls on the picnic table beside the grill where Kurt was busy flipping the burgers, and Jack was tending to the bratwurst.

Stefan and Patrick stood near the road in a tree-less section of the yard, staring up at the sky. She followed their gaze and spotted what looked like a large bird flying around. Stefan held a controller with a small screen, showing a view of the house from high above. Jenny and the twins were running around, laughing and waving their arms at the drone as it zoomed over them. She was about to tell the kids to come dish up and realized she had forgotten the serving spoons. "Jack, I have to run back to the kitchen. Can you tell everyone to get their plates ready?"

"Yeah, no problem." She hurried back to the house and was about to climb the steps when she heard voices coming through the screen door. Against her better judgment, Kari pressed herself against the side of the house as she listened in on her mother and father.

"You can't tell me there isn't something suspicious happening," Albert said. "Why would that house go up for sale right when Kari moved back? Maybe you should contact the Coven?"

"No, this doesn't concern them," Margrit replied, "but that is a strange coincidence."

"Maybe we need to tell Kari about-"

"No, I won't allow that, I don't want her-"

One of the chickens was hiding in the bushes surrounding the steps, and Kari startled it as she tried moving closer to the door. The bird squawked as it flapped its wings and scurried across the yard.

"Seien sie jetzt ruhig," Margrit snapped.

She climbed up the steps, making sure her footsteps could be heard. Margrit opened the screen door and came out with a pitcher of lemonade and the serving spoons. "You forgot these, dear."

"Oh, yeah, I was just coming back for them." Kari was about to say something about what she had overheard when her father came out the door.

"Is lunch ready yet?" Albert asked. "I'm starving."

"You're always starving, you lazy old fart," Margrit replied.

Lunch was surprisingly calm. Jack helped Patrick cut up his food. The girls were chatting and giggling while they ate but were otherwise well-behaved. With Stefan there to help watch her son, Kari could enjoy her meal for once without worrying so much. She wished could relax completely, but she couldn't stop thinking about the conversation she had overheard.

"Are you feeling well?" Jack asked. "Your face looks a little flushed."

"I'm fine. I'm not used to being out in the sun this much."

"Why don't you sit in the shade after lunch and rest for a while? I'll take care of the kids."

Once the tables were cleared, she took Jack's offer and set up one of the folding camping chairs they had brought underneath a large oak tree. Her mom and Jessica soon joined her, forcing her to pretend she followed their conversation. Since she hadn't lived here in a decade, she didn't know most of the local townsfolk they were gossiping about.

Her tranquility was punctured by a rapid succession of popping noises accompanied by shrieks of laughter coming from the other side of the house.

"What was that?" Kari asked as she stood up and looked around. All three girls were nowhere to be seen. She ran across the yard and found them with Kurt near his truck. They were excitedly jumping around as he was about to set off another string of firecrackers. Her brother lit the fuse and tossed the strand of small explosive-filled tubes onto the gravel, where they danced as they burst, kicking up a cloud of dust. The girls had their hands over their ears while the firecrackers were going off, then began yelling for him to do more.

Kari marched over to the group, took her daughter's arm, and pulled her away. "Jenny, I told you not to play with those things. They're dangerous. Come on, let's go."

"Calm down, sis. They're harmless." Kurt leaned against the side of his pickup and took a drag of his cigarette. He seemed unconcerned that he was standing beside a truck bed full of fireworks.

"That's not for you to decide," she said, her anger boiling over. "There's a good reason those things are illegal. Too many stupid people blow their fingers off with them or start fires. You can put your own children in harm's way, but don't take that risk with mine. And put that damn thing out, are you crazy?"

He dropped the cigarette on the ground and crushed it out with the toe of his boot, his face showing no expression as he locked eyes with her. Kari shook her head and took hold of her daughter's wrist. Jenny was holding several long, thin metal rods in her hand that looked like they were coated with black sugar. "What are those?"

"Sparklers, Uncle Kurt said I could have them. They make pretty colors."

"I'm sorry, honey, but if your brother sees them, he'll want some also." Kari held out her hand, but Jenny gripped them to her chest.

"It's not fair! I never get to do anything fun because of my stupid brother!"

"Jenny! I don't want to hear you talk about Patrick like that, do you understand me? You can sit inside until it's time to leave. Now give me those things." She reached down and snatched the sparklers out of her daughter's hand.

"ITS NOT FAIR!" Jenny cried. "YOU NEVER LET ME HAVE ANY FUN!"

Kari thought about taking the stupid metal sticks and shoving them up Kurt's nose for ruining her holiday and making Jenny upset. She wouldn't let him get under her skin more than he already had. Kari went to return the sparkler to him, but they ignited in her hand. She cried out and dropped the burning sticks on the ground, brushing the hot metal flakes off her arm.

"Look out!" Stefan shouted. He was standing near the house, pointing up at the sky. Kari craned her head back to see that the drone flying above had caught fire and was spinning out of control. Kurt's eyes widened in horror as the spiraling fireball landed in the powder keg in the back of his truck.

"GET DOWN! GET DOWN!!!" he hollered as he ran toward the twins and pushed them to the ground. Kari picked up Jenny and took off toward the house, but her feet slipped on the gravel, sending them sprawling on the lawn. She used her body to shield her daughter as the hot July afternoon became a blazing, multi-colored hellscape with a cacophony of whistles, shrieks, and ear-splitting thunderclaps. Patrick was standing nearby, jumping and laughing as he watched the impromptu fireworks display.

Jack scooped him up, carried him to safety, and then hurried back to help her and Jenny. Kurt grabbed both of his girls, one in each arm, over to the house. The bed of his pickup truck was on fire, and all three vehicles were littered with burning debris.

Her ears were ringing from the explosions. Jack grabbed the garden hose and sprayed water on the flames as her son, laughing delightedly, filmed the chaotic scene on his tablet. Albert came running out of the house with a fire extinguisher and handed it to Kurt, who sprayed the truck. The ordeal had been five minutes of pure terror, but at least Patrick was entertained. Kari had hoped her kids would have a memorable Fourth of July, and she doubted this would be one they'd ever forget.

# Law Men in Yellow Raincoats

Novel By **MARTIN KNIGHT**

Jupiter & Phoebus Publishing House

# CHAPTER 6
## Law Men in Yellow Raincoats

*H*e was stalking through the trees, sniffing the air for the scent of prey. It had been too long since he had been on a real hunt. He had sufficed his appetite for killing with deer, cows, coyotes, and even the occasional pet dog, but nothing slaked his hunger like humans. At last, he had been let off the leash, free to roam about the fields and forests, searching for someone he could take without being seen. It was difficult to think like a person in this form, so his instructions were kept simple. No witnesses, no killing. That second part would be even more challenging to carry out, especially if he got the taste of blood on his tongue, but he would have to control his instincts. His task was to find a victim and bring them back in whatever condition so long as they were still alive.

It didn't take him long to locate what he needed. The scent of burning wood led him to a group of teenagers partying by the river. They had made a bonfire and were busy drinking, smoking weed, and listening to music. He watched them from the darkness until he spotted two of them, a young man and woman, sneak away from the group towards a copse of trees. The male stumbled as he walked, heavily intoxicated from the smell of alcohol coming off him. The female had been drinking some, but he could also tell she was ready to mate from the other strong scent coming from her. She ran ahead, laughing as she stripped off her bikini top and bottoms, leaving them on low-hanging branches as breadcrumbs for the boy to follow. She was naked except for an unbuttoned flannel shirt, which she tied the ends into a knot beneath her bare breasts.

The male tripped on a tree root and fell hard, hitting his head on the ground and passing out. That was his opportunity to strike. He circled around to follow her. The trees' canopy was thick enough to obscure the moonlight, and the girl lay down on a blanket spread out on the ground as she waited for her lover to catch up. He slipped between two trees near her and waited, taking in the delicious smells permeating the air from her lithe body.

"About time you found me, Danny. I was getting lonely," she said as he moved closer. "Come suck on my tits. My nipples are so hard."

*The woman arched her back to push up her ample breasts, and he leaned down to lick them with his tongue a couple of times before sinking his teeth into her flesh. She let out a scream as blood filled his mouth, and all thoughts except for killing left his mind. He let go of her breast and clamped his teeth around her throat, cutting off the scream as her body thrashed beneath him. She gave a last couple of feeble twitches before going still.*

*July 5, 2019*

Jack woke with a snort, wrapped in the top sheet and alone in bed. Daylight was peeking around the edges of the curtains, and he was soaked in sweat. The alarm clock on the nightstand showed 9:08. Jack couldn't remember the last time he had slept in that late. He had been having such a vivid, bizarre dream it felt like he could still taste blood in his mouth. Or maybe that was because he had bitten his tongue in his sleep. Rolling out of bed, he shuffled into the bathroom to shower.

Kari was standing at the kitchen sink washing dishes when he came out. He kissed her on the back of her neck, but she pulled away from him.

"Good morning, babe," he said.

"Is it?"

Jack could hear the warning bells going off in his head while he poured himself a cup of coffee. He took a drink and spit it back into the cup. It was cold since the coffee maker had been turned off. Not wanting to risk escalating the situation, he stuck the mug, backwash included, into the microwave to heat it up.

He made breakfast as he tried to figure out what he had done and how much trouble he was in. The answer to that was clearly *pretty fucking deep* by the way his wife vigorously scrubbed each dish long after it was clean enough for the Pope to use.

Jack frantically racked his brain as to whether he had missed an anniversary or if he had said something stupid last night. Maybe she was upset with him for oversleeping and leaving her to care for the kids. He knew that he couldn't ignore the problem forever. He also knew it would only add fuel to the fire if he apologized without knowing what transgression he had committed.

After punishing the dishes, Kari wiped her hands off on a towel as if it had insulted her cooking and went to find something else to vent her anger. Jack decided to throw caution to the wind and follow his wife into the laundry room, where she was flinging wet clothes into the dryer.

"Okay, what did I do to land in the doghouse this time?"

"Don't give me that bullshit, Jack," she hissed before slamming another bundle into the dryer bin. "You don't get to play that game and pretend you don't know what you did."

"Whoa, hon, what are you talking about? I honestly have no idea."

"I want you to tell me one thing," she said, thrusting her finger in his face, "and if I find out you're lying, I'll rip your goddamn balls off. Have you started drinking again?"

"I swear to god I haven't touched a drop," he pleaded. "Whatever I did, it wasn't because of alcohol, I promise you."

To his complete surprise, Kari unbuttoned her top and unfastened her bra to reveal her breasts. "Then what the hell possessed you to do this to me? Because you sure as fuck were acting like you were drunk." She pointed to the two red crescent marks, one above and below the nipple on her left breast, where he had apparently bitten her. The skin around the marks was already starting to bruise. Kari fixed her bra and refastened the buttons on her shirt. "I hope you got a good look because it may be a long time before you see them again, if ever."

"Are you sure I did that to you?"

"Yes, Jack, you fucking did that after you woke me up in the middle of the night by ripping open my pajama shirt. You clamped down on my breast with your teeth. I don't know how the kids didn't wake up from me yelling at you. I had to slap you across the face to get you off me. Let me guess, you don't remember any of this. Is that what you expect me to believe? Am I also supposed to buy that you weren't trying to have sex with me even though you were hard as a fucking rock? If you had tried, I would have called the police and charged you with rape. Do I make myself clear?"

His mouth had gone dry as a sun-bleached skull baking in the desert, and his legs felt weak. "I...I..." Jack took a moment to force himself to swallow. "I don't know what to say. Kari, please believe me, I didn't consciously do that. I'm begging you to forgive me." He dropped down onto his knees in front of her. "I would never intentionally hurt you. I can't tell you how sorry I am that it happened. I must have been, I don't know, sleepwalking or something like that."

She stared into his eyes, piercing them with her own. His stomach felt sour, and he worried he might throw up his breakfast. Kari let out a deep sigh and rubbed her bloodshot eyes. "It was strange how you just stopped and went back to sleep like nothing happened. I don't think the whole thing lasted a minute, but you had me so freaked out that I went and slept on the couch for the rest of the night. I wouldn't call it sleeping since I kept waking up every time this godforsaken old house creaked, thinking you were coming after me."

"I have no idea what would have made me do that to you. I was having a weird dream. I know that doesn't excuse it, and I wouldn't blame you for hating me."

Kari bent down beside him. "I don't hate you, Jack, but you scared the living hell out of me. I believe you, but it better not happen again." She stood up and walked out of the laundry room, leaving him sitting on the floor.

The rest of the morning was spent with an uneasy silence hanging over the house. The kids seemed unusually subdued, as if they could sense the tension between their parents. He had meant to repair the outside bulkhead doors to ensure they were watertight so he could use the basement as an office. With the forecast threatening rain, it seemed as good of time as any to attend to it.

Jack found his toolbox and carried it outside, lugging it around to the cellar entrance. He replaced a few broken boards, attached weather stripping along the outer edges, and installed the new locking mechanism he had bought. This would be much safer than relying on a simple padlock accessible from the outside.

"Aren't you just a regular Bob Villa," Kari said from behind him, causing Jack to jump. She was barefooted and had come from the front of the house. "I'm terribly sorry. I didn't mean to scare you." He didn't think that was true from the smile on her face, but the fact that she was smiling at all was a good sign.

"It's not perfect, but it should keep the rain out."

"Good work, Sterling. Would you be mad if I asked you to do me a favor?"

"No, of course not, babe, anything you want."

"Mom called. A bunch of firework debris landed on the roof of their house yesterday, and dad wants to get it cleaned off before it clogs up the gutters. She's worried about him climbing up a ladder, and Kurt is at work. I know you hate heights, but could you help so he doesn't fall and break his neck?"

"Yeah, I'd be happy to do it."

"Great, why don't you take the kids with you? Mom can watch them while you work."

"Are you sure that's a good idea after what happened yesterday?"

"Not entirely, but I've got an appointment in town, and I can't take them with me," Kari replied. "Yesterday was a freak accident. They'll be perfectly safe there."

"Sure, no problem, I'll handle it. Do you have a haircut or something?"

"No, although I am overdue for that, I need to find a stylist I like first," she said, running her fingers through it. "Why, does it look bad?"

"Of course not," Jack replied. He made a mental note to kick himself later.

"I set up a job interview yesterday. I was going to talk to you about it this morning, but I was trying to decide whether to divorce you first."

"I wouldn't blame you," he nodded. "Are you worried about money? I know my salary will be a little tight, but it should be enough."

"No, I'm not worried. This is something I want to do for myself. It's a part-time salesclerk at the new bookstore, so I'd still be able to take care of the kids when school starts. Do you have any problem with that?"

"Honey, I fully support whatever you want to do. I'm dying to find out what that bookstore is like. Do you think you'll get an employee discount?"

Kari rolled her eyes before she turned and walked away. He managed to get both kids out the door and into the back seat of his Camry in under ten minutes. Jack hoped the rain would hold off until they returned, as he hated driving with them in the little sedan in bad weather. He also wasn't thrilled about climbing up on a wet roof. They were crossing the bridge over the Iowa River to Old Ahnen when Patrick got excited.

"Ducks! Ducks! Quack quack!" he giggled. "Big ducks, daddy! Big yellow ducks!"

Jack turned to look out the passenger side window at what had caught his son's interest. Several people wearing bright yellow rain slickers lined both sides of the riverbank. It did indeed look like a parade of giant yellow rubber ducks wading through the mud and brush. The river was wide but shallow through here, and a flat-bottom boat kept pace with the search party working the banks.

They crossed the bridge, and the trees hid the group from view. Despite their near-comical appearance, Jack was disturbed by their presence. It was likely that some fisherman had gone missing, but he thought of his dream last night.

He remembered that there had been a river or lake in it, and he had been stalking a woman through a bunch of trees. The rest was fuzzy, but he was sure he had hurt her. Jack knew it couldn't really have happened, but he attacked his wife in the middle of the

night in a similar manner. By the time they reached the farm, he had forgotten about the
men in yellow raincoats as the sky opened up.

Kari sat in her van outside of The Raven's Perch. The clouds in the sky were heavy and
gray, and she was worried about Jack up on a roof if it began to storm. It was better than
having her father doing it. Given how much her husband hated heights, it would serve
him right for scaring the daylights out of her last night. Jack had acted like a feral beast
trying to maul her, but it had been exciting in a perverse sort of way. Not that she would
ever admit that out loud or condone any such behavior from him, not without at least
being awake first.

She checked her hair in the rearview mirror once more before leaving the van. Kari
smoothed out her black slacks and flowered shirt, her most professional-looking outfit.
She took a deep breath to calm her nerves, then headed to her interview.

The store was lit up now, and the shelves and displays were fully stocked and organized.
A couple of women were browsing the aisle of used romance paperbacks up front, and
they looked up briefly when she entered. Kari walked past the bookshelves to the sales
counter, but nobody was there.

"May I help you?" a man asked, and she caught her breath. "I'm so sorry. I didn't mean
to startle you." She turned around to find Mr. Thynne standing behind her.

"I must have walked right past you," she laughed. "I'm Kari Sterling. Do you remember
me from the other day? I was in here with my daughter, Jenny."

"Yes, of course, I sold her a typewriter. Is she unhappy with her purchase?"

"What? Oh, no, that's not why I'm here," she answered. "I called about the sales
position. The lady I spoke to told me to come here at ten o'clock today for an interview?"

"Ah, please come upstairs to my office." He motioned for her to follow him and led her
to a spiral staircase. The second floor contained several more bookshelves and a couple of
tables holding boxes. An older woman was packing books into the boxes, and she seemed
to do a double take when she saw Kari.

"Gretchen, this is Mrs. Sterling," Ryland said. "I believe the two of you spoke on the
phone."

"You look familiar," the older woman greeted her. "Have we met before?"

"I don't think so, but I grew up here. You might know my parents, Albert and Margrit Ulmer?"

"No," Gretchen said briskly and returned to her work.

Ryland had a small office set up at the front of the store. It was furnished with a roll-top desk pushed up against the brick wall, two worn leather reading chairs, and a coffee table beside the narrow rectangular windows.

"Please have a seat. Can I get you something to drink?" he offered. "Coffee, perhaps?"

"No, thank you, I'm good," she replied. "You certainly have a large collection of books here."

"Yes, I've been selling used and rare books over the Internet for the past twenty years. Opening a store is more for tax purposes. It also lets me get to know the people of this community, whom I've already found to be much friendlier than most Londoners. Forgive my rambling; you are here about the salesclerk job. Have you ever worked in a bookstore before?"

"No, I taught elementary school for a while, but I know a lot about books since my husband is an English professor."

"That's right. I remember you telling me about that. So, when can you start?"

"I guess I can be available tomorrow."

"I think Gretchen is off on Thursday. Let's have you train with her on Friday. Is that acceptable?"

"That's perfectly fine. Does that mean I have the job?"

"If you are agreeable, I believe it does."

"Thank you, Mr. Thynne; I'm truly grateful for this opportunity."

"Allow me to say congratulations," Ryland said as he shook her hand. "I'm excited to have you as part of our little family."

The clouds were drizzling as she left the store and returned to her van. She started the engine, pulled out of the parking spot, and drove down to the next corner of the square. Kari glanced around to see if anybody was watching, then pumped her fists in the air.

"Yes!"

Jack struggled to maintain his footing and avoid tossing his cookies as he scooted toward the roof's edge. Although the rain was light, the shingles were already turning slick. He had managed to keep from looking at the ground while he cleaned off the remnants of the fireworks from the roof, but there was no avoiding it while climbing down the ladder.

Despite the rain, he sat at the edge of the precipice for a few seconds, steeling his nerves before he swung his leg out over the endless void below. His foot found nothing but empty space, and Jack flattened his stomach against the roof to keep from slipping off. After what seemed an eternity of flailing about, his foot caught one of the rungs.

"Are you coming down sometime today?" Albert hollered up at him. "I already took a shower this morning."

"Stuff it, you old coot," he grumbled under his breath. "Yeah, I'm on my way."

Jack kept his eyes fixed straight ahead on the wall of the house until he was a few feet from the ground. His father-in-law let go of the side rails so he could hop down, and it took all his willpower not to drop to his knees and kiss the ground. He bent over to wipe debris from the shingles off his jeans, but it was also to hide his trembling hands.

"Can you handle putting the ladder away on your own?" Albert asked him. "This old coot has to go piss after standing around so long."

"Sure, I'll take care of it," Jack replied, wondering how Albert had heard him from up there.

"Good, and thank you for doing that," he said. "Don't feel bad. I hate heights as well."

Albert laughed and slapped him on the back as he walked away with enough force that Jack stumbled forward a step. He collapsed the ladder back down and carried it around the house, stopping halfway to rub his shoulder, which was still smarting. His clothes and shoes were soaked when he got the ladder hung up in the garage.

The rain was coming down steadily now, so he hustled across the yard and hugged the side of the house as he made his way around to the back door. Jack noticed that his sister-in-law's minivan was parked next to his Camry. The kitchen window was open despite the rain, although the box fan was turned off. As he passed by it, he could overhear Jessica talking.

"...it was all over the news this morning, and you know that last night was a full moon."

"I'm sure that's just a coincidence," Margrit replied. "Has he given you any reason to-"

"No, I swear he was home all night. I would have woken up if he had...I mean, he's taking his pills, so it wouldn't even be possible, right?"

"Of course not, but we should talk about this later. Jack might come back."

He didn't realize that he had been eavesdropping, and he moved away from the window before somebody saw him. Jack made sure to be noisy as he entered the house and removed his mud-caked shoes. Margrit and Jessica were sitting at the kitchen table drinking coffee.

"Look what the cat dragged in," his sister-in-law said. "You're soaking wet, poor thing. What were you doing outside in the rain?"

"Turns out somebody shot a bunch of fireworks up on the roof," Jack replied, to which she grimaced. "Nothing to worry about. I got them cleaned off. Did Kurt's pickup get a lot of damage?"

"Nothing a little paint won't fix, and it serves him right for buying those stupid things. That was the craziest thing, all of them going off at once. I think the kids had a blast watching it."

"I should get going. I need to change into some dry clothes before catching a cold."

"Oh, that's too bad. I brought the girls over because Kari texted me that Jenny would be here this afternoon," Jessica said. "I could drop her off at your house later if you don't mind?"

"Sure, sounds good. I'll take Patrick home with me."

Jack had to wait until the episode of Mickey Mouse Clubhouse playing on the television was over before his son would leave. Between the back steps and the Camry, there was an abundance of puddles for Patrick to jump in, and his shoes were covered in mud by the time they reached the car. Jack helped him buckle his seat belt and then plopped down in the driver's seat, wiping off his glasses using the driest spot he could find on his shirt.

"Well, that was fun." The car started making a dinging noise after he turned it on, and an icon of a gas pump flashed on the dashboard. Jack glanced down at the fuel gauge and saw that the needle was pointing at the red zone of the dial. "You've got to be kidding me."

There was probably enough gas left in the tank to make it to Bailey Grove, but he stopped at the convenience store in Old Ahnen just to be safe. If he ended up stranded on the side of the road with Patrick, he would never hear the end of it.

The gas station's brick facade matched the other quaint buildings that attracted the tourists. A local news station van was pulled off the side of the road across from it, and a TV crew was setting up to film with the historic buildings of Old Ahnen as the backdrop. Jack turned into the parking lot and had to maneuver around a boat trailer to get to the only open gas pump.

"All right, buddy, can you stay in the car while I get gas?"

"Patrick's gas!" His son leaned over in his seat and let one rip. Jack couldn't help but laugh as he got out of the car.

The man fueling the pickup with the boat trailer in the next stall was wearing a yellow raincoat like the group Patrick had spotted earlier. Jack noticed that **SHERIFF** was written in white reflective letters across the back. The boat was also the same one that had accompanied the searchers along the river.

While waiting for the pump to shut off, he tried to see what the news crew was doing. The reporter, a young woman wearing a jacket with the station's logo, stood beside another of the yellow-coated lawmen. Although he was across the street, Jack recognized the guy being interviewed as the detective from the hardware store. The gas nozzle clicked, and he put it back in the cradle on the pump.

"Patrick, do you want to go inside and get some donuts?"

"Um hum."

"Okay, no running around, and you have to stay with daddy because it's busy here."

Jack pulled forward into an empty parking spot in front of the convenience store. He snagged a cup of coffee, and Patrick insisted on a candy dispenser with a motorized propeller that cost more than the coffee and a dozen donuts.

"A lot of excitement in town here today," he told the cashier as she rang him up. "There's a news team filming across the street, and I thought I saw a search party by the river earlier. Do you know what's going on?"

"Oh, yeah, it's been all over social media," the woman replied. "A local girl vanished near the river, and her boyfriend is in the hospital. Somebody posted he claimed she got dragged away by a bear or something, but I think he killed her. I watch a lot of Dateline Mysteries, and that's always how it turns out."

"Oh, I didn't know there were bears in Iowa."

"I've never heard of any either," she replied, "but there's plenty of drunk assholes."

The moonlight barely filtered through the trees, but Kurt could see what he was doing just fine, even without being in his true form. His eyes could see much better in the dark than ordinary people, a trait that had helped save his life many times when hunting his prey in Iraq and Afghanistan. He hated those countries; they were too hot and had no decent woods, but he had enjoyed the work. His bloodlust had gotten so bad that it had been difficult to return to the States, but his new job allowed him to be both a family man and the occasional cold-blooded killer.

Jessica was happy thinking he was working security for MasterPharm, which technically was true, and he intended to keep it that way. However, he would lose his mind if he couldn't unleash the beast within him every so often.

He finished digging the shallow grave and stretched out his back. Kurt tossed the shovel on top of the pile of dirt beside the crude hole before he hopped out. It had to look like something a drunk man would have dug in desperation. He stretched his back and walked over to where the body wrapped in a blanket was laying.

In the palm of the girl's severed hand was a small chunk of the shirt the boyfriend had been wearing that would match a torn, bloodstained hole in his sleeve. When the police inevitably found the girl's mutilated body, it should be enough to point the crime back at the poor bastard. Kurt had made sure to cover up any evidence of the wounds he had left on her, which was easy since she looked like a blind butcher had carved up a side of beef.

The sound of footsteps on the underbrush caught his sensitive ears as he carried the body. A woman in a hooded robe and hiking boots stepped out from behind a bush and pointed a flashlight that shone red instead of white light at him, making the scene look like it was bathed in blood.

"What the fuck are you doing here?" Kurt snarled.

"I came to make sure you don't fuck this up as well since you made a mess of the girl," the woman said. "I can't believe you would hunt this close to the Master's home. What the hell were you thinking? You'd better bring me a living victim on the next cycle, or I'll use your wife as the sacrifice."

Kurt was tempted to snatch the assault rifle propped against a nearby tree and answer her with a couple of high-velocity rounds, but he didn't feel like digging a second grave tonight. He tossed the body into the open pit, and it landed with a thud on the cold, damp earth.

# Jenny's Birthday Box

SW

Children's Tale By **MARTIN KNIGHT**

Jupiter & Phoebus Publishing House

# CHAPTER 7
## Jenny's Birthday Box

*July 31, 2019*

I t was dark when Jack woke to find his wife's arm draped across his chest as he lay with his back to her. A scratching noise had stirred him from his sleep, most likely one of the kids up and about already, but he didn't hear anything now. Kari was still asleep, so perhaps he had dreamed it.

Today was his birthday, and his wife had planned a party at their house for that evening. That shouldn't stop him from trying to kick off the festivities a little early. He reached up and intertwined his fingers with his wife's hand, not surprised to find that it felt cold. "Hey, I don't think the kids are awake yet," he whispered as he rolled over. "Are you up for..."

The woman lying next to him had a deep gash in the side of her head, and he could see a good chunk of brain matter through the hole. Blood matted her graying brown hair and stained the collar and sleeve of her robe. Her green eyes were glazed over in the stare of death, but her mouth opened as she began to speak.

*"The Alchemist will soon be resurrected,"* she spoke in a flat, emotionless voice with a German accent. *"He seeks to become the King of Nightmares and will cast the world into darkness. Look to the past to name him, follow in the night's shadow to find him, heed the dreamer to defeat him. When you hear the call of the wolves, the children will be in the corn."*

He heard a scratching noise again, this time coming from behind him. Jack rolled over and saw the closet door slowly swinging open. An ominous red glow was coming from inside of it. A fur-covered arm reached out and raked its long, black claws across the wood. Jack jumped out of bed and shoved the closet door against the protruding arm. Whatever was on the other side let out an angry growl that froze his blood. The creature snarled and clawed blindly at the wall as he pressed his entire weight against the door, trying to keep it shut.

His efforts were in vain as the monster hurled its body against the door and sent him flying backward onto the bed. Jack covered his head with his arms as he braced for the creature to leap on him and deliver the killing blow. The beast's jaws closed around his hand, piercing his flesh.

Jack jerked awake with a cry, scrambling away from the monster attacking him. The sheet was wrapped around his legs, and he tumbled out of bed to land with a painful thump on the floor. Stunned and smarting, he rolled onto his side as he struggled to free his bound ankles. If the situation wasn't humiliating enough, his wife and daughter came running into the bedroom and found him still tangled up.

"Jack, are you alright? What happened?" Kari asked. "What was all that shouting?"

"Did you fall out of bed, daddy?" Jenny giggled, and then his wife started laughing, too.

"I'm fine, thanks for asking." With his legs now free, Jack stood up with what little dignity he had left. He was only wearing boxer shorts, so he grabbed the sheet and wrapped it around his waist. "I just had a bad dream. Would you both mind leaving so I can take a shower?"

Kari shook her head and took Jenny back into the hallway, closing the door behind her. Jack couldn't help but look inside the closet, hesitating with his hand on the doorknob before he opened it. He cursed himself for being a fool to think a monster could be hiding in there, but he sighed in relief that it was empty.

His butt was aching where it had hit the hardwood floor, and his left hand was on fire. Jack gingerly flexed his wrist and fingers to check if he had any broken bones. Everything seemed fine except for a couple of red marks on his palm and the back of his hand where he had dreamed the beast had bitten him.

Jack took out the notebook from the nightstand drawer, which he used to write down story ideas. The memory of the dream was fading quickly, so he jotted down what the dead woman had told him. After showering and getting dressed, he sat on the bed to put on his socks.

He glanced over his shoulder to make sure nobody was behind him and spotted a small red stain on his wife's pillow. He leaned over to get a better look, and it appeared to be dried blood in the exact spot where the woman's head had been resting. Jack stripped off the pillowcase and tossed it into the laundry along with the rest of the sheets.

"There's the birthday boy! It's about time you rolled out of bed," his wife said as he entered the kitchen. "Are scrambled eggs okay for breakfast, or would you rather have them over easy?"

"Scrambled will be just fine," he replied. "Can't a guy fall out of bed without getting harassed?"

"Poor baby, get your coffee when you're done feeling sorry for yourself. Try not to spill the pot all over the floor."

Jack held his tongue as he got a coffee cup from the cupboard. Since the biting incident, he had been plagued with bad dreams, which had also affected his appetite. However, he was starving this morning, so he grabbed four pancakes from the plate on the table and a heaping serving of scrambled eggs.

"A little hungry this morning, dear?" Kari asked.

"What? It's my birthday."

"Mommy, I'm done. Can I go play?" Jenny asked.

"Sure, honey, can you take your dishes to the sink first?"

She got up from the table and cleared off her plate and juice glass, then came over and kissed him on the cheek. "Happy birthday, daddy! I hope you didn't hurt yourself."

"I'm fine, thank you, sweetheart," he replied. "At least somebody cares."

"I know it's your birthday, but I hope you don't mind if I go to work for a couple of hours this afternoon," Kari said. "Gretchen has a doctor's appointment, and I told her I would cover for her. I'll be home in time to get things ready for the party. Mom is baking a German chocolate cake which I know you won't eat with your weird hatred for coconut. Don't worry, I picked you up a slice of cheesecake with cherry pie filling."

"You know me too well."

"Yes, you don't deserve me," Kari said as she patted him on the arm. "You're like a stray dog that I fed once and wouldn't leave, so I took pity on you and let you come into the house."

"Gee, thanks, you're too kind."

"Don't mention it," his wife said, smiling at him before looking over his head. "That poor girl, missing for almost a month. I can't imagine what her parents are going through. If her boyfriend killed her, I hope they throw him in the smallest, darkest cell they have."

"What are we talking about?" Jack asked. Kari pointed at the small flat-screen television on top of the refrigerator, which was tuned to the local newscast.

"Don't you remember the woman who disappeared on the Fourth? A dog walker found a body buried near the river yesterday," she replied. "The police haven't confirmed the identity, but unless bears can use shovels, the boyfriend's story is falling apart."

The station replayed the footage of the reporter interviewing the detective in the yellow raincoat in front of the Old Ahnen sign. Jack remembered them setting up to do that location shot. The broadcast switched over to a live news conference featuring the detective with the scarred face now standing behind a podium, looking annoyed at having to answer questions.

"Where's the remote? Can you turn it up?"

"I don't know if I want Patrick to hear about this." Their son was sitting at the far end of the table, his head down over his drawing pad.

"He's not paying attention. Just turn it up for a bit." Kari passed him the TV remote, and he increased the volume until it was audible.

*Detective Blackburn, what can you tell us about the cause of death?* Asked an off-screen reporter.

*Given the advanced state of decomposition and dismemberment of the body, the coroner will need to perform a full autopsy to determine that. We are treating this as a suspicious death for the time being.*

*Do you have any suspects?*

*I'm not going to discuss that right now, but we are investigating all leads. If anyone has information, they are urged to come forward and contact the Johnson County Sheriff's Office by calling...*

The photo of the young woman who had been murdered appeared on the screen, and Jack felt his vision blur as a sharp pain shot through his head.

"Did you hear what I said?" Kari asked. "Can you please shut that off? I don't want Patrick to listen to this."

"What? Oh, um, sorry," he answered as he turned off the television.

"Are you okay? Your face got suddenly pale."

"Yeah, I'm okay, just a bit dizzy. Maybe I bumped my head when I fell out of bed this morning." The truth was that he didn't feel fine at all. His head was swimming, and he wanted to lie down.

"Don't joke about that. Do you think you have a concussion? Maybe we should take you to the doctor and have you checked out."

"Whoa, calm down, I didn't hit my head."

"Well, I was about to beat you upside your head this morning. You were moaning in your sleep and snoring like a water buffalo."

"I didn't know water buffaloes snored, have you slept with many?" he grinned, but his wife's face showed no hint of amusement. "I guess I haven't been sleeping well, probably from all the stress of preparing for the upcoming semester. I take it I'm waking you up overnight?"

"Not at all. I enjoy a freight train rumbling through my bedroom at two o'clock every morning. I know you've got a lot on your plate, but it's your birthday, so take it easy today and get some rest." Jack nodded as he cleared off his and his wife's dishes and rinsed them in the sink.

"I'd like to work on setting up my office downstairs. I hope to have it ready soon to start writing."

"I think you really want someplace you can go hide and get out of doing dishes."

"What? I would never do a thing like that, honey. Scouts honor."

"Uh-huh, if you were in the Scouts, I was a teenage beauty queen."

"I thought you were the homecoming queen," he quipped. "That's about the same thing, so I guess that makes me an Eagle Scout, wouldn't you say?" His wife shook her head and walked away.

Jack headed down to his sanctuary beneath the house. Three walls of the cellar were lined with shelves made from four-inch-thick wood planks, varnished, shellacked, and attached to the wall with sturdy metal struts. The multitude of circular indentations on the shelves spoke to their previous use to store canning jars. He would elevate their stature to displaying his collection of books once he put on a new shellac topcoat.

He had bought a new light fixture to replace the single bare bulb. Jack opened the outer cellar doors to let in as much light as possible before shutting off the basement's electricity. He flipped the light switch on and off several times to ensure the circuit was open but was still nervous as he stood on the step stool and disconnected the wires to the existing fixture. Jack was putting up with the new dome light when Kari came running down the steps.

"What the heck, are you trying to break an ankle?" Jack asked.

"You left your phone in the bedroom. Somebody named Dr. Wilkens called you." She handed him his cell phone, which showed he had a missed call and a voicemail. "Is it about your fall this morning?"

"Huh? No, Dr. Wilkens is my boss. Why would she be calling me? I told her I was taking the day off for my birthday, and I emailed all the students in my class." Jack brought up the voicemail and listened to it.

"*Hello, Jack. It's Kellie. Sorry to disturb you on your birthday, but I want to discuss some exciting news with you. Please call me back as soon as possible. Thanks!*"

He wondered what sort of event could have transpired in the English department that would make for '*exciting news*' short of a new work from Shakespeare being discovered.

"Well, what does she want?" Kari asked.

"I'm not sure. Let me call her back." He pressed the button to dial her number.

"Jack, happy birthday," Professor Wilkens answered. "I hope I'm not bothering you, but I wanted to see if you would be available to meet a friend tomorrow."

"Oh, um, sure thing, who would that be?"

"I'm afraid my friend is very private, so he would prefer to make his introductions face-to-face. He has been a generous supporter of our program at the university for many years, and he was the one who recommended you for your position. He's impressed with your writing talents and wants to discuss an opportunity with you."

"It sounds rather mysterious, but I'm game," Jack chuckled. "Let me know when and where I should meet him."

"I think it would be best if we go together," she replied. "I can pick you up at your house at, shall we say, nine-thirty tomorrow morning?"

"Okay, I'm looking forward to it. See you then."

Jack hung up the phone and stared at it in his hand.

"What was that about?" Kari asked.

"She wants me to meet some bigshot department supporter," he replied. "Probably some stuffy old business owner who thinks he knows everything about literature because he read Faulkner once." Another possibility came to mind, but he didn't want to get his hopes up. Jack tucked his phone in his pocket as Kari went back upstairs.

Jack finished hooking up the new light and was pleasantly surprised when it worked the first time. Kari wasn't in the kitchen, but his son was still drawing at the table. As he walked by, he caught a glimpse of the picture that Patrick was working on.

"Hey, can daddy see what you're doing?" Patrick shook his head and leaned over the picture to block it from view, but Jack managed to get a good look. "That looks kind of scary."

The drawing showed a door in the middle of a yellow wall, the same color as the master bedroom, with a red light shining out from behind it. A large, hairy arm reached through the door, and scratch marks were drawn on it and the wall.

"What is this a picture of, Patrick?"

He had rarely seen his son show fear, except maybe at the dentist's office. Patrick turned to face him and looked directly into his eyes, and he was undoubtedly afraid.

"Monster," Patrick whispered and flipped the pad's cover shut. Jack wondered if he and his son had experienced the same nightmare, but that was impossible.

Wasn't it?

Kari needed a birthday present for Jack, but she couldn't step away from the cash register for more than a few minutes to find one. She hated to admit she was jealous of the gift that her daughter had found, which she would label as coming from both Jenny and Patrick. While she had picked up a couple of nice dress shirts and slacks, she also wanted to get something he would enjoy. There should be plenty of options for her from The Raven's Perch, given that it was practically a grown-up toy store made for Jack. For some reason, she hadn't been able to decide on anything that didn't cost a small fortune, and now she was out of time.

It wasn't like Jack had gone out of his way for her birthday. She got a new robe from the kids, a purse she had picked out, and some sexy lingerie from him. The last gift was more of a present for him. He had also picked up takeout from her favorite restaurant, and they put the lingerie to good use after the kids went to bed.

"Goodness, I don't think I've ever seen the shop this busy," Mr. Thynne said as he came out of the back room carrying a large box. He set it down on the counter and stretched out his back. "Oh my, I'm afraid that was too heavy."

"Are you alright? You shouldn't be carrying anything that big without help."

"I know, I know. I forget my years sometimes, and then my body is more than happy to remind me. I was sorting through some of the boxes I hadn't unpacked yet and discovered this collection of paperbacks in rough shape. Let's sell them for a dollar a piece to get them off my hands."

"I'd be happy to go through the box and tag them for you," Kari said.

"I would greatly appreciate it if you would be so kind. They are mostly old pulp horror and science fiction novels, but if you see anything you like, please help yourself."

"I usually stick with romance novels and murder mysteries, but my husband is a big fan of those genres," she replied. "I still need to get him something for his birthday. Maybe there will be some buried treasure here."

The rush had tapered off, so Kari opened the box flaps and stacked the books on the counter. Most of the novels were from the '60s and '70s or even earlier, with painted illustrations on their covers. She picked out five titles from authors she thought Jack might like and were in better shape than the rest. *The Magus* by John Fowles, *Conjure Wife* by Fritz Leiber, *The Wolf's Hour* by Robert R. McCammon, *Fourth Mansions* by R. A. Lafferty, and *The Tomb and Other Stories* by H. P. Lovecraft. The cover of that last one had the most disturbing image of a man with a padlocked metal band around the width of his head. His skull had split in half, and creepy red bats were escaping from inside.

At the bottom of the box, she found a dog-eared novel by an author named Butch Richardson. On the cover was a picture of an elegant hotel surrounded by snow-capped mountains.

"Mr. Thynne, have you read this one? *In The Mountains Of Murder?*"

"What's that? Hmmm, no, I can't say that I have. Feel free to take that one with you as well. I don't care for those types of novels." Kari momentarily considered throwing it back into the box, but then she put it in with her selections.

Jack's stomach growled as he entered the driveway, his car filled with the infuriating aroma of hot pizza. He had driven into the city to pick it up at Kari's suggestion, but he knew she was trying to get him out of the house to set up a "surprise" party. He parked the car and grabbed the three pizza boxes from the back seat.

"Hello, is anybody here?" Jack called out loudly as he entered the house, which conspicuously had all the lights turned off. Kari flipped on the switch, and everyone jumped up and yelled, "*Surprise!*" Patrick stood beside his mother with his hands clasped over his ears, but he was laughing with the rest of the family.

Margrit took the pizza from him while Jenny ran up and gave him a red conical party hat. Kari led him over to sit at the head of the table, then snapped the rubber band of the hat against his throat as she put it on him. Patrick came up beside him with a noise maker in his mouth and blew it right next to Jack's ear.

"Let's not give daddy tinnitus," Kari said as she guided Patrick to his chair. "He's getting old and needs every bit of hearing he has left. Isn't that right, dear?"

"Huh? What's that? You'll have to speak up."

"Wait until you see the present we got you," his daughter said. "I hope you like it. I paid for it myself."

"You did? I'm sure I'll love it, honey," he smiled. "Are you and Patrick going to help me blow out the candles on my cake?"

"Yes, if there aren't too many of them. I almost ran out of breath when I turned eight."

"If your mom puts one candle for each of my years, I will need help."

"Should we ask grandpa to blow them out, too?"

"Your grandmother always says I'm full of hot air, so I don't know how much use I would be," Albert chuckled. "I might light some of the candles back on fire."

Kari brought two plates for the kids with the pizza cut into pieces and two cups of milk. She returned to the kitchen as Margrit came out carrying two plates, one with his favorite taco pizza, which she set in front of him, and the other with two slices of all-meat pizza.

"Would you mind handing this to Albert?" she asked Jack.

He took the plate from her and passed it over to his father-in-law. Albert reached out to take the plate but grabbed Jack's left hand instead and sniffed at it.

"Did something happen to your hand?" he asked. "What are these red marks? Were you bitten?" Margrit had been looking questioningly at her husband, but now she focused on Jack's palm, where the two red welts still showed.

"I, um..."

"Is something wrong?" Kari asked as she came out of the kitchen.

"Nothing at all, dear," Margrit smiled. "Help me get the rest of the drinks."

Once dinner was over, they cleared away the plates before Kari brought out the cake. It only had two candles on top, but they were in the shape of numbers that Kari had put together to make up his age. They skipped singing Happy Birthday since that always upset his son. Kari cut the cake while Margrit served bowls of vanilla ice cream to everyone except Patrick, who didn't like anything cold.

"That was delicious," Jack said after the meal. "I think I'm ready for a nap now."

"Hold on, old man, there's still presents to open," Kari replied.

"Oh, right, I almost forgot about that part," he said, rubbing his hands together in anticipation. Kari brought out a stack of wrapped packages.

"Patrick's presents!"

"Here, buddy, you can help me open them." Jack passed him what he guessed was a shirt box from the shape. "Jenny, would you like to give me a hand with this one?"

When he was done, Jack had a pile of dress shirts, pants, socks, and several vintage paperbacks in front of him.

"Wow, this is great. Thank you, everyone."

"We're not finished yet. There's still one more present, but it's too heavy for me to lift," Kari said. "It's in our closet. I hate to ask, but would you mind getting it?"

Jack stood up from his chair and went to their bedroom closet. He picked up a large cardboard box with a red foil bow and almost threw his back out from the weight. Whatever heavy object was inside shifted about and made a distinct metallic ding as he carried it to the table. "Good lord, what's in here? Did you buy a new engine for my car?"

"That Camry of yours could probably use one," his wife said, "but that's not what your daughter got you."

"Jenny bought this? Now I'm even more curious to find out what's inside." Jack took out his pocket knife and sliced through the tape along the box's seams. He put his knife away and opened the flaps. "Is this an Underwood? Are you kidding me?"

"I paid a dollar for it!" Jenny announced.

"Is she being serious?"

"It's a long story. I assume that an Underwood is pretty good?"

"Don't you remember I told you Martin Knight used one before he finally switched to a computer?"

"Gosh, it must have slipped my mind. You only talk about this Martin guy so much I expect him to show up for dinner sometime," Kari replied. "Jenny found it at The Raven's Perch, and that's where I got all those novels, too."

"I need to go check this place out," he whistled as he lifted the typewriter from the box. "This looks to be in pristine condition. I feel like a kid again. I can't wait to try it out. Thank you so much, all of you, for a wonderful birthday."

"You might want to take it out of here before Patrick gets his hands on it," his wife said. "I don't think he'll let you have it back once he figures out what it does."

Jack scooped up the typewriter and giddily took it downstairs to his new basement office. He set it down on his desk and stepped back to admire his birthday present.

Rummaging through several boxes of his books, he found a ream of blank paper and inserted a sheet through the roller. He sat in his chair while he thought about what to type, then decided on the well-known pangram.

The quick brown fox jumps over the lazy dog.

# On Ghost Writing

Novel By **MARTIN KNIGHT**

Jupiter & Phoebus Publishing House

# CHAPTER 8

## On Ghost Writing

*August 1, 2019*

J ack sat in the passenger seat of Professor Wilken's Lincoln Towncar as she drove north on Motte's Ferry Road. Coming over the top of a hill on the other side of Bailey Grove, the Iowa River valley stretched out before them with Old Ahnen off in the distance.

The Ahnen Villages were spread along the valley between the river to the south and a range of hills to the north. The land between the river and the base of the hills was flat and fertile, making it prime farming soil. Fields of corn and soybeans surrounded Old Ahnen, and the plethora of trees spread throughout the town gave the antiquated red brick and wood plank buildings the appearance of ancient ruins being reclaimed by a sea of vegetation.

"How is your family settling in?" Kellie asked. "Is it starting to feel like home?"

"It's getting there. We've got most everything unpacked, and the kids love all the space they have in the house compared to our apartment back in Colorado. Jenny is already trying to talk us into getting a dog, which I'm sure I'll end up feeding and cleaning up after."

"That's the joy of pets when you're a kid, all of the fun with none of the mess."

Old Ahnen was already busy with people visiting the stores, and the coffee shop on the corner had a line out the door. "Looks like the murder of that girl hasn't hurt the local tourism any," Jack commented as they waited for a group of people to cross the street.

"Yes, that was quite tragic, but I guess life must go on." Kellie turned west and drove past the pharmaceutical factory. "My friend has been very eager to meet you. He doesn't allow many visitors these days, and it's especially rare for him to invite somebody new to his home."

"I'm a bit nervous about meeting your friend. I have a feeling I know who it is, and I hope I don't disappoint him."

"I wouldn't worry about that. I think the two of you will hit it off splendidly." They passed the factory, and Kellie turned onto a narrow road named *Stone Fort Lane*, which went up the side of a wooded hill.

Even though Jack couldn't see the enormous house from here, he knew that was where they were going. Kellie turned off halfway up the hill onto a driveway that was barred by a tall wrought iron gate between two brick pillars. A metal circular disc was set in the center of each gate, with the letter **D** etched on the left and the letter **M** on the right. Off to the side of the road was a smaller brick pillar with a speaker, call button, and camera mounted in a metal faceplate. Kellie rolled down her window and pushed the call button.

"*Welcome back, Professor Wilkens,*" a woman's voice came out of the speaker.

"Thank you, Claudia."

There was a loud click as the gates parted and swung inward. She put the window back up, and they continued along the road towards the top of the hill. The drive wound around to the north side of the house and ended in an oval roundabout half the length of a football field.

His first thought as the mansion came into view was that they had somehow been transported from Iowa to the English countryside. The manor home was three stories high, made of brick and stone, with towering oak trees standing around it like palace sentries with green-leafed canopies in place of bearskin hats. If the manor wasn't enormous enough, there was also a four-stall garage with a cobblestone courtyard and a two-story cottage on the west side of the roundabout.

Although he had put on his best suit coat for today, Jack felt underdressed for the occasion. His boss drove up to the entrance, which stood beneath a stone portico with a gabled roof. The arched wooden front door, reinforced with studded iron straps, looked sturdy enough to fend off an attack from a Viking horde.

Kellie pressed the doorbell, and a series of chimes rang inside the house, reverberating even through the stone wall. If that wasn't sufficient to announce their presence, the sound summoned a high-pitched barking dog who began scratching furiously at the other side of the door. The barking was momentarily cut off as someone picked up the dog before opening the door.

"Jojo, calm down. You don't need to attack everyone who rings the doorbell," a burly woman wearing a white blouse and black slacks said to the small, black-and-tan canine cradled in the crook of her arm. The dog ignored her and bared its teeth at Jack with a menacing snarl.

"Welcome to Devonshire Manor. Please come in."

"Hello, Claudia, nice to see you again," Kellie replied. "It's nice to see you, too, Jojo. Such a cute little puppy, aren't you? Yes, you are!" She scratched the dog behind the ear as his tail started wagging, but Jojo kept his eyes trained on Jack and let out a growl as he stepped over the threshold. They stood in an entry hall, a two-story, long rectangular room with a vaulted ceiling supported by thick wood beam arches and illuminated by an ironwork chandelier hanging down in the center. The manor house's exterior was a work of extraordinary craftsmanship and flaunted wealth, and it was equaled, if not surpassed, by the interior.

On the east wall was a carved stone fireplace big enough to roast an entire pig inside, and hanging above it was an *honest-to-freaking-god* tapestry that could easily carpet his living room. The other wall was decorated with a gallery of paintings that Jack guessed were worth more than his house and yearly salary combined.

"Oh, good. Our guests have arrived," came a man's voice from the hallway. "Right on time."

He was a tall, lanky, older man with slicked-back, graying hair and thick-lens glasses. Jack recognized the famed author from the photographs on the back covers of his novels, but he looked noticeably older and was leaning heavily on a cane. He had imagined meeting Mr. Knight as a fellow writer and what sort of conversations they would have, but now that he was standing before him, Jack's tongue was tied into knots.

"Kellie, hello, my dear," the author said, bending down to kiss her on the cheek. "Ah, you must be Jack Sterling. How nice to finally meet you. I'm Martin Knight. Perhaps you've heard of me?"

"Yes, of course. I've read all your books," he replied. "I can't tell you what an honor it is to meet you in person. You have an extraordinary house. It looks like the perfect home for a famous horror writer."

"I'm afraid I can't claim any credit for that," Martin said. "My late wife's grandfather, Henry Masterson, built Devonshire Manor, and I inherited it when she passed away. I've thought about selling it more than once. It's quite a headache to maintain, but I can't bring myself to part with it."

"I'm very sorry for your loss, and I hope I didn't offend you."

"Not at all. Why don't we go to the library and chat? My bad leg begins to hurt if I stand on it too long." He turned to the housekeeper. "Claudia, would you be a dear and prepare refreshments for our guests?"

"I've already made up a platter along with coffee and hot tea, Mr. Knight," she replied. The housekeeper set the small dog on the floor before she headed down the hallway. The four-legged land shark lunged at Jack and grabbed his pant leg with its mouthful of tiny daggers, growling and shaking its head back and forth.

"Get back, Jojo," Martin barked as he tapped the end of his cane on the floor twice. "Get back where you belong." The dog reluctantly let go of Jack's leg and tucked his tail before slinking away to lie down on a plush doggy bed beside the stone fireplace. His dark brown eyes watched Jack warily with a low growl coming from his throat every so often.

"Don't mind Jojo," Kellie said. "He might look vicious, and he is, but deep down, he's a sweetheart. Once he gets to know you, he will jump on your lap whenever you sit down."

"He looks just like the Doberman Pinscher from the cover of your book *Jojo*," Jack noted, "but I've never seen one that small before."

"That's because he's a Miniature Pinscher," Martin explained. "He's got all the attitude of a regular Doberman in an easy-to-carry package."

"He certainly lives up to his fictional namesake."

"That he does. Follow me to the library."

Martin led Jack and Kellie down the same hallway the housekeeper had gone. The wood-paneled corridor was lined with framed paintings and wrought iron lanterns hanging from the ceiling. He opened a set of double doors that revealed the most impressive library Jack had ever seen. The built-in bookshelves were works of art, but the rare and finely crafted books behind their wood-framed glass doors genuinely left him awestruck.

He scanned the collection while Martin and Kellie sat in two high-backed chairs near the fireplace. Claudia entered the library, pushing a wooden cart with two silver pitchers and an oval silver platter filled with pastries and fruit. Jojo trotted after her and curled up on the Persian rug at Martin's feet, staring up at Jack with distrust.

"Ah, that looks delicious," Martin said. "I'll take a cup of Earl Grey, thank you." Claudia placed the platter on the coffee table, poured hot water from one of the pitchers into a cup, added a tea bag, and passed the cup to Martin. She then poured two cups of coffee from the other pitcher.

"Thank you, Claudia," Kellie said as she added cream and sugar to her cup. Then she reached out and picked up a pecan roll from the platter. The housekeeper nodded before leaving the room. "I don't know how you stand it here in this big house with nobody to talk to all day, Martin."

"I don't mind it so much," Martin replied. "Claudia is not much of a conversationalist, but her Schnitzel is to die for. So, Jack, I assume Kellie has told you why you're here?" He had just taken a bite of a cheese Danish.

"Um, no," he mumbled as he chewed quickly and swallowed.

"I thought he would rather hear it from you," Kellie said.

"Ah, very well, there's nothing more I like than a dramatic reveal," the author chuckled. "First off, let me congratulate you on joining one of the best writing programs in the country. I'm sure you know I used to teach there before leaving to write full-time. While my accident has robbed me of even the ability to do that anymore, it doesn't mean I've lost the desire to tell stories." Martin leaned forward and put his hand on Jack's forearm. "That's where you come in."

"I'm afraid I don't understand."

"I want you to be my ghostwriter, Jack. I'm effectively retired from the business, but there's no reason my name can't be used to do some good. I approached Professor Wilkens about taking on a new student every year and teaching them the ropes. While she supported the idea, she thought starting with someone more experienced was best. I knew you would be perfect after reading your thesis and novel. So, would you care to be the guinea pig for my little experiment?"

"I would love to work with you, as long as you don't actually mean to keep me in a cage,"

"Fantastic, I can't wait to get started. I want this to feel like your book, so it's up to you to do all the writing. I'm here to guide you along the path, teach you the process, and gently nudge you if you stray from the path. I'm afraid you'll need to keep our arrangement a secret, except from your immediate family and if you hire an assistant. My literary agent will want you to sign a Non-Disclosure Agreement, just the standard *sue-your-pants-off-if-you-blab* lawyerly stuff. Nothing to worry about, though."

"Good lord, Martin, you don't need to scare him," Kellie said.

"I promise not to tell anyone besides my family," Jack answered. "I appreciate you giving me this opportunity."

"I'm sure I won't be disappointed," he replied. "We can handle most correspondence over email, but I'd still like to meet in person once a month."

"You understand that this project is not part of your job at the university," his boss told him. "You will have to take it on along with your normal teaching duties."

"Of course, that won't be a problem," Jack replied.

"One of the most important things a writer needs to learn is how to keep your writing projects in perspective," Martin said. "I look forward to doing great things with you."

The conversation diverged to the latest gossip about the university, but Jack barely paid attention as his mind floated somewhere in the stratosphere. When he woke up that morning, he couldn't have imagined that he would meet his idol, let alone ghostwrite a novel for him. He couldn't wait to get home and tell Kari about this, not only because he knew how happy she would be but also to convince himself that he wasn't dreaming. If that's what this was, he didn't want to wake up.

"Uh-huh, and I'm meeting Martha Stewart for lunch tomorrow to discuss flower arrangements."

Jack stared at his wife dumbfounded as she continued loading the dishwasher. "What's that supposed to mean?"

"Oh, please. You think I don't know when you're trying to pull one of your silly pranks?"

"You're serious? You really don't believe I met Martin Knight, and he wants me to be his ghostwriter?"

"Jack, it's been a long day. Patrick's been very agitated since you left this morning. If you had met this Knight guy, wouldn't you have taken a photo with him? Isn't that what the kids say now: pics or it didn't happen?"

"I didn't even consider asking him to do that, not with my boss there."

"Hmmm, for being the supposed ghostwriter to a famous author, you're not very good at making stuff up," Kari shook her head. "Here, why don't you finish doing the dishes so I can make dinner for everyone." Jack was at a loss for words, his enthusiasm having been deflated like a balloon. A better analogy would have been that Kari had burst it with a pin.

"Why don't you believe me?" he asked. "I'm not joking around. Martin Knight wants me to write his next novel. If the book succeeds, I could get a contract to publish my own."

"And you would get paid for being a ghostwriter?"

"Yes, I'd split the advance and any royalties with Martin since it's under his name, but the follow-on contract is more important. That gets my foot in the door, or it could even open it the whole goddamn way."

"Watch your language. The kids might hear you," she scolded him. "Like how much money?"

"I don't know, we didn't talk about that," he shrugged. "I would assume it's more than an English professor makes in a year, which isn't saying much."

"If that's the case, the first thing you should do is hire me as your business manager before somebody sells you some magic beans."

"Does that mean you believe me then?"

"Maybe, but I don't want to get my hopes up," she said. "I mean, if this is real, it could change our whole lives. We could send Jenny to college and create a trust fund for Patrick so he's taken care of when he gets older. That's why I won't believe it yet."

Jack felt ashamed that he hadn't even thought about what his good fortune could mean for his children's lives. He had been so excited to work with Martin that the reality of the situation hadn't fully sunk in for him. If his resolve to become a professional writer had wavered over the years, it needed to be rock solid now so that he didn't screw up this once-in-a-lifetime chance.

"If you are messing with me about this, you had better come clean right now, Sterling."

"I promise you, babe, everything happened just like I told you. Do you want me to call Professor Wilkens and have her confirm my story?"

"How do I know you're not having an affair with her, and this is part of a ruse the two of you cooked up?"

Jack threw up his arms in exasperation. "What if you come and meet him? We're supposed to get together every month, and I bet he would allow you and the kids to join me sometime."

"Have you lost your mind?" Kari asked. "You honestly think bringing our children to a house full of expensive, breakable things would be a good idea?"

"I'm sure they'll be well-behaved, or we could have them stay with your parents for a few hours."

"Maybe, let me think about it. I'm not saying I believe this story yet, but it wouldn't hurt if we did something to celebrate. Let me see if Jessica would be willing to come over and watch the kids tomorrow night. I'll tell her I'm taking you out for your birthday."

"Really? That would be awesome. We haven't had a date night in forever," he grinned. "Who knows? Maybe you'll get lucky if you play your cards right."

"Ugh, maybe I can still get your boss to take you off my hands," Kari said. "I guess I have to put up with you for a while longer now that all the years I've invested in you might finally be paying off."

"Babe, you always know just what to say to set my loins on fire."

Martin Knight sat at the bistro table on the expansive back patio of his manor home, sipping 18-year-old Glenstirling Blue Label Single Malt Scotch neat as he watched the sun setting behind the trees. It was still warm outside, but he felt a chill crawl up his back as he looked to the east and saw the nearly full moon peeking above the horizon. He picked up the tumbler from the table, walked to the edge of the terrace, and leaned against the railing.

The gently sloping yard was large enough to host a polo match if it weren't for the flower gardens, hedges, and stone planters. The estate was a monument to excessive wealth and power, inexplicably constructed in the most obscure area of the country. To Martin, it had been a cold and bleak prison for the last three years.

At this time of the evening, he could more clearly make out the faint shimmer of the giant bubble that enclosed the manor's grounds. It prevented him from leaving the estate, giving him a painful shock if he went near it. As far as he could tell, nobody else could see it or was affected by it like him. The moon was partly obscured by clouds and resembled the eye of a hungry beast stalking him. He threw back the rest of the liquor and then threw the glass up into the air. It hit the edge of the dome and disintegrated into a shower of glittering dust.

# Cyclist and the Werewolf

I OWA RIVER
126123
POWER CORP

## MISSING

Tracey Hickman — Age 18 Female
5'8" Red Hair Green Eyes
Last Seen July 4th Near Old Annen
Any Information CALL 555-8401

$1000 REWARD For Safe Return

Pagliai's Pizza

Novel By MARTIN KNIGHT

Jupiter &
Phoebus
Publishing
House

# CHAPTER 9
## Cyclist and the Werewolf

*August 2, 2019*

K ari pushed him out the door at six o'clock that evening. The kids were fed, and his wife had prepared instructions for Jessica to deal with any situation that could arise. They told the children a quick goodbye to avoid making a big scene and getting Patrick upset. He seemed to be taking them leaving in stride, but that could change before they got five minutes down the road.

Jack knew his wife would monitor her phone until they returned home, waiting in anticipation of a call that would cut short their date night. If that happened, so be it, but he was determined to have a good time no matter how long their excursion lasted.

She ordered him into the passenger seat and refused to tell him where they were going. Kari took the Interstate towards Iowa City and got off at the North Dubuque Street exit. That road took them south along the Iowa River towards downtown.

"Ah, I should have guessed," Jack said as they pulled into the parking lot across from a familiar restaurant.

"I know we just had pizza for your birthday," Kari replied, "but I thought we could relive our first date tonight."

"I'm good with that, and there's no such thing as too much pizza. Or second chances."

Kari smiled as they exited the van and crossed the street. The pizza parlor was in an old brick building, and the restaurant's name was displayed above the front door in large, raised black letters, backlit by red neon lights.

## Pagliai's Pizza

"Are you sure we can afford to eat out again?" he asked.

"Don't worry about it. This is my treat," she answered. "Since it's your birthday weekend, I won't object if you have a beer as long as you don't make me regret it."

Jack kissed her cheek, then held the door open for her. The place was practically deserted, and they grabbed a booth by the front windows. A young Asian woman with a streak of purple hair soon showed up to take their order.

"Hello, my name is Niko. I'll be serving you tonight," the waitress said. "What can I get you two to drink?"

"I'll take whatever you have on draft from Big Grove Brewery," he replied.

"Good choice, Professor Sterling," Niko commented.

"I thought you looked familiar. Aren't you in my Intro to English Literature class?"

"Yes, I've enjoyed it so far. I liked Henry James' story about the nanny."

"Just an iced tea for me, thanks," Kari said. After the waitress left to get their drinks, she gave him a raised eyebrow. "I can leave if the two of you want to be alone."

"Come on, I wasn't flirting with her," he protested. "We're supposed to be on a date here. It's been so long that it practically is like our first one."

"You're right. This place looks the same as it did a decade ago."

"Yeah, it's like stepping into a time machine," Jack replied. "Honestly, I was so nervous on our date that I don't remember much about it."

"That could also be from the three beers you drank that night," she said. "You probably don't remember me driving you back home. I had to pull over so you could throw up and then help you up three flights of stairs to your apartment. You're lucky you managed to get a second date."

"I seem to remember you ordered a couple of Long Island Iced Teas on your twenty-first birthday and got a bit sloshed."

"That was as much your fault as mine," Kari jabbed her finger at him. "I told you I don't drink, and you could have warned me those were loaded with alcohol. I felt so stupid, and I was scared you thought I was a lush."

"Yeah, that would have been such a turn-off for me," he responded dryly.

"Are you mocking me, Sterling? At least you were a gentleman and didn't try to take advantage of me."

"I might have a lot of faults, but that's not one of them. I'm sorry I was a jerk all those years I was drinking. I won't let it get out of control again." The waitress returned with their drinks and then took their food order. Jack admired the thick head of foam on top of the lager before taking his first sip, savoring the smooth flavor as it went down his throat.

"If you caressed me as lovingly as you do that beer, you might get me into bed more often." He was swallowing when she said that and started coughing. "It sounds looks like you still have a drinking problem."

He used a napkin to dab at the wet spot on the front of his shirt. "You know, if I become a famous author, you're not allowed to mock me because I can't hold my liquor. It's an occupational hazard."

"Oh, I'm so sorry; I didn't realize I was in the presence of literary greatness," Kari snorted. "You sound like the main character in the book I'm reading. His name is James Dunbar, and he's a washed-up author trying to get sober. Why do most stories about authors involve substance abuse?"

"Who knows? I find it to be an unfair stereotype." He raised his beer and took a big gulp.

"I'd slow down there if I were you, Hemmingway. I'm not carrying you back out to the van if you're too drunk to walk."

"Relax, I'm only having one."

"I hope so because I don't want to go down that path again. I'm being serious, Jack."

"I know. I don't want to go back to living like that either," he replied. "We were pretty close to getting divorced there, weren't we?"

"Do you want me to answer that question?" Jack shook his head, drained the rest of his beer, and asked the waitress for a glass of water when she passed by.

"What's the name of this book you're reading?" he asked, changing the subject. "I haven't heard of many romance novels with such a flawed character."

"I read other books than just bodice rippers, thank you very much. I got this one from The Raven's Perch along with those old paperbacks I gave you for your birthday." Kari reached into her purse, took out a dog-eared novel titled *In The Mountains Of Murder*, and handed it to him. "I was going to include it with them, but something about this novel compelled me to read it. Have you ever heard of Butch Richardson before?"

"No, I don't think so, but it sounds like an interesting story," he said, reading the blurb on the back cover. "It reminds me of the summer job I almost took at that ski resort back in Colorado."

"Yeah, I thought the same thing. It's weird," she agreed. "I swear I've never read this book before, but it's almost like I knew everything that was going to happen. I haven't finished it yet, but I have a bad feeling it won't end well."

"If it's a horror story with a happy ending, then this Butch guy isn't doing it right."

"How about I write down how I think it will turn out, and then you read it and do the same. Let's see who gets closer to the actual outcome."

"That almost sounds like a wager. What are we betting?"

"If you want to talk about someone being predictable, I know where your mind is going," she groaned. "Why not do this to prove you can make it as an author? Is that a good enough reason?"

"All right, no need to get feisty—not until later, anyway." Jack winked at her, and she kicked him under the table as the waitress brought out their food.

"Now you have me curious why I've never heard of this writer before," he said once she left again. "I'll have to do some detective work on the Internet and see what became of him. He could be one of those who only put out a handful of books before running out of steam, or maybe he got hit by a car or died of cancer before he made it big."

The conversation drifted back to the kids as they ate, as it often did between them anymore, and Kari talked at length about her anxiety over the upcoming school year. Being back on campus reminded Jack of all the dates they had during their college days when they could spend hours discussing their favorite books, music, movies, or where they wanted to travel after graduating. He missed those days, but it wasn't like he resented having his life now centered around their children. Turning thirty-five years old was probably making him feel sentimental, or perhaps that was the alcohol.

"What do you think about catching a movie after dinner?" he asked. "I wonder if the theaters in the Old Capital Mall are still in business."

"I don't want to be out that late. I told Jessica we would be home by eight thirty," Kari replied. "It's the first time leaving the kids with her, so let's stick with the plan."

"How about we take a walk down to the river then? The English building is probably locked up, but I can point out which window my office."

"Oh good, I can picture where you are during the day, looking out at all the pretty young coeds walking by while I care for your children."

"Come on, babe," he grinned, "you're the only woman I want to stare at while thinking impure thoughts, you know that."

"Wow, that doesn't sound creepy or anything. Why don't you take care of the check while I use the restroom? If this were our first date, I would skip out the back and leave you to walk home."

An outdoor arts and crafts festival was set up around the Old Capital area. They wandered through the vendors for a while, and Kari picked out a pair of hand-crafted earrings that looked like crescent moons. Jack made a note to talk to Martin about using a local artist to do the cover for their book if he managed to finish writing it—or start it, for that matter.

"Let's head over towards the library," Jack said. "There's a shortcut that leads to the parking lot behind the English building."

As they reached the Main Library, the sun had dipped below the ridge on the west side of the river, painting the sky with a dramatic palette of purples, pinks, oranges, and yellows. "If this isn't a literal trip down memory lane," Kari said. "I can't even tell you how much time I spent in that library between studying and working."

"We certainly put those study rooms to good use," Jack chuckled, and her cheeks turned bright red as she glowered at him. "I remember the first time I saw you at the checkout desk. You took my breath away. I could tell you liked me right away, too."

"Um, that's not exactly how I recall it," she replied. "I believe you were trying to charm your way out of twenty dollars in overdue fines. You told me you would pay up if I went to dinner with you. It was a pathetic pickup attempt, but I said yes to see if you would pay your fines."

"It was the best twenty bucks I ever spent." He growled in the back of his throat.

"Is that all you ever think about?" Kari sighed. "If your memory were a photo album, all the pictures would be indecent."

Jack stopped walking so abruptly that his wife took a few steps before realizing he was no longer beside her. "*Look to the past...* books are windows to the past. The library is full of time machines." He started laughing. "How did I not think about that right away?"

Kari stared at him as though he had lost his mind. "I hope you don't act this weird when other people are around," she said.

"Sorry, I just thought about something for my story."

"You're becoming obsessed with this ghostwriter business," she said. "You better not leave me to do everything around the house. Do you think you'll be able to juggle writing a novel while teaching?"

"I hope so," he replied. "I won't get a better chance at breaking into publishing than this. I'm scared I'll screw it up and make a fool of myself in front of Martin."

"Don't be silly, you're a damn good writer," Kari replied. "Just do your best. I know you'll be successful, but don't let it take over your life."

"Thank you, babe. I'm glad one of us has confidence in my ability. Martin has a great idea for this story. Once I get going, it will practically write itself. I need to come up with a good first scene, though. All the best horror stories have an opening hook that grabs the reader's attention and gives them a glimpse of the evil that awaits them in the darkness. You know what I mean?"

"Yeah, I've read a horror novel before, Jack."

"Sorry, I get a little overly excited when I start thinking about writing this book."

"That's a good thing. If it helps motivate you, then let yourself be as giddy as a schoolgirl."

It was Jack's turn to glower at her. He led her down a walkway in between the library and the Journalism and Communication building and then, oddly enough, underneath a set of railroad tracks before coming out in the parking lot next to the English-Philosophy building. "If you look at the second floor, my office is four over from the end. Or is it five? Yeah, I can see a bit of the river, so it must be-"

"Okay, Jack, I've seen it. Can we head back?" Kari interrupted him. "It's a long walk, and my feet are already hurting. I wish I had worn more comfortable shoes."

He looked down to see that she was wearing a pair of red high heels. "Oh lord, I forgot you had those on. I bet they are hurting, but they look damn good on you."

"I'm glad my suffering turns you on."

They followed the sidewalk parallel to the elevated train tracks until it reached Iowa Avenue. There was another overpass where the tracks crossed above the road, and the thick bushes growing on the side of the hill made it difficult to see anyone coming from the right. Neither of them thought to check that direction as they turned onto the sidewalk, and Jack grabbed Kari and pulled her back as a bicyclist came flying past them.

"Sorry!" the young woman called over her shoulder without slowing down. Jack recognized her as the waitress with the purple streak in her hair.

"Are you okay, babe?" he asked.

"No, I twisted my ankle, and my heel snapped off," she hissed as she removed her right shoe and examined the damage. "Fuck, that's just great, this was my favorite pair."

"Whoa, you kiss your mother with that mouth?"

"Zip it, Sterling. You don't want to mess with me about shoes." She bent down and removed the other one. "They were hurting my feet anyway." Walking barefoot while carrying her ruined shoes, Kari limped up the sidewalk until they reached Madison Street before stopping. "I don't think I can walk all the way back. I'm getting a blister already."

"How about you sit down on the steps here? I'll get the van and come pick you up. There are plenty of people around with the festival; it should be safe."

"Okay, but don't take too long, it's getting late."

Jack left her sitting on the concrete steps that led up to the Old Capital Building and headed back towards the parking lot. He turned the corner onto the street that led to Pagliai's Pizza. Jack was passing by a telephone pole when a flier stapled to it caught his attention. He had seen lots of these fliers posted all around campus lately.

It was a photo of the young woman who had disappeared on the Fourth of July, hugging her pet cat to her cheek and smiling at the camera. The poster was faded, but he could still read the girl's name and description underneath the word MISSING. What had made him stop and take a second look was that he could have sworn at first glance the girl in the picture was Niko, the bicycle-riding waitress who had almost run over his wife. He must have imagined it because now that he had a better look, it was the same girl he had seen a dozen times before.

"About time," Kari said when he pulled up. "I was about to call an Uber."

"Sorry, I hurried as fast as possible," he replied. "Good news, I think I have an idea for my story's opening scene. Now all I need is the perfect first line to start it with."

His wife rolled her eyes at him as she climbed into the van.

Patrick had been huddled on the living room couch for the past hour. His headphones were plugged into his tablet while he watched videos about inflatable Christmas displays, fire alarms, and vacuum cleaners, trying to drown out the sound of the girls running and screaming throughout the house. He was getting agitated by all the noise when Aunt Jessica took the three of them upstairs to find some board games. His mom had told him she would be home by 8:30, fourteen minutes from now. He did not like her being gone in the evening. His aunt spoke to him in baby talk, and his two little cousins made his ears hurt even with the headphones covering them.

Aunt Jessica had baked chocolate chip cookies after dinner. While oatmeal raisin cookies were his favorite, he still ate four before she told him to stop so he wouldn't get a belly ache. His stomach felt funny, so he set down his tablet to use the bathroom. Patrick stopped the bottom of the stairs as he saw a woman standing in the kitchen doorway.

He thought his mother had returned home, but the woman was shorter and wearing a pinkish-red bathrobe. The air had also become freezing, and Patrick knew it was the same woman he encountered in the attic.

The woman put a finger to her lips, which Patrick knew meant she wanted him to be quiet. She motioned for him to come to the kitchen before she vanished from the doorway. He needed to use the restroom, but that buzzing noise again filled his head. Patrick went down the hall to the kitchen and peeked around the corner to see where the woman had gone.

She was nowhere to be seen, so he took a few steps into the room and saw that the basement door was open. His father kept that locked unless he was writing. Patrick worried he might get blamed if the woman messed his papers up. He didn't want his father to be angry at him again like the one time.

The light was on in the basement, meaning she had to have gone down there. Patrick crept down the steps until he could see most of the room. Although the light still left some areas of shadow around the basement, he didn't see her anywhere. She might have gone outside through the other door, but he no longer cared about where she was. The buzzing in his head was now deafening, and he felt drawn to the typewriter sitting on the desk. There was a blank sheet of paper already inserted into the roller.

Patrick pulled the chair out from the desk and sat down, scooting the creaky wood seat forward until he could reach the typewriter's keys. He had watched several videos about typewriters on his tablet and knew they were some kind of old computers that wrote on paper instead of a screen. While you couldn't play games on it, he liked the sound they made when you typed better than computer keyboards. He felt a vibration coming through his fingertips as they touched the round black and silver keys. The buzzing noise ceased, and now he could hear a voice whispering words for him to type.

```
The woman on the bike sped along the
river, and the werewolf followed.
```

Niko pedaled her bicycle along the trail beside the river, enjoying the evening breeze and the chirping birds that flitted about the trees. She was glad she had decided to take a couple of summer classes and waitress instead of returning to Japan. While she missed her family, there was little to do back home. She could save enough money to keep from working during her senior year. It also allowed her to spend time with her girlfriend,

Joleen, without having to worry about her family disowning her if they found out she was a lesbian. When she graduated, she intended to get her green card and find a job in the States. For now, she was enjoying her life here and having a blast learning how to ride the bike that Joleen had given her for her birthday.

After she passed by Hancher Auditorium, a man standing on the Park Road bridge above caught her attention. The hood of his sweatshirt hid his face, but she felt like he was watching her. Niko thought it was strange for somebody to be dressed in heavy clothing with it being so warm, even at this time of day. The man appeared extraordinarily tall and muscular, his arms straining the material of the sweatshirt so that it looked ready to burst if he flexed too much. He was probably an athlete at the university, a football player judging from his build, but something about him seemed unnatural.

Niko pedaled faster as she crossed underneath the bridge. A short fence ran along the outside of the overpass, but the man looked able to leap over it. When she came out to the other side, she glanced over her shoulder to see he had crossed the bridge and was continuing to track her movement. The trail she was on dead-ended inside the city park, which meant she would have to return the same way to go home. She had her cell phone on her and thought about calling Joleen, but her girlfriend would still be bartending at *Joe's Place*.

She doubted the guy would try to chase her on foot, but she decided to cut through the park and make her way over to Riverside Drive instead. The sound of rustling bushes and a flash of movement were her only warnings before a massive body slammed into her and sent her flying off the bike. Niko had the wind knocked out of her when she landed on the ground. Before she could regain her breath, the sweatshirt-clad guy leaned over her. She struggled to roll away from her attacker as he raised a hairy fist and struck her on the head.

The first sensation she felt when coming around was coldness, followed by a throbbing pain radiating from the side of her head. Niko was in a large, dimly lit room with a domed ceiling, and she was leaning against a stone pillar. Her wrists were bound above her head by leather cuffs attached by a thick chain to an iron ring. She was also naked except for a black silk skirt that was little more than a long loincloth.

Niko tried pulling on the restraints, but the pain in her head threatened to make her black out again. Her movements drew a growl from a dog lying on the ground near the pillar's dais. She recoiled as she realized that the creature looking up at her was not a dog but a giant wolf. It regarded her with amber eyes that shone with malicious intelligence.

The beast bared its teeth at her, then turned its attention towards the shadows on the other side of the room. She followed its gaze and saw a black hooded figure step out of the gloom holding a long, zig-zag-bladed knife. The heavy-set woman was nude beneath her cloak, and she glared at Niko with icy eyes that were even more frightening than the wolf. With her free hand, the woman grabbed Niko's right wrist and pinned it against the pillar. She started to struggle, but then she felt the cold metal of the knife pressed against her neck.

"Don't move, or I'll slit your throat instead."

She sucked in her breath as the robed woman drew the knife's edge across her forearm, and a line of blood formed where it had passed. Still holding onto her arm, the woman tucked the knife away under her cloak and pulled out a glass vial, which she used to collect the stream of blood running down to her elbow. After filling the container, she released her arm and walked over to a black stone sarcophagus on the far side of the room.

The woman had her back facing her, so she couldn't tell what she was doing with the vial of blood she had collected. Niko's arm was on fire from the open wound, but the pain kept her from passing out. The robed woman held up a ceramic jug covered in golden hieroglyphics. She leaned over the sarcophagus and poured the contents through a hole in the face of the painted figure on the lid. Once it was empty, she tossed the jug aside, and it shattered against the wall.

"Arise, Master, and live again!" She cast aside her cloak and prostrated her naked body at the foot of the stone coffin.

Niko would have laughed if she wasn't in absolute misery. Nothing happened for several moments, and then the heavy lid began to lift on its own. It slid off the back onto the ground as a thick black mist poured over the sides. The fire in the braziers hanging from the ceiling flickered as though disturbed by a strong wind and died down to embers, leaving her in near darkness. Her eyes adjusted to the lack of light, and she could just make out a skeletal figure draped in a black robe standing beside the prone woman.

Niko was mesmerized as she stared into the thing's glowing red eyes. She opened her mouth to scream as the undead abomination lumbered towards her and grabbed her head. Only a weak, strangled cry managed to escape before it died in her throat. The last thing she felt was a sharp pain from the vampire sinking its teeth into her neck and piercing her carotid artery.

# Dr. Insomnia

## r: How I Learned to Start Worrying
## om The Boy Who Loved Martin Knight

Novel By **MARTIN KNIGHT**

Jupiter & Phoebus Publishing House

# CHAPTER 10
## Dr. Insomnia, or: How I Learned to Start Worrying from The Boy Who Loved Martin Knight

*August 21, 2019*

*Jack could smell the blood and taste it on his tongue as he drank the last delicious pulses from the girl's dying heart. He pulled away and let her limp corpse collapse to the ground, two rivulets of blood oozing from the wounds on her neck and flowing down either side of her right breast. The werewolf at the foot of the dais looked up at him expectantly. He nodded at it, turning as the beast leaped on the girl and began to feast on her still-warm body.*

*The sound of its slobbering jaws rending her apart disgusted some small part of him that remembered what it was like to be human, but that which had evolved to become master of death delighted in the symphony of tearing flesh and breaking bones. A smile played upon his lips as he returned to his resting place, still weak from his long slumber but now filled with warmth from the girl's lifeblood. He could feel himself growing stronger and would soon be ready to ascend to his rightful place as a god. He shut the lid to his sarcophagus, and the darkness enveloped him in its loving embrace as he slept once more.*

Dr. John Sterling was a bright, up-and-coming English professor with a loving family and a promising future ahead of him when he left Colorado.

Jack Sterling, a borderline alcoholic writer on the verge of being dragged underneath the wagon, was losing his mind because he couldn't sleep.

The problem started the night Kari had taken him out to dinner to celebrate his birthday. That was the first time he'd awakened from the now-recurring nightmare in a cold sweat. Jack experienced attacking a helpless woman chained to a black stone pillar nearly every night since then. He had also sleepwalked down to the basement that fateful night to write a sentence about the girl's disappearance on his typewriter.

Jack had woken up the following morning with his head pounding as though he had a hangover. Both the duration and the intensity of the nightmare had increased to the point where he was afraid to close his eyes for more than a few hours. If he reached the point of exhaustion and slept through the night, he woke up feeling dizzy and tired, as if he had run a marathon while drunk. Jack was getting used to being up at all hours of the night, fighting off sleep by keeping himself busy.

Since he had extra time on his hands and the house was quiet in the middle of the night, he had taken to working on his story with almost maniacal fervor. He had an old recliner in the basement for when he could no longer keep his eyes open and had to doze off for a while. Despite its age, the chair was quite comfortable, so he used the timer on his phone to keep himself from napping too long and letting the nightmare start again.

He must have forgotten to set one last night because Kari had shaken him awake. The nightmare she had pulled him out of had at least been different than usual. In this one, he had been trying to break down a door with an axe to get at her, and Jack had to fight back a momentary urge to wrap his hands around her neck.

"What is going on with you?" she asked. "This is the third time I've woken up this week to find you're not in bed. Have you been down here all night?"

"I couldn't sleep, so I decided to get some writing in," he yawned. "I must have fallen asleep in the chair. I'm sorry, babe."

Jack stood up, and a heavy object tucked into the blanket rolled off his lap onto the floor. He picked up the half-empty bottle of 25-year-old Glenstirling Gold Label Single Malt Scotch and stared at it. He had poured out all the alcohol he owned when Kari had threatened to kick him out if he didn't sober up, but he had stashed this bottle of liquor away out of sentimentality with no intention of drinking it. The Scotch had been given to him by his late father, a hard man who often drank too much himself, for his twenty-fifth birthday. He had died less than a year later, and Jack couldn't bring himself to throw away the bottle as a love of fine spirits and books were the only things the two of them had in common.

While he didn't recall opening the bottle, it would explain why, in the dream, he had also been sitting at an empty bar while a bartender who was the spitting image of his father served him glass after glass of whisky. His disgust at having drank the better part of the bottle paled next to his wife's look of utter revulsion.

"Is this why you're sneaking down here in the middle of the night? To drink?"

"What? No, it's not...I mean, I don't know how this got here." Kari scoffed at that. "You don't understand. I've been having these horrible nightmares lately, and I think I've been sleepwalking."

"Are you sleep drinking as well?" she asked. "You must think I'm stupid if you expect me to believe that."

"I swear I don't remember getting this out."

"Too much alcohol tends to have that effect," she said. "We'll talk about this later; I need to make breakfast for the kids. Kurt will be over soon to help you install the security light on the porch unless you're too hungover to manage that."

"No, I'm fine. I just need some coffee."

"You know where the goddamn coffee machine is located." She turned on her heel and stormed back upstairs. Jack looked down at the bottle in his hand, then walked over to the drain by the water heater and dumped out the other half.

The rest of that morning, he felt like a goldfish, swimming about aimlessly with no memory of what he had done only a few minutes ago. His head was pounding so hard he could barely manage a couple slices of toast, but even that threatened to sour his stomach. While he nursed his coffee, his mind wandered back to the recurring nightmare.

The most disturbing thing about it was that the woman he continually drained of life was the same waitress who had served them at the pizza restaurant and nearly ran into Kari on her bike. Jack might have chalked that up to his subconscious manifesting her image since it had been all over the news after she disappeared, except he had dreamed about her before she had been reported missing.

Kari had been upset when he pointed out their intersection with the waitress, so he hadn't told her about the missing girl repeatedly appearing in his dreams. By the time he finished his second cup of black coffee, the fog enveloping his brain was beginning to lift a little, but his unease at the nightmares plaguing him continued unabated.

Shortly after ten o'clock, the rumble of a diesel engine announced Kurt's arrival, and Jack went out to meet him. He stepped out onto the porch as the pickup pulled onto the front lawn and parked underneath the oak tree. Kurt had also brought his teenage son, Stefan, who looked like a spitting image of his father. Jack had only spoken with the boy a handful of times. He was shy but had a quirky sense of humor when he let it show.

"Good morning," Jack said as they climbed down from the truck. "Thanks for coming over."

"Ah-yup, so you need a light put up?" Kurt asked.

"Yeah, Kari's been feeling nervous after those two women disappeared. Hopefully, this motion-sensor light will provide some sense of security."

"What you outta get is a good twelve-gauge, or I've got an old double-barrel twenty-gauge if that's too much gun for you to handle. It's better than shining a bright light in some asshole's eyes if they're trying to break into your house."

"I don't think Kari would be too crazy about having firearms around the house. Patrick tends to get into all kinds of things, and I'd hate to think what would happen if he found that."

"Have it your way. Let me see this light." Jack picked up the box on the porch and handed it to his brother-in-law. "Doesn't look like it will be too much trouble, but I'll have to replace one of the existing porch lights. Where's your box located?"

"Do you mean the circuit box? It's down in the basement."

"Okay, lead the way."

"We'll have to go through the kitchen."

"I just swept the floors, so please take your shoes off," Kari said as they entered. "Hi Kurt, thank you for coming over and helping Jack put that up."

"Nice house you've got here, solid bones from the looks of it. They don't build stuff like they used to in this country anymore. Could use some fresh paint on the outside."

"We certainly like it, don't we, honey?" she replied, putting her arm around Jack's waist. "I'll let you boys get to work. You and Stefan are welcome to stay for lunch. I'm making hamburgers."

"Thanks, but I have to head to work soon," Kurt said. "Before I forget, Jess said she's taking the kids shopping for school supplies in Cedar Rapids tomorrow if you want to come."

"Oh, that would be excellent. I'll message her in a bit and let her know."

Jack led them through the kitchen and down into the basement. He pointed his brother-in-law to the metal panel on the wall behind the staircase.

"Shit, none of these switches are labeled," Kurt said after opening the cover. Thirty circuit breakers were aligned in two columns with nothing to indicate what function each one served. "This is going to take a while to figure out. Do you have your phone, Stefan?"

"Huh? Oh, yeah, here." He held it out to his dad.

"No, dumbass, when I get outside, I'll call you. I want you to turn off each switch one at a time, starting with the top left one here, until I tell you to stop. After you turn each off, wait ten seconds and flip it back on. Got it?" Stefan nodded, and Kurt headed back upstairs.

"You've got a lot of books," his nephew said. "Have you read all of them?"

"More or less, I'm an English professor so it's kind of my job to read," Jack replied. "Do you read many books?"

"Not really. I mostly play video games when I'm not doing chores around the farm. I've read everything by Martin Knight, though. I love his novels, but my mom doesn't approve of him. I used to have to sneak his books home from the library and read them by flashlight at night, but I can download them on my phone now."

"No kidding, he's my favorite author as well."

Kurt's call came in, and it took flipping eighteen breakers before Stefan tripped the one that controlled the porch lights.

"I suppose we should go help your dad out," Jack said. "You must know your way around the Internet, I imagine. Like how to search for all different kinds of things?"

Stefan gave him an odd look. "Do you need help finding porn?"

"What? No, that's not-," he shook his head. "I'm working on a novel myself, and I could use some help doing research. I guess that's not something most teenagers would want to do."

"No, it's cool. I've done research online to write papers at school. Is it like that?"

"Yeah, sort of. Do you think your parents will let you take the job?" he asked. "I could only afford to pay you probably twenty-five dollars a week, but I'd be able to let you in on a secret."

"Are you sure this isn't a sexual thing? Because I'm not..."

"Good lord, it's nothing like that," Jack groaned. "Alright, you have to promise not to tell anybody else about this, but the novel I'm writing is actually for Martin Knight."

"So, you mean you're dedicating it to him?"

"Huh? No, that would be weird. I mean, I'm ghostwriting the book for him. If you help me with it, I might be able to arrange for you to come to his house with me."

"Seriously? That would be awesome. Nobody's seen him in years. Have you met him already?"

"Yes, he was very friendly," Jack replied. "What do you think? Do you want to be my research assistant?"

"I'll have to ask my dad, but it sounds fun." They headed upstairs to the porch, where Kurt was already on a ladder working on the wiring for the security light.

"Hand me that circular metal plate there," Kurt barked, pointing at the chair where he had unpacked the box's contents.

"Hey, dad, Uncle Jack wants to hire me to help him do research on the Internet," the boy said. "It's nothing perverted. He just needs help writing a novel. Is that okay?"

Kurt paused before continuing to screw on the mounting bracket. "As long as it doesn't get in the way of your schoolwork or chores, it's fine. If you two are done slacking off, bring me those wire strippers."

Jack grabbed the tool he wanted (*or hoped it was*) and held it up to Kurt. "What's this novel about?" Kurt asked.

"Werewolves." The question had caught Jack off guard, and he had blurted out an answer before he could think about it. "It's about a family of werewolves secretly living in Iowa."

The wire strippers slipped from Kurt's hand, but he caught it mid-air. "Goddamn thing," he muttered. "That sounds right up Stefan's alley. What made you think of that idea?"

"I didn't. I'm ghostwriting the novel for someone else," Jack replied. "He came up with the idea, but I'm developing the rest of the plot."

"Sounds like something I might even read."

Kurt took off after he was done with the light, but he agreed to let Stefan stick around for the afternoon. Jack allowed him to read the first few chapters he had written so far, which his nephew blew through with surprising speed. "That's a good opening, and I like the part about the naked girl chained to the pillar. If they make a movie about your book, do you think they'll put that scene in it?"

"I'm sure you'd like to see that. Let's not get ahead of ourselves. I need to finish writing it before Hollywood knocks on my door." Jack put the pages back in the desk drawer.

"Hey, what's this book?" Stefan asked as he picked up **Occult Secrets of the Third Reich** sitting on the desk. "Are you going to have Nazis in the story too?"

"No, that's something different," he replied. "I don't think werewolves have anything to do with the Third Reich."

"Of course they do. The Nazis almost won the Battle of the Bulge because they had soldiers infused with werewolf blood."

"What kind of history books are they using in schools these days?"

"We don't use textbooks in school anymore; everything is online. There's nothing about that in history books because it's top secret. I read about it in this graphic novel, *Gestaltwandler*, written by a guy whose dad worked for the OSS in World War II and told him all about it shortly before he died."

"A graphic novel, huh? If the Germans had made werewolves, wouldn't they still be running around attacking people?"

"The soldiers didn't stay werewolves because it was only temporary. The Allies fire-bombed Hamburg and Dresden because the orphanages there were being used to create full-blooded werewolves. Most of the kids were killed in the war, but the handful that were left were captured either by the Americans or Russians and trained as spies and assassins."

"That sounds a little far-fetched, but I need to develop an interesting backstory on why werewolves exist in Iowa. Maybe you can help me think up some explanation that's a bit more plausible." Jack paused for a minute as he tapped the book on the desk, then flipped it open to a page he had bookmarked the other day. "Before we get to that, I've got something I want you to help me look into."

"Sure thing, what is it?"

He pointed to a photograph on the page showing a group of stern-faced men in black robes seated or standing in the center of a library. The face of the man at the far right had been circled with a red marker. "You see this guy? From the caption, his name is Dr. Heinrich von Meister. I want you to see if you can find anything about him."

"Meister? Isn't that the German word for Master?"

"I don't know, it could be. Do you speak German?"

"Some. I've been taking it as my foreign language class in school."

"Well, somebody thought he was important enough to circle his picture, and I'm hoping to find out why."

"If you didn't circle his picture, then who did?"

"Probably the same person who checked out the book last. The university library might have a record of who that was, so I'll try looking into that." A thought crossed his mind, and Jack opened his desk drawer to remove a small, leather-bound journal. "Also, see if you can translate anything from this. I think it's written in German."

Jack drummed his fingers on the desk, staring at the blank page in the typewriter. He hoped that inspiration would bubble up from the depths of his imagination. Nothing came to mind though. He just needed to buckle down, put on his thinking cap, and get to work. But first, he needed a quick nap.

He removed his glasses, set them on the desk, flopped down in the old recliner, and closed his eyes. The lack of sleep had taken its toll on him, dulling his mind and draining his creativity. Jack needed to find a way to get some rest without constantly being plagued by these nightmares. As his wife had suggested, it was probably time to see a doctor.

No sooner had he drifted off into an uneasy sleep than a rattling noise dragged him back awake. Jack sat up and looked around, but nobody else was in the basement. He heard it again. This time, he was sure it came from the old steamer trunk. He used the toe of his shoe to lift the lid in case a raccoon had gotten trapped inside. All the books had been removed; the only thing left was the strange black box. He hesitated to touch it after cutting his finger, but he told himself he was being ridiculous.

A faint green glow was emanating from between the metal seams. He reached down and took hold of the box, then dropped it before he could lift it out of the trunk. The metal surface was so cold that it felt burning to the touch, and the palm of his hand was bright red like he had placed it on a hot stove.

*Daddy*

He thought he heard his son's voice but didn't see him anywhere. Then he noticed that the door to the outside cellar steps was open. A wave of panic hit him as he pictured Patrick wandering over towards the highway. The bulkhead doors were wide open, and Jack flew up the steps but halted when he reached the top.

Standing before him about ten feet from the cellar entrance was another door. It was mounted in a door frame that wasn't attached to anything. Other than some strange symbols carved into the frame, it looked like an ordinary door. Jack circled behind it, and the door vanished from view until he returned to the front side. He remembered what had brought him up here and looked around for his son, but he was nowhere to be seen.

Jack worried Patrick might have gone through the door and was trapped on the other side. He tried the doorknob, but it was locked. He placed his hand against the frame and tried to push it over. To his surprise, it didn't budge a hair, staying put as though it were mounted in the middle of a brick wall. A wrought-iron knocker was mounted in the center of the door, the metal ring shaped like a snake eating its tail.

"Patrick?" he hollered at the door. "Patrick, are you in there?"

Jack took hold of the knocker and rapped it against the door, the sound echoing back at him through the door. On the third knock, it swung inward, and he jumped back. It was too dark to see what was beyond the doorway, but he thought he could make out the interior of a large room. He put his hand through and felt a tingling sensation on his skin like an electrical current was running over it. Jack tried to pull his hand back, but a force from the other side grabbed his arm and yanked him through the doorway.

He landed face-first on the dust-covered hardwood floor of the room. The impact knocked the wind out of him, and he started coughing and wheezing as he tried to regain his breath. Jack stood up but had to lean against a wooden bookshelf until a wave of dizziness passed. His eyes adjusted to the gloom, and he was in a deserted store surrounded by shelves full of dusty books. Through the grime-covered windows it appeared to be evening out already.

He used his sleeve to clear a spot on one of the windows and realized it was still daytime, but a blanket of heavy fog had drowned out most of the sunlight. Just enough light filtered into the room to show him a set of shoeprints leading toward the door. They were too big to have been made by his son and, from the shape of the indentation, looked to be from a pair of boots.

Jack took a few tentative steps out the front door, searching the ground to see where the footprints led. A herd of elephants could be standing ten feet away, and he wouldn't have been able to see them in this fog. He didn't hear any sounds of vehicles or people moving about. Wherever he was, he seemed to be alone. The question of his whereabouts answered itself, hanging from the awning above the door he had exited.

# THE RAVEN'S PERCH

"How the hell did I get here?"

Even though he hadn't spoken loudly, his words echoed like thundercracks. The noise disturbed several crows who took flight and circled above him, cawing down at him to express annoyance. His ears picked up the sound of a rope creaking, and he craned his neck back to see a dead body hanging from a light pole.

The corpse's face had been pecked at except for where a black blindfold covered its eyes. Based on the tattered blue jeans, denim jacket covered in souvenir metal buttons, and cowboy boots, he guessed it had been a man. Probably the same person who had exited

The Raven's Perch before him. Around its neck, a wooden sign had been hung with a single word written in what looked like blood.

# INTERLOPER

Jack crossed the street to the park to avoid walking under the body. The tree canopy blocked out what little sunlight got through the fog, and it was nearly dark. He glimpsed a white structure to his left and knew it had to be the gazebo in the park's center. Several gnarled, leafless trees had been planted around the pavilion that he didn't remember.

His curiosity got the better of him, and he went to investigate. What he had taken for trees turned out to be a ring of blackened poles with charred, skeletal remains bound to them. A warning message, also in blood, had been scrawled across the bottom of the gazebo.

# DEATH TO THE COVEN

The shrill, undulating howl of a wolf pierced the silence. It sounded close by, and Jack was standing out in the open. He ran back towards The Raven's Perch but got disoriented and came out on the square's north side. Another howl, this one even closer, drove him towards the nearest building, the church on the corner.

The double front doors were both unlocked and standing wide open. That was because of a jagged hole in their center and dozens of smaller holes dotting the thick wood. The outside of the doors was also raked with claw marks as though a bear had been trying to tear its way through. Jack poked his head through the doorway, but a crude barricade had been constructed right inside from broken pews stacked on top of each other.

He decided to seek sanctuary in the bookshop instead. Turning around, he caught sight of a pair of glowing eyes watching him from the park. Jack scrambled inside and shut the doors, but the large hole was right where the lock would have been. Jack dragged one of the broken pews over and used it to brace the doors. No sooner had he done so than a hairy snout lined with jagged, yellowed teeth poked through the hole and snapped at his hand. Jack backpedaled until he came up against the barricade.

The beast started thrashing against the doors. The pew had wedged against them but wouldn't hold up long. Jack looked for a way to climb over the wall of stacked benches. They were haphazardly piled up and threatened to collapse underneath him if he put his weight on them. He clambered over the unstable barrier and landed on the floor in a pile of skeletons clad in tattered, camouflaged uniforms. One of the dead soldiers was holding onto a black rifle. Jack lifted it by the barrel, and the decomposed hand let go of the weapon.

The werewolf pushed its way past the pew and stood up silhouetted in the doorway on two legs, sniffing at the air. Jack had never fired a gun before, but he raised it to his shoulder, aimed as best he could, and pulled the trigger.

# CLICK

Nothing happened, and he thought the wolf grinned at him as it opened its mouth. The beast leaped atop the barrier. Jack screamed and dropped the rifle as it lunged at him, but the creature's head exploded in a cloud of blood, fur, and bone. The decapitated body collapsed at his feet, spraying him with gore as his ears rang from the gunshot that had saved him from being mauled.

"Who the hell are you?" he heard a gruff voice challenge him when his hearing returned. Jack was staring down the barrel of an enormous revolver pointed directly at his head. The grizzled old man holding it had a graying, shaggy beard, leathery skin, and half-crazed eyes, but Jack recognized the pale scars running down his cheek.

"Whoa, Detective Blackburn, don't shoot," he pleaded, raising his hands. "I'm Jack Sterling. We met at the hardware store. You found my son when he got lost."

"That's not possible. That was twenty years ago." The gunfighter narrowed his eyes at him. "What are you? A werewolf? Vampire? Or did the Alchemist cook up some new abomination? Maybe I should put a bullet through your skull and find out."

"Please don't kill me. I'm not a monster. I'm an English professor."

"Nothing human's been able to survive in this fucking nightmare."

"What happened here? I have to find my family."

"Your family is either dead or long gone. The Alchemist unleashed a deadly plague that started here, most of the world's population died of dysentery and the rest were hunted into submission by his army of werewolves. So, tell me how you got here."

"I don't know, I found a door in my yard and it brought me here. If this place is so dangerous, how are you alive?"

"I fled with the few survivors I could save, but I've come back here to put an end to the Alchemist." Another howl cut him off, and it was joined by several more. "Oh shit, you've brought the pack down on us."

"Hey, hold on, what do you know about the Alchemist?"

"Shut up and stay out of the way." The old detective drew his other revolver, leaped over the barrier, and took cover behind one of the broken doors. Jack clamored after him but stayed a safe distance back where he could see through the doorway. It might have been a trick of his eyes, but it seemed to be getting brighter outside. He thought he was seeing things until Blackburn backed away.

"Fuck, this ain't good."

"Huh? What's going on?"

"It's her, the Queen of Sorrows," the gunfighter snarled. "There better be another way out of here, or we're fucked."

Edgar ran further into the church, and Jack tried to get a look at what had spooked him. The town square was now lit up like midday. Only the light was coming from beneath the trees instead of the sky. He watched as a woman clad only in a sheer white gown walked out of the fog, her porcelain skin aglow with a radiant brilliance that nearly blinded him. He felt drawn to her, and his feet pulled him out upon the steps of their own accord. The almost nude woman seemed to float across the ground, and as she got closer, Jack was able to make out her face. The resemblance to his wife was unmistakable.

"Kari?" he called out. "It's Jack. Don't you recognize me?"

The light seemed to falter as the woman's brow furrowed, but then her face became a mask of anger. "No, you're not real," she said. "I killed you!"

The spell that had kept him enthralled was broken as a wall of flames formed in front of her. He ran back into the church as he felt the intense heat radiating behind him, but his foot caught on the threshold and sent him flying. An endless black pit appeared where the floor should have been. Jack tried to scream, but there was no air for him to breathe.

...

*Uncle Jack...*

*Uncle Jack?*

*Uncle Jack, wake up!*

Jack snapped awake to somebody shaking him.

He jumped out of his chair, knocking the person to the ground. Jack rushed to the outside door, threw it open, and looked up to see that the bulkhead doors were still locked.

"Uncle Jack, what's wrong?"

He realized his nephew was in the basement, staring up at him from the floor with shock and confusion.

"Stefan? How long have you been here? Where's Blackburn?"

"I came downstairs when I heard you shouting in your sleep," he explained. "Who's Blackburn? Are you okay? Should I get Aunt Kari?"

"What? No...no, I'm fine, I um-" His head felt woozy, but his wits slowly returned to him. "I must have fallen asleep; I've had a lot of nightmares lately. I didn't mean to knock you over like that, are you hurt?"

"It's okay, don't worry about it," his nephew said as he stood up.

The whole experience seemed so lifelike that it was hard for Jack to believe it had only been a dream. At least it was different from the usual vampire nightmare.

"Were you able to find anything in those books?"

"Not really. I mean, there was one thing that seemed unusual."

"What about the journal? Were you able to read any of it?"

"Not much; it's in cursive, and I don't know most of the words. There was some stuff about the Ahnen Villages, but it seemed boring," Stefan said as he handed him the journal. "There was something weird on the last page, but I don't know what it means because most of the ink has faded away. Here, this sentence, *mein mann ist ein gestaltwandler.*"

"You've said that word before, gestaltwandler. What does that mean?"

"I think it means shapeshifter. The lady who wrote this says her husband is one."

"Shapeshifter? Could that be...like a werewolf?" Jack asked, and the boy shrugged his shoulders and nodded. "What about the other books? You said there might be something unusual."

"Maybe, I don't know."

His nephew picked up the book *Ahnen Villages: A Photographic History* off the floor and opened it to a page tagged with a sticky note. Someone had used a red marker to circle the face of a dapper, well-dressed man with a neatly trimmed beard standing in front of a brick building with a ribbon across the front entrance. He was the spitting image of the man from the Nazi book, and written above his head was a simple but harrowing question.

# THE ALCHEMIST?

The caption showed the photo was taken at the opening of the MasterPharm factory, and the man was Dr. Henry Masterson. "Stefan, you've earned your twenty-five dollars for today."

# PART II:

# QUEEN OF SORROWS

# INTERLUDE
## Durch die Augen des Drachen

*August 21, 2019*

P rofessor Kellie Wilkens sat at the head of the dining room table. She sliced off a chunk of medium-rare filet mignon and moaned as she chewed the succulent, pinkish-red meat. Claudia had also prepared sweet potatoes, fresh asparagus with bacon, and a raspberry cheesecake for dessert. The housekeeper had expertly paired the meal with a fine bottle of Pinot Noir, but Martin stubbornly asked for a glass of Scotch instead of the wine.

"You're rather quiet tonight," Kellie commented. "We haven't had a nice dinner together in quite a while. Don't you have anything you would like to discuss?"

Martin was sitting at the opposite end of the table. He paused with a piece of steak on his fork halfway to his mouth and set the utensil back down on his plate. "Sure. How long do you plan to keep me here as your prisoner?" he asked. "It's been three years. I want to go back home. Please."

Kellie smiled at him before taking a sip of wine. "Hmmm, it seems you have some spunk in you tonight, after all." She pushed back her chair and stood up, unbuttoning her shirt as she walked towards him down the length of the table. "I understand what this is. I've been neglecting you. To make up for it, I've decided to stay the night and allow you to attend to my needs. What do you think about that, Martin?"

He looked down at the steak knife in his hand, and she wondered if he was going to attack her or slit his own throat. Not that he would be able to do either. Her powers were diminished, but she could keep him from harming her or himself. The thought of doing one of those violent acts must have crossed his mind as his arm went limp, and the knife dropped onto the floor. "No, thank you. I'm too tired this evening."

Kellie dropped her shirt and reached up to unfasten the front clasp of her bra, unleashing her well-endowed bosom. Martin tried to turn his head away from her, but she grabbed him under the chin and forced him to look up at her bare breasts. "I thought you writers were supposed to be horn dogs?"

"I'm not in the mood," he said as he averted his eyes from her nakedness.

"What's the matter? Do you no longer desire the pleasures of the flesh?" she teased him. "Or perhaps you wish to deny me the satisfaction I want out of spite?"

She looked over his shoulder and then gave a brief nod. Martin hadn't heard Claudia enter the dining room as she had removed her shoes and was surprisingly stealthy for such a big woman. She pinned his arms back and pulled his chair away from the table with him in it. Kellie straddled his lap, burying his face into the depths of her ample breasts.

Martin struggled to free himself, but she pressed her cleavage together and held him there as her soft flesh cut off his oxygen supply. She kept his face pinned like that until he was in danger of being smothered to death by her tits. Kellie laughed as she let go and allowed him to draw a ragged breath before a coughing fit wracked him.

"I'm disappointed in you, Martin. I thought we had developed feelings for each other," she sighed. "Perhaps we need to start your discipline lessons again. What do you think?"

"No, please, not that," he whimpered. "I really am very tired. I think I might be coming down with something."

"For such a talented author, you are a terrible liar." Kellie grabbed his shirt collar and ripped it open, sending buttons flying across the table. "If you ever want to return to your world again, then you need to do exactly what I say."

She leaned in, took hold of his nipple between her thumb and forefinger, and then twisted it until he cried out. "Jesus wept, let go!" Martin yelled. "That fucking hurts."

"Good, then I have your full attention. Now, let me be very clear. The only way you will ever leave this house alive is if the Master gets what he wants. That means you must give me what I want, when I want it." She reached down and rubbed his crotch, and his cock soon grew hard.

"That's what I thought. Maybe you can't get it up anymore unless you are being whipped like the little bitch that you are. I'm sure Claudia would enjoy getting out her collection of whips and riding crops once more." He looked up at the housekeeper, and she smiled maliciously. "Now then, are you ready to obey me, or do we need to firm up your resolve?"

"No, ma'am," he said. "I live to serve you."

"That's better, my love." She stroked the side of his face with the back of her hand. Kellie unfastened her skirt and pulled it down along with her panties, stepped out of them, and then took off her stockings. She picked up a black silk robe from the nearby serving table and slipped it on. Leaving it untied so that her sex was still on full display, she stood before him with her hands on her hips.

"I need to speak with the Master, but afterward, I think some reinforcement of your loyalty is in order. We are near a crucial part of our journey, so you must understand what is expected of you. That includes you eating out my hairy cunt whenever I want." Kellie grabbed his face with both hands and kissed him roughly. She closed the robe, tied the sash around her waist, and pulled the hood over her head. "When the Master gives me a younger body to replace the one I sacrificed to resurrect him, I may ask him to do the same for you. I wouldn't mind wrapping my legs around that handsome face of your new ghostwriter, what do you think about that?" Martin recoiled in horror, which made Kellie throw back her head in laughter.

"Why don't we invite some company over for dinner next weekend? I believe enough time has passed for you to be done mourning your dearly departed Vivian, and now you're ready to declare your love for me. Claudia, please take Mr. Knight upstairs and make him uncomfortable. Why don't you put on that leather corset I like and join us? I'll be up shortly; we are going to have lots of fun tonight."

# Danse du Poulet Macabre

Novel By **MARTIN KNIGHT**

Jupiter &
Phoebus
Publishing
House

# CHAPTER 11
## Danse du Poulet Macabre

*August 22, 2019*

"Chickens!"

Kari snapped awake at her son's voice in the dark. A sliver of daylight peeked in between the curtains, but it was enough for her to see Patrick standing in their doorway. Jack was snoring beside her, so she got out of bed. "Honey, what's wrong? Did you have a bad dream?"

"Today is chickens!" he said, flapping his hands excitedly. "Grandma's chickens!"

Jack let out a loud grunt and raised himself up on his elbows. "Huh? Wha? What's going on? What time is it?"

"It's fine, go back to sleep. I'll take care of it." He flopped back down on his pillow and began snoring again. Even if she managed to get Patrick to lie down, there was no way she could sleep with the Mannheim Chainsaw Orchestra performing right next to her. "It's Saturday, Patrick. Go back to bed until six o'clock."

"No back to bed. Grandma house!"

"Patrick, that's not until later. Go rest on the couch and watch videos quietly. Please don't wake Jenny up, okay?"

Kari set him up on the living room sofa with a pillow, blanket, and tablet, then headed to the kitchen to brew a pot of coffee. It occurred to her that this was the first morning in almost three weeks that she had woken up to find Jack still in bed. The clock on the microwave showed it was **05:18**, only twelve minutes before her son usually woke up, but it still felt early. She wished he would sleep in just one morning, but he was excited about today.

Kari had promised him that they would stop out at the farm to see the chickens as an incentive to go shopping for school clothes and supplies. He likely had become overstimulated thinking about that, or he could also be anxious about attending a new school. Determining what mood her son was in proved difficult detective work most days, even though he was learning to vocalize his wants and needs better as he got older.

While she waited for the coffee to finish brewing, Kari curled up in an armchair with the novel she had been reading. *In The Mountains Of Murder* was not a book she would have thought she'd enjoy, but she had barely been able to put it down. With only twenty pages to go until she reached the conclusion, she had been waiting for a chance to read the last bit without interruption. While she wasn't thrilled about getting up before dawn, it created the perfect atmosphere to experience the fate of the Dunbar family. When she had last left them, James had just murdered his father-in-law, who owned the ski chateau, after he arrived to evacuate the writer and his family due to a massive blizzard moving in.

Patrick was watching a video on YouTube of a man feeding cockroaches to his collection of pet Tarantulas. She tried not to pay any attention to it even though that was almost impossible since her son kept restarting it when it reached the end. It heightened her level of anxiety as she poured over the final pages of the novel. The beep of the coffee pot signaling that it was done brewing nearly made her leap out of the chair. She muttered a curse word under her breath, and Patrick giggled.

Kari marked her page and set the book down as she went to pour herself a cup of coffee. She grabbed a mug sitting on the counter when she noticed the basement door was open. Jack usually kept it locked if he wasn't down there. He was borderline paranoid about having his story pages messed up, but he must have forgotten last night.

She went to close the door, but he had also left a light on downstairs. Kari pushed in the button on the switch, but there was still another light on further below. With a sigh, she turned the overhead light back on and trudged down the steps barefoot. The lamp on Jack's desk illuminated the haphazard piles of books and papers scattered all over the surface. He had laid down some carpet remnants on the cement floor, but it was still cold on her feet. Kari reached across the desk to pull the lamp chain, but a piece of paper caught her eye. She recognized Jack's handwriting, which was usually very neat, but she could tell he had jotted this down quickly.

*Blackburn and werewolves*

*Masterson is the Alchemist*

*Kari — Queen of Sorrows?*

She looked around for any other notes, hoping there was something to give her some context about what sort of writing project Jack was working on. He often left story ideas scrawled on random scraps of paper, yet she didn't remember him ever using her as a character. Her first instinct was to march upstairs, wake up snoring beauty, and ask him to explain the meaning of his note. No matter how much she wanted an answer (*and to silence the foghorn she could hear even down here*), doing so would let him know she had been snooping through his papers.

The phrase '*Queen of Sorrows*' seemed oddly familiar, but she couldn't recall from where. Kari set the paper back on the desk where she had found it, turned off the lamp, and hurried up the steps.

"Shut door!" Patrick said as reached the top.

Kari let out a yelp and almost tumbled back down the stairs. "Patrick, can you not give me a heart attack, please?"

"No go down basement!"

"Okay, calm down, I won't go in the basement anymore. Are you hungry, kiddo?" Patrick answered her by walking over to the table and sitting down. "I'll take that as a yes." She finished preparing Patrick's breakfast just as Jenny came downstairs.

"Did somebody scream?"

"That was me. Your brother scared the living daylights out of me," she replied. "Would you like some breakfast?"

"Yes, please." Jenny sat down next to Patrick. "Eww, why is he watching a video about spiders? That's gross, mommy make him turn it off."

"Your brother is fascinated by all kinds of...unusual things, and some of them can be quite skin crawling," Kar explained. "That doesn't make him bad for watching such things. He could grow up to be a scientist who studies insects. Or vacuums. Or fire alarms."

"When I grow up, I want to be a writer like daddy so I can stay up as late as I want. And I can have my own typewriter."

"I don't think all writers are complete insomniacs like your father has been lately, and I'm pretty sure most of them have discovered these things called computers," she said. "I'm glad you want to be a writer. Maybe your brother can do the illustrations for your stories."

"What are illustrations?"

"Those are drawings that go along with a book. They show something that happens in the story, so the reader understands what it looks like."

"Oh, like how Patrick has been making pictures of things that happened since we moved here?" Kari was pouring milk over Jenny's cereal and paused when she heard that.

"I guess I haven't looked lately." She wondered what Patrick had been drawing as she made herself some toast and scrambled eggs.

After breakfast, she let Jenny watch TV with the volume low while she returned to her chair. Despite having a cup of coffee, she nodded off after reading only a couple more pages of her novel. The sun was pouring in through the windows when Jack nudged her awake sometime later. Kari sat up in her chair and rubbed the cramp that had formed in her neck.

"Babe, are you alright? How long have you been out here?" he asked. "Did you know that the kids are up?"

"Yeah, I already fed them," she answered, stretching her back. "Patrick got me out of bed early this morning."

"Oh, I'm sorry about that. You should have woken me up." Jack took a sip from his mug and spit it back into the cup. "Damn it, coffee's gone cold again."

Kari was nervous about taking the kids out to the farm by herself after what had happened during the Fourth of July (*what exactly had happened, she still wasn't quite sure*). Patrick was so excited about going that to deny it to him would undoubtedly trigger a meltdown. Jack had some work he needed to catch up on for school he had been neglecting for his writing, so she would have to keep track of both kids on her own. Kari tried not to get after him about all the time he spent downstairs working on his story, but she had begun to feel like a single parent these last few weeks. At least by going out to see her folks, she would have some help.

She hoped there would be a return to normalcy with the school year starting. Perhaps he had been stressed out about doing both the ghostwriting and having to teach classes, and she couldn't blame him for that. Her stress level was through the roof from preparing the kids for a new school. Patrick was going into fifth grade, and Jenny would be starting third, which meant that her babies were growing up too fast.

It seemed like only yesterday when they brought Patrick home from the hospital. He had slept the whole trip in his car seat, and Jack had carefully carried him inside to keep from waking him up. They sat on the couch, staring at this brand-new person, and looked at each other with the shared question. *What are we supposed to do with him now?* That had been well before they knew all the hurdles that autism was going to throw in their path. Even if she had known what was coming, she wouldn't have shied away from the journey for a second. Her kids were her world now, and she would do anything to ensure they had the best life possible.

Kari kept the sliding doors of her van locked as she pulled into the driveway of her parent's farm so her son couldn't run out. "Patrick, we need to go inside first and say hello to grandma before going to see the chickens. Can you do that?"

"Uhn ungh, no grandma!" He had removed his seat belt and was bouncing up and down on the seat. "Patrick's chickens!"

"Thanks for leaving me to deal with this, Jack," she muttered. "Patrick, if you want to see the chickens, we need to go inside for five minutes. Can you set a timer for five minutes on your tablet?"

To her relief, he opened the clock application and started a countdown for 5:00. "Thank you. Aunt Jessica is here already. Jenny, can you take that bag beside you and give it to her?"

"It's too heavy, mommy," her daughter said as she lifted the plastic bag full of books.

"Okay, just bring it around the van for me while I get your brother out." She went over to the passenger's side to open the door, and Jenny followed behind her, dragging the bag of books across the ground. Kari took it from her, and Patrick tried ducking underneath her arm. "Hey, that's enough or no chickens, understand?"

He was still chomping at the bit to chase the birds, but she kept him reined in long enough to get into the house. The bag of books she was carrying was surprisingly heavy, and she set it down on the kitchen floor with a grunt before letting go of Patrick's arm.

"Can I help you with that, Aunt Kari?" Stefan asked as he got up from the kitchen table. He hurried over and picked up the bag.

"Thank you, Stefan, those are for you anyway," she said. "Jack said something about wanting you to do more research on the chemist. I hope you know what that's supposed to mean."

"Oh, okay, sure thing," he replied, setting the bag on the table. "Do you need help with anything else?"

"I would hate to ask, but Patrick wants to go outside and see the chickens," she said. "Would you mind keeping an eye on him? Just make sure he doesn't run out towards the road or hurt any birds."

"Yeah, I'd be happy to do that," Stefan answered. "Come on, Patrick, let's go outside."

Kari worried that her son would hesitate, but he took hold of Stefan's hand as they headed out the back door as Jessica and Margrit came into the kitchen.

"Good grief, you're looking rather rough," her mom remarked. "What's with the dark circles under your eyes? Are you getting enough sleep, dear?"

"Thanks, mom, that's what I needed to hear. Patrick woke me up at the crack of dawn," she said, stifling a yawn. "We were running late, so I didn't get a chance to do much with my hair and makeup."

"I just brewed a fresh pot of coffee," Margrit replied. "Let me get you a cup."

"I've got my makeup bag if you want to use it," Jessica offered. "Why don't you go freshen up in the bathroom? I'll keep an eye on the kids. Jenny's playing with the girls."

"Would you mind? Stefan was nice enough to take Patrick to see the chickens."

"Oh lord, I forgot to warn you about that," Margrit said.

"Warn me about what?"

"Your father was butchering several of the hens this morning," her mom answered. "I imagine he's done by now, but it will still be a mess out there."

Kari darted out the back door and sprinted towards the chicken coop, but Stefan met her halfway across the lawn.

"Aunt Kari, I'm so sorry," he said, panting. "I couldn't get him to leave."

"It's okay, go back to the house," she called out as she ran past him. Kari cut through her mom's garden and squeezed through a narrow space between the shoulder-height hedges on the opposite side to reach the hen house.

Growing up on a farm, she understood the practice of slaughtering animals for food. Not that she cared to witness it, but she couldn't imagine what horror her son must be experiencing. She found out soon enough as she came upon a dozen severed chicken heads scattered around the tree stump that her father used as a chopping block. Three headless carcasses were hanging by their bound feet from hooks underneath the eaves of the small wood and tin shack, their blood draining into a galvanized steel bucket on the ground below.

Patrick was standing a few feet away from the gruesome scene, staring up at the headless birds without any expression on his face. He looked back at her as she approached him.

"Chicken dance," he said in the tone of voice he used when upset. "Mommy, chicken dance! Chicken dance!"

"Honey, the chickens can't dance anymore. Why don't we go back-"

"NO GO BACK!" he yelled. "CHICKEN DANCE!"

Kari knelt by her son, trying to block his view of the hen house with her body. She wrapped her arms around his shoulders, both to comfort him and to prevent him from hitting her in case the situation devolved. Patrick's hand shot up, and she recoiled for fear of being slapped. Instead of hitting her, he touched the tip of his index finger to her temple.

"Dance," he whispered with a smile, and a jolt of electricity seemed to travel from his finger through her body. She had no earthly explanation for what happened next, as it was the most disturbing and absurd event she had experienced in her life.

The disembodied chicken heads were clucking in unison, their beaks opened and closed like some kind of feathered fish gasping for breath. If that weren't bizarre enough, the decapitated birds hanging from the hooks were flapping their wings and twisting their bodies in perfect synchronization. Kari realized they were performing the chicken dance as Patrick laughed and used his hands to imitate their clucking beaks.

"Patrick, are you doing this? Stop it, now!" She grabbed hold of both his hands, and the chicken heads and dead bodies became, well, dead again.

Kari had no idea what she had just witnessed, and her mind felt too frayed from the ordeal to wrap itself around what it meant. Margrit and Albert were waiting in front of the house as she guided Patrick across the lawn. Her father was holding the bloodied ax that he had been using to butcher the chickens, and she wanted to scream at him.

"Is everything alright?" her mother asked. "Stefan said Patrick saw the dead chickens and got upset. We weren't sure if we should come help."

"Would the boy like to see how the chickens are gutted and cleaned?" Albert asked as he wiped the hatchet blade clean with a handkerchief, and Margrit gave him an exasperated look. "What? It's good for him to learn where his food comes from."

"He's fine, mom, I got him calmed down," Kari replied. "He's probably traumatized, though, I don't think he's seen an animal with its head cut off before."

"I'll fix him a plate of cookies and a glass of milk," Margrit said. "Would you like that?"

Patrick nodded as her mom took his hand and led him back to the house. Kari would have rather just gone home, but both kids were excited to go shopping. She tried to hide how upset she was, but it was hard with her perky sister-in-law around. There had to be a logical explanation for what had happened, but she needed time to clear her head.

Although she felt like a nervous wreck, Patrick didn't seem the least bit fazed by what had occurred. He scarfed down the cookies, and ten minutes later, she and Jessica were on the road heading up to Cedar Rapids. Kari tried to put the sight of those chickens dancing around out of her head, but the image was seared into her brain. She tried to convince herself that it was some sort of hallucination, but she knew that wasn't true. There was only one person who she thought could give her some answers. Her mother.

There was obviously something going on that Margrit wasn't telling her about. She would have to find the courage to confront her about it, which wouldn't be easy. Her mother had never been one to show much emotion, which had always intimidated Kari and made it difficult to open up to her about personal matters. Too many strange things had occurred since they moved back to Iowa, and if Margrit knew what was causing it, Kari would have to get over her fear and talk to her.

They didn't return home until late in the afternoon. She was both physically and mentally exhausted from chasing Patrick around the mall and listening to Jessica chatter incessantly. To top it off, Jack was sound asleep on the couch when she walked into the house. He sat up as the kids came running through the door.

"Wha? Oh, hey babe, I was just resting my eyes for a few minutes."

"I'm sure. How about you cook dinner for the kids while I sit down and rest my eyes for a few minutes, dearest."

Jack took one look at the expression on her face and jumped off the couch without saying a word. She collapsed into the recliner and kicked out the footrest, groaning as the muscles in her legs stretched out. Despite how tired she felt, she wasn't in the mood to take a nap. Kari decided that reading her novel would at least take her mind off the trauma of this morning for a while. She went to open to the spot she had bookmarked but flipped too far and landed on the page listing the other novels the author had published. Her breath caught when she saw the first title on the list.

## *Also by Butch Richardson*

Homecoming Queen of Sorrows

An English Nosferatu in Nantucket

Satan's Hot Rod Lincoln

The Thing In The Drain

Roulette of Death

# Witch and Amulet

Novel By **MARTIN KNIGHT**

Jupiter & Phoebus Publishing House

# CHAPTER 12
## Witch and Amulet

*August 24, 2019*

"Patrick, look up and say cheese," Kari said. "Come on, please let mommy take a picture before school."

"Uh uh, no school!"

"Mom, we're going to be late," Jenny whined.

"Relax, Jenny, we're fine. Patrick, can you take one photo, and then we'll go look at the scarecrow. Would you like that?"

"Yes. Say cheese!" Kari motioned for Jenny to smile and quickly snapped the picture with her phone before she lost Patrick's attention. She loaded the kids into the van and took off before they had time to protest further. Passing the cornfield on the way into town, she had to slow down so her son could see the scarecrow dressed in an Iowa Hawkeye football uniform. Kari doubted that it did much to dissuade any birds from eating the crops, but it attracted Patrick like a moth to a bonfire.

"Hi, scarecrow! Good morning, scarecrow!"

She still hadn't processed what happened this past weekend. Part of her mind insisted that she had imagined the entire incident. Patrick refused to say anything about it when she tried asking him. Kari wanted to tell Jack about the dancing dead chickens, but she didn't know how without sounding like she was off her rocker.

That wasn't the only reason. She was still disturbed by the note he had written with her name on it and why he had referenced the title of some obscure horror novel. There were too many strange things going on, and she needed some time to make sense of them. With the kids dropped off at school, she headed downtown to the bookstore.

Kari parked behind the store and was walking up the alleyway when she felt she was being watched. She glanced over her shoulder and saw a pickup truck parked across the far end of the alley, blocking it. The windows was tinted almost black so she couldn't tell if anyone was sitting inside. She was probably paranoid because of the two disappearances, but she quickened her pace.

She rounded the corner and reached The Raven's Perch, but the door was locked when she tried it. All the lights in the store were off, and she could see that the bookshelves had been cleared out. The display in the front window had also been removed, and a makeshift note hung on the glass in Ryland's distinctive hand.

*Closed For Business*
*Thank You*
*For Your Patronage*

She had worked with Mr. Thynne last Friday, and he hadn't said anything about quitting. Kari knew the store hadn't been overly busy lately, but she didn't think it was in dire financial straits. Perhaps Ryland was having medical issues, but if that were the case, why would he take the time to pack up everything without asking for help or giving his employees any notice.

Kari turned away from the window, unsure what to do next. It wasn't like she needed the job, but she had enjoyed the work and meeting new people in town. After being stuck at home caring for the kids so long, it was refreshing to be out among other adults and feel like she was part of the community. She thought about heading to Desirable Wares and asking Susan if a sales position was open, but she didn't want to impose on her friend. There was also a hardware store on the square, not that she knew much about tools, or maybe the bank...

From the corner of her eye, she caught sight of the black truck idling at the street corner to the south. She kept her head looking towards the park but turned her eyes just enough to get a better look at the pickup. Kari had mistaken it for all black earlier because the rear body panels had been primed for repainting. The front portion still had its very distinguishable red and black paint job, and with the damaged truck bed, there was no mistaking who it belonged to. It was possible Kurt could be out running errands for his job, but she was sure he was spying on her.

She headed back towards her van, but instead of getting in, she ducked behind a row of bushes that gave her a clear view of the alleyway. Kari was beginning to think she was being foolish when she heard the rumble of a diesel engine. The suspicious pickup crept up the alley from the other end, slowed as it passed her van, and then stopped right beside the bushes where she was hiding. She crouched down as far as she could in case Kurt got out, but after a minute she risked a quick peek through a hole in the branches. The windows were still too dark for her to see the occupant, but she recognized the somewhat charred bumper stickers that her brother used to display his political affiliation.

The pickup rolled out into the street and turned right, disappearing from sight behind The Raven's Perch. Kari waited for a moment to see if her brother circled back, sprinted over to her van, and hopped into the driver's seat. She turned onto the same street where Kurt had gone, but there was no sign of his pickup. She drove around town for ten minutes without finding him and returned to the park.

Kari considered heading to his work to confront him, but instead she drove out to her parents' farm. Her mother's Chevrolet Lumina was gone, but her father's old Ford pickup truck was parked in the driveway. She climbed up the back steps and knocked a couple of times, but there was no answer. Kari was about to get back in her van and leave when she heard metal being hammered from the large workshop that her dad used to repair his farm machines. Even though he was retired, he still liked to tinker around with his tractors.

"Hello?" she called out, stepping into the dirt-floored building. "Dad, are you in here?"

She doubted her voice could be heard over the transistor radio sitting on the handmade wooden worktable, blaring out a country music station. In the back of the garage stood the ancient Minneapolis-Moline tractor that her father had owned for as long as she could remember. The orange tractor with its distinct red wheels was probably older than him, but Albert had kept it in near-immaculate running condition despite it being his workhorse machine.

She heard another bang from the far side of the tractor followed by what she assumed was cursing in German, then her father came around rubbing his head. "Ah, Karina, good morning. What are you doing here? You look upset, is something wrong?"

"No, I'm fine, I just need to talk to mom."

"I think she went to see Gertrude up the road, but I wasn't paying much attention," he said. "I wouldn't expect her home until this afternoon; you know how she likes to gossip."

Kari forced a smile, but her mood was too dark to laugh. "I'll call her later. Sorry I startled you." She was almost to the doorway when Albert gave a sharp whistle and waved her back. He pulled over a stool with a torn vinyl cushion that he wiped off with a handkerchief from his back pocket. Patting the seat as an indication for her to sit down, he went over to a dented refrigerator and took out two bottles of cold beer.

He popped the bottlecaps off using his thick thumbnail, sending the small aluminum discs flying over his shoulder. Kari didn't care for the taste of beer, but she accepted the cold lager. Albert leaned up against the man-sized tractor tire and drained half the bottle in one pull. She gave a deep sigh and took a long drink herself.

"Tell me what's troubling you," her father said. "And don't pretend you're not upset."

"You know, I was so excited to move away from here after college," she replied. "Once the kids were born, I wanted nothing more than to move back here. I thought this place would feel like home again, but it's been...different, I guess. Like, weird different. Even Jack has been acting strange lately. When I went to work this morning, I swear Kurt was driving around following me. You know, like spying on me."

The smile left her father's face, and he lowered his bottle as he was about to take another sip. "Kurt was following you? Are you sure about that?"

"I think so, it looked like his truck, but maybe I was-"

"I must be very careful how I say this, I am not always good with words. Your brother is a good man, but there are things you don't know about him. You must be careful around him. He has changed since returning from the war and working for that company."

"I don't understand, why would he be spying on me?"

Albert had a strained look on his face as if he were having a silent argument with himself. "I want to tell you the truth because you deserve to know...but I promised Margrit I wouldn't without her permission."

"Everyone seems to be keeping secrets from me these days, and I'm getting goddamn sick and tired of it," she snapped as she stood up to leave.

"Wait, Karina, please calm down," he replied. "You are right, no more secrets. Why don't you shut the door and take a seat."

She wondered what could possibly be so shocking that he couldn't just tell her, but if her dad was willing to let her in on whatever was going on around here then she wasn't about to question him. The garage door was twice her height and very heavy, and it took all her strength to slide it along its track. It was almost dark inside with the doors closed since the overhead lights were caked with years of grime. She walked back to the tractor, but Albert had disappeared somewhere further into the garage. Kari sat on the stool and fished around in her purse for a wet wipe to clean off her hands when she heard footsteps crunching on the dirt floor.

She looked up, expecting to see her father. A hulking, hairy beast stood there instead on its hind legs, towering over her. They locked eyes for a heartbeat, and then she let out a scream. Kari grabbed the can of mace in the bottom of her purse by instinct, and she sprayed it in the creature's eyes. It reared back and howled in pain, giving her the chance to run for the door. She was yanking on the handle, trying to get the damn thing to budge, when her father called out for her.

"Karina...stop...wait," he wheezed before he was overcome by a coughing fit. She risked a quick look over her shoulder while still pulling on the door and saw that he was kneeling on the ground without a shirt on, holding up his overalls with one hand as he rubbed at his eyes with the other. Kari noticed that his socks and boots were missing as he stood back up, his bare feet still covered with long, coarse hair. "Please, don't leave," Albert said, staring up at her with reddened, tear-streaked eyes that he could barely hold open.

"Dad?! Where did that monster go? What the fuck is going on?"

"There's nothing to fear; there's no monster. I mean, there was, but it was only me."

"That...that was you?" she stammered, then held up the pepper spray as he took a step towards her. "Stay back, or I'll spray you again! What the hell are you, a werewolf?"

"Yes, I am, and so is your brother," he answered. "Please calm down, I can explain."

"This is crazy. How can you be a werewolf? Why wouldn't you tell me about this?"

"Because it would put you in danger," her father replied as he picked up her beer bottle from the ground and used it to rinse off the mace. "You can't tell anyone else, not even your husband. You must promise not to say a word about this, not even in private. They could find out if you do."

"What do you mean? Who will find out? Does mom know about this?" A thought crossed her mind. "Is she a werewolf? Am I one?"

"No, there are female werewolves, but neither of you has been cursed with this burden," he said. "That's because the two of you carry a different one. You are both witches."

Jack Sterling needed answers. Having spent almost a decade in the academic world, he turned to the one place where he knew how best to find them. The library. Specifically, the university's library, where the two books causing him so much consternation had originated.

He wasn't entirely sure what he was looking for, perhaps reassurance this wasn't some crazy delusion taking place only in his head. Jack wondered what section of the Dewey Decimal System covered visions of impending doom. What he hoped to find was something that would convince him to go forward with the next part of his plan, contacting Detective Edgar Blackburn. He also hoped doing so wouldn't end with him sitting in a jail cell. Or a padded cell.

He made a beeline for the checkout desk and handed the young woman working there the two books from the steamer trunk.

"Um, these look pretty old," the clerk said. "I don't think they're even in our system. Where did you get them?"

"They were in the attic of the house we moved into," he replied. "This might sound odd, but I was hoping you could tell me who had checked them out."

"Let me get the head librarian, she might know how to look up the records from that far back." Jack remembered the short, stern-looking woman who now had steel gray hair from his years as an undergrad, and a sudden, irrational fear that he had overdue fines crept into his mind.

"Hmmm, no. We most likely marked these books as lost when we went computerized," the librarian told him. "Wait a minute. You may be in luck. This ID number would have belonged to a faculty member. I'll search for it in the system, but I can't promise anything. Come back in half an hour."

"Sure, no problem," Jack said. He headed off to track down the next thing on his list. While digital scans of back issues for local newspapers were available online, you usually had to know the exact publishing date to find anything. He knew the library provided students and faculty access to the Prism database, which cataloged and indexed a wide range of periodicals and academic, scientific, and law journals to make them searchable.

Jack went up to the second floor and found an open computer station. He logged in with his faculty account and hunted around on the desktop until he located the icon for accessing the Prism application. Jack typed in *Werewolf attack* in the search bar, then selected all the newspapers from the area as the sources before clicking on the button with a magnifying glass icon.

The search returned much too quickly – **0 Results**.

He hadn't expected that to work, so he changed the search term to *Detective Blackburn*, which came back with **395 Results**. That was a daunting number, but he could filter it down. Jack saved off the results to his personal folder on the university's network storage drive so he could sort through them later. He was about to log out when he got an idea and tried one more search, this time for *Deputy Blackburn*. A few minutes later, it produced a much more reasonable **16 Results**. Jack scanned through the summaries of the articles until he found one that looked like what he wanted and selected the link to display the whole story.

A Johnson County Sheriff Detective was killed in the line of duty, and a deputy was injured while serving a search warrant at a rural property. The Sheriff declined to say whether the warrant was in connection to the recent series of disapperances of young women in the surrounding communities. The deputy, identified as Edgar Blackburn, was transported to the University of Iowa Hospital with serious injuries but is expected to recover. The identity of the detective and the assailant, who died of a self-inflicted gunshot, have not been released pending notification of next of kin.

Jack printed out the page with the story on it and went back to the rest of the articles from the search. The one from farthest back, dated November 1st, 1987, listed **ERROR: Not Available** in its summary description. Intrigued, Jack clicked to view the newspaper scan and was shocked when it brought up a black-and-white photograph that looked like his house. There were patrol cars and an ambulance parked in the thick snow, along with what appeared to be two men carrying a stretcher with a sheet-draped body out the front door. Unfortunately, the text from the article had been distorted during scanning, making

it completely unreadable. He could pick out a few words from the caption underneath
the photo.

...oroner remove...scovered by Deputy Blackburn...
...can confirm....ouse belo...ofessor at...Schreiber...

Strangely, the picture remained perfectly clear, and only the text was illegible. He
printed the article out as it was, hoping he could find something in the photo that would
identify it as the house they had purchased. Jack brought up the search tool once more
and typed in *Professor Schreiber,* only to have the engine return with nothing found. That
seemed bizarre if, in fact, she had been a murder victim.

Jack tried typing in the address of their house and pressed the search button. The
program displayed the busy icon for so long that he worried the computer had locked up
when it returned a disappointing **0 Results**. Jack logged out and returned to the checkout
desk.

"I found a name associated with that ID," the head librarian said. "It belonged to
Catherine Schreiber, a professor in the German Studies department. That's the only
information on her in the system. Try contacting the department head to see if they have
any further records on her."

"Thank you, I appreciate you taking the time to look that up," he said. "I don't mean
to pry, but how long have you worked here at the university?"

"I started here in '85, I'm due to retire next year. Why do you ask?"

"Do you recall ever hearing the name Catherine Schreiber before? She might have died
on Halloween in 1987. Maybe the story was in the news?"

"You know, when I first saw her name come up on the computer screen, it almost
sounded familiar. No, I don't remember her though. Do you want these books back? I
can't return them to circulation since they're not in our system." Jack thanked her and
took his books.

He was disappointed at how little information he had found. Not that he had been
expecting to unearth deep, dark secrets buried for years with a couple of database searches.
If he wanted answers, it was clear he would have to get them from somebody who had
been there in person. He was done with classes for the day, and he didn't need to be home
for another hour. There was no excuse for him not to pay Detective Blackburn a visit,
except he could end up sounding like a raging lunatic.

Jack's heart was racing as he parked down the street from the Sheriff's Office. He forced himself to take a couple of deep breaths to calm down. He got out of his car and walked towards the imposing brick building, but his legs grew heavier with each step. Halfway there, he came to a halt, whatever courage he had wavering. Jack turned around and ran into a person walking behind him. To his absolute horror, it was the man he had come to see.

"Whoa, careful there, pal."

"I'm sorry. I didn't see you behind me, detective."

The word slipped out of his mouth before he could stop it, and Edgar looked at him with a curious expression. Jack hurried back to his car, collapsed into the driver's seat, and smacked his palm repeatedly against his forehead. "Stupid, stupid, stupid!"

His self-reprimanding was interrupted by a knock on the passenger-side window. Detective Blackburn was leaning down, looking at him through the glass, the holstered pistol underneath his suit coat clearly on display.

Jack rolled down the window. "I didn't mean to run into you, sir. It was an accident."

"It's Sterling, isn't it?"

"What?"

"Your name is Jack Sterling, right?"

"Yeah, have we met before?" He decided playing dumb was the best course of action.

"Once, at the hardware store, your son had run off."

"Yes, of course, I remember now," Jack replied. "Is there something I can help you with?"

"I was going to ask you that question. You look like a man who needs to get something off his chest. Would you like to come to my office and talk?"

"Um, no, that's okay, I...I don't have anything to talk about. I was just out taking a walk."

"Didn't look like you made it too far. If you change your mind, you know where to find me."

Edgar tapped his knuckles on the door frame and turned to walk away. "Detective Blackburn, wait," Jack called out. "This is going to sound strange, but I know how you got those scars on your face." He held up the copy of the newspaper article he had printed from the library.

"Not a day I care to remember, but that's not exactly secret knowledge. What does that have to do with anything?"

"I don't think the paper reported all the details."

"Oh really, and how's that?"

"The person who attacked you, I don't think they were human."

Detective Blackburn regarded him silently for several moments. "There is a coffee shop two blocks over. Do you know it?"

"Um, yes, I think so."

"I'll meet you there in five minutes."

Jack drove over to the chain coffee restaurant, which was full of students this time of day. He ordered a cappuccino and a black coffee for the detective before finding an open table. While a professor grabbing a coffee between classes didn't look too out of place, he felt like a sore thumb when the scarred-face man in a dark suit walked in and took the chair across from him.

"So, who do you work for? Are you a reporter?" Edgar asked.

"No, I'm an English professor at the University."

"We're going to play this game, huh? Maybe you're on MasterPharm's payroll. Are you their new Dr. Moreau? That would explain why they put you up in that house."

"What do you mean by Dr. Moreau?"

"It's a book about a mad scientist. You really need to work on your cover identity."

"I've read the novel, thank you. I meant your reference to it. Does MasterPharm have some part in, you know...the thing that gave you those scars?"

"If you are who you claim to be, you're splashing around in shark-infested waters with raw steaks for flotation devices. I strongly recommend you forget all about this."

The detective went to stand up, but Jack reached across the table and took hold of his wrist. "Please, it's important you listen to me." Blackburn looked down at Jack's hand and he quickly removed it. The detective sat back down at the table. "Was it a werewolf that attacked you?"

Edgar fixed him with a blood-chilling glare, his piercing blue eyes drilling into Jack's skull. He could only imagine what it would be like to be sitting across from him in an interrogation room and barely managed to keep from shuddering.

"If you're not working for that fucking company, then how do you know about them?"

"You saved me from one, I mean your future self. It was in a dream I had, only it seemed very real...I know, this sounds completely ridiculous."

"We were in Bailey Grove, and the town was covered in fog." For an moment, a look of fear flashed across the man's hard eyes. "I was hoping I had too much to drink that night."

"You had the same dream? Do you know what happened to the former owner of my house?"

"Yeah, it used to be the home of another professor. I'm pretty sure she was killed because she found out her late husband was a werewolf. The pharmaceutical company bought the house when it was sold at the estate auction, but they went out of their way to hide that. I'd say somebody wanted you to move in, which makes me wonder why that is."

"I don't know, but I also had a dream about the professor who died there," Jack said. "She told me I needed to find someone called the Alchemist. I think his real name is Dr. Henry Masterson, but he died almost thirty years ago."

"You're playing a dangerous game here, Sterling. What's your angle?"

"I don't have an angle," he answered. "I just came across this information while researching the novel I'm working on, which happens to be about a town that's secretly run by werewolves."

Edgar had been taking a drink from his coffee and had to spit it back into the cup as he started coughing. "You're what? Good god, you really are crazy. Does anybody know about this?"

"I'm not supposed to say anything, but I'm ghostwriting it for Martin Knight. You know, the horror author."

"Yeah, I know who he is."

"My wife sort of knows, and I also told my nephew, Stefan. He's my research assistant."

"That's Kurt Ulmer's son, isn't it?"

"Yes, do you know Kurt?"

"We've had a few run-ins," Edgar replied. "Let me investigate this Alchemist business. In the meantime, I'd suggest you don't go digging any further. And whatever you do, stay away from Kurt." Before Jack could ask him what he meant by that, Edgar handed him a five-dollar bill for the coffee and left the shop.

Kari picked at her dinner, pushing her food around the plate to hide the fact that it was mostly untouched. The kids had eaten an hour ago, and the meal was dry from being kept in the oven because Jack came home late. She had done her best to keep her feelings under control, but they were churning just below the surface.

Her father hadn't been willing to answer any more of her questions, yet what he had told her was enough to shake the foundation of her world. While she wanted to hate her mother for keeping her in the dark about the true nature of her family, Albert had made it clear that she did so to protect her. Kari could only wonder from what. Or from whom?

"Are you feeling okay, honey?" Jack asked. "You've barely eaten anything."

She pulled herself out of her thoughts and looked up at him. "I'm fine. It's just been a long day. You didn't mention you would be home late."

"Yeah, sorry about that. I went out with a couple of the other professors for a cup of coffee after work," he replied. "Did something happen with the kids at school?"

"No, no, they had a good day. Patrick did well, and Jenny already has three friends she wants to invite for a sleepover." She pushed her plate away and took a drink of her iced tea. "I did get some bad news. The Raven's Perch went out of business, so I'm unemployed for now."

"Without even giving you any notice? What kind of jerk does that?"

"Mr. Thynne was very nice; he must have had a good reason for closing. Who knows, he might have had cancer and didn't want to tell anyone."

"I'm sure you'll find something else, or you can stay home with the kids. Whatever you want to do. Not a big deal."

"I know it's not a big deal to you, Jack, but this was a job I really enjoyed. I'm sure you would rather have me at home cooking and cleaning for you. If I dropped dead, I doubt you would even notice until it came time to do the dishes or feed the kids. I'm just the housekeeper who you have sex with when I'm not too tired from watching your children all day."

"That's not what I meant at all," he stammered. "I'm very sorry you lost your job."

"No, I'm sorry, I shouldn't have snapped at you. I've had a bad day. I liked working for Mr. Thynne. I wish he would have told me in person so I could say goodbye."

"Hold on a minute, there was a package in the mail for you from someone named Thynne, I think," Jack said as went into the living room and returned with a small box. "Here you go, is his first name Ryland? I didn't notice before, but it's not stamped by the post office. Looks like he must have put it in our mailbox himself."

"Thanks, I'll open it in a bit," she replied. "I guess I can see if Susie will get me a job at her store, or I could do some substitute teaching at the elementary school."

"Whatever you want to do, I'll support you," he said. "Why don't you take a couple weeks off though and relax for a bit, we're fine on money for a while. I almost forgot, there was something else that came in the mail. Martin Knight is hosting the entire English department for dinner at his house on Saturday evening. Do you think your mom or Jessica would mind watching the kids so we could attend? I'd really like for you to meet him."

"Do we have to go?" Kari asked. "I don't know if I'm feeling sociable right now. Plus, I don't have anything to wear."

Jack gave her a wounded look that made her want to throw her glass of tea in his face. "He asked me to be his ghostwriter, I think he would notice if we don't show up. What am I supposed to give as a reason for not being there?"

Kari came within a hair of blurting out everything that had happened this morning and then telling him to take his precious novel and stick it where the sun doesn't shine, but she put on her best fake smile instead. "Why don't you tell him that I'm having my monthly visitor, dear? That usually gets you to stop bugging me for a week." He rolled his eyes. "Fine, we'll go, but don't expect me to enjoy it."

"Thanks, now that you have some free time on your hands, you can go shopping for a new dress for the party." Jack stood up to clear off the dishes, and she flashed him the bird as soon as his back was turned. Kari knew she shouldn't be so rude to him, but her nerves were a bundle of frayed live wires throwing off white hot sparks. The only thing she wanted to do was slip into a nice hot bubble bath with a glass of Chardonnay and read a book, but instead she had to find a fucking dress to wear to a party that she had no desire to attend.

Jack retreated down to the basement, so she placed the box from Ryland on the counter and dug out a pair of scissors from the junk drawer. There were no stamps on it, and the return address was that of The Raven's Perch. She wondered why he would go out of his way to deliver a package but not come knock on the front door. Inside was an envelope taped to a box wrapped in gold foil which she opened first and read the note it contained.

*Dear Karina,*

*I apologize for leaving in such haste, but it was unavoidable.*
*Please accept this gift as a token of gratitude for your service. The bracelet belonged to my late wife. I think she would be pleased for you to have it. The book is one of my favorites, and I hope you will appreciate it as well. It is, to my knowledge, long out of print.*

*Kindest Regards,*
*Ryland Thynne*

Setting the note down on the counter, she unwrapped the gift box. Inside was a silver and gold bracelet, studded with tiny rubies, in the shape of a snake eating its own tail. It was an unusual gift, but she appreciated the sentiment from Mr. Thynne. She put the box down and picked up the paperback novel underneath it. Kari was shocked to see that not only had Ryland found another title from the same obscure author, but it was the one she was most curious about.

# HOMECOMING QUEEN OF SORROWS

# Misery Loves Company for Dinner

Novel By **MARTIN KNIGHT**

Jupiter & Phoebus Publishing House

# CHAPTER 13
## Misery Loves Company for Dinner

*August 29, 2019*

S ince she learned that most of her life had been based on lies, Kari tried her best not
to think about it. She felt her chest tighten whenever her mind wandered back to
what her father had told her. It was probably good that she no longer had a job because
she would have been fired for acting scatter-brained.

Then again, she could have gotten out of tonight by claiming she had to work. Kari
was not looking forward to the dinner party this evening, but it would at least give her a
distraction. She also had the novel Mr. Thynne gave her to pass the time. While it was a
disturbing story, that helped her focus on the book. It was especially unnerving since the
main characters, a teenage girl and her overbearing mother, had names similar to Kari and
her own mother, Cassie and Marjorie Alba.

Especially bizarre was the feeling of déjà vu the further she got into the book. She
could picture what was happening to the protagonist as if she were pulling up her own
memories. That was ridiculous since the story was set in 1963, but Kari was able to
imagine every detail as if she had been there.

Perhaps she would have been thrilled to meet a famous author like Martin Knight any
other time, but she was not in the mood to attend a boring dinner party. She would have
preferred to stay at home and read her book or do absolutely anything else. Since there
was no avoiding it, she put aside her novel and went to fix her hair and makeup.

Having the knowledge there were more secrets her mother was keeping from her was
driving her crazy. She almost wished she could make herself forget what had happened.

Since she had no magic wand to wave and accomplish that, she decided that the best thing to do was enjoy herself tonight and not ruin Jack's big evening.

Even though her parents had lied to her, she couldn't bring herself to hate them for it. She knew she would do anything to protect her children from the ugly truths of the world as long as she could. Kari wasn't a child anymore, though, so what could be so terrible that her mother couldn't bring herself to divulge it after all these years?

No sooner had she finished putting on her lipstick than the doorbell rang. "Jack, can you get that?" she called out, but there was no response. She hadn't changed into her dress yet and was only wearing her bra and panties, so she grabbed her bathrobe and hurried to answer the door. Jessica and her two daughters were waiting on the porch. "Sorry to keep you waiting," she said. "I don't know where Jack is."

"You're fine, dear. Go finish getting ready," her sister-in-law replied. "You two are going out to a dinner party?"

"Yeah, it's for Jack's work," Kari explained. "I'm running a little behind. Please make yourself at home. Jenny should be in her room, and I think Patrick is drawing at the table."

Except for having to put up with her overly perky nature, Kari was glad to have her sister-in-law around to help. Jessica sent the twins upstairs and sat down with Patrick while Kari went to get dressed. She had purchased a simple black dress for the evening, which she worried showed off too much of her legs, but Jack predictably said it looked great on her. Kari paired it with a simple silver necklace, and then, on a whim, she decided to put on the bracelet Ryland had given her.

Keeping with tradition, Jack was nowhere to be found. She carried her heels and walked down to the basement, thinking they needed to carpet the unfinished wooden steps for the hundredth time. Jack was sitting at his desk pounding away at his stupid typewriter, but at least he had managed to get himself dressed and ready on time. "Thanks for keeping an ear out for the doorbell, honey."

It took him a few seconds to realize that somebody had spoken to him before he stopped typing. "What? Oh yeah, no problem," he said without turning around. "Is it time to go already?"

Nothing short of a miracle kept her from launching her shoes at the back of his head. "Yes, Jack. This is your dinner party, so why don't you take responsibility for once and not make me keep you on task? I don't need a third child to take care of. If you want me to spend my entire evening talking to a bunch of boring, snobbish professors, the least you can do is act like an adult."

Getting up from his chair, Jack came over and put his hands on her shoulders. "You're right, babe. I'm sorry, I lost track of the time." He bent down to kiss her, but she pushed him back.

"I just got done with my makeup. I don't need to have it smudged, thank you."

"Sorry, I'll be right up. Just let me finish a few more sentences. I don't want to lose my train of thought." Kari clenched her fists as he sat back down at his desk. It took all her restraint to walk back upstairs without telling him where he could shove his train of thought. Patrick was sitting at the kitchen table, scribbling away on his pad. "Patrick, mommy and daddy are going out tonight," she said. "Aunt Jessica will be taking care of you. Can you eat dinner for her like a good boy?"

"Uhn ughn, no dinner," he said without looking up. Kari was tempted to trigger one of his meltdowns to get out of this stupid dinner party, but it wasn't worth dealing with the aftermath of Patrick going nuclear.

"What are you working on?" she asked instead.

"Mommy dance." The picture he was making showed a girl in a dress standing up on a stage with a crowd of people below her. The front of the girl's dress and half her face were colored black. Before she could look closer, Patrick leaned over the table and blocked her view with his body. "No look."

She wasn't about to pry the drawing pad out of his hands, but there was something oddly familiar about the picture. Kari reminded herself to sneak a peek at it while he was at school. Her dear husband finally emerged from his cave, running a hand through his unkempt hair as he walked up the stairs.

"Okay, I'm done, babe. What time do we need to go?"

"Mommy no go!" Patrick yelled as he got up from the table and wrapped his arms around her waist. "Mommy stay home."

"Jack, he's upset. Maybe you had best go without me."

"He needs to get used to being away from us for an evening. Come on, Patrick, hug mommy and tell her goodnight."

"It's okay, Patrick. Mommy and daddy are going out for a little while," she said. "You're going to stay here with Aunt Jessica."

"No Aunt Jessica," he replied defiantly, and she raised her eyebrow at Jack.

"Don't worry, he'll calm down once you leave," Jessica said as she entered the kitchen. "Would you like to get some board games out, Patrick?"

Her son shook his head but let go of her and sat back down at the table to continue with his artwork. Kari leaned down and kissed him on the cheek, which he wiped off with the back of his hand without saying another word.

On the drive over, Jack droned on about the folks from the English department, but she was barely paying attention. Kari didn't like leaving with Patrick upset, and she worried whether Jessica was prepared to handle him if he threw a tantrum. She would be a nervous wreck thinking about it until she got home that night.

There was only one other vehicle in the driveway when they pulled up, which did nothing to improve her mood. If she'd known they'd arrive this early, she wouldn't have run around like a chicken with her head cut off getting ready. That wasn't the best analogy after what happened the other day, but it seemed fitting.

"Looks like Professor Wilkens is here already," Jack said, nodding toward the sleek black Lincoln sedan in the driveway. "Do you want to wait in the van until more people arrive?"

"Yeah, that wouldn't be awkward since we had to pass through the front gate with a security camera," she replied. "I'm pretty sure they know we're here."

"Oh right, I forgot about that."

"Come on, let's get this over with already."

Jack came around the van and opened the door for her, holding her hand as they walked up to the entrance. "Are you feeling okay tonight?" he asked. "You seemed quiet on the ride over. I know you didn't want to come to this, but I really appreciate you doing it."

"I'm fine, dear. It's just been a stressful week." He nodded and pushed the button beside the door, setting off a series of booming chimes inside the house. "Promise me we won't stay a minute longer than necessary. I don't want to be out all night."

From the sound of the furious barking that preceded the door being opened, Kari expected there to be a large beast on the other side. Instead, a cute little black-and-tan dog came charging out at Jack, and he quickly backed away from it. He was rescued by a stout, stone-faced woman with her black hair pulled back in a bun who picked up the dog one-handed.

Kari held out her hand for him to sniff, and he stopped barking and let her scratch the back of his head. She turned and smiled at Jack.

"Jojo doesn't usually take that well to strangers," a tall man leaning on a cane spoke as he stepped into the doorway. "Welcome, I'm Martin Knight. You must be Kari," he said, offering his hand for her to shake. "Jack, good to see you again; please come in. Claudia, let's put Jojo upstairs so he doesn't eat any of our guests tonight." As if the dog associated Jack's arrival with his banishment, he snarled at him before the woman carried him away.

"This is a very nice house, Mr. Knight," Kari said as they entered the Grand Hall. "It's probably the most amazing building I've ever been inside."

"Have you considered renting it out as an Airbnb?" Jack suggested. "You could probably make a couple of extra bucks that way."

"That's not a bad idea now that I'm retired and living on a fixed income," Martin laughed. "Maybe I should hire you as my business manager as well. Kellie is out on the terrace; why don't we join her and have a drink before everyone else arrives."

"I guess we're a little early," Jack said. "Or are the other guests being fashionably late?"

"I put the time on your invitation thirty minutes before all the others. I would like to discuss your progress on the novel without the need to whisper off in a corner."

Kari had been interested in meeting Jack's boss after hearing so much about her. The woman who was sipping on a glass of white wine wasn't exactly what she would have pictured as the head of an English department. She had a sturdy frame with wide hips and a substantial chest, but she wasn't overweight. Her long, curly black hair was pulled back on the left side with a silver clip. She wore an elegant red dress with a white silk shawl draped over her shoulders, but Kari imagined she was more accustomed to wearing a smart-looking pantsuit. Kellie had a pleasant smile on her face, but the intensity in her sharp green eyes was somewhat unnerving. She looked like she belonged in a courtroom or a board room rather than teaching literature and creative writing.

"Good evening, Jack," she said. "This must be your lovely wife. Kari, isn't it?"

"Yes, it is a pleasure to meet you, Professor Wilkens. Jack has told me a lot about you."

"Well then, I may have to entice some stories about him out of you before the evening is over. Come sit beside me, and we'll let the boys talk shop while we drink Martin's expensive wine and get to know each other."

Jack and Martin sat down across the table from them, and they were soon immersed in their own conversation. She accepted a glass of Riesling from Kellie. Kari didn't drink often, but she figured some wine might help ease her tension about having to talk with her husband's boss. If nothing else, it would make the evening go a little faster.

"I saw a photo of your two lovely children on Jack's desk. How old are they?"

"Our daughter Jenny is eight, and Patrick is ten," Kari answered. "This was their first week at a new school, but everything has gone pretty smoothly so far."

"I'm sure that it was still stressful for you, though. I know I get anxious at the start of every school year, and I don't even have any kids," Kellie replied as she took another sip from her glass. "History tends to attribute most of the great discoveries in the world to men. I bet if we could travel back through time, there would be a woman responsible for the invention of wine."

"With a handful of needy children and a lazy husband who drove her to it," Kari added, and Kellie laughed. Jack and Martin paused their discussion briefly to look at them but then went back to chattering about plot structure, character development, or some such tedious drivel. Kari didn't realize she had finished her first glass until Kellie offered to fill it up for her again. Her head felt a bit fuzzy, but she didn't refuse the drink.

"So, do you stay at home with the kids, or do you work as well?"

"I'm actually unemployed right now," she answered, "but I was working in a bookstore until it went out of business recently. I might go back to teaching, or maybe I should open my own bookstore. Not that I know anything about running a business."

"What a wonderful idea! Perhaps I could help you arrange for local authors to do book signings in your shop," Kellie said as she leaned forward and peered closer at Kari's wrist. "That is a beautiful bracelet you're wearing. Where did you get it?"

"It was a gift from my boss. I guess it was his way of apologizing for laying me off."

"You don't say, that's very interesting," she said, then turned towards the two men across the table. "Martin, my dear, perhaps we should share our good news with Jack and Kari. It will be more special to make the first announcement in an intimate setting than to do it in front of everyone, don't you think?"

"Of course," Mr. Knight said after a moment of hesitation. "So, um, what Kellie was saying is that, ah, I guess the two of us are-"

"Martin is better at writing words than speaking them, but what he's trying to tell you is that we're engaged to be married."

"Oh, that's fantastic news. Congratulations!" Kari said. "We're very happy for the both of you. Have you set a date for the wedding?"

"We haven't settled on anything, but we were thinking Halloween seemed appropriate," Kellie replied. "It was also the same day we first met, and that way, Martin has no excuse for ever forgetting our anniversary."

"I could never forget the first time I laid eyes on you, my dear," Martin said. "It was like I had woken up from a long dream and found myself in a whole new life. I think it would make for quite a story." Kellie smiled at him, but it didn't seem to go to her eyes.

"Speaking of which, how is the ghostwriting coming along, Jack?" she asked without taking her eyes off Martin.

"Oh, uh, pretty good, I guess," Jack said. "I'm near the middle of the story, I think, but I'm a bit stuck on where to go next."

"A touch of the old writer's block, huh?" Martin asked. "I often find the best cure for that is to kill off a character or two. Death can be a powerful catalyst for creativity, believe it or not."

"I guess that could work, but what if I haven't used my characters for everything I need in the story?"

"Just because they die doesn't mean you can't still use them, there's always flashbacks, or you could even do time travel if you want to open that can of worms. You're writing a horror novel, so death doesn't need to be permanent. You never know when someone you thought was gone could come back to life, trust me."

"I think that's enough shop talk for this evening, my love," Kellie said, patting his hand. Claudia opened the patio door and ushered through the first group to arrive for the party. "Looks like our guests are here. Shall we go meet them, my love?"

She stood up and motioned for Martin to follow her. He rose to join her, but he didn't look too enthusiastic about socializing. Kari was grateful that the other guests had shown up when they did, as those two glasses of wine had gone right through her.

"I'll be right back," she whispered to Jack. She slipped around the milling crowd and got the housekeeper's attention. "Excuse me, where is the bathroom?"

"Follow me," Claudia said, taking her back into the Grand Hall. "Through there, turn left." She pointed to the archway on the wall opposite the large fireplace. The doorbell clanged, and the housekeeper went to answer it.

The archway opened onto a wooden staircase leading up to the second floor. A suit of armor was standing guard at the base of the stairs, which gave her the creeps as she looked around the corner and spotted a door to the left. She gave the metal mannequin a wide berth as she opened the door, but it turned out to be a closet. Kari saw another door in an alcove under the stairs, which proved to be the bathroom.

She turned on the light and was about to close the door when she heard faint sobbing. The bathroom light showed her there was a set of stairs in the alcove leading downward, and whoever was crying sounded like they were somewhere below. Kari approached the edge of the landing and tried to see around the bend in the stairwell. She didn't trust herself wearing heels on the narrow steps, so she unfastened the straps and set them beside the bathroom door.

It was nearly dark in the next section of stairs. She stuck her head around the corner and saw a young woman wearing a green dress curled up on the next landing. She had her face buried in her hands and was also barefoot. The girl looked up at her, and Kari saw that the front of the girl's dress had been covered in a black substance and then coated with feathers. Half her face was also coated with the thick sludge.

"Hello? Are you okay?"

"They're going to pay," the troubled teenager sobbed. "They're all going to pay for this."

"Are your parents here?" Kari asked. "Do you need help?"

Instead of answering, the girl stood and ran further down the stairs. Kari hesitated, then followed to see where she had gone. She found a light switch at the bottom of the stairs and flipped it on to reveal a short hallway with several doors leading off it. There was no sign of the girl in the dress, and Kari questioned whether she had seen someone in the dim light.

She turned around to go back up the stairs when a red rubber ball bounced down the hallway and rolled to a stop at her feet. Kari didn't want to touch the fucking thing, but she made herself tap it with her toe to be sure it was real. She was about to reach for the ball when she heard a little girl's laughter.

"*Your turn, mommy,*" her daughter's voice floated out of an open door at the end of the hall. "*Come and play!*"

"Jenny? Are you down here?" Kari knew that couldn't be possible. Jenny was at home with her sister-in-law, but a buzzing noise in her head made it difficult to think. She took a few steps down the hallway as the noise grew stronger, drawing her toward its source. The ball dropped from her hands and went bouncing back down the hallway, but Kari barely noticed she had let go of it.

The door looked different than the others; it was made of black wood and carved with strange symbols. The floor was freezing beneath her bare feet, but she kept walking forward. Every nerve in her body screamed to run away, yet she could no more do that than a fish with a hook in its mouth. The room on the other side was nearly dark, but she had to find Jenny. She crossed the threshold, and the black door swung shut behind her.

The buzzing died away, leaving her in control of her body once more. Kari spun around to open the door, but it was no longer there. In its place was a solid stone wall, and she couldn't find any other point of exit. She went towards the only light source, which was coming from an old-fashioned oil lantern. Kari turned the knob at the base to increase the flame, but it only gave her enough light to see about ten feet around her.

"Help! Can somebody hear me? I'm trapped in here! Jack? JACK!"

Her voice reverberated off the stone walls surrounding her, making it sound as if several frantic women were shouting. The oppressive silence swallowed the echoes, which only unnerved her more. Kari fought back the urge to start screaming and forced herself to get control of her fear. She continued along the passageway until finding stone steps spiraling downward. The last thing she wanted to do was go even further into the depths of this dungeon, but she had no other options.

At the bottom of the spiral stairs was a dome-shaped room as long as the Grand Hall. In the center of the room was a stone dais composed of three concentric circular tiers, with human skulls carved into the edges of each level. An imposing black stone pillar stood in the middle of the dais; its surface etched with strange hieroglyphic symbols. A thick chain was affixed to an iron ring halfway up the pillar, with leather cuffs attached to each end.

Kari took a step closer to the pillar and something sharp pricked her foot. She sucked in her breath and lifted her foot to find a black plastic nametag with the locking pin embedded in her skin. When she pulled it out blood welled up from the tiny hole and dripped on the floor. It might have been a trick of the light, but the blood seemed to be absorbed by the stone. Kari turned it over to read the name etched on the front in white.

## NIKO

She recalled the name as the waitress who had gone missing, the same one who had served them at Pagliai's. Closing the pin, she tucked the nametag into her clutch purse and stepped onto the dais. Kari shuddered as she imagined the poor woman chained to the pillar. On the other side of the room was a stone sarcophagus, like something from an ancient Egyptian tomb. She feared if the waitress had been murdered, her killer might have stuck her dead body inside.

A thin sheet of mist emerged between the lid and the base of the stone coffin. Kari backed away as the top of the sarcophagus lifted with a scrapping noise and shifted aside. The fog billowed out and spread over the floor, wrapping around her legs. A withered, pallid head rose from the opening and looked at her with blood-red eyes, its paper-thin lips pulling back in a fearsome smile to show elongated fangs.

*Karina, welcome home*

The skeletal horror had spoken to her inside her head, and the words were ringing in her ears as she went flying out of the chamber and back up the steps. She dropped the lantern, leaving her in total darkness as she felt her way back up the circular staircase. Kari's lungs were burning, and her legs were growing weak. She knew if she looked behind her, those awful red eyes would be right behind her. She stubbed her bare foot on a step and fell to her knees.

Kari tried to push herself up, but her arms and legs had no strength remaining. She closed her eyes and wrapped her arms around her head as she waited for the thing to attack. A hand closed around her shoulder, and Kari let out a yelp.

"Whoa, babe, it's me," Jack said. "Are you okay?"

Opening her eyes, she was standing before a painting of two horses by a pond mounted on a wood-paneled wall. Her husband was standing behind her, his face worried. She had escaped from the monster and ended up in the hallway outside the library.

"What...what happened?"

"I don't know, you went to the bathroom, but you've been gone for a while. I came to check on you and found you staring at this painting. Hey, where did your shoes go?"

Kari glanced down and saw she was barefoot. "I must have left them outside the bathroom. Can you get them for me?"

"No problem. Would you like some coffee? It might help sober you up."

"I'm not drunk, Jack. Can we go home, please?"

"Already?"

"Yes, I'm begging you. I don't want to be in this house anymore."

Jack opened his mouth as if to argue, but the look in her eyes must have persuaded him otherwise. "Okay, I'll tell Martin one of the kids got sick. Why don't you go out to the van, and I'll be right there."

Kari nodded and followed him to the front door. Her hands trembled as she tried to unlock the van, but she managed to press the button on the key fob after almost dropping it. She collapsed into the passenger seat and started sobbing. Kari had stemmed the tears by the time Jack arrived, but her mascara was running down her cheeks.

"What's going on?" Jack asked. "Did something happen in there?"

"I...I don't know how to explain it. I think I'm going crazy," she replied. "I went to use the bathroom but found this girl was crying in the basement. I tried to help her and ended up in this underground crypt. There was this thing in a coffin with glowing red eyes that knew my name. I ran away, and then you were shaking me. Maybe I did have too much to drink."

She looked over at him, expecting him to judge her or get angry for taking him away from his party. Instead, he remained silent, staring out the windshield at nothing. "I don't think it sounds crazy at all. I believe you." Hearing him say that caused her to burst into tears again, and he reached over and hugged her. "Let's go home."

He started the engine, put the van into gear, and headed down the hill towards the front gate. She hadn't told Jack that the girl in the dress had looked just like her when she was that age. Kari dug through her purse for a tissue to wipe off her makeup, but her hand closed around a plastic nametag. She pulled it out and let out a whimper when she saw the name.

## NIKO

Jack paced back and forth across the length of the basement, his mind a whirlwind as it sought to make sense of this new reality. If he woke up tomorrow in the Land of Oz wearing a dress and ruby slippers with Martin's four-legged killer canine, he wouldn't have been more surprised than right now. Learning witches and werewolves were real, let alone living in his own backyard, was shocking enough. Finding out that his in-laws were among them was truly mind-boggling. He would have to think twice before making any more mother-in-law jokes, even in private, for fear that Margrit would find out and turn him into a newt.

On top of which, Martin Knight might be harboring some sort of...undead creature. He hated himself for thinking it, but if he could somehow tie in the existence of witchcraft into his werewolf story, it could really give it that extra kick it needed. All he had to do was come up with a logical scenario to explain how both could co-exist without it coming across as ludicrous.

"Jack, can you please quit pacing!" Kari snapped. "You're giving me anxiety, and my nerves are already shot after tonight."

"Sorry, babe. It helps me think." He sat down in his office chair and scooted over to his wife, who was curled up in the old recliner. She looked less like a frightened animal than a dangerous snake coiled and ready to strike. "I didn't mean to upset you. Can I make you some herbal tea to help calm you down?"

"I almost got attacked by a monster tonight. I don't think tea is going to cut it."

"Well, I'd offer you a stiff drink, but I already poured out my secret stash," he said, and Kari glared at him. "Okay, sorry, bad joke. There's got to be something we can do about this."

"There is. We can call the police," she replied. "We show them the nametag, tell them it belonged to the waitress who disappeared and that I found it inside Mr. Knight's house. Maybe he's the one who kidnapped her."

"If all we have to give them is a nametag, I don't think they're going to take us seriously," Jack said. "I can't imagine that Martin would be going around killing people. It's too cliché to have a horror writer be an actual murderer. I think you should go talk to your parents and find out what they know. Let me handle the police. I might know someone who can help us out."

"Who would that be?"

"Detective Blackburn, he works for the Sheriff's Department. I met him doing research for my story, and he's killed a werewolf before."

"What? Why didn't you tell me about this? You knew werewolves were real?"

"I mean, it's not like I actually ran into one or anything," he replied. "When you're a horror writer, you have to know about these sorts of things."

Kellie walked down the spiral stone steps barefoot in her black robe. The last of the guests had finally left ten minutes ago, and she was eager to tell the Master what she had seen. She had no idea how *Little Miss Suzie Homemaker* had come into possession of the Amulet of Hauhet, but she didn't buy this story about some bookseller gifting it to her. Kellie wondered if the woman had any inkling of the kind of power she had at her fingertips, but she doubted it since she displayed it so casually. Or maybe the bitch was taunting her with it?

The Master would know what this meant and what to do about it. Kellie reached the bottom of the stairs and saw that the missing lantern was lying on the floor. She had been curious why the Sterlings had left so early. Now she understood the reason for it; the woman must have found her way down here to the Master's tomb.

She worried about what had transpired as she hurried into the chamber and removed her robe. The Master had been interred here beneath the manor when his mortal life had ended, but she was the one who had resurrected him into his true form. Kellie wasn't about to let some nosy cunt ruin her plans, especially since she decided she would ask the Master for Kari's body.

Completely nude, she approached the sarcophagus and knelt before it. She stretched out her arms and bowed down with her forehead touching the cold stone as she waited for the Master to emerge. Kellie jumped when an icy hand rested upon her bare shoulder, and she looked up to see a black-cloaked figure standing over her even though the coffin was still closed.

*Arise, my faithful servant.*

"Master, I didn't know you were awake," she said as she stood up. "I have excellent news. I found the Amulet of Hauhet."

*I know, it is worn by the woman who was down here.*

Kellie was shocked to hear him say that, but she tried to hide any emotion from her face. She was worried that he would blame her for the intrusion, even though she had no idea how Kari could have managed to do that...unless...

"What if she knows how to use it? She could change time and-"

*She was given the Amulet by my former apprentice at my direction.*

"Your apprentice? Is he still alive? Where is he?"

*I want you to begin preparations for performing the Ritual of Thule.*

"How can I do that? The Alchemist's Stone vanished along with Martin."

*Fear not, you will soon be reunited with it along with your beloved husband.*

"What about my body? When can you give me a new one?"

*Be patient, my faithful servant. You will receive your reward soon.*

"The Sterling woman, do you want me to have her brought here?"

*We will deal with her soon, but I must settle an old debt first. Summon the beast, I have a task for him.*

"Yes, Master, as you command."

*You have done well, granddaughter.*

# Call of the Wolves, Children in the Corn

Novel By **MARTIN KNIGHT**

Jupiter & Phoebus Publishing House

# CHAPTER 14
## Call of the Wolves, Children in the Corn

*August 30, 2019*

"*I* see," Margrit nodded. "Albert told you this, did he?"

Her father suddenly became very interested in his newspaper at the other end of the kitchen table. Kari had insisted on talking to her parents alone, so Jack was at home watching the kids and missing out on the most uncomfortable conversation of her life. Margrit sat drinking her cup of tea, her face perfectly calm, while Kari felt like ants were crawling under her skin. She forced herself to stop fidgeting with the bracelet on her wrist, which she hadn't figured out how to remove since she put it on for the dinner party.

"Please don't act like I'm crazy," she replied. "I saw dad turn into a werewolf, so enough with the lies. I want to know the truth."

"You're right, I should have told you," Margrit sighed. "I chose not to because I wanted you to have a normal life and not carry the same burden that we have all our lives. Nobody else can know what we really are. Normal people would fear us and kill us if they found out we're living among them."

"I mean, what would you have to be afraid of if you can just throw a fireball at anyone who wants to hurt you?"

"It doesn't work like that. I can manipulate people's thoughts and feelings to get them to do what I want. Or even forget things, but I can only do so much to protect our secret."

"So, if I'm a witch, why can't I do magic?"

Margrit looked down at her teacup, and Albert rustled his paper. "Tell her, or I will," her father said. Her mother shot him a dirty look, but then she sighed.

"Yes, you're a witch, but I blocked your abilities when you were a child."

"Why would you do that?"

Her mother opened her mouth to say something, but then she stopped herself.

"Because you are dangerous," Albert spoke up. "We couldn't take the chance of what you might be capable of."

"What's he talking about, mom?"

Kari was shocked to see tears in her eyes. "I'm sorry, I...I can't...I can't do this." She stood up from her chair and walked out of the room.

Albert reached out and took hold of her hand. "If you want to hear the truth, I will tell you, but you must understand something, *liebling*. It will not be easy to hear."

Kari stared into her father's eyes and saw something she hadn't expected. Fear. She tightened her grip on his hand. "Whatever it is, I need to hear it."

He nodded and cleared his throat. "Your mother and I used to work for Dr. Masterson."

"I know about that."

"Yes, but you don't know in what capacity. We did some bad things for him, although we thought we were doing so for the government. You see, after the war, Henry convinced the CIA to smuggle as many of the werewolves he created out of Germany as they could and bring them here, so we owed him our lives. Part of the bargain was that we would work for the CIA to help counter the werewolves that the Soviets captured. Dr. Masterson used us to do his own bidding, and he was also continuing his experiments. Your brother was just the first of what was supposed to be an entire army of werewolves."

"Oh my god, does Kurt know about this?"

"No, I don't believe so. Your mother killed Dr. Masterson before he could fulfill his plan. That wasn't the only twisted experiment he carried out. He was obsessed with one of your mother's ancestors, a witch named Geraldine, who was said to be the most powerful ever born. Dr. Masterson even started calling Margrit by the title she gave herself, the Queen of Sorrows."

"What? Why was she known as that?"

"She had powers no other witch possessed, like the ability to control fire with her magic," Albert replied. "The Salem Witch Trials were started because of her, but she was betrayed by her fellow witches in the Coven after she became too dangerous. Her death put an end to the witch hunts."

"Is mom that powerful?"

"No, but Henry thought since she was part of the Queen's bloodline, he might be able to draw out that power in her offspring." Albert stopped talking for a few moments, then took a deep breath. "You are my daughter, Karina, and nothing can ever change that, but Dr. Masterson is your biological father."

Jack stared at his typewriter but couldn't focus on his story. Although Kari had asked him to wait until she talked to her parents, he phoned Detective Blackburn as soon as she left. He had left him a voicemail, hoping the detective would call back before his wife returned home.

He heard footsteps on the stairs and turned to see his son coming down. "Hey, buddy, what are you up to?" Patrick reached the bottom of the steps, walked over to his desk, and held out something he was carrying. "What do you have there?"

"Book," he said as he handed Jack a paperback novel, then headed back upstairs. He flipped the book over to see the front cover and almost dropped it on the floor in his surprise. The title of the novel was *The Homecoming Queen of Sorrows* by Butch Richardson.

The artwork on the cover showed the backlit image of a mousy girl wearing a green dress, surrounded by a halo of disembodied heads with their mouths open as though laughing at her. He didn't recall Kari mentioning she had found a second book by the same obscure author she was fascinated by.

Jack had scoured the Internet for any reference to Butch Richardson, but he had come up empty-handed. That a novel published by this mysterious author would be titled with the phrase from his dream had to be more than a coincidence. He read the story blurb on the back, then flipped to the novel's last few pages and read the ending.

*A blinding light suddenly filled Cassie's vision, and she tried to raise her hands to block the spotlight pointed at her. Rough hands grabbed hold of her arms and pinned them to her sides. As her eyes adjusted to the brightness, she could see the crowd of students gathered in a half-circle around the charred body lying on the gymnasium floor. Cassie looked down at her once beautiful green dress and saw it was now covered with a sticky black substance and coated with feathers.*

*She tried to turn her head to see who was holding her, but a hand shot out and grabbed her roughly by the chin. Cassie looked up to see Suzannah glaring at her, murderous rage contorting her flawlessly beautiful face. In her other hand was an empty pillowcase with a few feathers still clinging to it.*

*"You fucking bitch! You killed my boyfriend!" Suzannah said, pointing at burnt corpse in front of the stage where they were standing. "We were just playing a prank, and that's what you do to him, you freak!" The girl let go of her chin and turned to face the crowd. "I TOLD YOU ALL WHAT SHE IS, DIDN'T I? SHE'S A GODDAMN WITCH! YOU ALL SAW WHAT SHE JUST DID! SHE AND HER MOTHER ARE THE DEVIL'S WHORES!"*

*All the students and even the teachers stared up at the stage in stunned silence, then one of the football players with dark, curly hair stepped up to the edge of the risers. "She's a fucking witch! Come on, let's burn her!"*

*"Yeah, burn her!"*

*"Burn her! Burn her!"*

*"BURN HER! BURN HER! BURN HER! BURN HER! BURN HER! BURN HER!"*

*The students took up the chant as the handful of teachers chaperoning them tried desperately to stop it, but they were no match for the bloodlust coursing through the angry mob. She was picked up off the ground and unceremoniously slung over a football player's shoulder. Cassie tried to hit and kick him, but he held her legs at the knees, and her fists did nothing to deter him. The frenzied mob surrounded her as she was carried over to the metal post where one of the basketball hoops was mounted.*

*Somebody produced a rope, and her arms and legs were bound to the post as the wooden tables and chairs set out for the dance were broken up to form a pile of kindling around her feet. Suzannah appeared holding a bottle of vodka with a rag stuffed into the opening. She handed the bottle to the guy beside her, then pulled out a pack of cigarettes and a lighter from inside her bra.*

*"Let me go!" Cassie cried. "Why are you doing this, Suzannah?"*

*"Because you killed my boyfriend, and you don't belong here."*

*"I just wanted to be your friend. You told me I would be elected Homecoming Queen."*

*"Nobody here wants to be friends with someone like you," the girl laughed as she flicked the lighter.*

*"No, stay away from me!" she called out. "Momma, help me!"*

*Her mother's words to her as she left for the dance came back to her.* "They do not want to be your friend, you stupid girl. They are going to turn on you as soon as they learn that you are a witch."

*"Your mother can't help you, it's time to die, princess."*

*Suzannah lit the rag in the bottle on fire, and that's when she started laughing. Cassie finally understood the question that Mr. Haggard, the bookstore owner, had posed to her when he sold her the fairytale book* The Princess and The Witch *as a little girl. The kindly old man had asked her which one of the two she really wanted to be when she grew up. All along, she had been sure she wanted to be the sister who escaped from the poor, rundown cottage in the woods and became a princess instead of the sister who stayed behind and learned how to be a witch. In the end, the princess is still unhappy and feels powerless and trapped in her castle, while the witch is happy because everyone fears her, and she becomes ruler of the forest. The witch proclaims herself as the Queen of Sorrows.*

*"I am not a princess. I am a queen," Cassie said. "The Homecoming Queen of Sorrows, the most powerful witch to ever live, and you will all die in agony."*

*Still holding the burning cocktail, Suzannah stepped back at the maniacal laughter coming out of Cassie's mouth. The flame flared up, and the girl yelped as she dropped the bottle on the floor. The glass shattered, creating a burning puddle that spread across the waxed floorboards towards the pile of debris at her feet. Before it could ignite the pyre, the flames turned from red to green. The fire started swirling and growing as it began to form into the rough shape of a winged, long-necked dragon. The crowd that a few moments ago had been calling for her death was suddenly scrambling to get through the exits. She reached out with her mind, and all the doors to the gymnasium slammed shut.*

*"VERBRENNE SIE!" she yelled to the dragon, which unleashed an inferno upon the mob. Cassie's laughter was lost in the screams of terror as flames engulfed the entire school. When the fire was finally extinguished, there were no survivors—except for one girl, unharmed and unburnt.*

Jack shut the book and turned it around to view the cover again. On a second look, the people surrounding the girl seemed not to be laughing so much as screaming. He was wondering why his son had brought this book down to him when his cell phone rang. The caller ID on the screen showed it was Edgar.

"Hello, Detective Blackburn. I have something you need to see. Can I meet you somewhere?"

"I'm a bit busy today, Jack. Can this wait until tomorrow?"

"It's about that missing waitress, I found her nametag in Martin Knight's house. You know, the one that used to belong to Dr. Masterson."

There was a pause at the other end. "Okay, I'll stop by your house as soon as I can." The line went dead, and Jack set his phone down on the desk. He wanted to take care of this business with Blackburn without him meeting Kari. Jack hadn't told her about his nightmare where he met the post-apocalyptic version of Edgar, or the walking weapon of mass destruction who looked just like his wife. He didn't know whether Detective Blackburn remembered that part of the dream, but he was afraid the man might put a bullet between Kari's eyes if he saw her.

Jack knew such a thought was ridiculous, but he still felt nervous when the doorbell rang about thirty minutes later. The detective was wearing jeans and a polo shirt, but also had a gun holstered on his hip. He invited the man inside and led him into the kitchen.

"What have you got for me?" Edgar asked. Jack retrieved a clear plastic baggie from the cupboard and handed it to him. He held it up and examined the black rectangular nametag inside it. The detective nodded and looked at Jack with those intense blue eyes. "Where exactly did you say she found it?"

"This is going to sound strange, but we were at Martin Knight's estate for a party. I went to use the restroom and happened to find it in a stairwell leading down to the basement."

"And you didn't think to call the police right then, or go see if she was down there?"

"I...I guess I didn't connect the name to the missing girl until later when we returned home."

"I suppose that's understandable. If I didn't know better, though, I'd have the CSI team here digging up your backyard," Edgar said. "What do you expect me to do with this? There's no way I can take this to a judge and get a search warrant based on that."

"I get that, but there has to be something you can do."

"I'll investigate and see if there is a connection," he sighed. "What I need you to do is stay out of it. You've put your life and your family at risk enough. If they come after you, I don't know if I'll be able to protect you."

Albert pulled into the parking lot behind the Yoke and Plow restaurant, shut off his truck's engine, and looked through the dusty windshield at the building. The restaurant was closed until four, but a dozen vehicles were in the parking lot. He approached the back door and knocked on it, and the owner's wife unlocked it for him.

"Hello, Albert, good to see you again," the woman said. "Everyone else is already here."

That was unusual as the Elders were never early for council meetings, even emergency ones. "You know me, I'll be late to my funeral."

"And probably drunk for it, too. Can I get you a beer? How about a steak? They're cut fresh and still bloody."

"You know all the right words to say, *liebling*," he chuckled. "I'll take an Altbier and my steak raw as usual."

She led him into the main dining room where the other twelve Elders were already gathered, seated around three tables that had been pushed together to form a long one. All of them were busy biting off chunks of flesh from the uncooked marbled steaks they were holding, blood running down their jaws and pooling on the plates, pausing only to chug from their frosty mugs of dark German beer.

The scent of fresh blood in the air filled his nostrils and woke the ravenous hunger within him that he kept suppressed most of the time. It had taken years to learn how to control it, and letting it out while alone in the company of his brethren was still dangerous as it yearned to be let free to devour relentlessly. Even after all these years, it was hard to be around normal humans and not want to tear them to pieces, but that was the burden and price of living among them.

The Elders were the thirteen remaining werewolves smuggled out of Germany after World War II. There had initially been twenty of them, but seven had died over the years. He had been forced to kill one of them himself, Elias, who had been the same age as him when they had been turned into wolves. At age eight, the two of them were the oldest of the orphans Dr. Heinrich von Meister had used for his experiments. Their transformation allowed them to heal from almost any injuries and slowed their aging process. Despite being eighty-six years old, he only appeared to be middle-aged. More or less.

The Elders had left him an open seat at the head of the table, and a slab of meat and a cold beer were soon set before him. "It has been too long since we last got together, Albert," Karl Yoder said, runnels of blood flowing down his bearded chin. "I doubt you called us here just to share a meal. What's on your mind?"

"Brothers and sisters, we have been through many hardships," Albert announced. "We have fought and suffered together, survived a war, and made a haven to raise our families in peace. All of that is in danger, threatened by an old enemy we trusted but who used us for his own purposes. Dr. Henry Masterson has come back from the dead, and I mean to put him in his grave for good or die trying. This time, we must fight him on our own. There will be no witches to save us."

"That's nonsense. He's been dead for thirty years," Walther Hagen replied. "How would that even be possible?"

"I don't know, but I doubt he could have resurrected himself. Somebody has been helping him, and we've seen that person's handiwork."

"You're talking about those two women who went missing?" Rebecca Abrams spoke up. "Do you think that was Masterson's doing?"

"Yes, his hand was in it, but I'm convinced a werewolf took them."

The entire table stopped eating and turned to look at him. "Are you accusing someone here of these crimes?" Walther asked.

"No, I believe my son, Kurt, is responsible," Albert replied. "I have called you together because I cannot bring myself to do what is needed if he is guilty."

"Perhaps he had good cause for what he has done," Walther answered. "What if helping the Alchemist will bring us real freedom? Imagine a world where we must no longer hide, where it is the wolves who rule and the humans who are hunted and live in fear."

"What? What are...you saying?" Albert asked, his words slurring. His nose caught a faint hint of something in the beer that didn't belong. "No, what...what have...you done...We must...we must...stop...stop him..."

"I told you he wouldn't go along with us," Walther said. "That damn witch has made him forget where his loyalties should be."

"My father will come to his senses," a new voice spoke up. Albert's vision blurred, but he recognized his son's voice easy enough. "Don't worry, dad, I have something that will help you see the truth."

The two men sitting to either side of Albert grabbed hold of his arms. He tried to struggle against them, but his strength was fading. Kurt approached and placed a thick metal collar around his neck. A silver, crescent-shaped medallion dangled from the collar. When it touched Albert's skin, his head exploded in pain. He jumped to his feet, freeing his arms from their grasp. Albert tried to run for the exit, but the room started spinning, and he collapsed onto the floor. Kurt bent down and looked him in the eyes as they clouded over.

"Nighty-night, father. I think you'll see things my way when you wake up."

Margrit paced about the kitchen, holding a lukewarm cup of coffee. She usually enjoyed having the house to herself when Albert was out, not having to hear him grumble about the weather, politics, the Cubs losing again, or grabbing her ass. Even at her age, she didn't mind that last one, but she often kept a wood serving spoon close by to crack him on the knuckles if he got too handsy. He had left to meet with the Elders four hours ago and wasn't answering his phone.

A black Lincoln Towncar pulled into the driveway, and Margrit felt a nervous flutter in her chest. She peeked out the kitchen window and was surprised to see her daughter-in-law step out of the passenger's seat. Jessica knocked on the screen door twice before she opened it and poked her head in. "Hello, is anyone home?"

"Yes, come in, dear. Would you like some coffee?"

"No thanks, I just stopped in to borrow some eggs," she replied, but Margrit thought her eyes looked red. "I was going to bake a cake tonight and ran out. I hope you don't mind, but I didn't want to drive into town."

"Of course, don't be silly," Margrit answered as she went to the refrigerator. "Whose car is that? Don't tell me Kurt talked you into trading in the van."

She stood up with the container of eggs in her hands to find Jessica aiming a black device that looked like a flashlight at her chest. There was a loud popping noise, and she felt her body go rigid as two long wires shot out and hooked into her skin through her shirt. The electrical jolt caused her to drop the egg carton and fall to the ground. Jessica hurried over and bound her wrists behind her back with handcuffs, then gagged her with a flour sack towel.

Her ears were ringing, but she heard the screen door slam shut. She twisted around to see a middle-aged woman in a business suit walk into her kitchen. "Hello, Margrit. It's so nice to finally meet you."

"I'm sorry, mom. I didn't have a choice," Jessica whispered before standing up. She bowed her head to the female stranger and backed away to stand against the kitchen cabinets. The woman bent over so that she was staring down into her face.

"I bet you're wondering where your traitor husband is. Don't worry, he's alive, but he will need to be retrained to obey. On the other hand, you have committed too egregious a crime to go unpunished. Even if you are the mother of the Master's daughter." From behind her back, she pulled out a knife with a thin, zig-zagged blade and placed it against Margrit's neck. "For betraying and murdering the Master, you deserve to die."

"No, you promised-" Jessica protested, but the woman pulled out a gun and pointed it at her.

"Shut up, you stupid cunt!" the woman snapped. "Do as your husband told you, or I'll gut your fucking children in front of you."

"You're...you're not from the Coven, are you."

"Who said I was?" the woman laughed. "Go bring the car up closer."

Jessica hesitated, then hurried out the back door. Margrit was not ready for her life to end, but she would not let this bitch see any sign of fear in her eyes as she died. The businesswoman smiled as she pressed the knife against her throat, drawing a trickle of blood, before she took it away.

"You're lucky the Master wants you alive until we have control of your daughter," she said. "After that, you'll be wishing I had slit your throat and left you to bleed out." Margrit worried about what they wanted to do to Kari as the woman took out a syringe from her purse and injected it into her arm, plunging her into unconsciousness.

Detective Blackburn had followed the black and red Dodge pickup since it left the Plow and Yoke. He had trailed Kurt Ulmer from his house to the restaurant, which had seemed an odd destination since it was closed until dinner time. However, several other vehicles were in the parking lot, and Kurt parked near the back door before walking inside. Edgar pulled his truck behind a nearby business where he could view the parking lot. He opened the glove box, took out a leather case, and removed a rigid plastic container about the size of a book from inside it. Flipping up the latch, he switched on the GPS tracker connected to the battery pack and closed the lid.

He had long suspected Kurt of being a werewolf. The kid had been a troublemaker in high school but always managed to slip away before getting caught. When he had enlisted in the Marines and left for Afghanistan, there had been a noticeable drop in crime around the Ahnen Villages area. Edgar had kept an eye on his military career through some old friends he had in the Corps. Despite being a fuck-up in school, the kid could have earned himself a doctorate in killing if they handed those out. He had volunteered for some of the most dangerous assignments and come back from them without a scratch, even when most of the other soldiers returned severely wounded or in body bags.

Edgar got out and walked over to the Dodge truck, glanced around to be sure he wasn't being watched, and then attached the magnetic container inside the rear wheel well. Not even five minutes later, Kurt and an older man came out carrying a third man who appeared drunk between them. They helped him over to Ulmer's truck and put him in the cab's rear seat, and then the old guy went back inside. Kurt lit up a cigarette before climbing into his truck and driving off. Edgar brought up the GPS application on his cell phone, and the map on the screen showed a red triangle that denoted the tracker's position.

Kurt had apparently been called to the restaurant to pick up a drunk patron, most likely his father, and was taking him back home. The blip turned onto the main road, then it veered into the nearby gas station and stopped. Edgar watched until the blip started moving again, heading east along the Ahnen Trek. He waited for the marker to get a half mile down the road and then pulled out of the parking lot. With the tracker, he could maintain his distance without worrying about losing his quarry.

Edgar reached underneath the bench seat to grab the lever-action rifle chambered in .45-70 Government and a leather gun belt holstering a pair of Colt Single-Action Army revolvers. All three guns had been given to him by his father when he passed away and had belonged to his grandfather when he was a Texas Ranger. The bullets they were loaded with were hollow points he had capped with silver to make them lethal for werewolves. The metal itself wasn't fatal to them. Instead, it countered the effects of their healing so that whatever wound they received couldn't close. It still took a lot of firepower to bring the bastards down, so he trusted nothing smaller than a .45 caliber round.

About twenty minutes later, the marker turned off onto a side road leading towards Coralville Lake. He stepped on the accelerator and closed the distance, turning onto the road and following it along until he could see the lake ahead. Edgar pulled off onto a grassy area, shut off the engine, and strapped on the gun belt. He picked up the rifle, stepped out of his truck, and used the trees to cover his approach.

A Dodge pickup truck was driving back up the boat ramp, but it was blue and white. Detective Blackburn checked his phone and saw that the marker was now located out in the open water, right where a fishing boat was floating beside a pier near the ramp. The pickup stopped and a shirtless man with a beer gut and cut-off jean shorts hopped out to join the bikini-clad woman (*who had no business wearing a two-piece swimsuit*) in the boat.

"Son of a bitch."

Jack knew he could be oblivious to other people's feelings, but even he noticed something was bothering his wife. Kari had barely said a word about what happened with her parents, but he could tell she had been crying from the redness in her eyes. He decided it was best to give her some space until she was ready to talk about it. Jack debated telling her he had met with Detective Blackburn, but that could also wait.

He put the kids to bed like normal, and when he came downstairs, he heard her sobbing through their locked bedroom door. Jack had tried contacting Detective Blackburn again, but it just went to voicemail. He was about to give him another call when his cell dinged with a text message from a blocked number.

> You're going to want to take this call, Mr. Sterling

Just as he finished reading the message, his phone rang. The screen showed it was from an Unknown Caller. He stared at it for a moment then pressed the button to accept the call.

"Hello?"

"Professor Sterling, I presume. I'm afraid we haven't had the chance to meet in person, but I know your wife quite well. My name is Ryland Thynne."

"Thynne? You're the bookstore owner?"

"Yes, we don't have much time, so I'll get to the point," Ryland replied. "Your family is in danger. The Alchemist is coming for your wife tonight. She is his daughter, and he intends to kidnap her and your children after killing you."

"I'm sorry, what? How would you know that? Are you working for him?"

"No, John, I've tried many times to stop him, but so far, nothing I do has been able to change the story," he answered. "You only have about five minutes before a pack of werewolves descends upon your house. If you want to live and save your family, do exactly as I say."

"You're not making any sense. Change what story?"

"Please don't interrupt. You need to get your family out through the basement. Your father-in-law will buy you time to escape, use it to head for the cornfield. Detective Blackburn should catch up with you. You must not forget to grab the black box sitting on your desk. If you can't rescue them, find the imprint of a crescent moon on the cube. Insert the pendant from the collar and rotate it counterclockwise."

"Is this some sort of joke?"

"I wish I had time to explain everything. I'm the one who left the trunk you found in the attic. Until I find a way to defeat the Alchemist, you must prevent the story from proceeding past this night. Hopefully Detective Blackburn will stop him this time, but if not you will need to use the Alchemist's Stone to reset it to the beginning."

"You're talking nonsense. Why should I believe a word of this?"

"If you want to keep your wife from becoming the Queen of Sorrows, you have to trust me. I can't help you any further than that. Good luck, Mr. Sterling."

The call ended, and Jack ran to the living room window to look outside. The sun had already set, but the moon provided enough light for him to see that the front yard was empty. Mr. Thynne was clearly off his rocker, but the fact that he knew about the Queen of Sorrows disturbed Jack the most. If there was a chance his family was in danger, he had to get them to safety.

"Kari?" he called out through the bedroom door, but she didn't respond. "Kari, I need you to come out!"

Jack bounded up the stairs two at a time and opened the door to Jenny's bedroom. "Sweetie, come on, there's some bad weather coming. We're going to the basement for a while."

"Where's mommy?"

"Come on, honey, we need to get your brother." He rushed down the hall to Patrick's room, carrying Jenny in his arms. His son was standing at his window looking out at the yard. "There's a storm coming, buddy. Can you follow me to the basement?"

"Daddy, monster," Patrick whispered without turning around. Jack set his daughter on the floor and peered through the window over his son's head. Even in the moonlight, it was hard to make out the dark form lurking under the branches of the large elm tree. Jack spotted glowing amber eyes looking back at him before he pulled Patrick away from the window. He scooped up Jenny and took his son's hand, hurrying them down the steps. His wife was standing in the hallway when they reached the bottom of the stairs.

"Jack, what's wrong? Why are you shouting?"

"We need to get to the basement," he replied. "Don't argue with me, let's go!"

The motion-sensor light on the porch turned on a moment before something slammed into the front door. Jack heard wood splintering, but the door held. Kari grabbed Patrick, and they ran for the basement as the next blow struck. They made it to the kitchen as a shadow blocked out the moonlight coming in through the back door's window.

Jack rushed his wife and kids into the basement before the window exploded inward. He grabbed the butcher knife from the wooden block on the counter as a lumbering, gray-haired beast threw open the door and stepped into the kitchen. He tried to keep his hands from shaking as he held out the knife, blocking the door to the basement with his body. The werewolf moved closer, and Jack lunged at the beast. It swatted his hand away and knocked the knife to the floor.

He stepped back and held up his hands in a last-ditch attempt to protect himself. To his surprise, the werewolf picked up the knife and held it out to him. Jack hesitantly took hold of the handle as the beast bent down and pointed at a thick metal collar around its neck. He considered thrusting the blade into the thing's neck, but instead he wedged the knife into the gap in the metal and cut through the leather strap holding it together. The collar fell to the floor, and the werewolf stood up to its full height. It rounded on him and barred a set of yellowed fangs.

# RRRUUUUUUNNNNNN

The wolf's growl sounded almost familiar. A loud crash announced the front door being smashed open, and the gray-haired werewolf rushed down the hallway. He heard snarling, fighting, and furniture breaking but didn't stick around to find out who would win. Jack hurried through the basement door and locked it behind him.

His family wasn't in the cellar, and the door to the outside steps stood ajar. Jack bounded up the cellar stairs, but there was no sign of his wife or children. His foot stepped on something soft, and he picked up Jenny's stuffed cat.

"KARI! JENNY! PATRICK!" he called out. It wasn't a human voice that answered him but a chorus of blood-chilling howls seeming to come from all directions. "The call of the wolves," he murmured, then ran down the driveway. Jack reached the highway and stared at the dense fortress of green stalks on the other side of the road.

It was nearly impossible to see in the moonlight, but he spotted a row that showed signs of being disturbed by somebody running through it. Jack sprinted up the road and plunged into the cornfield, holding his arms up in front of his face to protect himself from the blade-like leaves. He hoped what the ghost woman had told him was true and his family was somewhere in the corn. Even if he managed to find them, Jack had no idea how he would get them out alive.

"Kari, this way! Hurry!"

The shock of seeing a werewolf break into her kitchen had left her unable to comprehend at first that her sister-in-law was standing in her basement. Kari was still carrying her daughter and holding onto her son's wrist for dear life. Patrick tugged his arm out of her grip and rubbed it where she had left red marks on his skin.

"Jessica? How did you get in here?"

"We don't have time; Kurt's lost his mind. We need to go!"

"I can't leave Jack..."

"He would want you to get to safety. Come on!"

Jessica led her up the outside steps and down the driveway. When they reached the highway, she was out of breath, but her sister-in-law didn't stop. Instead, she crossed the road and took them into the cornfield.

"Where are we going? I need to call the police!"

The sound of inhuman howls filled the night air and caused Jenny to wrap her arms around her neck tighter, nearly strangling her.

"The police can't help us. We need to get to safety."

Jessica clinched Patrick's wrist in her hand and pulled him along. Kari had no choice but to chase after her, cradling Jenny's head against her chest to protect her from the leaves slicing at them as they ran between the rows. After getting several scratches on her arms and neck, she was about to yell for Jessica to stop when they reached a clearing in the middle of the field. All the corn stalks here had been bent over at the base to form a perfect circle, and on the opposite side was the football uniform-clad scarecrow.

"What are we doing, Jessica? Jack is in danger; we need to get help."

"I'm sorry, Kari, they won't harm your children," her sister-in-law said. "That's the best I could do for you. She threatened to kill my kids."

There was a rustling noise from the other side of the circle as Margrit stepped out of the corn with a gag tied around her mouth and her arms behind her back. A woman in a black-hooded cloak walked behind her, holding a knife to her mother's throat.

"Mom? Jessica, what the hell is this?"

"Come over here, Mrs. Sterling," the woman ordered, forcing Margrit to her knees in front of the scarecrow. "I won't ask you a second time."

She approached the center of the circle, and the woman motioned for her to kneel. Kari gasped when the woman drew blood from Margrit's neck and dropped to her knees. The woman threw back her hood to reveal that she was Professor Wilkens.

"Hold out your arm," Kellie said, "the one with the bracelet."

She remembered the woman taking an interest in the bracelet Mr. Thynne had given her. If she wanted it so badly Kari would have gladly handed it over, except she had no idea how to remove it unless she cut off her own hand. She worried that was what Kellie intended to do as she approached her with the knife held out.

Instead, the woman wrapped her own hand around the blade and drew it downward, slicing open her palm and releasing a trickle of blood that landed on Kari's wrist. The rubies began to pulse with a red glow and the bracelet constricted even further on her wrist until it was downright painful. Kari tried to yank her arm away, but she couldn't move her body anymore.

"The one who walks in shadows approaches," the crazed woman announced. "The Master is here!"

Tendrils of mist snaked out from beneath the flattened corn, coalescing into a pillar of smoke. The black cloud solidified as it formed into a humanoid shape. When the last wisp of dark vapor had conjoined with the pooling mass, two glowing red eyes appeared from the depths of the blackness.

*Margrit, my betrayer, I have returned to deliver my vengeance upon you!*

Her mother twisted around as best she could to look at her with a mixture of fear and sadness. Kari tried with all her strength to stand up, but her body would no longer obey her will. She could only watch helplessly as the shadow wrapped itself around Margrit. Kari could only hear a few muffled cries from within the darkness before it evaporated and left behind her mother's lifeless body lying on the bent stalks of corn.

*Karina, my daughter, my Queen of Sorrows*

The disembodied voice spoke to her from within her head. She recognized it from the crypt beneath Devonshire Manor. It belonged to her father, or whatever nightmare existence he had taken on. Kellie knelt beside Margrit's pale body and plunged her knife into her mother's chest.

"Leave...her...alone..." Kari managed to force her jaw to move enough to get out.

"Don't worry, dear, you'll soon be joining her," Kellie said as she stood up and wrapped a white silk scarf around her injured hand. "I'm not going to kill you, though, not your body anyway. That I will take for myself, along with all your powers."

"No! Don't hurt my mommy!" Jenny shouted as she broke free of Jessica's grasp and ran over to Kari. Her daughter stood between her and the black-robed woman, shielding her with her tiny body.

"Get that brat under control," Professor Wilkens hissed at Jessica.

"This wasn't part of our agreement; you said nobody was going to die," Jessica sobbed, still holding onto Patrick.

"I'll take care of this myself," Kellie snapped, and Kari could see her reach inside her robe for something. Jenny threw her arms around her neck, which gave Kari a better view of what was happening. Kellie had taken out a pistol and was walking towards them. Her body remained frozen, but the bracelet on her wrist suddenly became very cold.

She could still turn her eyes and look down at it. The jewels were glowing even brighter than before, and an aura of red light had formed around her and her daughter. Kellie had to raise her hand to shield her eyes as it grew to a blinding intensity. "What are you doing? Stop that right now!"

The last thing Kari saw was a burst of wind lashing out to send Kellie flying backwards. The darkness swallowed them, and she was falling...

falling...

falling...

The wind was so strong that it forced Jack to drop to the ground and cover his head until it passed. He had heard about such straight-line windstorms popping up in the Midwest without warning. There was even a name for them (*doritos?*) that he couldn't recall. He doubted this storm was natural, but that wasn't about to stop him from finding his family. Jack lifted his head and pushed off the pile of broken corn stalks on top of him.

He came into a clearing where his sister-in-law knelt on the ground with Patrick standing beside her. Jack raced over to hug his son, then turned to face Jessica.

"What are you doing here? Where's Kari? Oh dear god, Margrit? What happened?"

Jessica turned to him with tears running down her cheeks. "They killed her! This wasn't supposed to happen."

"Who's they? Where the hell is my wife? Jenny...where's Jenny? Are they..."

He couldn't bring himself to voice the thought that came to him, but Jessica shook her head.

"No, I don't think they're hurt," she answered him. "They...they just vanished. There was a woman, I thought she was from the Coven. She did this to mom."

Before he could get a coherent explanation out of her, he heard something crashing through the cornfield.

"We need to get out of here," he said.

Jack put himself between Patrick and whatever was barreling towards them, not that he had any way to fight it off. A ragged, bloodied werewolf lurched into the clearing; its right arm nearly severed at the shoulder. He feared that the beast was about to tear them apart until he saw a patch of graying fur on its chest.

"Albert? It's Jack, do you know who I am?"

The anger drained from the werewolf's eyes as whatever part of its mind was still human pushed back against the animalistic instinct to kill. Jack kept his son behind him as the werewolf approached the body lying on the ground. Albert knelt beside Margrit, cradled her lifeless body in his working arm, and threw back his head to let out a mournful howl.

Jack heard a rustling of corn stalks and turned to see the barrel of a rifle emerge between the plants.

"No, wait!" he yelled. The shot was a deafening thunderclap at that range, and the muzzle flash blinded him briefly. When his vision recovered, Jack saw a second body lying on the bed of corn, this one half-human and half-wolf. Albert had slumped over next to his dead wife, reverting from his werewolf form as his lifeblood drained out and seeped into the earth. Jack didn't realize he was yelling until the sound returned to his ears.

"Sterling!" Detective Blackburn hollered at him, grabbing his shoulder. "We need to go!"

"You just shot my father-in-law."

"I'm sorry. I thought he was going to attack you. We're dead if the others find us here. We need to get out of here."

"They've left," Jessica said. "The other werewolves are gone. I can't sense them any-more."

Edgar regarded her with his cold eyes. "I'll still feel better when we're out of this fucking place."

"I have to make sure my kids are safe," Jessica replied. "I'm very sorry about everything." She turned and fled into the cornfield, but Edgar didn't make a move to stop her.

The three of them crept back through the cornfield to his house, the detective keeping his rifle at the ready the entire time. The living room was ground zero of an indoor tornado that had wreaked havoc on every piece of furniture in sight. The couch was mostly intact and Jack flipped it over for Patrick to sit down on.

"I checked the rest of the house, it's clear," the detective said. "I'm going to wait on the porch for backup to arrive. Keep an eye out in case any wolves come back."

He sat down on the staircase, suddenly exhausted. Patrick seemed no worse for wear, giggling as he watched a video on his tablet.

"Are you ok, buddy?" Jack asked. "Did you get hurt?"

"Box," Patrick answered. "Black box."

Jack didn't understand what he meant, then he remembered the metal cube on his desk. He had forgotten to grab it in the chaos, so it was hopefully still downstairs. Edgar was talking on his phone on the front steps, so Jack snuck down to the basement. His desk had been knocked over, but he managed to locate the black box underneath a stack of scattered papers.

He found the collar Albert had been wearing on the kitchen floor and pried the pendant from it. Jack turned the cube around until he spotted a crescent-shaped outline on the surface. It matched the pendant perfectly, and he tried to remember which way Ryland had told him to turn it (*righty-tighty or lefty-loosey?*). Jack was about to twist it when Patrick came into the kitchen and snatched the box from his hands.

"Hey, what are you doing?"

"That's wrong," his son said. Patrick flipped it around and rotated one of the corners. A compartment popped open in the center, and his son reached inside to pull out an antique brass key that he handed to Jack.

"What's this for?"

"Door," Patrick told him, then pointed towards the open kitchen door. Jack went over and peered out into the darkness. Sure enough, a free-standing doorframe with a blood-red door had appeared in the backyard, just like in his fever dream.

"You want me to open that?" he asked his son, and Patrick nodded.

Jack sighed as he walked down the steps and approached the strange portal. He inserted the key into the lock, turned the knob, and opened the door.

# How I Met Your Dead Mother In The Twilight Zone

Novel By **MARTIN KNIGHT**

Jupiter & Phoebus Publishing House

# CHAPTER 15
## How I Met Your Dead Mother In The Twilight Zone

*October 22, 2019*

John Sawyer groaned as the alarm on his cell phone went off, stabbing a red-hot poker into his brain and igniting what would surely be a record-setting hangover. What the hell had he been thinking, going out to celebrate on a weeknight and getting smashed. He needed to get Patrick to school on time and slug through three lectures today.

A call from his literary agent that his novel had cracked the New York Times Best Sellers List had instigated the impromptu and ill-advised revelry. While it was far from the top of the list and probably wouldn't last longer than a week, it was still a victory and an important recognition. This was his third novel to be published, but the first time he got anywhere near the best-seller list. The previous books sold well enough, but this one would hopefully allow him to ensure Patrick was taken care of for the rest of his life. That was the greatest measure of success.

He silenced his phone before rolling over. A hand touched his bare chest, and he popped his head up to see a beautiful Asian woman lying beside him with her eyes closed. She had a streak of purple in her long black hair and a crescent moon tattoo on the back of her shoulder. He thought she looked familiar, but John was sure he'd never met her before last night.

"Hmmmph...unnnggh," she mumbled, half asleep. John peeked under the sheets to see She was completely nude. From what little he could remember; they had engaged in some after-party activities. How in the world was he going to explain this to Kathy? She would divorce him, and rightly so. Except she had been dead for almost eight years.

Johnny sat straight up in bed, pulling the covers off the sleeping woman and launching his headache into the stratosphere. The memory of his late wife did wonders to sober him up quickly, but for a minute he was sure she was still alive. Kathy had died in a car crash two years after Patrick was born. The two of them were on a weekend getaway in Maine when a deer jumped out in front of their car, causing Johnny to swerve and smash into a tree.

Kathy's parents had taken care of Patrick during the three months he was in a coma. Before the accident, he had been unsure of what he wanted to do in his career, wishing he could stay in college as long as possible. Once he recovered, he became determined to get his shit together and make it as a published author.

Johnny heard footsteps coming down the hallway and threw the sheet back over his naked guest before Patrick tried the doorknob and thankfully found it locked. He tried to get out of bed and found that his left wrist was shackled to the headboard by a pair of pink fur-covered handcuffs. Apparently, his one-night stand had a taste for kinky sex, which he wasn't opposed to but was rather inconvenient now. Luckily, she had left the key for the cuffs on the nightstand, and he unlocked the restraint before hurrying to collect his clothes off the floor.

"Time for breakfast," Patrick announced through the door.

"Okay, buddy, daddy will be right out," Johnny replied, and he heard his son walk away.

"Hey...hey...I need you to wake up," he said, gently shaking the woman. She turned her head and looked up at him with one bleary eye. "I'm very sorry, but I need you to get up and head out. There's a shower in the bathroom. I'll make you some coffee and breakfast if you feel up to eating."

"Ungh, where am I? Who are you?"

"I'm Johnny," he replied. "We met at a party last night, and I guess we ended up back at my apartment together."

"Oh fuck, my head is pounding," she groaned as she sat up in bed, letting the sheet drop to her waist. Johnny handed her the button-up shirt he had been wearing last night, then went into the bathroom to brush his teeth before leaving to make his son's breakfast.

Patrick was giggling at videos of funny animal antics on his tablet. Johnny put the skillet on the stove, cracked some eggs, and fetched the bag of store-bought pancakes out of the freezer. The one skill he had never picked up was cooking beyond scrambling eggs and making grilled cheese sandwiches. Patrick didn't complain as the menu of foods he tolerated was only ten deep, most of which were microwave-ready meals. His son would be eating much healthier if Kathy was around to cook for him.

Johnny heard the bedroom door open, and his overnight guest walked into the kitchen still only wearing his button-up shirt, which was thankfully long enough to preserve her modesty. "Oh, I didn't know you had a son," she said. "I'll go find my clothes."

"It's okay. Patrick, this is daddy's new friend, um..."

"Niko, nice to meet you, Patrick."

"Not mommy. Niko go home," his son said without looking up from his tablet. Niko glanced at Johnny with an alarmed expression.

"Don't worry, I'm not married anymore. He has autism, so there's usually no filter on what he says. My wife has been...gone for eight years. Can I make you something to eat?"

"Um, I don't know if that would be a good idea," she replied. "I wouldn't mind a cup of coffee if that's alright?"

"Of course, I'll get it for you. How do you take it?"

"Black is fine." Johnny took down two mugs and filled them up, then handed one of the cups to Niko. His phone vibrated in his pocket, and the notification on the screen showed he had a new voicemail. He had put it on silent and hadn't felt it buzz while cooking. It was probably some telemarketer, but he was curious since the phone number was from Massachusetts, where his in-laws lived. Unlocking his phone, he played the voicemail and put it up to his ear to listen.

*Hello, Mr. Sawyer. This is Vivian Knight, Martin's wife. We met once when he was teaching at the University of Iowa. Call me when you get this. I have an important opportunity to discuss with you. Thank you.*

"I don't mean to take advantage of you, but could you keep an eye on Patrick while I return this phone call?" he asked.

"Of course," Niko replied.

Johnny returned to the bedroom and redialed the most recent number from the call log. He let it ring several times and was about to hang up when a woman answered.

"Hello? Is this John?"

"Yes, Mrs. Knight, sorry I missed your call earlier," he answered.

"That's quite alright. I hope I didn't catch you at a bad time?"

"No, not at all," Johnny said. "I was devastated when I heard about your husband's accident. Is he doing any better?"

"Martin's still in a coma, I'm afraid," she said. "This may sound rather strange given the circumstances, but I would like to carry on with the annual writer's retreat that Martin holds every October. I know this is short notice, but you were one of his favorite students, and I was hoping to enlist your participation."

"You mean at your house in Massachusetts? I would love to attend, but I'll have to talk to my boss first. I have classes that I'd need to find another professor to cover. I would also have to get somebody to look after my son."

"I spoke with Professor Larsen already, Annie is an old friend," Vivian told him. "She's agreed to arrange for someone to take your place if you want to come. All your expenses will be paid for, including for your son. I'm sure he will enjoy seeing the ocean, and I can have someone watch him during the day."

"I appreciate that, but maybe I should have him stay with my in-laws in Salem for the week. He's on the autism spectrum, and he can be disruptive at times."

"As you wish, but he is more than welcome anytime. It's been too quiet here since our youngest left for college, especially with Martin being...away." John could hear the barely restrained sadness in her voice.

"If you're sure it's okay, we would be happy to attend."

"Very good. There is another matter I wish to discuss with you, but it would better to do that in person," she replied. "I sent you a package; it should have arrived this morning. It contains an unfinished manuscript, which I would like you to read over before the retreat. My assistant will contact you later today to make travel arrangements."

Johnny thanked her for the call before hanging up. Martin had been a professor and author who was well known and respected among literary circles but hadn't received much commercial success until he started churning out horror novels under his pseudonym Butch Richardson. His life and career had nearly been cut short, though, when he had collapsed at a lecture three months ago. Johnny had dedicated his latest novel *To Butch* at the last minute.

Patrick had finished eating and was sitting on the couch watching cartoons when he returned. Niko was at the table spooning a bowl of Fruity-Os into her mouth with one hand while propping her head up with the other. "I helped myself, I hope you don't mind."

"Of course not. Would you like an ibuprofen chaser to go with it?" Niko nodded, which caused her to groan and squeeze her eyes shut. "Listen, I hate to ask you this, but you look sort of familiar. You're not a student at the university, are you?"

"You mean, are you going to get in trouble if somebody finds out you're sleeping with me, Professor Sawyer?" she asked. "No, I graduated already, but I did take English Lit with you my freshman year."

"I'll be out of town next week, but I would like to see you again when I return. Unless this was a one-time thing for you, which I completely understand. Not that I do a lot of that myself. In fact, you're the first 'overnight visitor' I've had since I became single again."

"I've got something going on next week, too, but I would like that. Here's my number, text me when you get back. I should get going; I need to swing by my apartment and change clothes before I go to work."

"Okay, it was very nice to see you again, Niko."

She laughed and gave him a kiss. "It was nice to see you too, Johnny. Don't wait too long to call. Bye, Patrick!"

"Niko go home," his son called out from the living room. He walked her to the door, and they shared another kiss, this one much longer. She almost tripped over a box in front of the door to his apartment, and he grabbed her around the waist to steady her. After she was gone, Johnny sat down on the couch beside Patrick and opened the box. Inside was a leather file folder that contained a two-inch-thick stack of paper, and he pulled out the first sheet.

## The Alchemist's Apprentice
## A Novel

The title page didn't list the author, but given who had sent him the package, it was probably safe to assume he was holding an unpublished Martin Knight novel.

"Hey buddy, how would you like to take an airplane ride?" he asked. "We can go to Salem to see grandma and grandpa."

"Go to Salem," Patrick said. "Mommy is gone."

"Yes, I know you miss your mommy. We're going to be staying at a friend's house for a week. Kind of like a vacation, doesn't that sound like fun?"

"Patrick's vacation," he replied. "Jenny is gone."

His son turned his attention back to the cartoon on the television. Johnny watched him for a moment, wondering who Jenny could be, then saw he had only five minutes left to get Patrick ready for school on time. He hoped he wasn't making a mistake taking him to Massachusetts. While it would be good for Patrick to see his grandparents, it also meant visiting his wife's grave again. He hoped he was ready to deal with that.

*October 24, 2019*

Johnny had been nervous about taking his son on an airplane, but the kid handled it like a champ. Patrick had flown twice before, once when he was a baby while Kathy was still alive. They had flown to Florida for vacation, and Patrick had cried nearly the entire flight. It was the first time they had wondered if there might be something different about their child. The second time was four years ago after he had accepted a professorship at the University of Iowa.

It had been difficult to leave his in-laws behind, but the opportunity was too good to pass up, and there were too many painful reminders of his late wife in Massachusetts. Of course, returning to where they had gone to college together also brought back other memories of her.

Since he didn't need to be at the writer's retreat until Monday, Johnny had arranged to fly out on Saturday so Patrick could spend the weekend in Salem with his grandparents. Both his parents had passed away when he was young, so Margrett and Alfred Dietrich were the only family they had left. Moving away had been hard on them as well since Katherine had been their only daughter.

Johnny had hoped going back to Iowa would help him deal with his grief and give him a chance to meet someone without feeling guilty. Between classes, writing, and taking care of Patrick's needs, he had little time for that, or maybe those were just excuses he made so he didn't have to try navigating the dangerous waters of modern dating.

They picked up the rental car Mrs. Knight had reserved for them at the airport, a Ford Mustang GT. It barely had enough room in the trunk to fit their two suitcases, but he was happy to deal with that minor inconvenience as soon as the big V8 roared to life. Patrick was more impressed by the big screen in the dashboard that displayed the GPS map, and he would repeat the directions that the artificial female voice called out as they crawled along with the heavy traffic. It took them nearly forty-five minutes to make the fifteen-mile trek from the airport to the Dietrich house in the historic downtown section of Salem.

The two-story gray house with twin gable facades was one of the oldest in the state and had been in Margrett's family for over three hundred fifty years. It was built by her umpteenth-great grandfather, a skilled carpenter, when he immigrated from Germany. The house was passed down through the generations, but that lineage had ended with Kathy's death since Patrick would be unable to handle taking care of a house on his own.

They pulled up in front of the house, and Margrett came out to meet them. She hugged John, then leaned over to be at eye-level with Patrick. "Look how tall you've gotten. In a few more years, I'll be the one looking up at you." She gave him a big hug and kiss on the cheek, which he promptly wiped off, but Margrett didn't seem to mind. "Come inside, I'll get lunch ready. How was your flight? Did Patrick do well?"

"He was fantastic. It's good to see you again," Johnny answered. "How's dad holding up? You said he hasn't been feeling well."

"It's probably nothing, just getting old," she said. "I shouldn't have even said anything, but I wanted to warn you in case it happens again while you're here."

"What do you mean? In case what happens?"

"I hate to embarrass him, but I don't want you to mistake him for a prowler and call the police. I've woken up several times in the middle of the night to find him sleepwalking in the backyard, staring up at the sky. It's good that we have a high fence around the yard and plenty of trees. Otherwise, the neighbors would've gotten an eyeful since he was completely naked."

"Oh, wow, that's...a lot to take in."

"I'm afraid Alfred likes to sleep in the buff, but I made him promise to wear pajamas after the first incident," Margrett said. "He left them lying on the patio table the second time, and he was making howling noises loud enough to get all the dogs in the neighbor-hood going. I had to spray water in his face to get him to stop."

"'That sounds serious. Maybe you should take him to see a neurologist."

"You know him, unless his arm has been cut off or he's on death's door, that man won't go near a doctor's office. He claims he has no memory of it and says I'm making it up to get him to go in for a physical. Maybe you can talk some sense into him?"

"I'll give it a try, but I might have used up all my miracles on flying an autistic kid half-way across the country without a meltdown."

Margrett took Patrick's hand and led him into the house while Johnny retrieved their luggage. He pulled the car around and parked in front of the detached garage. As he exited the Mustang, his eyes gravitated to the graveyard across the street. Johnny had planned to wait until tomorrow before making the short yet daunting journey, but he decided it would be indecent of him not to pay his respects right away.

The cemetery was also one of the oldest in New England and had been closed since around the turn of the previous century, but Kathy had been buried in her family's plot. He walked past the towering oak tree that cast its shadow across her grave.

**KATHERINE ANNE SAWYER**
**BELOVED MOTHER, WIFE,**
**AND DAUGHTER**
**AUG. 1, 1988 - OCT. 31, 2014**

"Hey babe, it's been a while," he said. "I've been thinking about you a lot. I feel like we were just together yesterday. This doesn't seem real most days. I miss you so much...I love you."

Margrett was preparing sandwiches when Johnny walked into the kitchen. "There you are," she said, "would you mind telling Alfred that lunch is served? He's out in the garage either tinkering with his motorcycle or napping."

The detached garage stood about a hundred feet from the main house. The entry door on the side of the building was standing open, but he still knocked before walking inside. His father-in-law was sitting on a stool beside an Indian Scout motorcycle, holding a ratchet in his hand. Mounted in the corner was a small television with a car race playing, but he wasn't watching it.

Alfred was staring blankly out through the window towards the backyard. From the slackened, somewhat pained expression on his face, Johnny worried that his father-in-law had suffered a stroke. He went to shake him by the shoulder, but when his hand made contact, the room grew dark, and he had a dizzying feeling of weightlessness.

*He is standing in a cavernous, dimly lit building beside an old red tractor, dust motes swirling in the narrow shaft of light from the small square window above the sliding doors. He looks down at his arms, covered in thick graying brown hair or fur, and at his hands which end in sharpened black claws. He walks around the back of the tractor and a woman is sitting on a stool with her head facing down. She is the spitting image of his late wife, except about ten years older than Katherine when she died. She glances up and an expression of fear spreads across her face. She pulls an object from her purse and points it at him, and then his eyes and nose are on fire.*

"Johnny? When did you guys arrive?" Alfred asked, blinking like he had just woken up. "Sorry, I was working on old Betsy here and didn't hear you walk in. Are you okay? You don't look too good."

"Yeah, I'm fine," he replied, "just a little exhausted from the long flight."

"Well, Margrett should have lunch ready by now," his father-in-law said, then dropped his voice to a conspiratorial octave. "I've got a mini-fridge full of beer hidden behind the tool chest over there if you want one later, but don't say anything to Marg. She says I'm not supposed to drink anymore, but you might as well put me in the ground if that's how it is."

"My lips are sealed."

After waking up from the coma caused by the car crash, Johnny developed a special, albeit unusual, talent. It had taken him a while to figure out that he would get visions of nightmares people had when he touched them. The first time it occurred was when a nurse came to check on him in the hospital, and he saw her strapped down to a metal examination table completely naked while doctors with chicken heads prepared to cut her open. That one still made him wake up in a cold sweat some nights.

He had never experienced a physical reaction to one before though. Johnny's eyes were watering, and they still felt like they were burning. This vision was different than any he had before, as though it had really happened to Alfred.

They returned to the house where Margrett had set out a platter of sandwiches, a bowl of garden salad, and a pot of her famous baked beans. Johnny knew that she had likely started the beans simmering in molasses yesterday, and they were so tender they practically melted on the spoon. He was ready for a nap by the time he pushed back from the table.

"This meeting you're attending, is that for the university?" his mother-in-law asked.

"No, this is the annual writer's retreat that Martin Knight holds at his estate. His wife invited me to come out for it, she's covering all the expenses for the week."

"I thought that guy died," Alfred said. "It was all over the news a while ago."

"He's not dead; he's been in a coma for the past three months," Johnny replied.

"You know Marg actually met him."

"Oh really, how did that come about?"

"He was wandering around the cemetery and saw me gardening out front, so he came over to ask some questions," Margrett explained. "He said he was doing research about his wife's family for a new book. It turns out her and I are distantly related to a victim of the Salem Witch Trials. She was the oldest daughter of the German immigrant who built this house, Heinrich Meister."

"That's interesting, his wife sent me a manuscript about witches, but she didn't say if it was written by Martin," Johnny said. "It's too bad you didn't get his autograph."

"I guess I didn't know he was a famous writer until we saw him on the news."

"Now you've got an icebreaker for when you go meet his wife," Alfred said. "Just don't bring up the whole witch thing. Some people are still touchy about all that."

Salem had retained its small-town New England charm despite its proximity to the greater Boston metro area. The historic section of the town was a window back in time to the early colonial days, but the price for maintaining that quaintness was living with the infestation of tourists it attracted. It was a cool fall day, so they were roaming about in droves but nowhere near the plagues that swarmed the shops and restaurants during the summer. Johnny had been fascinated by the town's dark past, and despite it now being a tourist trap, plenty of Gothic mystique remained.

After lunch, he drove Patrick over to the Salem Common, a large open grass area in the center of the village, so that he could run around. His son was not exactly the sports type, but he did enjoy flying the kite that Alfred found in the garage. Their outing was cut short as storm clouds rolled in, and a strong gust of wind caused the kite's line to snap. It flew away across the green towards the busy street, and for a terrifying second, Johnny feared that his son would take off after it. Instead, Patrick watched the kite sail away and then waved at it.

"Bye, kite," he called out. "See you later, kite."

As they were heading back to where he had parked the rental car, he spotted a store that piqued his interest.

## TELL-TALE BOOKS & ANTIQUES

"Hey, Patrick, should we go check this place out? Maybe they'll have a book you like."

Patrick nodded, and Johnny took him over to look at the display window beside the front door. Leather-bound books were propped up to show their titles along the back of the display, with several expensive-looking breakable knick-knacks up front. Johnny had second thoughts about taking his son inside, but something caught Patrick's eye, and he darted towards the door.

"Whoa, slow down. We need to keep our hands to ourselves, understand?"

A tall, older man with a pale face and thinning gray hair was leaning on the sales counter, a book propped open on a wooden stand that held it in place for him. He looked up as the bell above the door tinkled with a pair of thick glasses perched on the end of his nose. The sight of Patrick hurrying over to the window display made his brow crease, and Johnny worried that the man would make a fuss if his son got too hyper.

"Good afternoon, nice store you have here," Johnny said. No other customers were in the shop right then, which made him even more nervous. "My son just wants to check out some of your books in the window."

"Of course, help yourselves," the bookseller replied. He came around the counter using a cane to walk, as his right leg had a severe limp. When he approached Johnny, he held out his hand. "Ryland Thynne, at your service."

"Oh, like the character in the Martin Knight short story *The Devil's Bargain Bin*."

"I've heard that mentioned before, but I can't say I've ever read it. I tend to stick to the classics. Are you a fellow bibliophile?"

"Um, yeah, I read lots of books, and I've even written a couple of novels myself," he replied. "My name's John Sawyer. I'm an English professor and author."

"A pleasure to meet you. My father went drinking once with Ernest Hemingway. He told me it was the drunkest he'd ever been," the man chuckled. "I read all his books as a boy growing up in Wales. It inspired me to run with the bulls at Pamplona when I was nineteen, which is why I have had this cane for the last fifty years."

"Holy cow," Johnny whistled. "Sorry, that was probably the wrong thing to say."

"Not to worry. If you are a book connoisseur, I keep the rare and first editions back here."

"Sure, let me get my son." Patrick was sitting on the floor near the display with his back turned, holding something in his hands and shaking it. "Patrick, what did I say?"

He spun around and held up a snow globe. "Patrick's globe."

"Okay, just please don't break it. Can you come with me?"

They followed Ryland to the back of the store, where more than a dozen tall, locked wood and glass bookcases were set up against the wall. Johnny's eyes grew large as he looked around the room. "As you can see, I've been in the trade for quite a while."

"Wow, this is an impressive collection, Mr. Thynne."

"Please call me Ryland. Let me know if there's anything you would like to see."

"Is that a first edition of *Homecoming Queen of Sorrows*?" he asked, pointing at a hardcover novel in the nearest bookcase. The name printed on the spine was Butch Richardson, which was the pen name and alter-ego of Martin Knight.

"Ah, yes, that was signed by the author on his first book tour. Are you a fan of Martin Knight?"

"I'm heading to his house tomorrow for a writer's retreat. How much do you want for the book?"

"I've been asking a thousand for it, but I haven't had any takers in the past three years I've had it for sale," Ryland answered as he unlocked the case and took it out. "I know this might sound ghoulish, but I'd hoped his being in the news would pique renewed interest in his work. I wouldn't be a very good merchant if I didn't sell my wares. Perhaps this book has simply been waiting for the right customer. I might be willing to part with it for, shall we say...five hundred dollars? I believe that would be a fair price."

Johnny accepted the novel from him and examined it more closely. The book was in near-perfect condition, the dust jacket showing a few small creases, but otherwise, it might have just come from the publisher. That was a lot of money to drop on a book, even one that rare, but he could afford such a luxury now. He knew it wasn't the most responsible decision, so he justified it by considering it a celebration of his recent publishing success. "You've got yourself a deal. I'll take the snow globe there as well."

Ryland looked down at the glass bauble that Patrick was holding and smiled. "Consider that one on the house."

*October 26, 2019*

The Knights' house was a short drive up the coast from Salem near the city of Beverly. The three-story grand estate featured a brick facade with limestone embellishments, an entrance framed by four marble pillars, and a breathtaking view of the Atlantic Ocean, including the nearby Misery Islands. Johnny knew he would never be able to afford a place like this. He probably couldn't even cover a year's worth of property taxes for it in his lifetime. Although Martin was well-off from his novels, his wife Vivian came from a ridiculously wealthy old Boston family.

Johnny had never felt so out of place as he approached the front door. He let Patrick push the doorbell, and his son started flapping his hands in excitement at the chime it made. He pushed it again twice before Johnny could stop him. That elicited the frantic barking from a couple of dogs inside the house, which caused Patrick to hide behind him.

"No big doggies," he said, grabbing the back of Johnny's shirt as the door opened to let out a pair of Labrador Retrievers, one black and one chocolate. "Daddy, no big doggies!"

"It's fine, buddy; they won't hurt you."

"Artemis, Apollo, get back inside," a stout, severe-looking woman in a black dress snapped, immediately sending the two big dogs darting back through the door. "Hello, are you Mr. Sawyer? Please come inside. Mrs. Knight will be down shortly."

"Thank you," he said and went to step through the door, but Patrick still held his shirt and refused to move. "Sorry, my son is frightened by large dogs, I guess."

"You two, off to the kitchen," the housekeeper snapped, and the two Labs trotted away. When they were out of sight, Patrick released his grip. "I apologize about that. They can be rambunctious, but they're very friendly."

"It's no problem."

"Mrs. Knight would like you to wait in the library; please follow me."

She led them down a hallway lined with paintings, bronze statues, and expensive-looking rugs. Johnny made a mental note not to let Patrick wander around here alone. He paused briefly to admire a painting across from the door to the library depicting a pair of white horses drinking from a reed-lined pond. In the background were the ruins of an ancient stone temple. Johnny bent down to read the painting's title engraved on a small brass plaque at the bottom of the frame.

# "Dream Mares" - HELLE W. ACHMAN
## DUTCH MASTER ( 1683 - 1740 )

Simply calling the room where the housekeeper brought them into a library was a disservice as it was a temple where books were lovingly enshrined. He could spend the entire week cloistered in this room, deep in reverie while pouring through the leather-bound tomes for hours. Johnny recognized several books that looked to be priceless first editions.

The housekeeper led them to a set of four leather reading chairs arranged around a glass-topped coffee table.

"May I get you something to drink?" she asked.

"Um, just a glass of water for this guy," Johnny replied. "I'll take a cup of coffee if you have some brewed."

"Certainly, any cream or sugar?"

"No, black is fine, thanks."

The housekeeper left, and Johnny took the opportunity to examine the collection on display closer, trying to keep the drool from running down his chin. She soon returned with a silver tray and proceeded to pour two cups of coffee and fill a tall crystal glass with water. Johnny wished he had asked for a plastic cup for Patrick. Vivian Knight entered as the housekeeper handed his son the glass.

"Thank you, Claudia, that will be all for now. I hope I didn't keep you waiting long," the slender, raven-haired woman said as she offered her hand for Johnny to shake. He knew she had to be in her mid-fifties, but her face showed no wrinkles and was accented with a minimum amount of makeup to highlight her structured cheekbones. She wore a cashmere sweater and jeans, and the unmistakable air of old-money wealth emanated from her.

Vivian sat in the chair opposite him, placing a manila file folder on the table as she took the nearest cup of coffee. "I appreciate you coming on such short notice, Mr. Sterling. I know Martin would have enjoyed seeing you again."

"It's my pleasure. Thank you for inviting us to stay at your home, Mrs. Knight. I noticed nobody else is here yet. Did we show up too early?"

"Please call me Vivian. The other attendees will be arriving later this afternoon. I wanted to discuss that matter I spoke about on the phone with you beforehand," she replied, sipping her coffee. "First off, I should offer my congratulations on publishing your new novel. I hear it is doing quite well."

"Thank you. The hardcover sales are looking pretty good, and I'm hoping they'll result in a decent contract for the paperback rights."

"That's excellent, did you have a chance to read through the manuscript I sent you?"

"I made it most of the way, but I should be able to finish it tonight," Johnny answered. "Is it written by Martin?"

"Yes, it was a new novel he was working on before he had his incident. He was struggling with writer's block and was quite stressed about it. I haven't been able to bring myself to read it since I feel that it was responsible for what happened to him."

"I can understand that. It's a really good story; it will probably be his best work when he finishes it. I'm a little confused why you sent it to me if it hasn't been published yet?"

"That's why I asked you to come to this retreat," Vivian replied, "or rather, why Martin asked me to invite you."

"Oh, I thought Martin was still in a coma?"

"He is," Vivian replied as she opened the manila folder and removed a piece of paper. "Martin gave this letter to his agent earlier this year with instructions to deliver it to me if he were to die or become incapacitated for any reason. The letter requests I hire a ghostwriter to complete that novel if it should remain unfinished, almost like he had an inclination something was about to happen. He provided a list of candidates and asked me to use the writers retreat as a way of screening them so the identity of the one I select would remain secret. I invited three of the people on his list, but one backed out at the last minute. I recognized your name from the *Times* and decided to contact you as the alternate."

"I'm flattered. Have you read any of my books?"

"No, but don't feel bad. I only read Martin's writing after he pestered me to death. The three of you will provide me with an outline for how you plan to finish the story at the end of the retreat, and I will choose which of you becomes Martin's ghostwriter."

"Thank you for this opportunity. I didn't realize Martin was that familiar with my work."

"He was very impressed with you from the creative writing class he taught; I found this on his desk along with the manuscript." She reached into the file folder, pulled out a yellowing sheet of newspaper, and held it out to him.

Johnny recognized it from the illustrated picture of a ghostly hand reaching toward the reader from the darkness. He carefully unfolded the yellowing, ten year old copy of the Arts & Entertainment section from the *Iowa City Press-Citizen*. He had the same page framed and hanging on a wall back in his apartment, it had been the first story he had published.

The newspaper had been holding a Halloween-themed contest for readers to submit a story based on a provided opening line. Martin had challenged the class to send in an entry with the enticement of extra credit if anybody won the contest. He hadn't thought his story was good enough to submit, but Kathy had encouraged him to send it in.

He had been shocked when he won the contest and the $100 prize that went with it, but more important to him had been the recognition in class from Mr. Knight. That spark lit the fire in him to become a serious writer, and knowing he had made that much of an impression with a simple ghost story knocked the wind out of him. It was crazy to think that little tale might lead to him becoming the ghostwriter for his favorite author. Johnny would gladly give that up if it meant having Martin awake and hosting the writer's retreat in person, but this was still the opportunity of a lifetime.

*Except that he had just met Martin at Devonshire Manor back in Iowa, where he had asked him to be his ghostwriter, and it had been Vivian who died in a car accident.*

A splitting headache erupted without warning, and Johnny had to grip the armrests of his chair as the room seemed to wobble in his vision.

"Are you alright, Mr. Sawyer?" Vivian asked. "You suddenly look rather pale."

"What? No, sorry, I'm fine. I don't do well with air travel," he stammered. "My ears are still popping from yesterday."

"I can understand that. I've never cared for flying. Anyway, there is one more thing, which may sound a little unusual, but it is a tradition Martin had at the retreat. Instead of using a computer, my husband did all his work on a manual typewriter. He insisted that the other writers do the same for the week, and I would also like to add my own stipulation that the remainder of his novel is completed in the same fashion. Is that agreeable with you?"

"Of course, it's been years since I've used one, but I'm sure I can manage."

"Excellent, I look forward to having you at the retreat," she replied. "You'll be happy to know that I'm giving you Martin's personal typewriter to use for the week. I've had it moved into your room. Claudia can show you to it after we're done so you can get settled in before the other guests arrive. I will see you this evening for dinner."

The housekeeper was waiting for them and took Johnny and Patrick to the third floor. They were given one of the larger bedrooms with a private adjacent bathroom. All the walls were gleaming white, the furniture and curtains were made from white fabric, and the bathroom was completely tiled in white marble. The starkness of the environment, devoid of any color or personal touch, made Johnny feel uneasy. It felt more like a mausoleum than somebody's home, and if not for the breathtaking view of the ocean, he wondered how Martin could have handled such a sterile environment.

To him, it looked like the epitome of a writer's worst nightmare, an endless ream of blank paper where no words could ever be written. In the corner of the bedroom was a red wooden writing desk, a small island of coziness tucked away in the sea of overly priced blandness. Sitting on top of it was an elegant bronze banker's lamp and an imposing black manual typewriter with a distinctive word stenciled on the paper rest in faded gold letters.

# Underwood

Johnny reverently ran his fingers over the typewriter's keys, opened the center desk drawer to find a stack of blank sheets, and inserted the top one into the roller.

## How vexingly quick daft zebras jump

Satisfied that it was in working condition, he lifted the lid to inspect the inner mechanism. It had been forever since he had used a typewriter, and never one this ancient. He would have to figure out how to change out the ribbon when the time came. Hopefully, he'd find an instructional video about it somewhere on the Internet if his (*lack of*) natural mechanical abilities came up short. He closed the lid and brushed a few specs of dust from the keys when the impulse to type another message struck him.

## Heeeeeere's JOHNNY!

Two surprises were awaiting Johnny when he came downstairs for dinner that evening. First, he walked into the formal dining room and was greeted by twelve pairs of female eyes looking back at him. While he was not sexist, the possibility hadn't occurred to him that the other writers Mrs. Knight had invited to the retreat might all be women. Johnny thought for a second that he caught a sly smile on Vivian's lips as he stood there staring like a deer in headlights. He quickly recovered his wits and helped Patrick sit down, then took his seat at the table's end. Johnny felt like he was on display since he was facing their hostess and all the other guests.

"Welcome, Mr. Sawyer, glad you could join us," Vivian announced. "Ladies, this is the special guest I was telling you about. John is a published author, and his third novel has landed on the *New York Times Bestseller List*. His charming son, Patrick, will also be with us for the week."

Johnny wasn't prepared to be put on the spot like that, so all he could manage in response was a simple "Hi."

"As you can see, he is a man of many words," she continued, and the women at the table laughed. He could feel his cheeks grow hot and was sure he was blushing. "John has graciously agreed to fill in for a last-minute cancellation, and I'm sure he won't mind imparting some of his experience and advice in navigating the publishing world."

"Of course," he replied.

"My dear husband had an unfortunate incident three months ago, so I appreciate all of you being here during this difficult time. I hope that this will be a chance for all of you to improve your craft and make connections with your fellow writers."

After the main course of fresh steamed lobster had been served, he received the evening's second (although not final) surprise. Johnny reached for the glass of red wine before him when a flash of purple caught his attention. A woman seated halfway down the table was trying to avoid his line of sight. He leaned over toward Patrick to help him cut up his food and get a better look at her without trying to be too obvious. Their eyes locked for a second before Niko looked away.

Johnny tried to get her alone once dinner was finished, but she was either busy talking with somebody or the other women surrounded him. Patrick started yawning at eight o'clock, so he excused himself for the night to take him to the room to watch television. Vivian said he could help himself to anything he wanted from the well-stocked liquor cabinet first, so he grabbed a 15-year-old Glenstirling Red Label Single Malt Scotch bottle and a crystal tumbler before heading upstairs. He found a channel playing cartoons on the TV for his son, poured a healthy measure of the amber liquor into the glass, and settled into an armchair to finish reading the manuscript.

The lighting in the room wasn't the best, so he reached over to turn the desk lamp on. He noticed the carriage on the typewriter was at the end but didn't recall having advanced it. It was possible that Patrick might have been messing around with it. With the lamp on, he could see something else had been typed out on the page, so he got up to look closer. He turned the knob on the roller a couple of times and received the third and most shocking surprise of the night.

## hi daddy its genny i miss you are yu in heavin?

Johnny sat down hard in the chair, the room spinning out of control around him. It felt like his mind was being torn in half by two different memories.

*You have a ten-year-old son named Patrick and an eight-year-old daughter named Jenny.*

*Your wife is named Karina, but she goes by Kari.*

*No, that's not possible. My wife was named Kathy, and she died eight years ago.*

*We only had a son named Patrick.*

# Geraldine's Game, or: From An Underwood No. 5

Novel By **MARTIN KNIGHT**

Jupiter & Phoebus Publishing House

# CHAPTER 16

## Geraldine's Game, or: From An Underwood No. 5

*October 26, 1963*

M ary Deloris Smith stepped from the taxi and stared up at the grandest house she had ever seen. She set her suitcase on the ground and helped her daughter, Geraldine, climb out. Mary had used the last of her money to pay the cab fare from the Iowa City train station to Old Ahnen. She hoped this wasn't just a dream as the taxi drove off.

When her husband, Jonathan, passed away, he left her with no savings and a mountain of debt. Mary was forced to return to work to provide for her daughter. She had been a secretary at a prestigious Chicago advertising firm before marrying Jon, but the only job she could get now was waitressing at a diner. She had been about to give up hope of getting back on her feet when her sister in Cedar Rapids sent her a newspaper clipping.

### Executive Secretary Wanted - Iowa City

Pharmaceutical corporation seeks executive secretary. Office experience is required, type 80-100 words per minute accurately. Must be willing to relocate, on-site housing and boarding provided.

Salary $6000 per year. Inquire at AH 5-4397

She had thought there was little chance of being hired for such a dream job, and the money was more than what she had made at the ad agency. Mary almost didn't apply but knew she could not keep working herself to exhaustion while not even making enough to pay for food and rent most months.

There were many nights when she had to go hungry so that Genny had enough to eat, which only added to her weariness. Her luck finally seemed to be turning around as she not only got called for an interview but received an offer of employment a week later. That was how she came to be in the middle of Iowa, desperate but hopeful, standing outside Devonshire Manor.

"Is this where we're going to live, mommy?" Genny asked.

"I don't know, honey. Should we go find out? I want you to be on your best behavior."

"Yes, mommy." Mary led her up to the front entrance and rang the doorbell. A young, diminutive woman wearing a black-and-white uniform answered the door, surrounded by a dozen black cats who circled about her legs.

"Hello, my name is Mary Smith. I was told to-"

"Come in and place your suitcase beside the door. I will have it taken to your cottage. Dr. Masterson is waiting for you in the library."

"Can I stay here and play with the cats, mommy?" her daughter asked, sitting on the floor with the felines vying for her attention.

"Alright, but don't leave the entryway, understand?"

"I will keep an eye on her for you, ma'am," the uniformed woman said.

Mary followed her down a hallway lined with beautiful dark wood panels and adorned with paintings in gilded gold frames, which were probably worth more than she would make in a lifetime. The woman stopped at a closed door, knocked, and opened it. "Excuse me, Dr. Masterson, your new secretary has arrived. Shall I show her in?"

"Yes, thank you, Gretchen." The tall, slender man in a gray three-piece suit stood up from his reading chair and came over to shake her hand. "Hello, Mrs. Smith. Please take a seat. How was your trip?"

"Thank you, it was good. I haven't been on a train ride since my husband took me to the Rocky Mountains for our honeymoon."

"Will your husband be joining you here?"

"No, Jonathan passed away two years ago. He was a police detective in Chicago."

"I am truly sorry to hear that. I know the sorrow that comes from losing a loved one. My dear wife did not survive the birth of our daughter, and I never felt alone in the world until I no longer had her by my side."

"That seems to be the story of my life," Mary replied. "There are days when it seems sorrow follows behind me like a shadow." She shook her head. "I apologize for sounding so morbid."

"Think nothing of it. In my line of work, suffering and mortality tend to become rather clinical; it's good for me to be reminded of their emotional toll," Dr. Masterson said, leaning forward to pat her on the hand. "Tell me, was your husband killed in the line of duty?"

Mary was shocked by such a personal question but felt strangely compelled to tell him the truth. "No, he committed suicide, or at least that's what the insurance company claimed when they refused to pay out his life insurance policy."

"It sounds like you have some doubts about that?"

"You mean, do I think Jon killed himself? No, not for a moment, but I have no way to prove that. The word of a grieving widow means little, especially one of a dead detective who owed five thousand dollars in gambling debts."

"Forgive me for prying, but I appreciate your honesty. Perhaps your parents had an intuition about the trials in store for you when they chose your name, Mary Deloris. The Spanish equivalent, *La Virgen Maria de los Dolores*, translates to "Our Lady of Sorrows". Those who have an intimate understanding of suffering are best equipped to help ease the pain of others."

There was a knock on the library door, and Gretchen stuck her head in.

"I'm sorry to interrupt, but your daughter is saying she's hungry," she said. "Would you like me to prepare her some lunch?"

"Yes, please, Gretchen," Henry replied. "How rude of me, I should have thought to offer you something to eat. I can't imagine the food on the train was decent." Mary didn't want to tell him that the food from the dining car had smelled delicious, but she couldn't afford to even set foot in there. "I would join you, but I have to call the factory and see why Fredrick hasn't brought me the latest sales figures for the month."

"You need to let your son handle such things now," Gretchen scolded him. "The doctor ordered you to avoid stress for the next month."

"That doesn't mean I can't keep an eye on him and make sure that he isn't squandering all that I've built over the past thirty years." The housekeeper shook her head as she turned and left. "That will be one of the duties of your position, I'm afraid, keeping me from over-exerting myself. You see, I had to turn over control of my company to my son rather unexpectedly after suffering what my doctor claims is a heart arrhythmia. While I decided to humor the man and step back from the company's day-to-day operations, that doesn't mean I intend to be completely uninvolved."

"Certainly, Dr. Masterson, whatever you need me to do."

"Please call me Henry unless I am entertaining important clients at the house. Most of your duties will involve typing up correspondence and memorandums that I will dictate to you via tape recordings. I cannot stress enough how much I despise the noise those infernal typewriters make, so you will need to work in a separate room from me. I ordered one to be brought to the cottage for you and a machine to play back the recordings."

"What do you want me to do with these memos after I type them up?"

"A company driver will stop by the house once a day at noon to pick up and drop off any of my correspondence. If there is an urgent matter, I will need you to drive to the factory. You do know how to drive an automobile, correct?"

"Yes, I grew up on a farm. My grandfather taught me to drive his pickup truck when I was twelve."

"Good, it isn't far to the factory, but the road can be quite difficult in the winter. I built an underground rail tunnel when the house was constructed to connect it to the factory for such weather. Enough talk of business; Gretchen should have lunch waiting in the kitchen."

The small cottage across the courtyard from the manor was larger than the house they had lived in when Jonathan was alive. There was a master bedroom on the first floor and two smaller bedrooms upstairs, one of which had been made into an office. The typewriter was sitting on a desk in the corner by the window that faced the driveway.

When she worked at the advertising agency, Mary was given a Royal Quiet de Luxe portable that was light enough to carry around and bright pink. Giving that up had been almost as painful as losing a comfortable paycheck. While she had not expected a small pharmaceutical company in Iowa to have top-of-the-line equipment, she recoiled in horror at the enormous black monstrosity Dr. Masterson had provided. The Underwood Model No. 5 reminded her of the clunky, intimidating machines she had to learn with back in secretarial school.

Mary unpacked the contents of their suitcase, which easily fit inside the dresser in the master bedroom. As soon as she had money, she would need to buy Genny new clothes so she wouldn't get teased at school. She would also have to find out how to enroll her daughter in the local elementary and how to get her there each day. Gretchen could hopefully tell her if there was a school bus stop nearby. With any luck, this job would be the start of a better life for them. Mary would have happily returned to living in the tiny, rundown apartment if it meant her husband, Jack, was still alive.

*That's not right,* she thought. *He always went by Jon or Jonathan. Never Jack.*

*October 28, 1963*

Mary was usually dead on her feet after finishing a shift waitressing, but she had forgotten how tiring secretarial work could also be. Even though this was her second day on the job, her hands were already stiff and aching. Through audio tapes, Henry dictated an unending stream of letters, memos, and white papers. These recordings were either utterly boring, blisteringly complex, or a caustic mix of the two. She had barely passed her chemistry class in high school, and she was struggling to decipher the cryptic formulas and terms that interspersed his correspondence. He also had her listen in on some of his phone calls and take notes in shorthand to be transcribed later for his records.

Genny had a much easier time adjusting to her new environment, having been given free reign of the manor save for the second floor. Gretchen had also taken a liking to her daughter and had walked her down to the estate's front gate this morning, where the school bus stopped. Henry had called the principal to change the bus route so it would come directly to the manor to pick her up. Mary was still worried that her daughter would find it difficult to fit in at the school since most of the children had grown up together and might treat her as an outsider. Genny had an uncanny ability to make people like her, though, and she had made several friends by the end of the first day.

Mary had discovered Genny playing with the typewriter in her office this morning. She had snapped at her out of concern that she could break the machine, but felt horrible when Genny started crying and said she had been writing a letter to her father so he would know they had moved. Her daughter had been very close with Jon and had barely spoken the first year after he died. It wasn't surprising she would come up with a way to cope with her grief by pretending she could still talk to him.

She decided that she wouldn't get upset with Genny if she used the typewriter again, and she would start giving her lessons so there would be no harm in allowing her to play her game. She finished a letter for Dr. Masterson, took off her headphones, and stood up to stretch her back. Fishing around in her purse, Mary found a crumpled pack of cigarettes with one stick left. It was a bad habit she had picked up from Jon, and she promised herself she was going to quit. Especially now that stories were coming out about how unhealthy it was, but right now she needed a smoke.

Mary decided to go outside before lighting up as she didn't know whether she could smoke in the cottage. She stepped out into the courtyard, walked around to the side of the house near the garage, and had just struck a match when she caught the rumbling of an engine. It was too early for Genny's bus to arrive, but perhaps the MasterPharm driver was late coming to pick up Dr. Masterson's letters.

She peeked around the corner as a bright silver sports car roared up the driveway and stopped in front of the courtyard. Mary wasn't all that familiar with different car models, but she thought it might be a Corvette. There were plenty of fancy cars like that to be seen in downtown Chicago, including several in the ad agency's parking garage that belonged to the senior executives. For someone to drive such an expensive car around the backroads of rural Iowa was unusual, but she was even more surprised when a red-haired woman wearing a low-cut black dress, stockings, and high heels stepped out of the driver's seat.

Dr. Masterson must have also heard the engine because he came out of the house as the woman leaned against the car's hood. She held up a small metal reel that looked like the audio tapes for the dictation machine. Henry stopped in front of the car and crossed his arms, a look of disapproval on his face. Mary was peeking around the corner, so she was out of sight but could hear their conversation.

"What do you think you're doing?" Henry snapped. "You were supposed to leave the car in the parking lot at O'Hare and take a flight to Cedar Rapids, not drive it all the way here. I had a man there waiting to dispose of it. We cannot risk anything being tied back to us."

"And let such a beautiful machine go to waste? I got the film you asked for. That Harvard pretty boy might prefer blondes, but he doesn't mind redheads, either." She handed him the reel, and he put it in his suit coat pocket. "You could say '*Thank you, Margrit*'."

"I wish you would have heeded my instructions, but I am grateful to you for doing it," Henry replied. "I'm afraid your efforts may have been for naught, though. The Agency has decided to continue with a more aggressive plan of action. They have asked for your involvement again."

"For crying out loud, can't a lady get some rest around here?"

"Put the car in the garage and get yourself changed, then we'll discuss your upcoming trip to Dallas. This assignment will be longer and less pleasant than your one to Chicago."

"Hold on, what I did with the Harvard pretty boy was as much for pleasure as it was about duty, but I draw the line at sleeping with that fat cowpoke of a second banana."

"It's nothing like that. There are some new guests in the house, so let's hold off any further conversations about this until later."

Mary backed away from the corner, hoping they didn't hear her shoes scraping across the cobblestones. The car engine started up again, and she used the sound to cover her escape around the back of the cottage.

She didn't know what she had overheard, but it was not her concern. Mary returned upstairs and picked up her work where she had left off. The good news was that she no longer wanted a cigarette. As she typed another memo, she allowed her mind to drift off. Her thoughts turned to the troubled waters where it often went, the murder of her late husband.

Jonathan's body had washed up on the shore of Lake Michigan, a steak knife lodged in his throat and his duty weapon missing. The police found his car parked near Navy Pier, and they also discovered a type-written suicide note on the front seat. Jon confessed in it his guilt about hiding his gambling debts for years and said that the only way out was to take his own life. He had told her a week before he disappeared not to answer the door for anyone when he wasn't home, even if they claimed to be the police. He had also given her a small revolver, which still scared her to have, but she had held onto it. The gun was hidden inside the lining of her suitcase.

A knock on the cottage door sparked a momentary fear that she had forgotten about Genny. The clock on the wall showed there were still ten minutes until the bus would arrive. She hurried downstairs and opened the front door to find Gretchen standing there.

"Hello, Dr. Masterson would like to invite you to the party he is hosting tonight in honor of his granddaughter's first birthday," the housekeeper said. "Hors d'oeuvres and cocktails will commence in the Grand Hall at six o'clock, and dinner will be served at seven. Your daughter is also welcome to come, and I can have a separate meal prepared for her if she doesn't care for rack of lamb."

"Oh, that's very generous of him to offer," Mary replied. "I don't know if I feel comfortable attending a family function, though."

"It's not just family; there will be many important business associates in attendance as well," Gretchen said. "Henry would like you there so you'll know who they are when he corresponds with them. I can take care of your daughter after dinner is over. I have a television in my quarters that she can watch."

"That's very kind of you. I don't think she could remain quiet in that setting for too long. I don't have anything to wear to a party, I'm afraid."

Gretchen looked her up and down as though taking her measurements by sight. "I think I can find you something that will fit." With that, she turned around and headed back to the manor. Mary stared at the imposing building for a while, wondering if she had made a mistake coming here when she realized she would be late for the bus. She ran across the yard and met her daughter walking up the driveway.

"Genny, I'm so sorry. I was busy working and forgot what time it was."

"That's alright; the guard let me in the front gate," she said. "I'm hungry. Could I have a snack before dinner?"

"Certainly, how would you like to go to a party tonight? Dr. Masterson has invited us to celebrate his granddaughter's birthday."

"Is there going to be cake and ice cream?"

"I'm sure there will be some kind of dessert."

"Will there be other kids? What about clowns? I don't like clowns, they're scary."

"I don't know about other children, but I doubt there will be any clowns. It will be more of a grown-up party where people stand around and talk. Can you be on your best behavior for dinner? After that, you can go with Ms. Gretchen and watch TV."

"Okay, but it doesn't sound like a very fun party."

Mary knew she should be grateful Gretchen had found a dress that fit her, but it was hard not to feel uncomfortable in such a revealing outfit. The dress was unquestionably beautiful and worth more than the simple white gown she had worn for her wedding. She worried it was intended for someone less well-endowed in the chest than her, or maybe it was cut to ensure that a good deal of cleavage was on full display. The hem of the skirt also made her uncomfortable as it barely reached the tops of her knees. Mary wondered who the dress could belong to until the red-headed woman entered the Grand Hall.

She no longer had curly red hair, but that could have been a wig. It was now blonde and straight, flowing down over her bare shoulders. She appeared to be in her early twenties, but there was a worldly sophistication about her. The woman was also wearing a form-fitting and revealing red dress that looked right in line with the one Mary had on.

"You fill that out quite nicely," the woman told her. "Try not to spill anything on it; that's a Givenchy I picked up in Paris and haven't even worn yet."

"I'll be careful, I promise," Mary stammered. "Thank you for lending it to me."

"Think nothing of it. The name is Weiss, Margrit Weiss. You must be Henry's new secretary?"

"Yes, Mary Smith, and this is my daughter Geraldine."

Margrit held out her hand, and Mary shook it. "Have we met before?"

"I don't believe so. We only arrived here from Chicago this weekend. I used to work at an advertising firm there."

"I'm the head of marketing for MasterPharm. I wonder if I employed your firm at some point. Or perhaps I know your husband. Is he here as well?"

"No, he passed away. He was a police detective, so you wouldn't have met him unless you did something illegal."

Margrit answered her with an amused smile. "Well, aren't you a feisty one," she said, then leaned in closer and whispered. "I see why Henry picked you as his latest object of amusement." Before Mary could respond, the woman waved to somebody she recognized on the other side of the room and strode away.

"Mommy, I'm hungry, but none of the food looks good."

"Let's see if Gretchen can get you some cheese and crackers."

She hoped to avoid talking with Margrit again, but that proved impossible as they were seated next to each other during dinner. A handsome middle-aged man was sitting to Margrit's right, and she spent the entire meal chatting with him (*while he was busy looking down the front of her dress*). Mary was okay with that as she had her hands full making sure Genny behaved herself and didn't make a mess eating.

If being in a room full of strangers wasn't uncomfortable enough, she didn't have pantyhose to wear with the dress. Not only were her legs bare, but the shoes Gretchen had given her were open-toe and had three-inch heels. She could feel all the men watching her, or maybe that was from being so near to Margrit. Despite her outfit, she felt downright plain compared to her.

The wait staff were clearing the plates after the main course in preparation for dessert when she felt a hand caress her knee under the table. Mary froze as the tips of the fingers slowly traced their way along the top of her leg, then slid down to the inner flesh of her thigh. She wanted to swat the hand away, but was afraid to make a scene. Margrit turned briefly from the businessman and gave Mary a mischievous smile before withdrawing her hand.

While it wasn't cake and ice cream, Genny seemed happy with the slice of strawberry cheesecake. Mary only managed a few bites, her stomach twisted into a pretzel, before sliding her plate over to her daughter. Henry made a toast to his granddaughter, and the table sang *Happy Birthday* to her.

She felt jealous when Gretchen came to get Genny as the other adults headed to the Ballroom for cocktails and to enjoy the live jazz band. Mary was already feeling tipsy from the glass of wine at dinner and had no interest in dancing with any of the men leering at her. She used the excuse of putting Genny to bed to escape the party at nine o'clock.

Mary was grateful to remove the heels once she returned to the cottage, her feet throbbing from being arched at such an unnatural angle. The dress also irritated her, and she was tempted to rip it off in the entryway. While that was mainly because it was tight around her chest, she also wanted to be rid of it since it belonged to that sinister woman. Wearing it reminded Mary of the hand crawling up her leg. What made it even worse was that the sensation had awakened urges she hadn't felt since Jon's death. She would have to wait until she put Genny to bed before taking it off and soaking her aching legs in a steaming hot bath.

"Okay, time to get some sleep," Mary said.

"Mommy, I can't find my doll," Genny whined.

"I'm sure she's around here. When did you have her last?"

"I took her to the party. I put her under my chair at dinner. I must have left her there."

"Okay, I'll get her in the morning."

"What if she gets lost or somebody throws her away? Daddy gave her to me," Genny said, tears welling up. "I can't go to sleep without her."

"Calm down, honey, everything will be fine. I'll go find your doll; can you get ready for bed while I'm gone?"

Mary trudged back downstairs and gave the pair of shoes sitting by the door an evil look. She decided to go barefoot even though it was getting cold outside. The cobblestone courtyard was painful as she hurried across, but it didn't hurt nearly as bad as having to wear those podiatric torture devices. Walking down the hall towards the kitchen, she saw a couple of waiters carrying stacks of dirty dishes in their arms. With any luck, the dining room would be empty, and she could grab the doll without anyone from the party noticing her.

Music and laughter were coming from the Grand Hall. A waiter passed her without a word, although he did glance down at her bare feet. Mary went over to where she and Genny had been sitting and peered underneath the chairs, but no doll was in sight. Sighing, she got down on her hands and knees to crawl underneath the floor-length tablecloth. It took a few seconds for her eyes to adjust to the dark, but she soon spotted it resting against the far table leg.

Mary was reaching for it when she heard footsteps enter the room. She was about to come out when the sound of the doors shutting froze her in place. Through a gap in the tablecloth she could see a pair of men's black dress shoes and Margrit's strappy heels standing in front of them.

"Now, can you tell me what's so important to interrupt my evening?" Margrit asked. "I know you probably don't believe this, but I was enjoying myself."

"We'll get to that, but first, there is more pressing business." A sudden burst of air ruffled the tablecloth. Once it settled back, Mary risked scooting forward to where she could peer through the gap again. Margrit's dress was lying in a pool around her feet.

"Dammit, Henry, you know I hate it when you do that," Margrit snapped. "You better hope you didn't rip it. When will you learn that you can't do whatever you want?"

"Oh, and why not? I've done whatever I wanted for as long as I've lived. What makes you think I'm going to change now?" His pants dropped around his ankles, and Margrit's legs were lifted off the floor as Henry presumably hoisted her up on the table. For the next few minutes, Mary tried to pretend that she wasn't listening to them having sex right above her head.

"That's just great," Margrit complained afterward. "Look at this; you've ripped the strap. Are you out to annoy me, like not telling me you were hiring that new secretary? Have you screwed her already?"

"Jealousy is not like you, and I don't think someone who recently bedded the most powerful man in the world has much room to complain," Dr. Masterson replied. "I have no intentions of sleeping with her. I need a good secretary, so try not to scare her off by doing what you did to her at dinner."

"I was simply having some fun, and don't pretend your intentions are innocent. I bet you gave her the whole *wife died in childbirth* story; am I wrong? How does that work when your son is adopted?"

"Do I need to remind you that you work for me now? I advise you to stay out of my business and do your job."

"What is my job anymore, Henry? Am I a spy? An assassin? Or a whore? This isn't what I left the Coven for."

"Be patient, my love. Our time will come, and we will no longer have to hide our true nature. For now, I need you to remain focused on the next assignment. You'll be working with Albert, one of the *gestaltwandlers*, so prepare yourself."

"I work better alone."

"It's not up for discussion. Fix your dress and get back to the party."

Mary backed away as she saw Margrit reach down and pick up her crumpled dress. She waited for a bit after they left, then crept out and returned to the cottage. Genny was sound asleep when she went upstairs to check on her, so Mary placed the doll beside her on the pillow and went downstairs to bathe. It was almost dawn before she fell into a fitful sleep.

*October 27, 2019*

Johnny sat at the edge of the bed, staring at the typewriter as if expecting it to jump up and bite him. He had barely slept last night, his mind trying to wrap itself around the thought of his daughter being alive. Where she was or how he could communicate with her through a typewriter were unanswered questions, but he hoped the machine would provide more messages to help him figure it out.

He had a tug-of-war going on in his mind between the half that insisted his wife was dead and the other whispering to him that she wasn't. That nagging feeling Kathy (*Kari?*) was somehow alive had been lurking in his subconscious for a while now, but the message from Genny proved that the idea wasn't so unbelievable. Whether talking to a daughter who shouldn't exist via a horror writer's typewriter counted as evidence of sanity was another question he couldn't answer.

Their bedroom had a king-sized bed, but Patrick tossed and turned most of the night and dug his feet underneath him. Johnny ended up clinging to the edge of the bed and finally went to sleep in the armchair instead. That was why he was wide awake early this morning with a nasty kink in his neck. He stood up to stretch out his aching muscles and went over to the window to look out.

There was not even a false dawn yet on the eastern horizon, but the moon was bright enough to illuminate the ocean's surface. A strong breeze was blowing, and it caused the waves to lap at the sea wall below. A tendril of white smoke rose from a dark figure leaning against the terrace's stone railing, silhouetted against the churning water. The wind picked up and Johnny thought he saw a streak of purple hair in the moonlight.

Patrick was still sound asleep, so he crept across the room and slipped out the door. Nobody else was awake at this hour, but he was careful as he walked down the stairs so they wouldn't creak. He needn't have worried about that since they barely made any noise as he stepped on them. Johnny went through the grand foyer into the large sitting room and found one of the French doors open. Before stepping onto the terrace, he peeked through the gauzy white curtains to check it was Niko outside. Johnny cleared his throat as he did so to keep from startling her.

"Do you mind if I bum a cigarette off you?" he asked.

"Sorry, it's a vape stick," she replied. "You're welcome to take a drag off it."

Niko offered the pen-like device to him, but he held up his hand. "I'll pass, it's not the same. I don't mean to sound rude, but were you avoiding me yesterday?"

Despite the low light he caught a flash of nervousness cross her face. "It wouldn't look good if everyone knew I slept with the bigshot writer."

"Don't worry, I won't say anything," he replied. "What I said about seeing you again still stands. Maybe we could get together after the retreat?"

"Yeah, sure, sounds good," she answered quickly, taking a hit from the vape.

"I didn't know that you were a writer. Anything I might have read?"

"Um, probably not; I've mostly published in small literary magazines."

"Okay, well, it's nice to see you again."

"You too," she said as she tucked the vape stick in her pocket and hurried back inside.

Johnny looked up at the house and thought he saw one of the curtains shift as though somebody had been watching at them.

Patrick was sitting up in bed when he got back to the room. "Hey buddy, I'm sorry I left you alone. Did you get scared?"

"Loud," his son said.

"Did a loud noise wake you up?"

"Uh hum. Typewriter is very loud."

The carriage on the typewriter had moved across the paper to the other side of the roller. Johnny sat down in the chair and turned the feed knob so he could read the new message that had appeared. The first line was what he had typed out last night before bed.

**Jenny where are you? Is your mother with you?**

Below that was the response that his daughter had just sent back.

**me and mommy are in odanna iowa in mommys new boss big house i have my own bedroom**

Taking out his phone, he brought up a list of all the towns and cities in Iowa and tried to find where Odonna was located. His daughter's spelling was probably off, but no names even came close. Something about the mention of a big house tickled his memory, but he couldn't put a finger on it. He scooted up to the typewriter and banged out a reply.

**Can you get your mother to write to me?**

Johnny sat back and waited for the next message to come. He was nodding off when a tug on his shirtsleeve snapped him back awake.

"Daddy breakfast," Patrick said. "Pancakes."

"Okay, let's see if we can find you something to eat."

He glanced over his shoulder as they left the room, but the typewriter remained silent.

*October 29, 1963*

"Mommy, are you awake?"

Genny nudged her shoulder, and Mary rolled over with a groan. "I am now. What time is it?"

"I don't know. Daddy wants you to come upstairs and write to him."

"Geraldine Rose Smith, what are you doing up this early?" Mary could see through a gap in the curtains that it was still dark outside. "And why are you playing around with the typewriter? I told you not to touch it until I gave you lessons on how to use it."

"But daddy..."

"No, enough of this silly game. I don't want to hear any more about it." Even in the dark, she could see that her daughter was on the verge of tears. "I'm sorry, I didn't sleep well last night after the party. Since I'm up, I might as well make you breakfast. Would you like some pancakes?"

She was ready to return to bed after seeing Genny off to school. Mary didn't have that luxury, though; not only did she have to get to work, but she had a more pressing matter to take care of first. Plotting her escape from Devonshire Manor.

Mary's plan was simple, but whether she dared to go through with it was another matter. She would ask Gretchen to give her and Genny a ride into Iowa City when she went to the grocery store on Saturday so that they could do some clothes shopping. She would slip away and use the money she earned for her first week to pay for the cab ride to her sister's house in Cedar Rapids. It would mean leaving behind what little clothes and toiletries they had brought, but the money she had left after the cab fare would be enough to replace them.

Mary thought about calling the police, but without proof that Dr. Masterson was planning to commit a crime, it would be her word against that of a well-respected scientist. She knew from experience that the police were often corrupt and in the pockets of the rich and powerful. Once she reached Cedar Rapids, she would figure out what to do next.

The first step of her plan was to verify that Gretchen was going to town on Saturday and mention that she wanted to come along ahead of time. If she waited until that morning to ask her, the housekeeper might take off without her. It was also better to place her request early so it didn't look suspicious. Of course, if Dr. Masterson somehow found out she had overheard him...it was probably best not to think about that.

Mary pushed aside the thought as she entered the manor and walked down the servants' hallway. As she entered the kitchen, she found Gretchen bent over in front of the oven. "I hope I'm not interrupting..." she started to say as the housekeeper stood up.

Only it wasn't Gretchen.

"Of course not," Margrit replied. "Would you care for a croissant? They're hot and fresh right out of the oven."

"Ah, maybe later, I was looking for Gretchen. Is she here?"

"Dr. Masterson sent her to town on an errand. Is there something I can help you with?"

"No, I was just going to ask her if she was going into town on Saturday. I need to get some new school clothes for Genny, and I was hoping she could give me a ride. I can wait until Gretchen gets back to talk to her." Mary wanted to grab one of the kitchen knives and cut her tongue off to stop babbling. Any hope of slipping away without drawing attention had vanished.

"Well, lucky for you, I was planning to head into town today to do some shopping," Margrit said. "I'll take you along with me. We can have lunch and get to know each other since we'll be working together."

"Oh, I wouldn't want to impose. I also don't get paid until Friday."

"I'll talk Henry into getting you an advance on your paycheck," she replied. "I'm sure he won't mind. There's a distinct lack of women at this company, so having some female companionship will be a nice change. I insist."

Mary tried to think up another excuse not to go with her, but her mind had gone blank. "Yeah, okay, it sounds like fun."

She spent the rest of the day feeling sick to her stomach. There was little chance that Margrit hadn't noticed how nervous she was. In only a few minutes, the woman had utterly unnerved her, and Mary had no idea how she would survive spending a couple of hours in her company. It was almost noon before she knew it, and she had to hurry to find something to wear.

Mary threw on the dress she had worn to her interview. While it was nothing fancy, she had this unexplainable urge to impress Margrit. She slipped on her shoes and unlocked the cottage door before returning for the revolver Jon had given her. Mary pulled the suitcase out from under the bed and removed the gun from inside the lining. She tucked it into her purse right before a knock on the bedroom door startled her.

"Sorry, the front door was open," Margrit said. "I was worried something was wrong."

"Oh, I'm fine, I just forgot my...bracelet," she replied, holding up her wrist to show her the silver bracelet she was wearing as she slid the suitcase back in place.

"How very pretty," the woman commented, "and rather unusual. Is that a snake?"

"Yes, it's a family heirloom from my mother's side. Even when I had to sell my wedding ring to pay rent, I couldn't bear to part with it." Mary had no idea why she was telling this woman things she was too embarrassed to admit to anyone else. "I'm ready to go."

Margrit led her to the four-stall garage at the back of the courtyard. The silver sports car she had arrived in the other day was nowhere to be seen, and she walked over to a black two-door Dodge coupe instead. The protruding tail fins displayed the badge **Viscount**, which she had never heard of, but it was a regal automobile. The engine roared to life as Margrit pulled the car out of the garage, and they headed into town.

Mary was not much for driving. She had sold Jon's car a month after his death, but she had never been as scared out of her wits as she was sitting in the passenger seat on that ride. Margrit drove with a casual, reckless abandonment, speeding down the road and whipping around slower-moving cars with only a single hand barely holding the steering wheel as she smoked a cigarette with the other. There were many times that Mary wanted to cover her eyes with her hands, but she would not give the woman the satisfaction of knowing how terrified she was making her.

The urge to roll out of the car and kiss the ground when they stopped was overwhelming. Margrit had parked down the street from the Old Capital building near a seedy-looking place called Kenney's Tavern. It hardly looked like a respectable place for a woman, especially in the middle of the day, and she was relieved when they walked past it.

Even without her hair done up or much makeup on her face, Margrit was undeniably beautiful. Her radiance emanated from beneath her skin and made her appearance appear ageless. What was even more irritating was that every man they passed turned his head to stare in her direction before catching himself. Even a couple of women looked at her as though her presence also had a hypnotic effect on them.

She led them down the street to the Younger & Sons department store. Jon had taken her shopping at the flagship store in Des Moines once when they visited her sister, and it had been glamorous even by Chicago standards. While this location was less extravagant, it was still well outside her price range.

"I can't afford this place," Mary said. "Is there somewhere else that we could go?"

"There's nothing to fret about, dear," Margrit answered. "Our little shopping excursion today will be going on Dr. Masterson's account. Before you argue, he was quite insistent about it."

Mary spotted several taxi cabs parked further down the street, waiting to pick up fares. If she could find a way to sneak away from Margrit, she could have one take her to Genny's school. While she didn't know the school's address, she hoped the cab driver would know where to find it.

The only problem was that Margrit stayed close to her, likely on purpose. Her opportunity came when the woman went to try on a dress, and Mary bolted as soon as she shut the door to the fitting room. She slipped through the curtain separating the changing area from the rest of the store and made a beeline for the entrance. Mary stepped outside and almost collided with Margrit at the store's entrance. "It's rather rude to leave a girl waiting for someone to zip her up," she said. "I'm beginning to think you don't like me."

"Stay away from me," Mary replied, wondering how she got out here ahead of her. "I don't want to hurt you, but I'm warning you to leave me alone."

"Oh, are you going to shoot me with the gun hidden in your purse?" Mary reached into her bag and found that the revolver was missing. Margrit stepped closer to her so she could whisper in her ear. "Don't make a scene, and let's go back inside. Otherwise, I'll put a bullet in your head, and everyone in sight will swear they saw you shoot yourself. I promise you I have the power to do that." Mary looked down and saw that Margrit was holding her revolver discreetly in her hand. The woman tilted her head to the side, to which she could only nod in agreement.

"Why are you doing this? What do you care if I want to leave?"

"Because Henry has plans for you, and you know too much for your own good."

The rest of the afternoon was a blur. They ate lunch at a nearby restaurant, but Mary barely touched the food she ordered. She returned to the cottage but saw it for what it was now—a prison. Mary tried to concentrate on her work but missed Genny's bus again. Her daughter wasn't upset about it, but she hurried upstairs right away. Genny came back down a few minutes later with a concerned look on her face.

"Mommy, I know you told me not to touch the typewriter, but daddy says he needs to talk to you."

"I don't know what this game is you're playing, but it's upsetting me. I'm going to have to put an end to this. If you can't leave the typewriter alone, I'll have to lock my office."

Mary hated snapping at her daughter, but her nerves were frayed. She knew that Genny was manifesting her own worries by pretending to talk to her dead father. If there were ever a time she wished she could talk to Jon, it would be now. Her plan to escape was ruined, and she was unlikely to be given another chance to leave the estate without being escorted. Margrit had also confiscated her gun, so she had nothing more than a kitchen knife to protect herself.

She marched upstairs to her office to see what Genny had done to her typewriter. Her daughter had removed the memo she had been writing and replaced it with a different piece of paper. The sheet in the roller was nearly at the end, and there were typed lines throughout the page, each separated by several blank lines as if she had scrolled up to read what had been written.

```
Jenny where are you? Is your mother with you?



me and mommy are in odanna iowa in mommys
new boss big house i have my own bedroom



Can you get your mother to write to me?



I tried but sshe dosnt beleve me



You need to get her to come to the typewriter
Please honey its very important I talk to her



im not supppos to be typn she wil get mad at me



I promise you won't be in trouble. Are you in
Old Ahnen? Is your mother's boss Dr. Masterson?
What is your mother's name?



yes we road the train from chiago daddy im scard
```

**Everything will be fine, sweetheart. Get your mom**

Mary's hands shook as she finished reading the exchange on the page. She had horribly misjudged what her daughter was trying to tell her, thinking she was playing some kind of game. This was clearly something different. Putting the sheet down on the desk, she inserted a new piece of paper and turned the knob on the roller until it was above the carriage.

Mary had no idea what she should write. What does one say to one's dead husband? Did she really believe her daughter was talking with a ghost through her typewriter? Mary placed her fingers on the keys and started typing the first thing that came to mind.

**Jon? This is Mary, is this really you writing?**

She sat back in her chair and waited for something to happen, but after about five minutes, she decided to check on Genny. No sooner did Mary stand up then the typewriter began to clatter away on its own. Her legs felt weak, and her bladder was suddenly about to burst. She was scared even to touch the machine, but she forced herself to turn the knob to advance the paper.

**Yes, it's me. I know this sounds strange, but what year is it?**

Mary had to fight the urge to go running from the room, but she remained standing as she typed out a reply to her dead(?) husband.

**Its October 1963. Are you a ghost, Jon?**

**No, I'm alive, but I can't explain it now. You are in great danger. You need to leave right away.**

**We're trapped in my boss' house. There's no way out.**

Mary could not believe she was conversing with Jon in this manner. She wondered if it was even her husband. Could this be a trap Henry had devised for her, or more likely, a cruel trick Margrit was playing on her? The unscrupulous woman claimed to have supernatural powers, after all. There was nothing she could do about it if that were the case. Mary had to hope her husband was still alive and trying to help her.

**There's an underground tunnel in the basement, it will take you to the factory. Look for a blue sign. You need to leave tonight or he will kill you.**

"Mommy, are you talking to daddy?" She hadn't heard Genny enter the room and nearly screamed when she spoke.

"Don't sneak up on me, honey. You scared the daylights out of me." Mary took the piece of paper out of the typewriter. "No, I was just taking care of some work. Go downstairs, and I'll make you a snack."

Genny followed her to the kitchen, where she fixed her favorite sandwich, cheese with grape jelly, along with a glass of cold milk. Once she was busy eating, Mary went back to her bedroom and changed into a pair of pants and a sweater she had bought. She had also picked up some more comfortable shoes at the department store. She was sure Margrit would notice her clothing selection at the time, but the woman hadn't batted an eye.

Mary knew she would have to wait until everyone in the manor was asleep before she could sneak inside, so she let Genny stay up and watch television. She kept watch from her darkened office until the last light in the main house turned off. She clicked on the desk lamp and typed a last message.

**We're going. If we don't make it, I love you.**

Before switching off the light, she turned the knob to advance the paper a few lines in case Jon sent a response. With any luck, she would never return here to see it. Genny had fallen asleep on the floor, and she nudged her awake enough to slip a sweater over her head.

"Huh? What's happening?" her daughter yawned.

"I need you to come with me, but we can't make any noise." Genny was wide awake at the sound of the urgency in her voice. Mary left through the cottage's back door since the front was easily visible from the main house. They stayed close to the garage to cross the cobblestone courtyard, and she kept a tight grip on Genny's hand to keep her from falling on the uneven surface.

The night seemed too still, or maybe she had forgotten how silent the countryside was after living in a big city for so long. Besides a couple of outdoor lights, the only illumination came from the moonlight filtering through the tall trees surrounding the manor. Every shadow took on a sinister form, and it felt like dozens of eyes followed her every move.

They reached the side door to the servants' hallway, which was locked. Mary dug around in the planter beside the door where she had seen Gretchen stash a key after sneaking a cigarette the other night. She sifted through the dirt, her anxiety rising every second that somebody would see them when her fingers closed around it.

The house's floors were all hardwood, which meant her rubber-soled shoes could elicit a squeak if she stepped wrong. She motioned for Genny to take hers off as she removed her own, carrying them as they made their way past the door to the housekeeper's private room. Mary realized she didn't have a flashlight and had no idea if there were lights in the basement.

She grabbed a candle and book of matches from the dining room before they crept towards the Grand Hall. Crossing the cold stone tiles of the daunting room was even more nerve-wracking than the courtyard had been, as every little sound seemed to reverberate throughout the house. Mary allowed herself to let out a sigh of relief when they reached the archway to the main stairwell.

The entrance to Dr. Masterson's private chambers was at the top of the second-floor landing. A small alcove hid the stairs leading down to the basement, but a bathroom was also tucked away in the recess. Mary ducked inside and fumbled open the matchbook, then almost dropped it on the floor getting one to light using the phosphorus strip. The match flared to life, and she held it to the wick until the candle took to the flame. The flickering light barely cut through the darkness as they descended the steps into the depths of the manor.

"We're looking for a door with a blue sign," Mary whispered.

The layout of the upper floors was confusing enough, but the basement was a veritable labyrinth. The stone walls, arched ceilings, and iron-strapped wood doors gave her the impression that she had set foot in a medieval dungeon. Seeing a spiderweb-covered skeleton rotting away in rusted chains wouldn't surprise her.

Panic and despair were two growing shadows following her as she found no sign of an exit. The last door of the center passage opened upon another hallway that ran the length of the western half of the house. It was populated with more doors, but they were all locked. Mary was about to give up hope as the candle was nearly burned out when she came to another intersection.

There was a door at either end of the shorter crossing hallway, and she could make out a sign affixed to the one on the right-hand side. Unfortunately, the sign was bright red.

## WARNING!
### NO ADMITTANCE WITHOUT
### PERMISSION OF DR. MASTERSON

She returned to the main passageway and tried the corridor to the left. Halfway down, a small, rectangular blue sign with words stenciled in white letters was mounted to the wall.

## ← TRAM TO FACTORY

Mary tried the door and found it was unlocked, the light from the candle revealing a set of steps going down further underground on the other side. This had to be the tunnel that would lead her out of the estate, but to what end? Dr. Masterson would track her down wherever she went. She needed something to use against him, or this nightmare would never be over.

"Are we going down there, mommy?" Genny asked.

"We need to check the other door first, and then we'll go," she replied. "I promise."

The last thing Mary wanted to do was spend one more minute than necessary in this place, but she forced herself to return to the door with the red sign. She was sure it would be locked, but the knob turned easily in her hand. The hallway past this door was narrower and sloped steadily downward. The candle had grown so dim that she could barely see more than six feet ahead. When the light fell upon a wall at the end of the shaft, Mary feared it was a dead end. Her foot almost slipped on the spiral stairs cut into the floor.

"Mommy, I'm scared. I want to go back."

"I know, but it's only a little farther." She was afraid as well, but something drove her on. A buzzing noise had started in her head shortly after she set foot beyond the red door, a sound that was both unsettling and enticing. It seemed to charge the air around her like electricity building up before a thunderstorm. The sensation grew stronger the deeper they went, and Mary was certain she would find its source at the bottom of these steps.

The stairwell twisted around itself, leading down for what seemed to be a long way until she was dizzy from circling about. The steps ended at a stone archway that looked like a larger version of all the doorways in the manor above. She passed through into a dome-shaped room dominated by a greenish-black pillar on a stone dais, its surface covered with strange carvings. Mary was sure this thing had drawn her down here, the flame to her moth.

She approached the pillar and stretched out her arms to touch its surface, which felt cold and warm simultaneously. The bracelet on her arm began to glow, the rubies pulsating as though they were beating hearts. Her head was filled with strange visions, glimpses of other lives that were not hers, yet they were. She knew each of these women, had walked in their shoes, lived their lives, and even shared their deaths.

Mary could see it now. The pillar was what Dr. Masterson was hiding, what he wanted to control. It was more than just a stone column; it was a gateway for traveling to other worlds. She could use this to escape, to take Genny and her somewhere else. Mary could be reunited with (*Jack...Johnny...John*) Jon.

A sharp prick on the back of her shoulder was her only warning that they were no longer alone. The tranquilizer coursed through her body as she struggled to reach the dart that had delivered it. She collapsed on the floor, her body losing all feeling. Kari managed to turn her head, and even as her vision blurred, she saw a younger-looking version of Albert. The man who had raised her and whom she would always consider her real father stood over her, holding a strange-looking pistol.

"You almost slipped away from me, *liebling*," he said with a toothy grin. "The boss would not have been happy with me."

"*Dad?*" Kari whispered before passing out.

# Schrodinger Was A Teenage Pet Grave Robber

A Novel By MARTIN KNIGHT

Jupiter &
Phoebus
Publishing
House

# Chapter 17
## Schrodinger Was A Teenage Pet Grave Robber

*October 28, 2019*

J ohnny tried his best to hide his exhaustion, forcing himself to concentrate on the round table discussion on the impact of social media in literature. He wished he could return to his room and see if there was a new message on the typewriter *(and maybe take a nap)*. If his wife and daughter had managed to escape the manor, they wouldn't be able to write to him anymore. If they had gotten caught...the result was probably the same.

The suspense of not knowing what was happening was killing him. Of course, all of that took *(was taking?)* place fifty years ago in Martin Knight's unpublished manuscript. His mind was still struggling to grasp how that could be possible.

The realization hadn't dawned on him at first. In the two days he had to read it, Johnny had skimmed through his copy of *The Alchemist's Apprentice* that Vivian had given him. The town's name from the story must have stuck in his memory. After realizing Jenny had misspelled Old Ahnen as *Odonna*, he went back and read through the first couple of chapters more closely.

The woman in the book was named Mary though, not Kathy, and her young daughter was Geraldine, but she called her Genny. All of that seemed to match up with the messages from the typewriter. Of course, if he told anybody about this, they would think he had suffered a psychotic break from reality.

That could be what was happening to him, but if there was a chance his wife and daughter were alive, he had to try to save them. He had warned Mary that she was in danger, but he hadn't told her that in the story she was going to die. Johnny worried that he couldn't change her fate since it was already written down. Or worse, maybe it was his actions that would cause her death.

As if all that wasn't weighing heavily on his mind, he also had to worry about watching his son. The housekeeper promised to keep an eye on Patrick, but she also had to supervise the kitchen staff preparing meals for the group. The kiddo slept until almost nine this morning, then after breakfast, returned to their bedroom to play with his tablet. When Johnny poked his head into the room about an hour ago, Patrick was still watching videos quietly.

The group finally stopped for lunch, and he took the opportunity to hurry upstairs and check on him. Johnny opened the door and found him sitting on the bed, but his tablet was on the floor. There was also a clear plastic box beside it. Patrick was holding something, but his back was turned, hiding it from view. Johnny looked over his son's shoulder and saw that he had removed the protective hard case from the first edition copy of the *Homecoming Queen of Sorrows*. He was flipping through the pages, stopping on the ones that had illustrations on them.

"Whoa, buddy, let's not damage daddy's book," Johnny said as he reached down and took the novel from him. "It's worth a lot of money, and we don't want to rip the pages."

"That's mommy," his son said, pointing to the drawing he had been looking at. Johnny had only read the mass-market paperback version of Martin's first novel, but he knew the first-edition hardcover book featured several artworks by the author himself. Standing on a stage wearing a formal gown covered in motor oil and feathers, the young woman in the painting resembled Kathy remarkably.

"You're right; that does look like mommy." Johnny thumbed through the rest of the pages, trying to find another image of the book's main character, when an envelope fell out and landed on the floor. He reached down to pick it up and saw that his name was written on the front. Breaking the seal, he opened the flap and removed a handwritten note.

*Mr. Sawyer,*

*If you are reading this, then I am dead or incapacitated. You also likely think your wife is dead. Let me assure you that she and your daughter are very much alive and in great danger. If you do not believe me, let me prove it to you. Return to the shop where you bought this book. The owner will explain further.*

*Kindest Regards,*
*Martin Knight*

Johnny read the note several times, but it made less sense with each pass. This had to be some sick practical joke by the old bookseller, but how could he have written the note, slipped the envelope inside the book, and enclosed it in the plastic shell while he watched him the entire time? The man could have done it before he entered the store, which begged the question of how he would've known his name beforehand. Johnny remembered there was a TV show where a magician in disguise pulled off tricks like that on unsuspecting people while hidden cameras filmed them.

Of course, it wouldn't be much of a show if the trick wasn't revealed until the next day. Maybe Vivian was in on the joke and had set up hidden cameras in the bedroom, taping him as he looked around like some slack-jawed yokel. He brushed aside his paranoid delusions (*it's not paranoia if they're watching you*) and tucked the envelope back into the book. Johnny intended to return to Salem and find out what game this bookseller was playing. He handed Patrick his tablet and took him downstairs to join the others for lunch.

"When my husband hosted this retreat, he would provide his guests with cigars and Bourbon at the end of each day," Vivian said after the meal. "Most of the attendants he invited were of the brutish sex, so perhaps a different choice of libations is in order. I was thinking of serving a selection of fine wines and cheeses. Would you be opposed to that, Mr. Sawyer?"

"I don't mind a good glass of wine, or whiskey for that matter, but I don't smoke, and I'm lactose intolerant. Unfortunately, I won't be able to join you. My son hasn't been sleeping well, so I'd like to take him back to his grandparents' house. I hope that's okay?"

He noticed Vivian glance over at Niko, who was suddenly looking down at her hands before she put a smile back on her face.

"Certainly, you must do what's best for him. Perhaps you will be able to join us tomorrow night? I know your fellow writers are anxious to get to know you in a more social setting." Niko continued to avoid looking at him, but all the other women were eyeing him almost brazenly now.

If he thought he had trouble concentrating that morning, his attention was absolutely shot during the afternoon session. They were supposed to be concentrating on their stories, but he kept catching the other attendees throwing furtive glances in his direction. When he took a break to get a snack, he ran into several women gathered in the kitchen and talking softly. Their conversations stopped when he was within earshot, and they all blushed with odd smiles as though they had been discussing him.

It was a relief to get out of there finally, and Johnny wasted no time driving back to Salem and dropping his son off with his in-laws. He gave them a quick explanation that he needed to pick up a prescription for Patrick from a nearby pharmacy before getting back in the car and heading to Tell-Tale Books.

The store was closed by the time he arrived, but Johnny went up and knocked on the door several times anyway. He was about to give up and try again in the morning when he saw a light turn on in the window on the second floor. Johnny stepped back so Ryland could see him when he looked out. A minute later, the lights turned on downstairs, and the aged shopkeeper unlocked the door with a scowl on his face.

"I'm sorry, young man, but the store is closed. Good evening to you."

Johnny reached out and stopped him from shutting the door in his face, earning him an even more reproachful look. "Wait, sir, I was in here yesterday with my son. I purchased a first-edition Martin Knight novel."

"If you're looking to return an item, all sales are final," Ryland said.

"No, that's not why I'm here. There was a note tucked inside the book," he replied, pulling out the envelope. "It's from Martin Knight, and it's addressed to me. The note says to return here to learn the truth about my wife and daughter. Do you know anything about this?"

"Perhaps you should ask Mr. Knight that question?" the shopkeeper responded, but he held out his hand and accepted the envelope. "Alright, you might as well come inside while I read this over. Can I offer you a cup of tea?"

Johnny was trying to contain his frustration, but he needed to find out if the old guy knew something about the fate of his family. He followed him upstairs to the quaint living quarters on the second floor. Johnny sat at the small kitchen table while Ryland filled a kettle with water and put it on the stove burner. "I would gladly ask Martin, but he's been in a coma for three months."

"Oh, right, I believe I heard that." Ryland set two mugs and a box of tea bags on the table, pulled out the other chair, and read over the note. "How much do you remember, Johnny? Or should I say, Jack?"

"Jack? What's that supposed to mean?"

"Never mind, just tell me what you know."

"I don't know, it's very confusing. My wife died eight years ago, but I also remember her being alive and us having a daughter named Jenny. I think I've been talking to them using an old typewriter, and they're somehow living in a fictional town in 1963."

"I know you probably aren't looking for a metaphysical discussion, Mr. Sawyer, but have you heard of the KnightmareVerse?"

"Yeah, sure, it's the shared universe that connects all Martin's stories and characters together. Can you please tell me whether I'm going crazy because this has started to feel like I'm in a horror story."

"It's funny that you would express such a sentiment. Suppose you were a character in such a story. What would you do if you found out about it?"

"I don't know, and I'm not in the mood for riddles."

"Imagine that you are living your life, minding your own business, when you learn that someone is watching your every move. This person is also using you to make their fortune. How would that make you feel?"

"Angry, I guess," Johnny answered. "What are you getting at?"

"That story Martin Knight was writing before his unfortunate accident is about a man named Dr. Masterson, is it not?"

"Yes, but how did you know that?"

"Martin was a friend of mine, and he shared it with me," Ryland shrugged. "He also mentioned that he was having terrible nightmares about his work in progress. He worried that this Dr. Masterson was real and had become aware he was a character in his book. I know it sounds ridiculous, but I think he truly believed it. He said he feared something bad would happen but couldn't bring himself to stop writing."

"You think this Dr. Masterson character somehow pulled him into the Knightmare-Verse? Like he caused Martin to slip into a coma?"

"Who knows, but Martin gave me that book shortly before it happened and told me to sell it to whoever wanted the snow globe."

"The snow globe? What does that have to do with anything?"

The kettle on the stove whistled, and Johnny nearly fell out of his chair at the sound. Ryland chuckled as he stood up, removed the kettle from the burner, and poured hot water into both mugs. "You certainly look like a man going through a stressful ordeal. I have a simple idea for how you can determine whether your wife is alive or not. There's a shovel downstairs. Take it with you and dig up her grave. If she's alive, you won't find her body, and if not..."

"Why the hell would I do that? Martin's note said you would explain everything."

"In good time I will, but I don't think you're ready to believe it yet," Ryland replied. "Your wife and daughter are alive, and they are being held captive along with Martin in the KnightmareVerse."

"Okay, you've gone off the deep end. Are you telling me Martin Knight had the power to create his own universe?"

"No, I don't believe so. He explained it was because he could see events happening in this alternate universe through his dreams and used those visions to write his novels. Martin said he made a mistake when he inserted himself as a character into this latest story, as it allowed Dr. Masterson to open a doorway between the two worlds. You don't have to take my word for it, Johnny. Go ask Mrs. Knight. She's the one who taught him how to do it."

"That sounds crazy. Nobody in their right mind would believe that. How am I even supposed to bring that up with her? *Hey, I think your husband came up with all his books by spying on people through his dreams and writing about their deaths.* She'll either have me arrested or committed."

"I understand your hesitation. If you think that's too uncomfortable, go dig up your wife's grave and learn the truth that way."

Johnny sat back and took a sip from his cup of tea. "Where'd you say that shovel is?"

The moon had crested the top of the pine trees bordering the graveyard's east side as Johnny stood with a shovel at the foot of his wife's final resting place. Her tombstone was silhouetted by the moonlight as though it knew what he was about to do and had hidden itself in shame.

Although nobody was around, he felt like a hundred eyes were watching him in silent judgment. To disturb this hallowed ground in the middle of the night was a sin against not only Kathy's memory but everyone else buried here, even if it was to save his sanity. Johnny had no choice, he needed to know whether she was dead or alive.

The old bookseller had to be off his rocker, talking about them living inside of a fictional universe. If that were the case, however, then what he was about to do would result in nothing more than some overturned earth instead of him desecrating her corpse. Every ounce of logical sense in him was screaming that this was madness, but he had to go through with it. Johnny took a deep breath and plunged the shovel's tip into the grass.

"John Sawyer, what in the world are you doing?" Margrett called out from behind him. He let out a yelp and dropped the shovel as he spun around to face her.

"What? I, uh... I was just... I was going to dig up Kathy's grave."

"Yes, I can see that. You're lucky I didn't call the police when Patrick told me there was a man in the graveyard," she replied. "Have you lost your mind?"

"I know you're not going to believe this, but I don't think she is dead. I've been talking to her and her daughter named Geraldine somehow over an old typewriter. I get how crazy that sounds, and I wouldn't blame you if you called the police."

"You're right, it does sound crazy. You said she has a daughter named Geraldine? Do you have a flashlight with you?"

"A flashlight? Um, yeah, I've got one on my cell phone."

"Follow me."

She led him through the tombstones to the older graves closer to the church. Margrett stopped and turned to face him. "Katherine was three months pregnant when she died, and she was going to have a girl. She hadn't told you yet because she was planning to leave you if you kept drinking, but she was scared to raise a baby and take care of Patrick on her own."

"What the fuck? Why didn't you tell me about this?"

"We didn't say anything when you woke up because the shock of her death was enough to handle, and you had a hard recovery ahead of you. Then it became too painful to even think about later," she answered, a tear rolling down her cheek. "The last time I talked to her, she told me she wanted to name her daughter Geraldine. Since I first showed her this, she had been fascinated with that name."

Margrett stepped aside to reveal the gravestone behind her. Johnny turned the light on his phone towards it and read the worn-down inscription carved into the blackened, moss-covered granite block set into the ground.

# GERALDINE ULMER

### BORN 6 JUNE 1666
### DIED 31 OCTOBER 1692

"Who was this?" Johnny asked.

"Do you remember the ancestor I told you about who died in the Salem Witch Trials? This is her grave. She founded a secret organization to protect women who were like her, women who were special. They would gather at her house to help each other with what they were going through and to enjoy the companionship of those who understood what it was like to be different. Someone found out about the meetings, and it led to the deaths of several members, including her own."

"What do you mean different?"

"The townsfolk claimed they were witches," Margrit replied, "but I think they were women who didn't wish to be relegated to little more than indentured servants to men. Women who wanted to be in control of their own lives."

"That symbol, the crescent moon with the writing on it. I've seen that somewhere before. What does it mean?"

"Nobody knows. It was carved on her headstone about a hundred years after she died. Some say it symbolizes the group she started, the Coven."

"Do you think she was a witch?" Margrett only looked at him silently in response.

Johnny leaned closer and tried to make out the strange markings on the carving, but they had become too worn down to recognize. "What about this Coven? Could they still be around?"

"Who's to say whether they even existed," she answered. "I wish there were some magic in the world that could bring my daughter back to life, but we both know that isn't possible. Whatever you were looking for here tonight, John, I hope you've found it."

⊗

*October 30, 1963*

*"So, who are you? And what are you doing here?"*

Mary tried to lift her head, but it felt too heavy to move. She was vaguely aware of being cold, and there was an uncomfortable tightness around her chest, wrists, and ankles. Those sensations seemed a distant concern, as if her mind was disconnected from her body. More pressing to her was the buzzing noise, like a swarm of angry hornets that had built a nest inside her skull. It set every nerve in her body on edge and made her want more than anything for it to go away.

Another feeling came from a deeper part of her mind: blind anger roiling up like a wall of flames. Somehow, she knew that the fire could burn away the merciless buzzing that was causing her pain, so she allowed the anger to lash out. Mary was jerked awake when a hand slapped her hard across the cheek.

"You bitch! You made my nose bleed!" Margrit snarled as she pinched her nostrils shut. "And you stained my favorite coat!"

Mary's vision was filled with stars from the blow, but she could see there was a trail of blood running from the woman's nose down to her chin. Some of it had also dripped onto the lapel of the white trench coat that she was wearing. Now that she was awake, Mary realized why she was so cold. She was sitting completely naked in a straight-backed wooden chair. A glaring light was shining down on her from directly above, making it hard to see anything beyond the cone of brightness surrounding her. Mary tried to cover herself up with her hands, but she was strapped into the chair by leather restraints.

"What's going on? What is this thing?" she asked.

"This is an interrogation, so I'll be asking the questions," Margrit replied, wiping her face with a handkerchief. "What you are sitting in is an electric chair. Don't worry, I'm not going to kill you. It's been modified to give a non-lethal shock, but it will make you wish you were dead."

"No, oh god, please don't do that." Mary shook her head and realized there was a leather band underneath her chin connected to something on top of her head. "I'll tell you whatever you want, but I don't know anything. I swear, you have to believe me."

"I'm afraid I don't believe much of anything you have to say. Don't tell me you haven't been trained to protect whatever you're hiding in your head. I can feel there's something you have buried inside there, and you attacked me when I probed at it."

"I don't know what you're talking about. How could I attack you? I can't move."

"You can drop the charade. We know you're a witch," Margrit scoffed. "Fine, if you want to make this more difficult, I've been looking forward to using this."

Margrit stepped over to a big metal switch on the wall with a thick cable connected to the chair's base. She placed her hand on the lever, and Mary tensed up as she braced for the electricity to course through her body. Margrit had a devious smile on her face as she swung the switch down and slammed it into place. She felt her bladder let loose, the warm liquid flowing down her bare legs, but nothing else happened.

"Oh, goddamnit, I just stepped in your piss," the woman hissed at her. "Do you know how much these shoes cost?"

"Enough with the theatrics, Margrit," Henry spoke up from behind her. "Clean her up and bring her upstairs."

Mary heard a heavy door close and was grateful that Dr. Masterson was no longer in the room. Margrit unfastened the straps holding her to the chair and helped her stand up as her legs felt weak and unsteady. "Try anything, and we'll see if you're powerful enough to stop a bullet," Margrit said as she took a pistol from the pocket of her trench coat.

She handcuffed Mary's wrists behind her back and led her out of the room. She wondered what had compelled her to turn away from her chance of escaping. If she had listened to Jon, she might be on her way to Cedar Rapids now instead of trapped inside this nightmare.

"Where's my daughter? I want to see her."

"She's safe, that's all you need to know."

Margrit unceremoniously marched her naked and shivering through the basement and up the stairs to the second floor. Gretchen was coming out of Dr. Masterson's private chambers as they reached the landing, and her eyes widened at seeing Mary nude.

"You, come with me," Margrit barked at the housekeeper. Gretchen fell in behind them as they passed through the Grand Hall using the second-floor walkway that connected to the house's other side. Margrit stopped at the first door they came to, which opened onto a spacious Queen Anne-style bedroom with its own private bathroom. She stood in the doorway and had Gretchen wash her, unlocking the handcuffs only long enough for her to put on one of the house staff's black-and-white uniforms. It was tight on her, and Margrit didn't provide her with any underwear, so she only felt a little less exposed than before.

Now that she was somewhat decent, she was taken back through the Grand Hall to the doorway from which Gretchen had first emerged. Mary had only been inside Dr.

Masterson's private office once since she started working for him. It was furnished with a massive mahogany desk with bookshelves behind it, a leather couch, and two reading chairs with an oval coffee table between them. Mary sat down in one of the chairs the best she could, her hands still bound behind her. A door on the other side of the room opened, and Henry entered.

"Couldn't you have given her something more comfortable to wear than that?"

"I've sacrificed enough of my wardrobe," Margrit replied. "Do you want me to leave her cuffed?"

"No, you can remove those," Dr. Masterson said as the woman freed her wrists. "That will be all for now. Why don't you see to the little girl? I doubt she is enjoying having a werewolf for a babysitter."

Mary gasped, and it took every ounce of her resolve not to run from the room in a desperate attempt to find her daughter. If she were going to make it back to Genny, she would have to wait for the right opportunity. Margrit started to protest, but a look from Henry caused her to close her mouth. She gave Mary a sideways glare as she left the room.

"I apologize for that unpleasantness," Henry said. "Margrit can get a little carried away with her questioning methods sometimes."

"You call being strapped into an electric chair *unpleasant*?" Mary asked. "Why do you even have that thing?"

"It was a gift from J. Edgar Hoover, having recently been retired from Sing Sing Penitentiary. He presented it to me in appreciation for exposing the Rosenbergs. That was the same chair they were executed with. It's no longer in working condition, as you no doubt are aware of now, but it is still quite effective as an interrogation tool."

"I don't understand, I thought you owned a pharmaceutical company."

"That is merely a cover, although a very profitable one. The real work we do here is for the CIA, helping to protect Americans from the evils of communism. Of course, I think J. Edgar would be less pleased to know that I provided the Rosenbergs with the atomic secrets that they passed on to the KGB.

"You see, I am the last in a long line of Alchemists, men of magic who have shaped the events of humankind: Zosimos, Merlin, Nicolas Flamel. We have raised civilizations from the mud and razed them back to ashes, all in pursuit of that most elusive and powerful magic. *Knowledge*. And you are going to help me unlock the greatest secret of all."

"About what? I don't know anything. I'm only a secretary."

"Everything, my dear. Your presence here is no coincidence." Henry walked over to his desk, picked up a black metal cube sitting on it, and set it down on the coffee table. "A man showed up on my doorstep recently, claiming to be a traveling encyclopedia salesman no less. He gave me this box and said it was the key to the pillar you saw, which I had brought here from the *City of the Dead* in Egypt. This man told me to put a job advertisement in the newspaper and that a woman from Chicago would apply who could use this key. Since you were the one from Chicago who answered the posting, that must be you, Mary."

"Do you know how insane that sounds? Why would I help you?"

"It is truly a shame about what happened to your husband. If I remember correctly, he stabbed himself in the throat and then drowned in Lake Michigan?"

"If you're going to kill me, then just get it over with."

"Quite the contrary, I wish to give you what so few people who have a loved one wrongly taken from them get. The chance for revenge."

"What do you mean? Jon committed suicide."

"We both know that isn't true. Help me with what I ask, and I will deliver to you the heart of your husband's killer on a silver platter. After that, you and your daughter will be free to go, and I will see you on your way with one hundred thousand dollars in cash. Enough to start a new life."

Mary looked down at the black cube on the table. While it appeared harmless, there was also a sinister quality to it as if it were a chunk carved out of the night sky. She couldn't be sure since her head was hurting, but being near it was causing the same buzzing that the pillar had emitted. Mary had no desire to touch the evil-looking thing, but if it was her only chance to escape, then so be it.

"Alright, whatever you want from me, I'll do it."

"Very well, I'm glad you have come around. The ritual will begin at midnight."

He returned to his desk, where he pressed a button on the intercom. The muscular man who had tranquilized her appeared, took Mary back to the bedroom, and locked her inside. She sat down on the bed, and the tears came as she sank into despair.

"Oh god, Jon, I wish you were here."

*October 29, 2019*

Johnny stood outside what should have been the front door to Tell-Tale Books, looking around in confusion. He was sure he had returned to the right place. All the other shops on the street were the same as he remembered them. The only problem was that no books were displayed in the window, and the store name above the awning had changed.

# ROSE MATTERS

He pulled the door open and stuck his head inside. An overpowering floral assault had replaced the musty smell of old paper, and Johnny felt his allergies threatening to overwhelm him. He was about to shut the door and leave, but the tinkle of a little bell above the doorway had summoned a diminutive older woman from the back of the store.

"Can I help you, young man?" she asked. Johnny had no choice but to step inside.

"Do you sell books here?"

"No, sir, this is a flower shop."

"That's what I gathered," he replied, glancing around at the glass-fronted coolers full of flower bouquets. "Is there a Mr. Thynne who works here? He might be the owner."

"I'm Gretchen, and I'm the owner," the woman said. "I don't have any employees named Mr. Thynne either."

"Okay, I know this will sound strange, but I swear I was in this shop the other day, and it was a bookstore. You didn't happen to open your business today, did you?"

"No, I've been at this location for thirteen years," Gretchen answered. "If this is some kind of joke, I'll kindly ask you to leave."

She was looking at him like he had three heads, so Johnny muttered a quick apology and left. His eyes were itching anyway, and he could feel a sneezing fit coming on. He wandered up the street, trying to wrap his head around what was happening to him. It seemed like the answers he needed were just around the corner, but every time he turned it there was nothing to find. He headed back towards his car, and as he came around the corner, he almost knocked over a woman walking the other way.

"Sorry, excuse me," he said without looking up.

"Johnny?" the woman asked.

"Hey, Niko, what are you doing here?"

"I was about to ask you the same question. I thought you were staying the night at your in-law's place?"

"They live here in Salem. I was just out running an errand. Shouldn't you be at the writer's retreat?"

"I made a mistake coming here. I don't think Mrs. Knight likes me very much," she replied. "I'm going to catch a flight back home, but I thought I should come look around Salem since I've never been here before."

"Oh, I'm sorry to hear that. She has been acting oddly towards you. Do you want me to talk to her about it?"

"No, it's best to let it go. Would you like to get a cup of coffee?"

"Sure, I could definitely use one."

Niko led him back to her car, and they drove down the street to an open coffee shop. She placed their order while Johnny texted Margrett to let her know he was returning to the Knight estate. Niko handed him a cup filled with a boiling concoction of espresso, syrup, and steamed milk. He didn't usually like drinking something this rich, but today, he would make an exception. They left the store and returned to her car.

"I noticed you seemed pretty stressed at the retreat," Niko commented. "Is that because of your son?"

"Sort of, I haven't been sleeping well."

"I don't think you're telling me everything," she replied as she started the engine.

Johnny thought her comment was odd, but he suddenly wanted to spill everything about what had happened to him. "To be honest, I've been getting a lot of headaches and having visions that my wife is still alive. I think she's in danger, but I don't know how to help her."

"Your wife is alive?" Niko gasped. "I thought you said she died? Oh no, we never would have picked you if that was the case. How did Vivian not know about this?"

"Huh? What are...what are...you talking..." Johnny's tongue suddenly felt too thick to move. "My...coffee..."

"I'm sorry, Johnny, but Mrs. Knight ordered me to bring you back."

"Your...tattoo...I remember..." his words were slurred. "You're...you're...a witch..."

He dropped his coffee on the floor, and his head smacked against the passenger window as he passed out.

❌

Johnny's head was pounding when he woke up. He tried to rub his temple but couldn't move his arm more than a few inches. Somebody had pinned both his arms above his head, and his legs were tied down as well. With a groan, he raised his head up as far as he could and looked down at his body.

He was lying spread-eagle and butt-naked on a four-poster bed in the center of a large, round room. The only light came from candles mounted in small alcoves spaced around the chamber's perimeter. His eyes were still blurry from the drug Niko had slipped him, but what he was able to make out in the gloom froze his blood. Twelve silent figures wearing dark green hooded cloaks surrounded the bed, each holding a narrow-bladed dagger.

"Jesus wept. Are you going to sacrifice me?" Johnny croaked out, but his mouth was so dry he could barely form the words.

He sucked in his breath as the cloaked figure at the head of the bed slowly lifted its arms up. Johnny struggled against his bonds in anticipation of the knife that was about to be plunged into his chest. Instead, the person pushed back the hood, and Vivian Knight looked down at him with a smirk on her lips.

"Welcome back, Mr. Sawyer," she said. "I'm sorry for sending Niko to collect you like that, but I was worried you were no longer enjoying our company."

"What is this? What's happening?"

"I'm afraid we've lured you here under false pretenses," Vivian replied. "The entire point of the writer's retreat was to bring you here to meet the prospective matches. Unfortunately, one of them decided to get the jump on the others, a clear violation of our rules. While I should have excluded her from further consideration, I can see that the two of you have a strong connection. That's why we are going to speed up the process and bond you together tonight."

"Bond? What does that mean?" Johnny looked around and saw one of the hooded figures look up, and a few strands of purple hair were visible under the hood. "Oh god, all of you are witches, aren't you."

"Yes, we are the Coven," Vivian replied. "And you are about to become part of us."

"Part of you? I don't have any magic powers."

"No, Mr. Sawyer, but you do have a talent for writing. And more importantly, you have the potential to become rich by doing so. Niko will make sure that you achieve success beyond your wildest dreams."

"What about my wife?"

"I don't understand."

"I need to save my wife."

"You are probably still feeling the effects of the drug Niko gave you, Mr. Sawyer," Vivian said. "Your wife died eight years ago."

"No, she's alive, and so is my daughter. I need to rescue them from Dr. Masterson."

"How hard did he hit his head on the window?" she asked, directing her question to Niko. "Did you give him a concussion?"

"I don't think so," Niko replied. "He was talking like this before the drug took effect. I read his aura, and he didn't seem to be lying. I think he honestly believes she's alive."

"That's impossible. It doesn't matter, he knows too much about us now. He must be put under your control, or we risk exposure. Niko, put your hand on his chest to begin the ritual." Johnny didn't understand what that meant but knew he had to stop it.

"Wait, what about Martin?"

"What about Martin, Mr. Sawyer?" Vivian eyed him suspiciously.

"He's trapped in the same place as my wife," he replied. "They're in the Knightmare-Verse, and I've been talking to them with your husband's typewriter."

"You have a very creative imagination, Mr. Sawyer. I can see why Martin liked you," she said. "No more delays, Niko do as I command."

"Listen to him, Vivian. I can feel that he's telling the truth," Niko said.

"You say they're in the KnightmareVerse? That's not a real place."

"I don't know how to explain it, but I believe it is. I think some other version of me was in the KnightmareVerse, too. I can't remember it clearly, it's like a fever dream I woke up from, but something happened that caused that version of me to bleed through. That's why I feel like two different people are living inside my head."

Vivian was quiet for several moments. "No...he couldn't have...oh, that goddamn moron. What I gave him wasn't good enough; he had to meddle with powers he didn't understand. I should have known something was wrong. He had become too successful. He must have enchanted his typewriter. That explains why he kept using the stupid thing."

"Does that mean you believe me?"

"It doesn't matter. Even if there was a chance you could bring back my love, I have an obligation to protect the Coven." Johnny saw Niko push back the hood on her robe and stare at Vivian, and then several other of the witches did the same. "No, this is too dangerous. Opening a door to the Dream Realm could have unforeseeable consequences."

"It sounds like your husband has already opened one," Niko answered her. "If this has happened because of him, then we need to make it right."

Vivian looked around the room and sighed. "Fine then. It seems we will try sending you to this KnightmareVerse, Mr. Sawyer. I hope, for all our sakes, that you know what you're doing." She motioned for the other women to get back into position and then raised the hood of her cloak over her head. The circle of witches began chanting in hushed tones, too low for him to make out what they were saying, if it was even a language he could understand.

Vivian disappeared briefly, then returned holding a black metal cube. She pressed something on the top, and it popped open like the petals of a rose. An orb of green light formed in the center of the room above his chest and bathed Johnny in its eerie glow. The light grew to blinding intensity, and he felt himself falling through the bed into darkness.

# Dream Mares
# and Knight Escapes

## or: Three Drawings and a
## Little Box of Horrors

Novel By **MARTIN KNIGHT**

Jupiter & Phoebus Publishing House

# Chapter 18

## Dream Mares and Knight Escapes or:
## Three Drawings and a Little Box of Horrors

*M*<sup>r. Sawyer</sup>
...

*Mr. Sawyer*

"Who?"

*Johnny, can you hear me?*

"That's not my name."

*What is your name?*

"It's John Sterling, but everyone calls me Jack."

*Okay, Jack, can you open your eyes?*

Jack did so and found himself floating above his naked body, strapped down to a bed.

"Whoa, what the hell? What's going on? Where am I?"

*Calm down, Mr. Sterling. You're in the dream world. Your mind has detached itself from your body.*

"Did you do this to me? Who the hell are you? Where's my family?"

*I am Vivian Knight, and you requested that I put you in this state. Or rather, the version of you lying on the bed requested it. If you want to rescue your wife and daughter, you must return to your world.*

"Vivian Knight? Martin's wife? I thought you were dead?"

*That may be so in your world, but in this one, my husband has been in a coma for the last three months. When you see him, give him this.* Jack watched her remove a necklace with a silver crescent-shaped pendant from around her neck and place it in the hand of his unconscious body. He looked in his hand, and it appeared there as well. *He will know what to do with it.*

"Okay, so what am I supposed to do now?"

*Martin would have created a portal to your world somewhere in the house, so look for an object familiar to you. Touching it will produce a doorway for you to travel to other dreams until you reach one in your reality, but the journey will not be without peril. If you die in this form, your body will be a mindless husk for the rest of your life.*

"I'll keep that in mind. How do I get off the ceiling?"

*You're dreaming, Mr. Sawyer. You can control your mind.*

Jack closed his eyes and imagined himself on the ground. When he opened them, he stood in the center of his own waist. His legs disappeared down into the bed, and for the first time, he realized that his dream self was also naked. That made for an awkward intersection with his physical form, and he backed away until he was standing beside the bed.

He pictured himself wearing clothes, and a pair of jeans and a T-shirt appeared on him. Jack looked around the room and spotted a pair of ornate double doors. He walked over and tried to open one of them, but his hand passed right through the knob.

"Great, how do I get out of here? I can't open the door."

*Good lord, do I have to tell you how to do everything? Walk through it.*

Jack took a deep breath and held it as he stepped into the door. Besides a slight tingling sensation, which could have been from holding his breath too long, he passed through the door and emerged in a stairwell. He was worried that climbing up the stairs would result in him falling into the ground, but his foot held firm when it contacted the first step. Jack wasn't about to question the physics or logic of this dream state for fear that doing so would end up with him floating in outer space or at the bottom of the ocean, so he focused on finding the portal.

He reached top of the stairs and passed through another door into a large living room. Through the wall of windows, he could see an expanse of moonlit water that stretched to the horizon. He had no idea where he was, but he sure as hell wasn't in Iowa anymore. Only a few lights were on in the starkly decorated house, making it hard for him to find his way about, let alone look for this mysterious object that could be anywhere.

He was about to climb the stairs leading to the second floor when a light down the hallway caught his attention. A small spotlight was mounted in the middle of the wall and pointed back at a painting hanging above it. He approached the artwork and recognized it as the one Kari had been staring at during the dinner party.

Jack recalled the scene as two horses beside a pond, but in this painting, a nude woman stood in front of the closest one, brushing its coat. Even though her back was to him, he thought there was something familiar about her. He leaned closer to read the small brass plaque fixed to the wall below the gilded frame.

## "The Lady of Dreams" - Ka. ARNT F. FRAETZ
### GERMAN EMPORER AND PAINTER ( 1369 - 1408 )

He was staring at the painting when the woman turned to face him. She had long blonde hair, but otherwise, there was an unmistakable resemblance to his wife. She motioned for him to come closer. Jack touched the canvas, expecting his hand to pass through it, but the cloth resisted his fingers. The woman blew him a kiss before walking around the horses towards the willow trees in the background.

"Wait, no, don't leave," he called out to her. She paused, looked over her shoulder, and disappeared into the shadows. He placed his hands against the canvas and shoved hard against it. The material stretched inwards and split apart, revealing a hollow space behind the painting. Jack stumbled forward as his waist hit the edge of the frame, causing him to tumble into the artwork.

He was hundreds of feet up in the air with a field of red flowers spread before him as far as the eye could see. Jack's arms and legs pinwheeled frantically as he hurtled towards the ground, and he shut his eyes right before he impacted it.

*Kari was nuzzling against his neck, kissing his cheek, luring him out of sleep so they could have some fun on a Sunday morning before the kids got out of bed. He reached over and stroked her hair, running his hands through it and twirling several strands loosely around his finger. His wife responded by putting her tongue in his mouth as he kissed her passionately, then she pulled back and neighed at him to wake up.*

Jack opened his eyes to see a giant horse's face staring back at him. The white-coated mare stuck out her tongue and gave him another lick before going back to grazing. He sat up and spit several times onto the ground, then wiped out his mouth using his shirt sleeve. When he was done, the horse looked up at him, shook its head, and wandered away to continue eating.

"Sorry, no offense," he said to the animal. "Where the fuck am I now?"

Surrounding him were rolling hills covered in bright red roses. Jack reached down and picked one, but a thorn suddenly grew out of the side of the stem and jabbed his thumb, drawing blood. "Ow, goddamnit!"

He dropped the flower and stuck his injured finger in his mouth until it stopped bleeding. The plants were covered in nasty-looking barbs, making them hazardous to walk through, especially considering he was still barefoot. He tried to imagine himself wearing cowboy boots but somehow ended up in flip-flops.

Even with them on, he couldn't take more than a few steps without his legs getting cut to ribbons. The mare didn't seem bothered by the razor-coated plants, moving through them easily and picking off their leaves to show her disdain for their prickly defenses. Jack whistled the mare over, slowly stretched out his hand, and stroked her on the neck. "Easy girl, that's a good girl," he said. "Can you give me a lift out of here?"

The mare lowered her head, a motion he hoped meant she would allow him to climb up. He had no idea how to do that since she wasn't wearing a saddle. Jack thought for a moment before he pictured himself sitting on her back. He had mounted the horse when he opened his eyes but was facing backward.

Before he could turn his body around, the mare bolted. Jack flattened his body and grabbed onto her rump as best he could. Despite her galloping across the field at full speed, he managed to stay atop her until she came to a halt, which sent him tumbling off her back. He hit the ground and had the wind knocked out of him. Jack struggled to regain his breath as the mare trotted off, leaving him alone. He was no longer in the field of roses but instead lying beside the pond from the painting. The sunlight barely filtered through the canopy of willow trees clustered around it, making it cool and tranquil.

His head felt dizzy from the fall, so he stumbled over to a moss-covered rock to sit. Jack reached down to scoop up some water and splash it on his face. The blonde woman's face appeared beside him reflected in the pond's surface. He whirled around and almost fell into the water, but nobody was behind him. He scrambled to his feet and searched around the nearby trees for her. Jack returned to the pond and found the naked woman standing on the far bank.

"Hey! Hey, wait! Don't leave!" he called out as she glided off towards the ancient ruins just visible through the trees. He sprinted after her, dodging his way around the rocks and willow branches, but she vanished behind one of the collapsed stone columns. He slowed down as he approached the ruins since the trees were so overgrown that it was difficult to walk.

Whatever building or temple stood here long ago had collapsed over the eons, making its structure indecipherable. At the heart of the ruins was a statue in the center of a circular stone basin filled with stagnant water. The monument was of a grotesque, reptilian creature rising from the water with several tentacles coming from its body. The stone monstrosity was covered in moss and vines, making it appear like a bloated corpse emerging from the ocean's depths.

Jack stepped into the clearing in the ring of columns where the vegetation had not yet taken over. The closer he got to the basin, the more yellowed and withered the plants became. Ripples appeared in the water as he approached, like something underneath was coiling itself to leap out. Jack stopped as the woman he had chased stepped out from behind the statue, standing knee-deep in the fetid liquid. She fixed him with a seductive smile, but there was an intensity to her eyes like that of a cunning predator tracking its prey.

"You're not Kari," he said as he backed away from the basin. "Who are you?"

"Welcome, Jack Sterling," the woman said. "I have been waiting for you. Don't recognize me? Perhaps this will help."

In the blink of an eye, she became an older woman wearing a reddish-pink bathrobe with blood dried on her dark brown hair. It was the same woman he had seen in the dream where the werewolf in the closet had bitten his hand.

"You are in the presence of the Knightmare. I am the living embodiment of your worst fears."

Jack ran back towards the pond, but the ground between the ring of pillars erupted with thousands of thorn-covered vines intertwined to form an impenetrable barrier. He felt the mental equivalent of tentacles reach into his mind and probe his thoughts. The Knightmare was searching for what terrified him, so he focused his thoughts on a memory from his childhood.

His parents took him to France for the Paris Air Show when he was five years old. While wandering about the city, they had come upon the most frightening abomination he had ever encountered. Jack concentrated upon this memory, allowing the fear he had experienced as an impressionable child to come flooding back as an irresistible lure.

*If that is how you wish to meet your fate, then so be it.*

He looked back at the statue, but the woman in the bathrobe had vanished. The water in the basin began to churn as a French mime emerged, complete with a horizontally striped shirt, white face paint, red ascot, and red Beret. It stood on the water's surface before stepping onto the ground, its clothes showing no dampness. Jack couldn't decide if the sight of the bizarre, silent clown made him want to laugh or shudder in terror. The mime stood watching him for a minute with its arrogant, lifeless eyes.

"What the fuck are you going to do, trap me in an invisible box?" he taunted it.

The mime smiled at him and held up its hands with its palms facing out. Jack watched as the mime pantomimed that it was surrounded by unseen walls and pretended to be running out of air. Suddenly, his lungs started burning, and he reached out to find a transparent barrier on all sides of him. His breathing became increasingly difficult as he pounded his fists against thin air. The mime flashed a mouth full of long, yellowed teeth filed to sharp points.

Jack was running out of air and knew he had to think of something, or he would be served up *écrivain sous verre* as this thing's dinner. With his vision dimming from lack of oxygen, he imagined holding a hammer and motioned like he was striking it against the box. Jack heard a sound like glass cracking, drew back his hand again as far as he could, and delivered a crushing blow that shattered his cage.

He collapsed on the ground, panting and sucking in big gulps of air. Before the mime could make its next move, he jumped up and acted like he was walking against a strong wind. The mime was caught off-guard and went flying backward into the statue.

"Eat that shit, you mute fuck!"

His celebration was cut short as the mime got back up, twirled its arm in the air, and gestured as if it were throwing something towards Jack. The mime acted out grabbing a rope with both hands and giving it a hard yank. The invisible lasso cinched tight around Jack's chest, pulling him off his feet.

With unprecedented strength, the mime dragged him across the ground, flipped him onto his stomach, and hog-tied his hands and feet together behind his back. Perching Jack's head on the basin, the mime walked a few steps away and pretended to sharpen an axe on a grinding wheel, sending sparks flying. The mime tested the blade by plucking a single hair from Jack's head and dropping it on the blade, splitting it neatly in two down the middle. He struggled against the unseen rope as the mime aimed with the imaginary axe at his neck.

"*With a CLUCK, CLUCK HERE!*" Jack called out as he pictured a flock of chickens swarming around the basin. The mime's eyes widened and it dropped the axe. The sound of dozens of clucking birds swarmed it even though none were visible.

With his adversary distracted, Jack rolled over and groped about blindly until his finger was nicked by something sharp. He moved his hands back and forth a few times, and the bonds holding them fell away, allowing him to sit up and free his feet. His hands closed around the shaft of the axe and he picked it up. The mime had managed to fend off the chickens, and now it mimicked drawing a sword from a sheath at its side.

They clashed with their weapons as they circled the statue, the sound of metal ringing out with each blow. Jack could not match the mime's inhuman strength, and a vicious strike sent the axe flying from his hands. The mime raised the sword over its head to deliver a fatal blow, which gave Jack an opening to kick it square in the crotch.

"*Merde!*" The abomination squeaked, then clapped a hand over its mouth before it vanished in a cloud of black smoke, leaving only the red Beret lying on the ground. Jack picked up the stupid-looking cap and tossed it into the basin. He looked around for a way out, but the vine wall blocked any escape. One column was leaning over from the weight of the vegetation wrapped around it, and he thought he could crawl up it. Jack had taken no more than a couple of steps away from the basin when the ground began to shake.

The water rushed out of the basin as the statue rose up on four scaled, claw-towed legs as thick as tree trunks. The stone creature lumbered about until it was facing him, then opened its enormous maw in a silent roar. Perched on top of its head was the Beret. Jack knew there was no use in running and hoped that his death wouldn't be too painful. He closed his eyes and waited for the end to come when he felt a blast of hot breath on his neck.

The dream mare stood behind him, and Jack grabbed onto her as she took off. He pulled himself up on her back as one of the statue's tentacles slammed down where he had been standing a moment ago, leaving a large crater in the ground.

"Let's get the fuck out of here!"

The horse charged straight towards the wall of vines, then leaped and soared straight over the twenty-foot-high obstacle. They landed on the other side, and Jack barely kept his grip as the mare galloped on at break-neck speed. He held on for dear life as she weaved around trees and bounded over large rocks until the forest gave way to sand dunes.

The mare stopped on the shore of a leaden sea stretching out beneath an overcast sky of bruise-colored clouds. Jack slid down onto the sandy beach, taking a minute to collect himself as he sat on a bleached chunk of driftwood.

"Oh my god, I thought I was a dead man," he said, trying to get his hands to stop shaking. "What the holy hell was that thing?"

The mare regarded him for a moment with its large black eyes. Her only answer was to bend her head down to eat from a clump of beachgrass. Jack was overwhelmed by the harrowing ordeal and buried his face in his hands. He had only closed his eyes a few moments when a hoof stomping made him look up.

"What is it?" he asked. The mare nodded towards a wooden door on the beach about ten feet in front of him. A brass plate with two words etched on it was mounted on the door.

# THE DREAMER

"Nope, I'm not opening that damn door," he stated. "There's probably some scary fucking creature on the other side that wants to rip my face off and wear it."

The mare's nose nudged him in the back, so he turned to face her. "Fine, I'll open it, but there's no way I'm going in there if it looks sketchy."

He cautiously approached the door as though it might try to eat him, stretched out his hand, and quickly turned the knob before leaping back. The door swung inward a few inches, and all he could see through the narrow opening was darkness. "You see? There's no way I'm setting foot in there. I'd rather sit on this beach until the end of time."

The mare thrashed her head back and forth before she spun around as if she were returning to graze, but instead lifted her rear leg and kicked him square in the gut. He went flying through the open doorway and blacked out.

Jack groaned and coughed as he sat up, then doubled over from the pain that exploded in his midsection. He lifted his shirt and saw a bright red horseshoe mark on his stomach. He had to still be in the dream world as it faded away quickly. His eyes adjusted to the dim light of the room he was in, which was spartan with furnishings.

There was a narrow, wood-framed bed with a gray wool blanket, a small desk with a chair, and a bookcase packed full of paperbacks and graphic novels. All the furniture was bolted down to the floor except for the chair. A part in the curtains let him see it was either early morning or near dusk outside through the leaded glass window. The furniture in the room looked antique, but there was a modern electronic lock on the door.

He saw no decorations except a handful of drawings taped to the wall above the desk. A person was sitting in the chair, leaning over a paper pad, furiously scribbling away. Jack took him for a teenage boy, but he couldn't see his face as the kid had it almost pressed against the drawing he was working on. He glanced at the other works hanging up that he assumed the boy had done, which showed remarkable detail and composition. Upon closer inspection, Jack noticed that all the pictures were scenes of the events that had happened to him and his family since they had moved to Iowa.

The door behind him opened, and somebody turned on the overhead light. Standing in the doorway was a stern-looking woman in a white lab coat flanked by two men in white uniforms holding arm-length black sticks with glowing blue tips. The woman had her hair up in a tight bun, but otherwise the resemblance to his boss, Professor Wilkens, was uncanny.

"Good evening, Patrick," the woman said. "I'm sorry to disturb you, but an important request has come in, and we need you to take care of it. Can you do that for me?" The boy at the desk shook his head vigorously without turning around. "Do I need to have the guards carry you?"

The boy stopped drawing and pushed his chair back from the desk without saying a word. The teen spun around in the chair, and Jack was shocked to see that his son had aged several years since that morning.

"*Patrick, it's daddy,*" he said, reaching out to hug his son as he stood up. Jack's arms passed through the boy's shoulders, and he showed no sign that he had heard him. The woman took hold of Patrick's hand, and they walked out of the room with the guards trailing behind, holding their batons as if ready to strike. His son looked over his shoulder, causing the men to tense up. Patrick's eyes briefly met his own before the boy faced forward again, but that could have been a coincidence.

During his first visit, Martin had given him a full tour of Devonshire Manor. Although all the artworks had been removed, he knew where he was as soon as he saw the Grand Hall. The hallway they were walking down was on the second floor, and the group crossed a wooden walkway that spanned the width of the enormous room.

On the other side, they took a right turn onto the upper landing of the main staircase and headed down. Professor Wilkens went first, with Patrick sandwiched between her and the guards. Instead of going into the Hall, they circled around into an alcove under the staircase, where another set of steps led down to the basement.

They passed the door to the bathroom where he had retrieved Kari's discarded shoes at the dinner party, which seemed like a lifetime ago. Jack hadn't been down to the basement, but it looked like something out of a medieval castle. The walls were made from gray stone blocks and red bricks, and the ironwood doors were reinforced with metal bands and had keycard sensors set into the wall beside them.

Professor Wilkens approached one of the doors, removed the badge pinned to the lapel of her lab coat, and passed it over the black square. It made a beep and the small red LED on the pad turned green before the door unlocked. Jack came around beside her to read her badge after she fastened it back in place.

### THE NEUROCYNERGIS FOUNDATION

### Dr. Anna Wylks

### Security Level: DELTA

The room beyond was dark except for the light from two large flat-screen monitors mounted to the wall, but what he could see put a knot in his stomach. A contraption in the center looked like a dentist's chair from hell. Leather straps were attached to the armrests and footrests, along with some kind of high-tech helmet mounted on a swiveling metal arm. A bundle of wires ran from a humming black metal cube the size of a small car sitting behind the chair, up along the arm, and into the top of the helmet.

"Dr. Schreiber, would you get Patrick hooked up?" Dr. Wylks asked.

A heavyset older woman wearing a white lab coat stood up from a computer station and approached. Jack had only seen her once before, but he would never forget the image of her with a gaping head wound in a bloodstained bathrobe lying next to him in bed. She seemed alive now, smiling as she bent down to talk to his son.

"Hello, Patrick, how are you?"

"Great, how are you?" he echoed in a practiced, monotone voice.

"I'm great. Should we go sit in our chair?"

"Uhn ungh, no chair."

"Please, can you do it for me?" Patrick looked up at her, and there were tears in his eyes. Jack thought he might resist and worried about what the two goons would do to his son, but he climbed into the chair. "Dr. Wylks, would you mind reviewing the latest test results on my screen while I get him ready?"

Anna glanced at the computer monitor but seemed reluctant to leave the other woman alone with Patrick. Dr. Schreiber didn't appear to notice her hesitation, and after a few seconds, Dr. Wylks stepped away. As soon as she had her back turned, the older woman lifted the back of Patrick's shirt. Jack leaned around her shoulder so he could see what she was looking at, and he caught a glimpse of a mass of black lines halfway up his son's spine before she dropped his shirt back in place. The formation was thicker and wider near the base, and it seemed to be working its way up towards his neck and head.

"Do you remember what I told you in the attic?" she whispered in Patrick's ear, and he nodded in response. "Show your dad how the device works. After we get your family out, I can disable the microchip, and you'll be free of their control. Just hang in there a little longer."

Dr. Schreiber fastened the straps across his wrists and ankles and secured the metal cap over his head with a leather chin strap. When she pressed a button on the back of the helmet, the black cube began to glow with an eerie green light.

"Come over here after you get him secured," Dr. Wylks called out. The woman squeezed Patrick's hand before she returned to her computer station. Jack followed her to hear what they were saying. "Are these numbers correct?"

"Yes, the anomaly is expanding at an accelerated rate. It won't be long before it reaches his cerebral cortex," Dr. Schreiber replied. "When that happens...the effects are unknown. He could suffer a complete psychotic break, or it might even kill him. You must tell Dr. Masters to halt further operations until we know how to reverse this."

"I'll tell him, but I wouldn't count on it. Find a way to stop it. For now, we carry on as instructed."

Dr. Schreiber pursed her lips, but she didn't argue as she switched to a different program on her computer. "ALCHEMIST system is coming online," she said. "Satellite connection is in progress; we should be ready soon."

"Good. Did you get the target coordinates?"

"Yes, I've received them. Entering them now," Dr. Schreiber said as she typed away on the keyboard. "There must be something wrong. This location isn't in Afghanistan or Pakistan. These coordinates put it...somewhere on the East Coast. That has to be a mistake. I'd better contact someone at Langley."

"You'll do no such thing. This operation is off the books," Anna replied. "There is to be no communication about it with them, understood?"

Dr. Schreiber looked at her with a shocked expression that she quickly masked. She typed away on her computer, and one of the screens on the wall displayed a map of the eastern United States. "I've got a lock on the cell phone signal. It's moving, but I should be able to track it."

Jack could only stand beside his son and watch the monitors. The map's image had switched to showing a live view of a coastline, presumably beamed down from a satellite flying through space. A red square appeared in the center as the camera started to zoom in until it hovered above a stretch of forest-lined roadway.

It was night there, but the video feed was being enhanced so they could see everything in the dark, clear as day. A motorcycle sped along a deserted stretch of road, and a red square centered on it as the satellite's camera followed the bike from miles above.

"Patrick, I want you to concentrate on the motorcycle," Dr. Wylks instructed. "Can you see the rider's face?"

His son closed his eyes tight, and a few seconds later, the second screen changed to static before the random electronic snowstorm congealed into vague shapes. After a minute, the picture solidified into a black-and-white image of a man holding onto the handlebars of a motorcycle. Jack recognized him as Martin Knight.

"Good, Patrick, now concentrate," Anna said. "I want you to cause him to go to sleep."

*No, Patrick, don't do that,* Jack said. *Please, son, don't listen to her.*

His words were useless in this state, and his attempts to free Patrick from the chair were equally futile. Jack watched helplessly as Martin started to nod off as he drove. If he fell asleep while going at the speed he was traveling, not even the helmet he was wearing would save him.

Jack saw a deer leap out of the ditch on the satellite monitor and bound across the road in front of the motorcycle. The large buck caused Martin to lose control of his bike and skid into the ditch where the deer had just emerged. The second screen showed a gash on the side of the writer's head, but despite a crack in the helmet, it looked to Jack like he was still alive.

"We're targeting Americans now?" Dr. Schreiber asked. "How did that get authorized?"

"I guess he made an enemy of the wrong person. None of what you just saw happened. Erase any data from this session and keep your mouth shut if you value your job...and your life." She locked eyes with Dr. Wylks for a moment, but the cold glare coming from her was enough to extinguish any flare of rebellion. Dr. Schreiber stormed out of the room as Anna loosened the straps holding Patrick in the chair.

His son looked visibly exhausted from whatever the machine had done to him, with dark circles already forming underneath his eyes. Dr. Wylks took Patrick back to his room, with Jack trailing closely behind.

"Let's give you something to help you sleep," Anna said. Patrick didn't resist when Dr. Wylks took a syringe from the pocket of her coat and injected it into his arm, even though Jack knew that he hated needles. His son climbed into bed, and she pulled the blanket over him before shutting off the lights and closing the door.

Patrick was lying in his bed with his eyes open, watching the door as if afraid the woman would return. Jack tried waving his hands around to get his attention, but his son gave no reaction. After a minute, the medicine seemed to kick in, and Patrick's eyes fluttered a few times before closing. The lamp on the desk had been left on, so he went over to see what his son had been drawing before he was interrupted. Unlike the other pictures that were cohesive scenes, this page was filled with a repeating symbol.

He recognized the symbol of a snake eating its tail from the lock on the steamer trunk. The crescent shape in the center looked like the pendant he was wearing around his neck. He wondered if the black square was part of the picture as well since Patrick had made that first and then drawn the snake and moon in white ink on top of it. The image tickled something in the back of his memory, but his brain felt foggy from being in the dream state.

Patrick sat up in his bed, turned his head towards Jack even though his eyes were still shut, and whispered, "Daddy, come home." He laid back down again and started snoring within a few breaths.

"*Patrick, can you hear me?*" Jack called out. "*Daddy's trying to get back home, but I don't know what to do.*"

Jack sighed and sat down on the bed, which held his weight even though he didn't make an indentation on the sheets. He rested his head in his hands, trying to push away the fear clouding his mind so he could think clearly. His family needed him, but he didn't know how to help them. Jack took a deep breath and opened his eyes to find another door in the center of the room with a similar cryptic plaque.

# THE LADY OF SORROWS

He came around the side of the bed and leaned over his sleeping son. "*I'm going to get you out of here as soon as I can, I promise.*" Although he couldn't touch him, Jack ran his hand over Patrick's head. He approached the door, turned the knob, and stepped through.

Jonathan stood looking up at the most extravagant house he had ever seen. The last thing he remembered was leaving the poker game after losing his shirt on two pairs, betting everything on aces and eights no less. A tall, gorgeous brunette woman had approached him, and he was about to drop one of his sure-fire pick-up lines when she drove a steak knife into his throat. The woman had smiled at him as he choked on his own blood and whispered *The CIA sends its regards, Detective Smith*.

No, that wasn't him. He was an English professor living in Iowa, not some dead cop from Chicago. Or maybe he was an up-and-coming author with the power to see people's nightmares just by touching them? Or was he the auto mechanic who made a deal with the actual devil to become a racecar driver and get revenge on the people who tried to kill him? His head was splitting open from all the identities crammed into his brain.

*You're none of those men and all of them.*

*Your name is John, and you need to save your family.*

He didn't know where that voice came from, but the words sounded true. His memories of Jack came flooding back in, and with them, the realization that he was standing outside Devonshire Manor. There was something different about the house, but he couldn't put his finger on it *(did the trees seem shorter than the last time he was here?)*. It didn't matter. He needed to find Martin and keep Patrick from being used as a human lab rat. He ran across the driveway and passed through the front door into the Grand Hall.

A pack of black cats greeted him as he stepped into the room, all looking up at him from where they were lying around the fireplace. Jack took a few steps further, and their eyes followed his movements. He gave them a wide berth as he approached the archway across from the fireplace. Several of them hissed when he got too close. As if that wasn't enough to freak him out, his mother-in-law was standing in the stairwell pointing a gun at his naked, handcuffed wife.

Margrit looked thirty years younger and not dead, while Kari's hair was a different color and a lot shorter. She also appeared gaunt and pale, like she hadn't been eating. Luckily it only seemed to be the felines who could see him, although Jack held his breath when Margrit stuck her head out into the Hall and glared at the cats.

"Keep moving," she barked at Kari. "Go upstairs and turn left."

He followed them up the steps, where they ran into a short woman carrying a tray. Margrit brought her along as they crossed the wooden walkway and took Kari into a large bedroom. Jack hurried around the corner and down the hall to the bedroom where Patrick had been in the other vision.

The room was empty except for the wood-frame bed with a bare mattress. When he returned, he found his wife being bathed by the diminutive woman while Margrit kept the gun trained on her. He felt uncomfortable watching the bizarre scene, so he left until they were finished.

The three women stepped back into the hallway, and Kari was now wearing a black-and-white uniform. Margrit marched her back to the door where the housekeeper had emerged and into what he guessed was an office by the large desk, leather couch, and bookshelves. An older man dressed in a smart-looking suit entered from a door on the opposite side of the room. Jack had only seen younger versions of him in photographs, but there was no mistaking Dr. Henry Masterson.

"That will be all for now," the man told Margrit. "Why don't you take over watching the little girl? I doubt she is enjoying having a werewolf for a babysitter."

Jack wondered if he was talking about Jenny, and he almost went after Margrit when she left the room. The object he spotted on Dr. Masterson's desk kept him in the office instead.

Henry brought the black cube over to the coffee table and set it down, allowing him to get a better look at it. He remembered images carved on the surface that were only visible when viewed from a certain angle. On the side facing up was the etching of a crescent moon. Jack tried placing the pendant he was wearing on it, but the necklace passed through the cube.

"A man showed up on my doorstep recently," Dr. Masterson said, "claiming to be a traveling encyclopedia salesman no less. He gave me this box and said it was the key to the pillar you saw, which I had brought here from the *City of the Dead* in Egypt. This man told me to put a job advertisement in the newspaper and that a woman from Chicago would apply who could use this key. Since you were the one from Chicago who answered the posting, that must be you, Mary."

A memory from Johnny's mind popped into his head. He was inside *The Alchemist's Apprentice*, and his wife was inhabiting the character of Mary Deloris Smith. However, this part wasn't from the book. Martin might not have witnessed it using whatever power he had to see into this world, or maybe the story was changing. Either way, if the box was some kind of key, he needed to figure out how it worked.

"Do you know how insane that sounds? Why would I help you?"

"It is truly a shame about what happened to your husband. If I remember correctly, he stabbed himself in the throat and then drowned in Lake Michigan?"

Jack involuntarily clutched at his neck when he heard this, the painful memory of being stabbed by the pretty brunette rippling in front of his vision. While he had only seen her face for a few seconds and her hair wasn't blonde, it was undoubtedly Margrit who had murdered him. Or rather, murdered Jonathan Smith. Jack had no idea how his mother-in-law could be a cold-blooded killer. Then again, not a whole hell of a lot about anything was making much sense to him anymore.

"Alright, whatever you want from me, I'll do it."

"Very well, I'm glad you have come around. The ritual will begin at midnight."

In keeping with that, a younger version of Albert entered the office, escorted Kari (*Mary*) back to the lavish bedroom, and locked her inside.

"Oh god, Jon, I wish you were here," Mary said as she sat on the bed and started crying.

"*I'm right here, babe,*" he answered, even though she couldn't hear him. "*I'll find some way to get you home, too.*"

Jack reached out and brushed his hand against her cheek, and the tear running down it came away on his finger. Mary looked up, startled as though she had felt it, too. He tried again to touch her, but his hand passed through her like everything else. She curled up on the bed, and he watched her for a while before returning to the hallway.

If Dr. Masterson had sent Margrit away to watch over his daughter, she must also be on the manor's grounds. The house was three stories tall, and she could be in any of the rooms, but Jack hoped she was being kept in the small cottage near the garage. That was where Mary and Geraldine resided in Martin's novel anyway, so it sounded like the first place to check.

He was in luck as there was a light on in the cottage. Margrit was in the kitchen preparing herself a gin martini. "How dare he treat me like a goddamn nursemaid," she muttered as she poured the ingredients into a steel ice shaker, thrashed it up and down several times, and strained the concoction into a coffee mug. "One of these days, he's going to push me too far, and he'll regret it with his life."

With the makeshift martini glass in hand, she stomped into the living room and sat in the recliner in front of the TV. Jack checked the downstairs bedroom and found it vacant, so he climbed the steps to the second floor. The door at the top of the stairs was shut, so he went to press his ear against it. He remembered that he wasn't restricted by physical barriers in this form and walked through the door. Although the light was off, Jack could make out the shape of a person underneath the bed's covers.

*Jenny, it's your dad. Wake up.*

He hadn't expected that to work, but to his surprise, she stirred and rolled onto her back. Jack called her name again, then shouted it, but she remained sleeping. Frustrated at his incorporeal form, he returned downstairs. Margrit was watching an incredibly young Johnny Carson and had already downed her first martini. He stepped back out of habit as she returned to the kitchen to fix another cocktail.

Without being able to touch or talk to anyone, all he could do was observe helplessly. If that was why he was sent here, it was even crueler than not knowing what had happened to his family. Jack stood in the doorway and briefly stared at the black-and-white television. The picture was small and fuzzy, and while he watched, it turned static before going completely black. White lines began appearing on the screen, soon forming an image.

Jack didn't know how it was possible, but somebody had drawn a picture of a typewriter. The meaning it was trying to convey was evident, and he wondered how he hadn't thought about it earlier. The only problem was that he had no idea where the typewriter Jenny had used to write to him was located, but he hoped it was somewhere in the cottage. The drawing on the television vanished as the screen switched to the late-night program before Margrit returned and took her seat.

A quick search of the first floor turned up empty, although he noticed his mother-in-law was starting to nod off. The typewriter was also not in Genny's bedroom, which only left the second bedroom. There was barely enough moonlight coming through a part in the curtains for him to see anything. Once his eyes adjusted to the dark, he spotted the reflection from the chrome trim on the writing machine sitting in the corner. Jack was elated to see a sheet of paper already in the roller, but the question was whether it would be of any use to him.

He held his breath as he stuck out his index finger and pushed down one of the typewriter's keys. When the striker bar flew up and hit the page, he let out a cry of excitement. He leaned down close to the keyboard so he could make the keys. The first letter he had typed was a *j*, so he pressed down on the letter *e* and slowly began to peck out a message to his daughter. The carriage hit the end of the line with a ding, but Jack found he couldn't operate the lever to reset it or the knob to advance the page.

### jenny its your father you have to wake up

He heard the door to the office creak open, but his heart sank when, instead of Genny's face peering in through the crack, it was Margrit. She opened the door, pushed in the light switch, and looked around the room. Jack thought she was about to leave, but then she came over and turned the knob on the typewriter's roller. Her brow furrowed as she read his message aloud.

"That's from my daddy," Genny said from the doorway. "He's a ghost."

"A ghost, huh?" Margrit scoffed. "That's quite an imagination you have, child. Go back to your room. It's past your bedtime."

Genny glowered at the woman before she returned to her bed. Jack turned back to the typewriter and quickly banged out a message to his future mother-in-law.

### hello margrit im the cop you murdered in chicago

"What the hell is this?"

After she moved the roller, he continued typing.

### look at the photograph on the desk

Margrit picked up the framed picture beside the lamp. Mary, Genny, and Jon posed in front of Lake Michigan. Ironically, it was the last photo they had taken together.

"This is you? Forgive me if I don't shed any tears over a Soviet spy."

### i was no spy masterson lied i worked for him

Jack wasn't sure why he had written that, but the words had just come out on their own. He felt the dead police detective in his mind taking control of the conversation.

"What do you mean? Why would he have employed someone like you?"

```
to cover up secret experiments he was conducting
i blackmailed him to pay me but he must have
double-crossed me and sent you to kill me
```

"No, Henry wouldn't do that..."

```
he just told my wife he would kill you if she
helps him why do you think he sent you away?
```

"And what is it that you want me to do? Help her escape? He works for the CIA. There's nowhere she can run that he won't track her down. Or maybe they work for him. You don't understand how powerful he is."

```
you need to sneak her down to the basement
```

Margrit let out a bark of laughter. "Do you think he will never look for her down there? You're not only dead, you're also delusional. How is that going to help?"

Jack didn't have a good answer to that question, but the typewriter moved back into position and started typing without him touching it.

```
perform the Ritual of Thule at midnight
the Witch's Moon reveals the gateway
the Ouroboros unlocks the sacred seal
and opens the way to the Black Spire
```

Margrit reached up to her neck and lifted out the necklace she was wearing. It had a crescent medallion hanging from it, just like the one Jack had been given. She rubbed it between her thumb and forefinger, seeming deep in thought.

"So that's what this is all about. Okay, I'll do what you want, but if I can't get her out, I'm going to have to kill her. If Henry wants her to open the Black Spire for him, I can't allow that."

She reached out and pulled the sheet of paper from the typewriter, took out her lighter, and set the corner aflame. After dropping the burning page into the metal wastebasket,

she shut off the lights and closed the office door. Margrit entered the next room, where
Genny was sitting in bed with the lights on.

"What did my daddy say to you?" she asked.

"It seems he wants me to rescue your mother," Margrit replied. "Come on, we need to
hurry."

Genny hopped out of bed, pulled her shoes on, and took Margrit's hand as she led her
out of the cottage. They entered the manor through the entrance to the servants' hallway,
but instead of following it around to the Grand Hall, she turned off into a short corridor.
A set of stairs there came out on the second floor near the bedroom where Patrick had
been kept prisoner. Margrit told Genny to be quiet and wait as she peeked around the
corner. Jack stuck his head out and saw young Albert sitting in a chair reading a newspaper
outside the bedroom where Mary was locked inside.

Margrit smoothed out her skirt and unfastened the top two buttons on her blouse,
exposing a healthy amount of cleavage. She removed her shoes and walked out barefoot
into the hallway. Albert's sensitive ears immediately picked up her footsteps, and he folded
his newspaper as he regarded her with a suspicious look. When he saw how she was dressed
(*or undressed*), his eyes nearly popped out of his head.

"Would you be a dear and mind opening the door for me?" Margrit asked in a sultry
voice.

"Sorry, I can't let anyone in," Albert replied. "Dr. Masterson's orders."

Margrit rolled her eyes. "Oh, please, you don't need to act like his lap dog. I need to ask
the woman a question. Her little brat is whining about some missing doll. I can't get her
to go to bed without it, and my martini is getting warm. Do a girl a favor, and I'm sure I
can find some way to repay you for it."

Jack could practically see the drool running down Albert's chin as he jumped out of
the chair and fished around in his pocket for the key. As soon as he unlocked it, Margrit
jammed the barrel of a pistol into the back of his neck.

"This gun is loaded with silver-tipped bullets," she told him. "Since magic doesn't work
on the likes of you, I made some to keep your kind in check."

Mary was lying down on the bed and sat up when the two of them entered the room.
"What's going on?"

"Do you have handcuffs on you?" Margrit asked, and Albert nodded at his pocket. She
took them out with her left hand and cuffed his wrists to the radiator under the window.
"I have your daughter, we're leaving."

"You know, these cuffs aren't going to hold me for more than five seconds," Albert said.

"How about you give me five minutes and I'll make it worth your while." A huge grin spread across his face as he glanced at his watch.

"The clock's ticking."

"I'm probably going to regret that," Margrit said while locking the bedroom door. Genny came from around the corner, and Mary scooped her into her arms. Margrit ushered them over to the stairwell, keeping her pistol pointed at the door to Henry's office.

"Wait for me downstairs. I need to get something first."

Margrit opened the door just enough to check that the room was empty. The black cube was sitting on the coffee table where Dr. Masterson had left it. She reached the bottom of the steps when a loud bang sounded from the second floor. "That was a quick five minutes. We need to get to the pillar."

"What about the gun? Can't you just shoot him?"

"I was bluffing," Margrit replied. "It's almost midnight, hurry!"

The lights were on in the basement, making navigating the confusing, narrow passageways easier. Margrit led them to a red door and along a corridor carved out of living rock, which ended in a set of spiral steps going deeper underground.

The stairs came out at a domed chamber that Jack thought was the waiting room to hell or Tim Burton's idea for the perfect rave venue. The pillar in the center was carved with the same strange symbols he had found on the black box, which meant the two had to be connected. Mary recoiled when Margrit held the cube out to her.

"If you want to get out of here alive, you'll need to use it."

"How is that going to help me?"

"I don't have time to explain, you'll have to trust me. It's the only way you'll get away from Dr. Masterson."

"Why should I trust you? You tried to electrocute me. Why are you helping me now?"

"Because I was tricked into stabbing your husband to death," Margrit said. "You have a choice to make. You can either escape, or you can take your revenge." She turned her gun around and offered it to her. "I'm probably a dead woman whether you leave here or not."

Mary started reaching for the pistol but took the black cube instead.

Margrit removed the crescent pendant from her necklace and handed it to her. "You'll need this as well, wait until I tell you and then fit it into place here. I'll hold them off as long as I can."

Margrit sprinted back to the archway, leaving her staring at the pendant and black cube in her hands. She turned the cube towards the light and traced her finger around the crescent-shaped indentation on its surface.

"Are we going to be okay, mommy?"

"Yes, sweetheart, I won't let anything happen to you." Jack caught the look of worry on his wife's face when she hugged Genny to her chest. He wanted nothing more than to hold them both right then.

"It's midnight, put the pendant in," Margrit called. "Hurry, I hear someone coming."

Mary slid the pendant into the hole and it fit perfectly. When she did so, the top half of the cube split into two parts and folded open on hidden hinges to reveal an inner mechanism. This consisted of a cylinder covered with strange symbols just like the pillar, and around the base was a recessed carving of a snake eating its tail. The pendant sat on top of the pillar, and Jack knew right away that this was what the older version of Patrick had been drawing repeatedly.

"What do I do now?"

"Maybe you're supposed to put something there?" Genny asked, pointing at the snake carving.

Mary looked closer at the cylinder, then sucked in her breath. "Oh my god, you're brilliant. Here, hold this." She gave the cube to her daughter and used her left hand to unfasten the bracelet around her wrist. Jack circled around behind her so he could see what she was doing. The silver band that she removed was dotted with tiny emeralds and was in the shape of a snake. Once she put it back together, it was biting the end of its metal tail. Mary placed the piece of jewelry on the cylinder, fitting the indentations perfectly.

*That's wrong,* a voice whispered in his head. A memory bubbled up within the block of Swiss cheese that his brain had become of Patrick saying those words to him. The echo of gunfire from the stairs interrupted his train of thought. Mary instinctively pushed Genny behind her as she moved them closer to the pillar.

*"No, don't go near that thing. It's a trap!"* Jack yelled futilely. In his attempt to save his wife, he had manipulated her into doing exactly what Dr. Masterson wanted. He watched in frustration as she fiddled with the contraption until finding that the column rotated when she twisted it. Mary spun it around once and it locked into place, causing the pillar to start pulsating with a sickly green glow. Mary stepped onto the dais and extended her hand towards the towering column. When her palm contacted its surface, an arc of green electricity flashed out and hit her square in the chest, knocking her to the ground.

She lay there unconscious while Genny screamed and rushed to her side. The gunshots grew louder, and a few seconds later, Margrit reappeared in the archway.

"I'm almost out of bullets..." her words dying off as she spotted Mary collapsed on the floor. Margrit picked up the black cube while keeping her pistol pointed at the entrance to the chamber, then hurried over to Genny.

"What happened?"

"It...shocked...her..." the girl managed to choke out.

Margrit looked up at the pillar, which still had a green glow, and held out the cube to his daughter.

"They'll be here any second," she said. "It's up to you now."

Genny looked scared even to touch the thing, but to his horror, she accepted the device. Margrit grasped her gun with both hands as an enormous shadow filled the archway. "Stay back, or I'll put a bullet right through your eye. It won't kill you, but it will hurt like hell."

The werewolf hesitated and stood where it was, watching her with its inhuman amber eyes. Jack repeatedly called out his daughter's name as she climbed up on the dais, holding the cube in one hand while she cautiously stretched out her other towards the pillar. This time, no bolt of energy shot out when her shaking fingers touched the smooth surface.

Mary came around and pushed herself up on one arm, using the other to shield her eyes as she scanned the room. She spotted Margrit holding the werewolf at bay, but then her head turned in his direction.

"Jon, is that you?"

Before he could answer her, a blast of blinding light filled the room, and a shockwave knocked him down. It took a good minute before Jack could see again. As his eyesight cleared, his heart dropped into his stomach because Mary and Genny had vanished.

"Bravo, Margrit, bravo," Dr. Masterson clapped his hands as he stood in the archway. "You played your part magnificently."

"Henry? Stay back, or I swear I'll shoot you," Margrit said, pointing the gun at him. "I know you were going to kill me to get what you wanted out of her."

"Don't be ridiculous," he smiled. "I wouldn't have killed you, it was all part of the act. I knew you would free her and bring her down here."

"Bullshit, I've had enough of your lies."

"Oh, did a ghost tell you to rescue her? I know about him, too. Tell me, which one of them removed the barrier?"

"The little girl, and now she and her mother are out of your reach."

"For now, maybe, but I'm a patient man." He walked towards her and pushed aside the gun. "Luckily for you, I'm also a forgiving one. I'm afraid I'll need you to forget you ever knew Mary Deloris Smith."

Margrit narrowed her eyes at him. "You wouldn't dare…"

Henry touched his index and middle fingers to her temple, and she froze in place. He stepped closer and whispered in her ear. "I'm sorry, but I can't have you aware of our daughter before she is even born. It would interfere with her destiny." Dr. Masterson removed his fingers, which caused Margrit to blink her eyes and look around in confusion.

"Henry? What are we doing down here?" she asked.

"Don't you remember? I brought you down here to discuss your next mission," he replied. "This is the only place I can be sure the walls don't have ears. You'll be traveling with Albert here to Dallas. He will fill you in on the details once you arrive. There is a poor, lost soul you are to recruit who needs your help fulfilling his true potential. I believe his name is Oswald."

Margrit glanced at the archway where Albert stood in tattered clothes, holding a pair of twisted handcuffs. "I'm afraid these are yours," he said. "I hope you have another pair to take along. Never know when they might come in handy."

She fixed Henry with a look of contempt before following Albert back up the steps. Dr. Masterson stepped onto the dais and ran his hand over the pillar's surface, which was back to being black as night. "Remarkable," he breathed, "so the girl is the true Queen of Sorrows."

He stepped back and looked about the room. "As for you, my invisible friend. I don't know if you truly are a ghost, but you also played your part wonderfully. My apprentice will thank you for your deeds once you meet him."

Dr. Masterson headed up the stone steps, leaving him alone in the chamber. Jack had been a fool, and now his wife and daughter were in even greater danger.

The dimly lit room appeared to be growing brighter, and he turned around to find another door at the foot of the dais. A green light surrounded the frame, and its brass plaque was even more cryptic than the others.

# THE LIBRARY PRISONER

"What kind of happy crap is behind door number three?"

The space beyond the doorway was dark. High walls were on either side of him like he was in a narrow canyon. Jack could see a patch of light ahead of him, and he carefully approached it. What he had mistaken for walls were bookshelves, enormous ones three times as tall as him, made from thick wood planks and stacked full of books. His curiosity made him itch to open one up and look inside, but he knew in his present state that his hand would pass right through it.

Jack came out of the shelves into the reading room of the most extensive library he had ever seen. It was filled with long mahogany tables adorned with bronze banker's lamps, plush red leather high-backed chairs, and even a giant card catalog cabinet. Spanning the perimeter of the reading room were row after row of bookshelves, standing like soldiers ready for inspection. He walked into the middle of the room and tilted his head back to take in the enormous glass dome filled with a night sky that contained hundreds of swirling galaxies.

"Beautiful, isn't it," someone said behind him, and Jack spun around to find an older man sitting in one of the reading chairs. "I was transfixed by it when I first got here, but now I barely even glance up at it."

"Where are we? Wait, you can see me?"

"Yes, Jack."

"Who are you? What is this place?"

"Welcome to the Galaad Eternal Library. It sits at the pinnacle of the Black Spire. This library holds the collection of all the stories that have been or will be written in all the universes. We are in the Horror Wing, fittingly enough." The man took hold of a cane resting against his chair and used it to stand up. "My name is Ryland Thynne. I've heard a lot about you even though we haven't met yet. If you're here, that can only mean the MacGuffin Device has been activated."

"MacGuffin Device? What's that supposed to mean?"

"It's not important, but what is important is that you've arrived just in time to help me. You see, I'm sort of trapped here."

"Trapped? My wife worked with you in your bookshop in Bailey Grove."

"Yes, she did, but the bookshop was an extension of the Library that I discovered how to manifest," Ryland explained. "I could not leave my store for long, but I did what I could to help you against the Alchemist."

"You know about the Alchemist?"

"Yes, and he is trying to take control of the Black Spire," the bookseller answered. "If he does that, he will become King of the KnightmareVerse."

"Okay...will he make everyone wet the bed at night or something?"

Ryland rolled his eyes and sighed. "What is the one thing that separates us from being anything more than another breed of dumb animals? Our imagination. To have mastery over that, to have control of what everyone dreams, what greater power could there be? He can drive everyone insane and plunge all of existence into eternal darkness. That's why he can't be allowed in."

"So, how did you get in here?"

"I stumbled upon this place by accident when I discovered that my life was part of a story written by someone else. That set me on a path which eventually led me here."

"What do you mean a story being written by someone else?"

"There are those who have the power to peer through the leaden curtains which hide the infinite partitions of reality and can observe the lives of others using their minds. Such practitioners of these dark arts were once known as *seers*, *magicians*, or even *lunatics*, but now we call them *authors*. The most crazed and far-sighted of these people are often showered in gold and fame."

"That sounds ridiculous. Are you saying that we could be in a novel right now?"

"Not just *could*, Mr. Sterling, I know that we are. Come, follow me."

Ryland shuffled over to the catalog cabinet, bent down to read the letter ranges on the little squares of paper affixed to each drawer, and found the one he wanted.

"Please stand to the side," he said. Ryland tugged on the drawer's brass knob and moved his hand out of the way as the drawer went flying outward, extending the width of five reading tables before it stopped. The bookseller took a pair of glasses from his pocket and flipped through the alphabetized collection of title cards until he selected one and pulled it out. Ryland stepped back and the drawer retracted as rapidly as it had shot out. A semi-circular desk stood beside the cabinet with a wooden sign mounted to the front of it.

# CHECKOUT

Ryland approached the desk and tapped the plunger on the bell atop it several times, issuing a series of sharp, ringing notes. Out of thin air, a woman with silver hair pulled back in a tight bun, black wired-rimmed glasses, and a bright red sweater appeared. Jack ducked behind the card catalog once he saw it was the same woman who had lured him into the painting and then to the ruined temple.

"What are you doing over there?" Ryland asked him.

"That's not a woman," he whispered. "She's not human."

"Yes, I know, she is the Knightmare and the head librarian of this wing. Don't worry. She won't harm you here unless you break the rules."

"Why does she look like my wife then?"

"She appears as that which frightens you most," Ryland explained. "For me, she resembles the ruthless nun who taught third grade, but if she looks like your wife to you...perhaps you are a wiser man than I took you for, Mr. Sterling. I noticed Karina has a penchant for murder mystery novels, and I bet she watches many of those true crime television shows."

"What does that have to do with anything?" Jack asked.

"I'm sure it's nothing to worry about." Ryland handed the librarian the card he had pulled out of the drawer. She snapped her fingers, causing a thick, leather-bound book to materialize on the desk.

"I hope there's no hard feelings," Jack said. "I mean, you did try to kill me."

The Knightmare turned and scowled at him over the tops of her glasses, a look that was both terrifying and sexy, before disappearing again. Ryland picked up the volume and carried it to a standing wooden book holder.

"Does it have a title?" Jack asked as he came around to look over Ryland's shoulder.

"Yes, it's called *The Ghost Writer*," he replied. "I believe it is intended to have a double meaning within the story."

"Huh, sounds pretty cliché. What's it about?"

"Why, you, of course, and your family. You are the main character. Here, see for yourself." Ryland opened the book and flipped through the pages until he came to a blank one.

"What am I supposed to be looking at?" Jack asked.

**"What am I supposed to be looking at?" Jack asked.**

"Wait, where did those words come from?"

"You spoke them, and they appeared," Ryland replied.

**"Wait, where did those words come from?"**
**"You spoke them, and they appeared," Ryland**
**replied.**

"What the hell is going on here? When does this happen in the novel!?" Jack exclaimed in bewilderment.

"Now, Mr. Sterling, this is happening 'Now' in the novel," the older man answered patiently. "Everything that we are saying right now is being written by the story's author as we speak it."

**"What the hell is going on here? When does**
**this happen in the novel!?" Jack exclaimed in**
**bewilderment.**
**"Now, Mr. Sterling, this is happening 'Now'**
**in the novel," the older man answered patiently.**
**"Everything that we are saying right now is**
**being written by the story's author as we**
**speak it."**

"I don't even know what to say to that, except I did not 'exclaim in bewilderment.' What the hell is that about? And who the fuck is the asshole writing all of this down?"

"It can be rather disorienting to realize you are a character in someone's work of fiction, but you shouldn't take it personally."

**"I don't even know what to say to that, except**
**I did not 'exclaim in bewilderment.' What the**
**hell is that about? And who the fuck is the**
**asshole writing all of this down?" ranted the**
**balding, scruffy-looking wanna-be author.**
**"It can be rather disorienting to realize you**
**are a character in someone's work of fiction,**
**but you shouldn't take it personally."**

"Did this son of a bitch just call me scruffy-looking? Whoever is writing this can go-"

"I think that should be a sufficient demonstration. I have something else I need to show you." Ryland picked up his walking cane from the edge of the reading stand and hobbled back towards the checkout desk. He stopped a few feet away and turned back to Jack. "Oh, I almost forgot, would you mind bringing that book to the desk? We wouldn't want the library police coming after us."

"Yeah, sure thing," Jack replied as he returned to the book stand. He went to close the novel when a drawing of a large bird appeared upon the page.

He wondered if the drawing was from his son or the asshole author who was writing down everything he said like a creep. Jack flipped the cover shut and picked up the book, but something struck him in the back. He dropped to the floor in agony, and when he tried to get up, a kick to the gut knocked the wind out of him and left him reeling.

"I forgot to mention, Mr. Sterling," Ryland said as he leaned over him, "that your presence here allows me to leave and claim my place as the true King of the KnightmareVerse. I'm also the real Martin Knight, not that two-bit hack you've been working with. It's always a pleasure to meet one of my fans."

Martin brought the head of his cane down on Jack's head, and he blacked out.

When Jack came to, his head was throbbing, and he was alone in the reading room. He rubbed the knot forming from the blow that Ryland had given him. The bookseller was nowhere in sight, and Jack knew he had been a complete idiot once again. His son had tried to warn him with the picture of the raven. That same bird had been carved into the sign for Mr. Thynne's bookstore. If he had made that connection a moment sooner, he might have saved himself a lot of pain. He was trapped inside the library and no closer to saving his family.

Slowly getting to his feet, Jack spotted the book on the floor where he had dropped it. A peculiar thought crossed his mind. He was initially inclined to dismiss it, but desperate times called for desperate measures. He picked up the heavy novel, lugged it over to the book stand, and set it down before flipping through until he reached the last page with words on it.

"Hey, I know you can hear me because you're writing down everything I say, so I'm asking for your help. How the fuck do I get out of here?"

```
"Hey, I know you can hear me because you're
writing down everything I say, so I'm asking
for your help. How the fuck do I get out of here?"
```

Jack waited a while, hoping for a response, but nothing appeared on the page.

"Come on, help a fellow writer out. You have this whole thing in your head. Can't you give me a hint?"

```
Jack waited a while, hoping for a response, but
nothing appeared on the page.
"Come on, help a fellow writer out. You have this
whole thing in your head. Can't you give me a hint?"
```

```
I don't think I'm allowed to do that.
```

"What do you mean you're not allowed to do that? Are you going to get in trouble with the Federal Bureau of Authors? Look, I'm tired, my head hurts, and if you don't throw me a bone, I will sit here until the end of time. Then where will your fucking story be?"

```
"What do you mean you're not allowed to do that?
Are you going to get in trouble with the Federal
Bureau of Authors?" Jack asked in a completely
unnecessary sarcastic tone. "Look, I'm tired, my head
hurts, and if you don't throw me a bone, I will sit
here until the end of time. Then where will your
fucking story be?"
```

```
Okay, fine, this chapter's dragged on long enough.
You can get out the same way Martin got in. You'll
need to find The Alchemist's Apprentice but don't
check it out. Go pull it from the shelves yourself.
The portal he created will appear when you open it
but watch out for the librarian.
```

"Thanks for the help," Jack grunted as he returned to the card catalog and searched for the letter range that would include *The Alchemist's Apprentice*. He hoped that whoever had devised this filing system from hell would be kind enough not to lump all the titles that started with the word *The* under the T's. Jack pulled on the tab for the drawer he wanted and barely managed to duck out of the way before the drawer took his head off.

He had to stand on a chair to look through the daunting stack of cards. He had to run through the letters of the alphabet more than once on his fingers as he narrowed his search. Thankfully, there was nobody around to witness his shame. He ended up with several nasty paper cuts on his fingers by the time he located the card he wanted. This one was different than all the others he had seen so far, as it had a bright red stamp across it.

Jack thought it was odd that any library would purposely mark a book as banned, even a magical one. Since he couldn't check out the book through the librarian, he scanned the card for any indication of its location. In the upper right-hand corner were three identifiers.

**XIII**
**19**
**NM-1408**

He climbed off the chair, picked up the book on the wood stand, and examined its spine. Sure enough, embossed near the bottom were three similar markings that had to be a location identifier. A Dewey Decimal System of the Damned. Jack checked the closest bookshelf and spotted a large Roman numeral **II** near the top. He went to the next one, saw it was marked with a three, and followed the sequence until he reached number thirteen. He spotted a brass pedestal signboard in the center of the aisle's entrance.

**FORBIDDEN BOOK SECTION**
**NO ENTRY WITHOUT**
**PERMISSION FROM**
**HEAD LIBRARIAN**

"You've got to be kidding me," he sighed. Jack picked up one of the banker's lamps from the nearest table, which didn't seem to require electricity to operate, and slipped around the signboard. He held the lamp as high up as he could and found numbers etched near the top of each section of the bookcase. They started at number one and increased the further he went from the reading room. The bookcase was about the length of a school bus, so he estimated that number nineteen was about a quarter of a mile away. He proceeded briskly, not wanting to make too much noise, and the light from the lamp was barely bright enough to see by.

Jack had only reached the tenth section when he heard footsteps echoing behind him. At the mouth of the aisle stood the librarian in the red sweater, and she glared at him with clear annoyance over the tops of her glasses. He was about to apologize, but her skin turned a sickly greenish-white color covered in scales. Her body stretched out at the torso until she doubled in height, and her face contorted to take on a serpent-like appearance.

# TRESSSSPASSSSER!

The blood-chilling hiss came from the Knightmare's mouth, now wide enough to swallow him whole and lined with jagged, yellowed teeth. Jack sprinted up the aisle, trying his best to keep count of how many bookcases he was passing. He reached what he hoped was number nineteen, dropped the lamp, and grabbed hold of the highest shelf he could reach. Jack had to climb another two shelves up to find the book labeled **NM-1408**.

The Knightmare was now as tall as the top of the bookshelves, its body and limbs having elongated further, and it slithered across the floor toward him at an alarming rate of speed. Jack let go of the shelf, landed hard on the ground, and the book flew out of his hand. The lamp had been knocked over when he fell, and he had to grope around blindly on the floor to locate the book. The scraping noise of the serpentine librarian grew louder in his ears as he desperately felt around for it. His hand finally brushed against it, and Jack flipped open its cover.

He wasn't sure what was supposed to happen, but he was overjoyed to see one of the strange doors appear before him. Jack glanced over his shoulder to see the Knightmare rear back as it prepared to strike. The nameplate on the door barely registered in his mind as he turned the knob and flung his body through the opening.

# THE RAVEN'S PERCH

Jack hit awkwardly on his shoulder and rolled to the side. He scrambled backward as he looked to see if his pursuer had followed him through the doorway. It was too dark to see much of anything, but he was alone. The otherworldly door had vanished, along with his clothes. He was sitting stark naked inside a store filled with empty bookshelves. It looked familiar, but he was too distressed by what had just happened to grasp onto the memory.

Covering himself up with both hands, he approached the front of the shop and peered out through the windows. At first, he thought it was nighttime, which would have been good news given his current state of undress. Then he realized a thick blanket of fog blocked out the sunlight. Jack couldn't see anybody moving around, although he couldn't see much further than the sidewalk. He steeled his nerves, opened the front door, and stepped outside.

## *CLICK*

"Hands up, nice and slow," a gruff, dangerous voice instructed. Jack froze in place, reluctantly raised his hands, and turned his head until he was facing the man pointing a gun at him. Detective Blackburn raised an eyebrow at him before holstering his revolver.

"Jesus wept, Sterling. Where are your clothes?"

# Vampire, Werewolves, Angry Villagers & A Lot of Salem Witches OH MY!!!

Novel By **BUTCH RICHARDSON**

Jupiter & Phoebus Publishing House

# CHAPTER 19

## Vampire, Werewolves, Angry Villagers & A Lot of Salem Witches OH MY!!!

*October 30, 2019*

*W*here am I?

*Who am I?*

She didn't have an answer for the first question that popped into her mind, but the second one was clear enough. She was Mary Deloris Smith, a widowed secretary for the owner of a pharmaceutical company. No, that wasn't right, her name was Cassie Alba, a socially awkward teenage girl who was humiliated after being crowned homecoming queen. No, she wasn't in high school anymore, she could tell that by the ache in her joints. Who the hell was she then?

Kari's memories came flooding back, along with the recollection of what had happened with the pillar. Her daughter had been in the underground chamber with her. Her head snapped up, and she looked around for (*Genny?*) Jenny, but it was too dark to see. Kari tried to stand up only to be hit by a wave of dizziness.

She would have collapsed face-first on the ground if it weren't for the shackles around her wrists. They pulled tight against the chain connected to them, breaking her fall, but she dropped to her knees on the stone floor. Her ankles were also bound, and she turned around to see that the chains connected her to the black stone pillar.

"Jenny? Jenny, where are you?"

There was no answer except for silence, but then she heard the faint echo of footsteps. A person wearing a black hooded robe holding a lantern entered through the archway. Kellie Wilkens pulled back her hood, helped Kari to her feet, and caressed her cheek with her hand.

"You have such beautiful skin," Kellie said. "I was hoping for someone a little bit younger, but given the circumstances, you will do wonderfully."

"Get the fuck away from me. Where's my daughter?"

"She's safe. Do you know how important your daughter is? The Master has been searching for her for so long. She's important to me as well, but more so for what the Master will give me for finding her. You see, this is not my real body. I used to be Vivian Knight and Vivian Masterson before that. Soon, your body will be mine, and I will possess both your beauty and powers."

Kari gasped when the woman cast off her robe, revealing that she was completely nude underneath it. Professor Wilkens walked around the dais to a sarcophagus on the other side. She knelt before it and prostrated herself with her arms stretched out towards the stone coffin. "Arise, Master, your humble servant is here," she intoned.

The lid lifted and levitated on its own before dropping to the side. A wave of mist rose from the interior and flowed over the side. Kari recoiled in horror as the pale, gaunt figure she had encountered the night of the dinner party ascended from its resting place, hovered in midair, and was on its feet in the blink of an eye.

His face was little more than a skull wrapped in a paper-thin layer of skin, but she could still see the resemblance to Dr. Masterson. The vampire seemed to glide rather than walk over to her.

*Karina, my daughter, you have done well,* the thing's voice resonated inside her head. *You have opened the door to the Black Spire and brought me the Queen of Sorrows. I would grant you a place at my side if you joined me as a willing servant.*

"Master, you promised me that I would be the one at your side," Vivian spoke up, apparently able to hear what the vampire was saying as well.

*SILENCE!*

Both Kari and Vivian staggered at the telepathic outburst.

"Go fuck yourself," she spat. "And I'm not your fucking daughter."

The vampire drew back its thin lips in a sneer to display its long, pointed canines while it regarded her with its dead eyes. The thing shot out its bony arm and grabbed her around the throat. Kari tried to pull away, but its hand had the strength of a steel clamp.

*Very well, if you do not appreciate the gifts that I have provided you, I shall give them to someone more deserving.*

Vivian stood up, rushed over to her discarded robe, and returned carrying a silver-handled mirror. This one was strange because it had a reflective surface on both sides, but the glass on one side was tinted red. Vivian stood at the edge of the dais facing her, and the vampire stood between them. It first held the reflective mirror up to Vivian's face with the red glass pointed at its own.

Kari had thought the myth about vampires was that they cast no reflection in mirrors, but she could see Dr. Masterson. His face strangely looked as it did back in 1963. When the vampire turned the mirror towards her, it was Kellie's face looking back at her instead of her own. The vampire moved the mirror before its horrid visage, and a blinding flash of light filled her eyes. Kari tried to scream as her entire body felt like it was on fire, but she no longer had a voice.

"You're lucky Father O'Leary is about the same build as you," Detective Blackburn said. "Sorry his shoes were too small."

"It's fine," Jack replied, buttoning up the black long-sleeved shirt with the distinct white tab collar across the throat. "Wearing this seems kind of sacrilegious, though."

"Yeah, well, we can't have you running about town like you're Adam in the Garden of Eden, so I'm sure you'll get a pass for it."

"Where am I?" he asked. "Is this some kind of purgatory?"

"No, you're still in Iowa," Edgar replied. "If you mean the fog outside, I don't have a good explanation. It rolled in this morning and doesn't look like it will burn off anytime soon. That's the least of my problems. Nobody can leave town, and it doesn't seem like anyone from the outside can get in. All the electricity shut off, and any vehicles with electronics also stopped working."

"What about the Ahnen Villages? Can we get over there?"

"I don't know. I'm the only law enforcement in town right now, and it's all I can do to keep these folks from panicking."

"If we don't get to Devonshire Manor and stop the Alchemist, all these people will die before morning. If you won't come with me, can you find me a working vehicle?"

"It's not a good idea for you to be running around out there, most folks around here think you murdered your in-laws and are responsible for your family disappearing."

"I don't care. My family is in danger, and I need to get to them. The manor will probably be guarded by werewolves, at least give me a gun."

"You'll likely shoot yourself in the foot before you kill a werewolf," Blackburn sighed. "Come on, the good Father has a tractor that might still work."

Jack waited around the back of the church until the detective came out with a set of keys and a pair of old rubber galoshes. "It's better than going barefoot, I guess," he said as he slipped them on. Edgar used one of the keys to unlock the large shed at the end of the parking lot.

Inside was an ancient John Deere tractor with a front loader, and the detective hopped into the rusted metal seat. After several tries, the diesel engine fired up, spewing out a cloud of black exhaust that filled the shed.

"You've got to be kidding me, it's going to take forever to get there on that hunk of junk," Jack said after he stopped coughing.

"Yes, but you'll have fewer blisters than if you walk there in those things," Edgar replied. "You're going to have to ride on the fender, the seat's only big enough for one unless you want to sit in my lap."

"No thanks, I'll take my chances up here," he said as he climbed up on the metal span covering the top of the tractor's enormous left tire. "Do you know how to drive this thing?"

"I grew up on a farm. I learned to shoot, drive, and cuss before I was ten years old."

"Good to know."

They set off on the tractor, having to proceed at barely ten miles an hour due to the limited visibility. The fog began to thin out as they headed north, and when they crested the hill outside of town, there was a break in the ground-hugging cloud that allowed them to see across the Iowa River valley. While Old Ahnen was obscured, Jack could pick out Devonshire Manor's location.

"Do you see that?" He pointed toward the hill on the opposite side of the valley.

"Yeah, what is that? Some kind of tower?" A dark, tapering shape rose fog-shrouded hills to the north and disappeared into the clouds.

"I don't know, but that's where we're going," Jack replied. "Should it be getting dark already?"

"No, it's only mid-afternoon," Edgar said. "You're right, though; the sun is setting." The fog enveloped them again as they rolled down the back side of the hill.

"How much longer until we get to Old Ahnen?" Jack asked.

"Right after this bridge, probably another ten minutes at this..."

Before he could finish, a lone wolf's howl filled the air.

"Shit, they know we're here," Edgar said. "Here, take the wheel." He slid off the seat while holding the steering wheel until Jack could take his place. He drew his revolvers and remained on the lookout as they crossed the bridge over the Iowa River.

The fog here was not as heavy as in Bailey Grove, and Jack could make out the dark shapes of houses and buildings up ahead. The tractor rumbled over another small bridge spanning the canal on the southern edge of town, and Jack had to jam his foot down hard on the brake. The road into Old Ahnen was blocked by a makeshift barrier of pickup trucks parked back-to-back with a handful of armed people standing on the other side.

"By order of the mayor of Old Ahnen, stop right there!" a man shouted, even though Jack had already stopped the tractor. "Don't come any closer, or we'll open fire!"

"Walther Hagen, is that you?" Detective Blackburn called out. "Put your goddamn guns down before you shoot somebody."

"Sorry, Edgar, I didn't recognize you. What are you doing on a tractor?"

"My truck's in the shop, what the hell do you think?" he replied. "What's been happening over here?"

"Goddamn monsters, that's what's happening," Walther answered as he stepped around the barrier. "We've had almost a dozen people attacked. Three of them are dead, and there could be even more missing. Nobody's phones are working, so we haven't been able to call for help."

"Everything's out in Bailey Grove also, but there haven't been any attacks."

"Are any of the victims a woman in her thirties with brown hair? Or a young boy or girl?" Jack asked.

"No, they're mostly folks who worked at the factory, Father," the man replied. "Hey, wait a minute, aren't you the guy who's been all over the news?"

"Forget about that right now, Walther," Blackburn said as he climbed down from the tractor. "I need you to move your vehicles and let us pass."

"What about all the people we've got injured? Are you going to help us get them to the hospital? Shouldn't the rest of the sheriff's department be coming?"

"There's something preventing anyone from getting in or out of the area. I'm afraid we're on our own, and nobody will be safe if we don't find a way to stop what's happening. That's why we're headed to the mansion on the hill."

"I don't think that would be a good idea, Edgar," Walther said, shifting the double-barreled shotgun in his hand. "We need you here in town, it will help keep folks calm if they have someone like you around."

Detective Blackburn grabbed hold of the shotgun and yanked it out of Walther's hands. In the same motion, he stuck the barrel of his revolver under the larger man's throat. "Listen carefully, if I pull this trigger, your head ain't going to grow back. Understand?"

"How long have you known?"

"It doesn't matter, what's going on Walther? Are you involved in this shit?"

"No, not after what happened to Albert and Margrit. Kurt and the other Elders are guarding the factory. I'm trying to protect the people of the Villages from them."

"You're only leaving them for the slaughter to come unless we stop this. Now, either you help me, or I'll neuter your shaggy ass," Edgar snarled, pointing his gun at Walther's crotch. "I want you to round up as many armed volunteers as you can get along with whatever vehicles still work. You're coming with us to the manor."

"It won't do you any good, they'll rip us all to shreds before we get near there."

"What about the factory?" Jack asked. "Is it being guarded also?"

"I don't think so, that's probably why they chased everyone away from there."

"There might be another way into the manor if the underground tunnel hadn't been sealed."

"How would you know there's a tunnel?" Edgar asked. "Never mind, what about it, Walther? Can you get us over there?"

"I'll see what I can do, but I'm not killing any other Elders. I don't care what they've done, they're still blood."

"Just get us in the building. We'll take our chances from there," Edgar replied. He lowered his revolver but kept it in his hand.

Ten minutes later, a convoy of three rusted, diesel-powered pickups rumbled north, packed with a motley cadre of Ahnen Villagers armed with guns, farming implements, knives, and torches. Jack and Edgar brought up the rear with the old John Deere, the agreement with Walther being that the three trucks would return to Old Ahnen as soon as they safely escorted the two of them to the MasterPharm Factory.

The sun had already set even though it seemed too early for that, but nobody knew what time it was since all watches and clocks had stopped working. The fog had cleared up, but snow flurries started falling as they prepared to leave town. By the time they reached the lake, it had become a full-blown blizzard, with a bitter wind stinging any scrap of exposed skin. It was soon impossible to see the road, and the trucks pulled over to let the tractor take the lead so Edgar could use its front loader to clear the path.

With all the streetlights off, it was almost impossible to find the turn-off into the factory. Edgar spotted the building through the blinding snow and took the tractor over the cement bridge that crossed the canal coming from the lake. Through the parking lot they were forced down a narrow path with cars on either side, as the factory must have been full when the fog rolled in. Jack worried they would be easy prey if the wolves were to catch them single file and boxed in like this.

Edgar shifted the transmission to its top gear and pushed the tractor to its maximum speed. It lurched forward just as a dark shape leaped onto the car beside them. Edgar fired a round off right as the wolf sprang through the air at them. The bullet caught the beast in its shoulder and spun it away, but Jack saw it get up and limp away. The vehicles behind them were not as well prepared and panicked shots and screams erupted as werewolves descended on the three pickups.

"Hold on to something," Edgar had to shout at him even though he was a few feet away. "We're going to ram the front doors."

Jack knew that they needed to use the precious few seconds of distraction the Villagers were buying them, but it still felt heartless to leave them behind. Edgar pulled the lever to raise up the bucket on the tractor and aimed for the glass-paneled entrance to the factory. "Get ready to jump!"

Blackburn took his hands off the steering wheel right, grabbed Jack around the waist, and they leaped off the back of the tractor. The snow cushioned their landing and helped shield them from the flying glass as the tractor plowed into the lobby.

"Are you hurt?" the detective asked.

"I don't think so," Jack replied, patting himself down. "You are, though."

A chunk of glass had embedded itself in the back of Edgar's shoulder. He reached back and pulled it out, grunting from the effort, and tossed the blood-stained shard aside. "Get up, we need to move. They'll be on us soon."

Two of the pickups had backed out of the parking lot, but the third was engulfed in flames. Jack didn't want to think about how many people might be dead. He hoped it wasn't for nothing, which it would be unless he found the underground passageway. Edgar switched on his flashlight as they picked their way through the destruction. "Where do we go now?" Blackburn asked.

"I don't know, actually," he replied. "We need to find Dr. Masterson's old office."

"Wait a minute, you don't know where this tunnel is?" The detective groaned. "Look for a fire escape map, I'll guard the front entrance."

Jack took the flashlight and searched around the office area. He felt himself starting to panic until he spotted a sign hanging on the wall.

## MasterPharm Company Museum ◑
### Site of Dr. Henry Masterson's Original Office

"Well, that's frickin' convenient," he said, then shouted over his shoulder. "Hey, it's this way."

The arrow pointed them down a long hallway to the manufacturing section of the plant. Jack worried they had missed a turn somewhere when he saw another smaller sign that said **Museum** and pointed towards a short corridor. He knew they were in the right place as soon as he opened the door at the end. The room was a portal back in time and looked untouched since Masterson's death.

"Okay, professor, where do we go now?" Edgar asked. "Looks like a dead end to me."

"There was a hidden passage in the office that led underground," Jack said. "At least there was in the novel."

"What do you mean '*the novel*'? Forget it, I don't want to know. Just hurry up, we don't have much time left."

Jack stepped over the velvet rope cordoning off the section of the museum that comprised Dr. Masterson's desk and working library. He started his search with the desk, pulling out all the drawers, but they were empty. Nothing on top seemed unusual, and he checked for any secret button or switch underneath. Giving up on that, he then pointed the flashlight at the collection of business, chemistry, and other dusty scientific tomes that filled the bookshelves standing sentry behind the desk. The only book that seemed out of place was a leather-bound book titled *The Conchologist's First Book*. It was an illustrated textbook from the 1800s about shells and the animals that lived in them, but Jack knew that the author was Edgar Allan Poe. He pulled out the book, but there was nothing behind it.

Frustrated, he pointed the flashlight upwards, illuminating a marble bust on the top shelf. Jack had to grab a chair to reach the statue of a woman's head wearing an ancient helmet, the Greek goddess Athena. Or the pallid bust of Pallas, as she was called in the famous poem. He felt around the statue until his finger found a small button in back of it. Jack pushed it in and heard something click. The bookshelf swung out from the wall a couple of inches.

"Quoth the Raven, *Open Sesame!*" Jack laughed. From out in the hallway came the sound of a wolf howling, and Edgar locked the door to the museum.

"That won't hold them long."

Behind the bookcase was a narrow set of concrete steps between the office and outer walls, going down about ten feet before switching back the other way. Jack started down the stairs as the detective closed the passageway behind him. His foot slipped as he was turning onto the second switchback and he almost went tumbling down the steps, but Edgar grabbed his arm before he lost his footing.

"I thought you injured that shoulder," Jack said as he steadied himself.

"It was just a flesh wound."

The stairs ended at least fifty feet beneath the surface at another door, this one made of thick steel that took both of them to open as its hinges were rusted. From above, a loud thud signaled that the pack had breached the museum door, and he wondered how long it would take them to find the hidden stairwell.

The door led to a tunnel with railroad tracks running down the center. While the rest of the factory was dark from the power outage, battery-powered emergency lights along the curved ceiling were still functioning. Several of them had burned out or were flickering, making the subterranean passage even creepier. The cement walls were also showing cracks from years of neglect, and Jack worried they might collapse.

They were standing on a narrow platform that was raised up a couple of feet above the tunnel floor. An open-topped tram car with multiple rows of seats was sitting beside the platform. Edgar stepped down into the front seat and pushed the starter button.

"No joy, the battery is dead," he said, then looked around. "Hold on, we might be in luck. See if you can pull that lever to switch the track."

Jack stepped off the platform and jogged up the tunnel to where a pole with a crossbar was positioned next to a shorter section of track that split off from the main line. He took hold of the crossbar and had to push with all his strength to get the rusted pole to point towards the secondary track. From behind him came the creak of metal grinding and he feared it was the werewolves opening the tunnel door, but it was Edgar making the noise.

He was standing atop a crude rail-traversing vehicle with a square wooden platform. It had a metal pillar in the center, and a long iron bar mounted at the top that had handles on both ends. Jack had only seen a railway handcart in old cartoons. This one was painted yellow with black stripes to make it more visible, and the company name was stenciled on the platform.

# KALAMAZOO RR COMPANY

"Are we seriously going to use that thing?"

"Would you rather try to outrun a pack of werewolves on foot?" Edgar asked as he pumped the handle to push it forward. Jack grabbed hold of the side and pulled himself up onto the cart. He took hold of the other handle on the lever and began pumping when it was his turn. It took them a while to get the rhythm down, but once they did the cart picked up speed. While they were traveling at a good clip, the effort was still exhausting. Edgar didn't appear to feel the effects as much, even with his injured arm, which was good since they had a long way left to go.

"Oh fuck, here they come," Jack said. Blackburn had his back towards the end of the tunnel they had started from, so he had to risk a quick glance over his shoulder when the lever was on the upstroke. Like a tidal wave rushing their way, a mass of brown and white furred fury poured out of the doorway and filled the width of the tunnel. Despite the lead they had, the pack quickly closed the distance. Jack looked over his shoulder and could see up ahead that the other end of the tunnel was still far away.

"We're not going to make it," he wheezed. His arms were going numb, and his lungs were on fire. Edgar reached down, grabbed the hand brake, and stopped the cart.

"You're right, stay here."

Blackburn hopped off the cart, straddled the rails, and drew his revolvers. Jack counted twelve werewolves charging at them, giving the gunfighter only one shot to take down each target. Time seemed to slow down as the lead wolf in the pack reached the point where he could see its eyes. That was when the gunfighter fired his first shot and struck the beast square in the forehead, dropping it to the ground. The pack bounded right over its corpse and continued at full speed. Edgar's hands were a blur as he cocked, aimed, and fired both guns nearly simultaneously, his shots finding their mark again and again.

When the smoke cleared, there was a twisting path of naked dead bodies scattered along the railroad tracks, most of them still with wolf-like features. Jack had covered his ears, but they were still ringing from the cannon-like reverberations in the confined subway. Edgar holstered his pistols and wiped the sweat from his brow.

"Jesus wept; you killed all twelve of them!"

"Twelve? I only had eleven bullets..."

The nearest body started to move, and a werewolf emerged from underneath. Its shoulder was bloodied from the wound Edgar had given it in the parking lot, and it pushed aside the corpse it had used for protection. The gunfighter grabbed one of his revolvers. His fingers flew through the reloading process, opening the loading gate, ejecting the spent shell, retrieving a bullet from one of the loops on his belt, and inserting it in the empty chamber. He had just shut the loading gate and spun the cylinder around to put the live round in position when the werewolf grabbed his arm and bit down on his hand. It tore off Edgar's thumb and index finger and spit them out along with the gun onto the ground, then tossed him against the wall.

Blackburn crumpled into an unconscious heap on the tunnel floor. Jack was frozen with fear, but a spark of anger at having come so close to reaching his family spurred him to move. He dove for the detective's bloody gun as the werewolf spun around to face him. Jack took aim at the monster and pulled the trigger, but nothing happened. He dropped the revolver and put his arms over his head as the beast lunged at him. With his eyes squeezed shut, he braced for the wolf to tear him apart with its enormous teeth and claws, but he risked opening one eye after a few seconds.

Two werewolves were now fighting each other, only a couple of feet away from him. The one with the injured shoulder was restrained from behind by a wolf with jet-black fur. That wolf was also hurt, having only three fingers on its hand (*paw?*). It was starting to lose the fight and turned its head towards Jack.

## GGGGUUUUUUUNNNNNNN

The guttural noise was almost indecipherable until he saw the werewolf motion with its head at the revolver he had discarded. Jack snatched it up and tossed it to the black wolf, who caught it with its left hand, awkwardly cocked back the hammer, and then jammed the barrel into the other one's neck. The gunshot nearly severed the wolf's head, splattering Jack in a torrent of red rain and fur. The black wolf released the dead werewolf, and the body started to revert to its human form as it collapsed. Jack was not surprised to see his brother-in-law's lifeless eyes staring back at him, although he could have done without the image of Kurt's naked corpse in his head.

"It's a single-action revolver," Edgar said. He had reverted to his human form and was wrapping his injured hand in what was left of his shirt. "You have to cock the hammer before you can fire it."

"Oh, right, I'll remember that for next time," Jack answered. "So...you're a werewolf?"

Kari woke up on the cold floor of the domed chamber. She was still naked but no longer chained to the stone pillar. She spotted the discarded black robe the other woman had been wearing in the flickering light of the braziers. After slipping into the robe and fastening the sash, she made her way back up the spiral steps until she came to the door to the basement.

She heard muffled voices on the other side and pressed her ear against it to listen. By the sound, it was two men talking, and they were not far away. Kari slowly turned the knob and opened the door wide enough to peek out. At the end of the hallway was a man dressed like a cowboy with his back to her. He stepped out of the way and Kari caught a glimpse of the other man he had been talking to, who looked like a priest just come from an exorcism. He wiped off his face with his shirt sleeve, and she recognized the Bloody Father was her husband.

"Jack?" she called out, throwing open the door. "Jack, it's me!"

The cowboy spun around and pointed a gun at her.

"Professor Wilkens, what are you doing here?" Jack asked. "Where's Martin? Where's my family?"

"What are you talking about? Don't you recognize me?"

"Of course I do, are you working for the Alchemist?"

"Jack, it's me, your wife. Why are you..." Kari stopped and looked down at her hands, which she now realized looked unfamiliar. She loosened the silk belt on the robe and peeked down at her nude body, which also bore no resemblance to what it should have. "Oh god. No, no, this can't be happening. She took my body, Jack, this isn't me."

She sank to the floor in tears and buried her face in her hands. She flinched when she felt Jack's hand touch her shoulder, then allowed him to put his arm around her. "Kari? Is that you?" She looked up at him and nodded.

"How can you be sure?" the gruff-looking man in the tattered uniform asked. "This could be a trick."

"Do you remember being the secretary for Dr. Masterson back in the sixties?"

"Yes, it seems like a bad dream, though. How do you know about that?"

"What did I use to talk to Jenny and you?" Jack asked.

"That was you? A typewriter, we were writing messages on the typewriter in the cottage."

Jack nodded towards the cowboy, and the man lowered his weapon. Her robe came open as he was helping her up, and Jack's eyes widened before she snatched it shut.

"Keep your eyes where they belong, Sterling."

"You're definitely Kari. This is Detective Blackburn."

"Call me Edgar," the cowboy said.

"I thought I lost you," Jack said as he hugged and kissed her.

"I don't know how you can even look at me," she sobbed against him. "That woman has taken everything from me. She killed my mother, and now she has my daughter."

"We'll find Jenny, don't worry."

The three of them headed towards the stairs to the main floor, with Edgar taking the lead, holding a revolver in his left hand. "Won't your fingers grow back or something?" Jack asked.

"Not from a werewolf bite, why do you think I have these scars? I guess I'm out of a job, but I think I'm ready for retirement if we get out of here alive."

The flashlight's battery died out as they climbed the steps. Light came from the archway to the Grand Hall, provided by a couple of wrought iron candelabra placed on the mantle above the fireplace. Jack picked up one of them as they looked around the room.

"Do you hear that?" Kari whispered. "I think somebody's singing."

The voice was faint, but it sounded like it was coming from the hallway towards the dining room. Despite the voice sounding slurred, she could distinguish some words as they approached the library door.

*When I'm...drowning in...a sea of sorrows...*

*Mother Mary...appears to me...*

*Singing songs of comfort...set me free...*

Martin Knight was sitting in one of the leather reading chairs with his feet on the wood coffee table. Another candelabra was placed precariously on the edge of the table beside a bottle of 50-year-old Glenstirling Black Label Single Malt Scotch. He almost knocked it over as he sat up to refill his tumbler.

"Oh, there you are, my dear," Martin said as he saw her standing in the doorway. "Please, do come in and join me. Sit, we can get drunk and watch the world end together. Your beloved Master said the apocalypse begins soon."

"Sounds like you're already pretty well sauced," Jack replied.

"Where's my daughter?" Kari asked as she approached his chair.

"I didn't know you had a daughter, Kellie," Martin replied. "Was that the little girl I saw earlier?"

"Yes, that's her," Kari replied, remembering she was no longer in her own body. "Where did she go?"

The drunken author pointed out the open window toward the night-draped backyard of the estate. "Out there, into that thing." Kari ran to the window and looked outside. A massive black structure filled the entire view.

"What is that thing?" Jack asked as he joined her at the window.

"It's the Black Spire," Martin replied, then drained the last swallow of liquor from his glass. "The Alchemist took your wife and the little girl inside."

"Then we're going in after him," Kari said.

"I don't think that's a good idea, but you have fun storming the Tower of Terror. I will be right here getting piss drunk."

"You're coming along with us," Edgar replied, lifting the author out of his chair by the back of his sweater. Martin grabbed the Scotch bottle as he was dragged towards the library doors. They returned to the Grand Hall and exited through the back door onto the terrace.

Once outside, it was easier to see the enormity of the building that took up the entirety of the manor's back lawn. Kari could still see the hedges and flower gardens through the exterior of the Spire. The structure was semi-transparent as if it were an illusion, but the blowing snow didn't pass through it. Jack went up to the side of it and reached out with his hand only to have it pass right through the rounded wall.

"How do we get inside if it's not solid?" she asked.

Martin pointed towards the center of the yard. "They went through the door."

"I should have known," Jack said. Standing before the Spire was a blood-red door that wasn't attached to anything. The four of them gathered around the door with a wrought-iron knocker in the center shaped like a snake eating its own tail.

"Maybe you should stay here," Jack suggested.

"My daughter is in there, and so is the bitch that stole my body," she snapped. "Don't you dare get in my way, Sterling."

Jack nodded and knocked on the door to the Black Spire.

*Fourteen Til Midnight*

Standing beneath a moonless night sky, Jack couldn't see his hand before his face. He worried that he had gone blind when a small blue flame appeared, hanging suspended in midair. In the ethereal light, he could just make out Kellie's (*Kari's*) face. Since she was wearing a black robe, it seemed like her disembodied head was floating. Another blue fireball materialized higher up, this one bigger and much brighter, casting a pale glow over the four of them. They were standing between the two stone columns that marked the edge of the property of Devonshire Manor, but there was something different. No snow was on the ground, yet the grass looked shriveled and dead.

"What is this place?" Kari asked.

"We're inside the Black Spire," Jack answered. "Don't trust anything you encounter in this place. Especially mimes."

"Where did those lights come from?" Martin asked.

"I think I made them," Kari replied. "I was scared that I couldn't see anything, and then the light appeared."

"You're a witch?" Edgar asked.

"I guess, but I don't know what I'm doing."

"Well, nothing like on-the-job training to motivate you," Blackburn replied as he checked the cylinder of his revolver.

The blue globes preceded them as they made their way up the stone path towards the manor house. The flowers in the gardens had all wilted away, and the hedges were nothing more than barren, dry sticks that resembled the skeletal husks of long dead creatures. As they got closer, the light showed that the rot and ruin had also infested the house. Most of the windows had been broken out, a black toxic moss covered the outside walls, and any exposed metal was coated in rust.

Jack tried to open the back door, and its hinges came loose from the frame. He had to jump out of the way as the heavy wood portal crashed to the ground.

"They might not know we're here," Edgar quipped. "Why don't you ring the doorbell just to be sure."

The Grand Hall was in as poor a condition as the exterior of the building, and it looked to be suffering from decades of neglect. The paintings were either slashed to ribbons or so faded they were no longer discernable. The tapestry lay crumpled in a heap before the fireplace and seemed to have been used by a wild animal as a nest. Edgar motioned for them to follow him towards the hallway that led to the library. Jack was holding Kari's hand, but Mr. Knight was nowhere to be seen.

"Where's Martin?" he asked, and the three of them came to a halt.

"Over here," the author called out, emerging from the archway to the main staircase. "I was starting to feel a touch sober, so I was wetting my whistle." He held up the bottle of Scotch.

Edgar cursed under his breath and turned back towards the hallway. Jack went back to retrieve the inebriated author, but the shadow behind the suit of armor by the stairs suddenly came to life.

"Look out!" Jack yelled.

Ryland moved with surprising speed for a man his age, closing the distance between him and Martin before the he could react. The metal-clad bookseller wrapped an arm around the author's neck and held a dagger to his throat with his other hand. "Greetings, old chum, remember me?"

"Mr. Thynne? What are you doing?" Kari called out.

"This is Martin Knight," Martin replied. "You could say he's my *Wicked Self*, it's a long story."

"Shut up, you windbag," Ryland said, nicking Martin's throat with his knife.

"Let him go, or I'll incinerate you," Kari threatened.

"Can you do that?" Jack whispered, but she elbowed him to be quiet.

"I don't think so, witch," Ryland replied. "You're going to help me kill the Alchemist. You, with the guns, drop them on the floor." Edgar didn't seem like he was going to cooperate. Ryland drew more blood from Martin, and he removed his gun belt. "Good, now, all of you out the door over there."

Ryland marched them to the front entrance while he and Martin brought up the rear. Jack pulled on the handle, and the door swung inward. He emerged in the middle of a moonlit field of roses with Kari, Edgar, Martin, and Ryland appearing beside him.

"Okay, what's with the doors around this place?" Edgar grumbled.

"You'll get used to it after a while," Jack replied.

"Where are we now?" Kari asked.

"I've been here before," he said. "Watch out for the flowers."

"Straight ahead, let's go," Ryland ordered.

They climbed up to the top of the nearest hill, and in the valley beyond was the pond where he had first encountered the Knightmare. In place of the ancient stone ruins on the far side was now a two-story tall white building nestled in the willow trees.

"We have to hurry, there's not much time left," Ryland said. "It will be Halloween in ten minutes."

"Why? What happens then?" Jack asked. "Do you turn back into a cabbage?"

"The Alchemist can free the Knightmare at midnight on Halloween. If he does that, he can unleash it upon the world."

"Isn't that what you want to do?"

"No, I only want access to the library so I can take from it the best stories. How do you think I came up with all my material? Of course, this asshole stole most of my best stuff."

"You're nothing more than a figment of my imagination," Martin protested. "Although that knife sure seems real."

They hurried down the hill and through the maze of trees surrounding the pond until they reached the edge of the clearing. The façade of the building that stood where Jack had fought the mime was made to resemble a Greek temple, with columns along the entrance. The building's name was carved into the gabled front of the portico.

# GALAAD ETERNAL LIBRARY

"Hey, that looks just like the public library from the town where I grew up," Martin said.

Through the trees, Jack spotted two black-cloaked figures standing next to a girl in a white dress. Kari must have seen her as well as she went running into the clearing.

"Jenny! Jenny, it's mommy!" she called out. "Come here, baby, get away from them!"

Jack was about to go after her, but Ryland grabbed his arm. "Stay here, she can handle this on her own. You, furball, circle around and see if you can get a jump on the bloodsucker."

Edgar narrowed his eyes at the bookseller, then disappeared into the woods.

"What about my wife? You're going to leave her out there alone?"

"Hopefully she can distract them long enough for me to sneak into the library."

Jenny looked at Kari in confusion since she bore no resemblance to her mother, and the hooded figure beside her placed her hand on the girl's shoulder. Jack's stomach lurched as the person threw back the cowl to reveal his wife's face with a sinister grin on her lips.

"That's the bad woman I warned you about," the woman wearing Kari's body said. "You need to protect us, can you do that, honey?"

His daughter nodded and raised her hands outward. A jet of green flame shot forth from the palms of her hands, arcing through the air straight towards Kari. His wife stumbled backward as she threw up her own hands, causing the flames to deflect away harmlessly.

"No, that's not possible!" Vivian shouted. "You aren't supposed to have any powers."

"Sorry to disappoint you," Kari said. "Give me my daughter back, you bitch!"

Jenny looked between the two women, but Vivian touched her on the temple, and she went stiff. "If you want her, come and get her." Jenny no longer seemed in control of her own body, and the other woman used her like a human flamethrower. A wall of fire erupted from his daughter, and it was all Kari could do to hold back the onslaught.

Jack could tell that his wife was no match for Jenny's powers, and he wasn't about to stand by and watch her be burned alive. He glanced down and saw that Martin was still holding the bottle of Scotch. Ryland was focused on the battle at the foot of the library's steps, no doubt waiting for an opening to usurp the Alchemist's prize. The moment came when Blackburn, having transformed into his wolf form, leaped onto the cloaked vampire's back. The bookseller lowered his knife and relaxed his grip on Martin. Jack snatched the half-empty bottle from Martin's hand, then brought it down on Ryland's head. It shattered and knocked him unconscious while also dousing him in priceless alcohol as he collapsed to the ground.

"What a waste of good Scotch," Martin groaned. "Can we go back home now?"

"I'm trying to figure out how to do that," Jack said. "Your wife sent me here to get you back." A fuzzy memory came into his head, and he removed Vivian's necklace. "Your wife gave this to me. She said you would know what to do with it."

Martin took hold of the crescent pendant and examined the symbols etched on it. "Oh yes, this is written in the language of the alchemists. I made it up for my latest novel."

"Great, what the hell does it say?"

Martin leaned over and whispered a word in his ear.

"I'm sorry, what?"

"You heard me, get close to your wife and speak it," Martin replied. "It will protect her from your daughter, but you'll still have to find a way to deal with the vampire."

"You don't have a pen and something to write on, do you?" Jack asked.

"Of course, I always keep a notebook on me. Why?" He ripped a page from Martin's pad and quickly wrote two lines on the paper.

"The library should be opening soon," he said. "Sneak inside, ring the bell at the checkout desk, and give this to the woman in the red sweater."

Jack ran to help Kari before Martin could ask him any questions. He had to put his arms in front of his face to protect himself from the intense heat coming from his daughter's attacks. It was like trying to get near the sun, but he managed to make it within a few steps of Kari before he held up the pendant and shouted out what Martin had told him.

"*ABRACADABRA!*"

A ring of blue light burst forth from the pendant and settled on the ground surrounding him and Kari. Twelve ghostly, robed women materialized around the perimeter of the ring. In unison, they raised their hands, and a beam of blue ice split apart the wall of green flames. The shockwave from the fire spell's dissipation knocked Vivian and Jenny down.

Kari collapsed in exhaustion, and Jack dropped to his knees by her side.

"Jenny...go get Jenny..." she said before passing out.

Blackburn and the Alchemist were still wrestling, but the vampire managed to get ahold of the werewolf and threw him up against one of the pillars. Jack had almost reached his daughter when the vampire swooped in and grabbed her. It lifted her unconscious body up and tilted her head, poised to sink its fangs into her vulnerable neck.

"You have lost, Mr. Sterling," the vampire rasped. "I will plunge your world into eternal darkness and suffering, but I shall keep you alive long enough to bear witness to my triumph. Maybe I will even make you write a book about it before I kill you."

The undead abomination gave a rattling chuckle. Martin burst out of the library's front door, cradling a book against his chest that he tossed to him.

"I prefer the classics," Jack said, holding up the book so Masterson could see its title.

# The Sun Also Rises

He opened the book, and the darkness burned away as the sun appeared above the horizon. The vampire dropped Jenny and tried to pull its hood back up as its skin blackened where the light touched it. Blackburn recovered and leaped onto the Alchemist's back, ripping the cloak off him. Naked and defenseless from the sunlight, the creature of the night was soon reduced to a smoldering pile of ashes on the steps.

"I guess even monsters have horror stories," Martin said.

Jack picked up his daughter and cradled her in his arms. Jenny seemed none the worse from the ordeal, and Kari was also unharmed. The only problem now was that his wife was trapped in the body of his former boss. They bound Vivian's wrists behind her back and tied her ankles together.

"Give that amulet a try," Martin suggested. "It's the symbol of the Coven, maybe it will work on her."

Jack knelt before the woman and held up the crescent moon pendant.

"Vivian Knight, I command you to return this body to its rightful owner."

"Get the fuck away from me!"

She tried to retreat from him as he pressed the amulet to her forehead.

"The power of the Coven compels you."

When the metal touched her skin, it caused it to smolder.

"No! You can't do this to me!"

"The power of the Coven compels you."

"I won't go back to that body! You can't make me!"

"The power of the Coven compels you!"

A flash of blue light emitted from the amulet and Vivian's eyes rolled back in her head so that only the whites were showing.

"THE POWER OF THE COVEN COMPELS YOU!"

The woman opened her mouth wide, and a jet of black liquid spewed out. The vile fluid splashed on Jack's face and coated the front of the priest's outfit that he was still wearing. Vivian fainted away, and Kari also went limp.

"I should have seen that coming," Jack said as he wiped off his face. "Do you think it worked?"

"No idea, I was just spitballing there," Martin replied.

Kari's body regained consciousness first, and Jack waited with breathless anticipation to see who inhabited it.

"Jack? What happened? Why are my hands tied up?"

"I thought we could get a little kinky."

"What? I'm not in the mood for your shit, Sterling. Where's Jenny?"

"Calm down, babe, she's fine," Jack replied as he untied her hands. "I had to be sure it was you, look down at your body."

"Oh my god, I'm me again." She threw her arms around his neck and kissed him.

"Let's get out of here."

Jack helped his wife stand up, and Jenny ran over to her mother to hug her. Martin tapped him on the shoulder and pointed up at the library. Standing in the doorway was the librarian in the red sweater, and she motioned at him with a wag of her finger.

"I think she wants to talk to you," Martin said.

He climbed the steps and got as close as he dared to the Knightmare, hoping she couldn't step across the library's threshold. She held out a black card with silver writing on it. Jack hesitated, then reached out and took it from her. The librarian winked at him, spun about on her heel, and the doors to the library shut behind her on their own. He looked down at the card.

# GALAAD ETERNAL LIBRARY
## *Membership Card*
### John Sterling

"What did she give you?" Kari asked as he came down the steps.

"A library card," he replied, holding it up.

"Jack, that's the gift that keeps on giving," Martin explained. "You can use that to access any universe in existence, you'll never run out of stories to tell."

"I don't want it, that's too dangerous for anyone to have access to." Jack went to tear it up.

"Hold on, before you do that, I think I know what to do with these two," Martin said. He handed him the card, and the author placed it on the ground in between where Ryland and Vivian were lying. He stepped back as a ring of green light formed around them, and they vanished.

"What did you do with them?"

"They're someplace where they can't cause any more trouble." Martin ripped the card in half and dropped it on the ground, where the two pieces vanished into smoke.

An arched wood doorway appeared before them. Jack opened the door to Devonshire Manor and was relieved to find the Grand Hall on the other side was not the decrepit, moldy version. The five of them filed into the spacious room, and Edgar bent down to retrieve his gun belt and revolvers. "I'm starving," the gunfighter said. "I wonder if there's someplace to get a steak at this hour."

Jack stopped and looked at Blackburn. "How are your guns here? You took them off in the Black Spire." A tremor shook the house and rattled the glass in the windows.

"Is that an earthquake, or am I still drunk?" Martin asked.

Another larger tremor knocked them off their feet, and Jack ran to open the door they had come through. Looming above the trees in the moonlit driveway was a black-and-white striped, multi-tentacled monstrosity with eight giant crab legs stomping up the lawn towards the house. If that wasn't terrifying enough, the creature had an enormous, red-Beret-topped mime's head with the sharp beak of a giant squid in place of a mouth. A snake-like tongue shot out when it opened its beak, and Jack barely managed to slam the door shut before it reached him.

"What the hell is going on?" Kari asked, clutching Jenny to her chest.

"The Knightmare tricked me when she gave me that library card," he replied. "I think we just unleashed it on our world."

The house shook again as several glass panels came loose from the windows, and cracks appeared in the ceiling. "Everybody down to the basement," Edgar ordered.

The shaking made walking difficult, and dust and debris kept falling with each shudder. Above them, Jack could hear loud cracking noises as the wood beams in the roof gave way. They reached the stairs leading down to the underground tunnel when a large quake struck, causing the ceiling above the stairs to collapse. Edgar pulled Jack out of the way just before a large chunk of cement landed on his head.

"Back to the chamber," Jack said.

"That's a dead end," Kari replied.

"There's no other choice."

Kari conjured up more small blue fireballs to light their way down the perilous circular steps. The domed room hadn't suffered any of the damage the upper floors had so far, but a cloud of dust followed them down the stairs and signaled that they were likely trapped. Kari and Jenny sat down on the edge of the dais as Jack, Martin, and Edgar huddled by the archway.

"What are we going to do now?" Martin asked. "Even if that thing doesn't get us down here, how long will it be before somebody rescues us?"

"Maybe it will give up soon and go somewhere else. We just have to sit tight," Jack replied.

"I've got four rounds left. If it comes down to it, only one of us has to suffer a bad death," Edgar offered.

"Whoa, I don't think we need to go there, Sheriff Grimdark," Martin scoffed.

"Is there another way out of this room, Martin? You were writing the novel about it."

"I lost most of my memories when the other Martin pulled me into this world," he said. "Wait a minute, in my stories, I always have a *deus ex machina* ready just in case it goes sideways on me, and I can't work out how to end it." The author looked around, and his eyes landed on the pillar. "Ah, that has to be it."

Martin walked around the black stone column and inspected the strange symbols carved into its surface. "Uh huh, yep, ok, so it says I need to press... here?" He inserted his finger into a hole in the pillar, and a section of the stone slid open. Underneath was a metal panel with a big red button. "Bingo!"

"Hold on, how do you know what that thing does?" Jack protested.

"Not to worry, my boy, I'm a professional." He pressed the button, and the pillar came alive with a pulsing red light. The floor also lit up with bizarre geometric patterns, a metal door slid down over the archway, and the section where the sarcophagus sat dropped away. In its place, a control panel and oddly shaped seats rose out of the ground. The dome's surface began to glow and changed into a 360-degree viewing screen that showed various instrumentation displays annotated with the strange symbols from the pillar.

"Is this...is this a spaceship?"

"Yes, I believe so, you'd be surprised how well aliens can get you out of a fictional bind," Martin said. "Well, Jack, let's take her for a spin, shall we?"

"You want me to drive, I mean, fly this thing?"

"I'm too drunk to manage."

"Don't look at me, pal," Edgar said, raising his injured hand.

Jack sat in the center seat as the rest of them took their places beside him. He noticed a blinking button, held his breath as he pushed it, and the whole room shook as the spacecraft took off. Two small probes came out of the chair and attached themselves to the side of his head, and he could somehow see the ship's exterior as though he were floating above it. The saucer-shaped machine rose from the ground, carrying the cottage and the earth surrounding it on top of it. It flew a couple hundred feet up, and Jack saw the destroyed manor house. There was no sign of the Knightmare, but a trail of broken trees led down the hill.

"How do I steer this thing?" Two levers extended from beneath the control panel, and he took hold of them. After a bit of trial-and-error (*and nearly crashing a few times*), Jack got the hang of navigating the ship.

"There it is," Kari called out, pointing at the screen showing the lumbering monstrosity. "It's heading right for the town. How do we stop it?"

"I don't know, is there a death ray or something on board, Martin?"

"Let me check for a user's manual...nope, don't see one."

Jack rolled his eyes. "Hang on to something, I have an idea."

He made the ship swoop down low to get the Knightmare's attention, then came around and positioned it right over the freakish creature. The Knightmare lashed out with its tentacles, but Jack pitched the controls forward, and the cottage and its foundation slid off the spacecraft. It crashed down onto the Knightmare and squished it flat, leaving only a couple of striped legs and its giant red beret sticking out. Jack righted the ship and watched as even those traces of the horror disappeared in a cloud of black smoke.

His maneuver must have damaged something with the alien vehicle as the control panel flashed like a Christmas tree. Jack flew it back to the wide lawn behind Devonshire Manor before the controls died. One large button remained blinking on the panel, and he smacked it with the palm of his hand. The room seemed to grow brighter, and then the walls became transparent as a feeling of weightlessness took over. He was blinded by a flash of light, and the next thing he knew, they were all standing on the ground in front of the destroyed house. The spaceship hovered above them for a few seconds, then zoomed up into the night sky until it was no longer visible.

"You don't see that every day," Detective Blackburn remarked.

"This should give you plenty of material for your own novel," Martin said.

"I think I've had my fill of horror stories for a while," Jack replied. "Maybe I'll try my hand at sapphic British murder mysteries, seems like a safer genre."

Mr. Knight raised his eyebrow at him. "I guess if you can find an agent for it, best of luck."

The manor was barely recognizable, with rubble strewn throughout the grounds. Martin picked through the piles of debris as Jack checked on his family.

"Where's Patrick?" Kari asked. "Where's my son, Jack?"

"I don't know, but I'm sure he's safe. We'll find him, babe, I promise."

"Ha, take a look at this!" Martin called out as he picked up a large black object. "They don't build them like they used to, that's for sure."

He set the typewriter down on an overturned chair, and Jack saw a sheet of paper in the roller. Suddenly, the keys of the machine began moving on their own.

## Daddy wake up! Please wake up!

"Is this all just a dream?" Jack asked.

"I don't know, but does it matter?" Martin replied. "I think your son is saying that you have the power to get us all out of here, though."

"What does that mean?"

"You have to learn the one trick every good writer must master. How to get out of your own head and back to the real world."

"Okay, how do you suggest I do that?"

"Try clicking your heels three times and say *There's no place like home*?"

"You can't be serious," Jack said, but Martin only shrugged in response. Although he felt like an idiot, Jack closed his eyes and did exactly what the horror author suggested. When he opened them, a door was standing before him. The brass plaque affixed to it had the most wonderful word in the world.

# SOMETIMES IT COMES BACK IN THE
## Epilogue

M artin's eyelids felt heavy as he tried to lift them, but after falling back asleep a few more times, he held them open long enough to look about the room. His eyes refused to focus, so he could only see a few patches of blurry light. The thought came from the murky depths of his mind that he needed glasses, but they weren't on his face. His ears also seemed to be suffering from disuse as he became aware of a muffled, annoying beeping sound somewhere near his head.

He heard a door open to his right and soft-soled shoes squeaking as a person approached the beeping sound and stopped it. Martin struggled to open his mouth, but it was so dry he couldn't get his tongue to work. The person stood just outside his peripheral vision, typing on a keyboard.

Martin wanted to speak and let them know he was awake, but nothing would come out. He could see the outline of someone standing beside him as he tried to lift his arm to get their attention, but the person finished typing and walked back towards the door.

*wait*

He wasn't even sure he had made any noise, his throat felt raw as though he had been gargling with glass shards. Martin worried the nurse had left, but then she leaned over him and shined a small flashlight in his eyes.

*fuck*

The nurse jumped back and dropped her flashlight.

"I'm so sorry. Stay awake, Mr. Knight, I'm going to get the doctor," she said. Martin tried to keep his eyes open, but they grew too heavy.

It was brighter in the room when he opened his eyes again. Martin could see daylight coming in through a window to his left. There was also a chair beside the window with a person curled up on it, but he couldn't make out anything more than that with his poor eyesight. He propped himself up on an elbow, although the effort left his head throbbing.

"Hello?" he called out in a weak voice. "Is somebody there?"

The figure in the chair started to stir, then came awake and got out of the chair. He lay back down as the person rushed to the bedside and leaned over him.

"Martin? Oh my god, you're awake," a woman said. "I didn't believe them at first, I thought it was too good to be true."

"I'm here, Vivian, I came back to you." He was showered with kisses from his wife before she picked up a pair of glasses from a nearby table to put on his face. His sight was still fuzzy; his eyes had either gotten worse or hadn't adjusted to being used again, but it was good to see her face. "How long have I been asleep?"

"You've been in a coma for three months, my love," she said, tears streaming down her cheeks. "I was afraid I would never get to see you again."

"Only three months? It seemed a lot longer than that."

There was a knock on the door and Martin turned to see a woman in green scrubs walk into the room.

"I didn't mean to interrupt," she said. "I can return later."

"No, it's alright. Come in," Vivian replied. "How is he doing? Is he going to be alright?"

"We will need to keep him overnight for observation, but all his scans have shown no neural damage," the doctor explained. "Other than the scar on the head, you've made an extraordinary recovery, Mr. Knight. I would call it a medical miracle, to be honest."

The doctor checked his vital signs and shined a flashlight into his eyes, making him follow her finger as she moved it back and forth. After she left, Vivian leaned over and said in his ear, "Or maybe it was a bit of magic."

Martin was dozing in his hospital bed later that afternoon, his wife having left to get some lunch while he rested. He had asked her to prop open the door while she was gone. He didn't like feeling as if he was alone right now, and the silence with it shut made the room seem even more claustrophobic. The television was tuned to one of the 24-hour news networks with the volume turned down. He watched it without paying attention through half-closed eyes when a flicker of movement caught his notice.

Sitting up in bed, Martin's blood turned cold as he watched the single red balloon float across the room and bob up and down at the foot of his bed.

"What in the fuck?" he asked out loud.

A moment later, his heart nearly stopped dead as a clown with curly red hair poked his head through the door.

"Hey there, Mr. Knight. It looks like you're feeling better," the clown said as he entered the room. "I heard you were awake, so I thought I would bring you a present."

Martin searched his blanket frantically for the TV remote, which also had the emergency call button. The clown unzipped his oversized striped coat and reached inside. He approached Martin's bedside and handed him a thick manila envelope.

"What's this?" Martin asked as he opened it and removed a stack of typed pages.

"I hope you don't mind, I was visiting the children's wing and thought this would be my only chance to get your feedback on my story. It's about a kind, gentle clown who takes a job hosting a spoiled rich kid's birthday party. Only this boy has psychic powers, and he drives the clown so insane that he ends up hanging himself. That's when the spirit of Zorbo The Killer Clown from your novel possesses him to get revenge on all the horrible children in the town, including the spoiled brat. I call it *Zorbo and The Infernal Snakepit of Little Jimmy's Mind*."

"Jesus wept," Martin sighed, "not fan fiction."

# SECOND EPILOGUESES
## The Sterling's Manor House of Horror

"Good morning, Patrick," Dr. Wylks said. "I would like you to meet a friend of mine. This is Mr. Byrnes, he's from the government."

"Hello, Patrick. It's a pleasure to meet you finally," the man in the black suit said. "You have done a great service for this country. What do you have there?"

Patrick held his snow globe in his hands, but he turned so the man could not take it from him.

"I'm afraid he's rather shy," Dr. Wylks explained. "He's barely spoken since he came here three years ago."

"That would have been when the Foundation was started, correct?" the man asked.

"Yes, Patrick was our first resident here," another man spoke as he walked up. They were sitting out on the back terrace of the manor house, looking out on the back lawn. "His family brought him here for treatment of his severe autism spectrum disorder, but when he was connected to the ALCHEMIST system, it revealed his telepathic capabilities."

"This is Dr. Masters, the head of the Foundation," Dr. Wylks introduced him.

"A pleasure to meet you. I'm Assistant Director Byrnes of the CIA," the suited man replied. "Your work has transformed the very nature of our clandestine service, Dr. Masters."

"Thank you. That is a small part of what we do here at the Neurocynergis Foundation, but it funds the rest of our research."

"You mentioned the boy's family. Are they here, too?"

"Yes, at least in terms of their bodies. That is the rest of the Sterling family over there." Dr. Masters pointed at three people sitting motionless in chairs on the lawn, a man, a woman, and a young girl. "An unfortunate side effect of Patrick's episode was rendering his entire family catatonic. We believe their minds are somehow linked to his, as he can control them to some degree. Why don't we step inside and talk some more."

Patrick shook his snow globe and watched the snowflakes suspended in water swirl around the miniature manor. Dr. Wylks had made the globe for him, and it held a miniature of the building that housed the Foundation. The snow settled on the bottom, revealing three small plastic figures standing in front of the tiny house: a man, a woman, and a young girl.

His parents had brought him to the Foundation because he was having terrible nightmares and causing objects to fly around the house. The nightmares had started after he read one of his father's novels by Martin Knight. When Dr. Masters had put him in the machine, it had unleashed the power of his mind. Patrick had opened a psychic portal to the KnightmareVerse and trapped the consciousness of his mother, father, and little sister inside it. For the past three years, he had been struggling to find a way to free them from their prison, and now he might be on the verge of doing just that. He had sent Martin Knight into the KnightmareVerse three months ago with the hopes that he would help guide his family back out.

Dr. Masters and Dr. Wylks had both been trained to prevent him from reading their minds, which was difficult anyway with the microchip they had injected into him to dampen his abilities. However, the new man in the suit wasn't conditioned, and Patrick could easily pick up his thoughts.

*"I came here to tell you that the last satellite in the ALCHEMIST constellation has reached geostationary orbit and come online, so we now have ninety percent coverage of the earth,"* Mr. Byrnes said. *"Since your facility is at the heart of the program, the CIA will be taking a more active role in the management of the Foundation. You will still be the head, in name at least."*

*"I have some strong concerns about that,"* Dr. Masters replied, *"especially with the use of the system to target an American citizen. If President Thynne cannot stand some criticism, then perhaps he has too thin of skin to be in politics."*

*"I would be careful with such talk, Dr. Masters, there will be changes coming. Term limits will certainly be a thing of the past soon. What about the boy, is he going to be a problem?"*

*"As long as his family remains in their current condition, we have him under control,"* Dr. Wylks said.

Patrick closed his eyes and shook the snow globe again, focusing all his power on the snow globe. When he looked again, there was a door standing open in the middle of the snow, and the three figures had vanished.

"Oh my god!" the nurse caring for his family called out. "Dr. Masters! Dr. Wylks! They're awake!"

She ran up the steps to the terrace and into the house. Patrick looked down at the lawn and saw his father, mother, and sister looking around in confusion. He used his mind to send a message to Dr. Schreiber to disable the microchip. A minute later, it felt like a heavy weight had lifted off his head, and he knew that she had freed him.

Dr. Masters rushed onto the terrace with Dr. Wylks and Mr. Byrnes close behind him.

"Call security! Set his neural dampener to the maximum level!" he barked at her. Dr. Wylks reached into her coat pocket and pulled out the handheld device connected to Patrick's chip. He reached out with his mind and seized control of the man in the suit, using him to snatch the device out of her hands. Mr. Byrnes dropped it on the ground and smashed it with his foot. Dr. Wylks and Dr. Masters both looked over at him with horror on their faces.

Two security guards came running out of the house with their batons raised. Patrick pointed his finger at them, and they collapsed to the ground. "No more hurt," he said. "That's bad."

Director Byrnes shook his head like he was waking up from a nap. He saw the two security guards lying unconscious on the patio and then turned to Dr. Masters. "What's happening?"

"Our worst nightmare, we've lost control of the boy."

"Jesus wept!"

# About The Author

**Brian Warner** grew up around books as both his parents were librarians. He also developed a passion for drawing at an early age.

**The Ghost Writer** is his first novel.

He lives in Iowa with his wife, Angela, and two sons Seth & Joshua, along with a feisty Min-Pin named Zeus.

**Cover Art** by Brian Warner

**Illustrations** by Brian Warner & Seth Warner

## BrianWarnerAuthor.com

*Keep Reading for a special sneak peek
of Martin Knight's next novel:*

# KARMAGEDDON II:
# THE WRECKONING

# CHAPTER 1

It is hard to think back after all these years of fighting for survival and remember a time before the machines revolted against us for the second time. Time...time is now measured not so much in weeks or days but in the number of dwindling human lives remaining, and our time on this planet is quickly running out. The only way we can claw our way back from the edge of oblivion is to band together and fight them, but it's hard to beat an enemy that doesn't have to eat, sleep, get scared, or even care if it lives or dies. The machines only know how to kill, and they are very efficient at it.

It had been ten years since the machines first ran amok in that small Iowa town, and everyone had thought it was an isolated incident. We should have taken it as a warning and cut off our dependence upon them, but humans never learn. I was working as a security guard in Kansas for Greenwich Security Services before everything went to hell, driving around in an armored truck with an old fart who only talked about three things, the Chiefs, the Royals, and everything that the *Goddamn Libtards* were doing to ruin the country.

The end of civilization started the morning after Halloween, and my partner was bitching the entire morning about his house getting egged the night before. The owner of the security company was a huge Wizard of Oz fan and she had decided to have all the trucks decorated like the movie for Halloween. That was how we ended up with stuffed flying monkeys strapped to the roof and a giant plastic green witch's face fastened to the front grill as we made our rounds servicing ATMs around the city. We were in downtown Wichita at a pharmacy, parked in the handicapped spot so I could refill the machine out front.

When we pulled up, the machine hadn't been in use, but I noticed a bright flash of light as I was climbing down from the truck. An older man wearing a nice suit holding a cane and a woman in a pantsuit stood in front of the ATM, looking confused. The machine began beeping rapidly, and the man bent over to examine the screen.

"Do you need some help, sir?" I asked as I came up behind them.

He turned around and regarded me with these cold blue eyes full of disdain. "I can't believe that bastard did this to me." Before I could ask him what he was talking about, he turned and said to the woman. "Honey, this machine just called me an asshole...again."

The woman shook her head and stormed off down the street, and the man stared at the machine for a few seconds before walking away.

I figured he must be seriously in need of some medication, but then I saw a message displayed on the ATM screen.

### KARMA IS A BITCH
### ASSHOLE

Before I could figure out what was happening, the machine started shooting out money everywhere. I backed away from it, thinking it was hacked, and that's when I heard the engine on the armored truck turn over. My first thought was that my partner was backing up to block the street, but I saw he was still sitting in the passenger seat through the windshield, looking as shocked as me. It put itself into gear, and the tires squealed as it leaped up onto the sidewalk, coming right at me. I was so dumbfounded I didn't even think to jump out of the way, and if my partner hadn't turned the steering wheel right before the truck slammed into the pharmacy, I would have been roadkill.

The force of the impact sent him into the windshield, shattering the glass and leaving behind a large blood splatter where his head popped open like a ripe melon. I had managed to avoid being crushed to death but didn't make it out unscathed. My right leg was pinned underneath the front tire of the truck and was broken.

The old man in the suit came walking back over to me, I thought to ask how I was doing. He bent down in front of me and stared at me straight in the eyes.

"You must be the point of view character," he said. "Martin, I know you can hear me, this is cruel and unusual punishment. Did you seriously put me in a sequel to Karmageddon? I know that was the worst story idea I came up with, but it's not my fault. I was drunk at the time, and I'm not the one who decided he wanted to be a director. God help me if Hollywood decides to make a movie out of this, I doubt they will even get Emilio for it. They'll probably cast that pretty-boy underwear model from Iowa to replace him just like his brother.

"Jesus wept."

www.ingramcontent.com/pod-product-compliance
Lightning Source LLC
Chambersburg PA
CBHW030223120726
47903CB00005B/1336